May all of your dreams come true!

Of Dreams and Nightmares

Shirley A. Roe

PublishAmerica
Baltimore

© 2004 by Shirley A. Roe.
All rights reserved. No part of this book may be reproduced, stored in a retrieval system or transmitted in any form or by any means without the prior written permission of the publishers, except by a reviewer who may quote brief passages in a review to be printed in a newspaper, magazine or journal.

First printing

ISBN: 1-4137-4337-4
PUBLISHED BY PUBLISHAMERICA, LLLP
www.publishamerica.com
Baltimore

Printed in the United States of America

Dedication

This book is dedicated to my family: Jim, James, Kelly and Laura for whom I am eternally grateful.

A special note to Haley, Erik, Zack, John and Angela:
"Never stop believing in magic."

There is in every true woman's heart a spark of heavenly fire, which lies dormant in the broad daylight of prosperity; but which kindles up, and beams and blazes in the dark hour of adversity.
~ Washington Irving (1783-1859, American Writer)

Acknowledgment

With a special thanks to Kelly, for pointing the way and to my dear friends, Stephen and Lillian P. who lovingly imparted both critique and support.

This is a work of fiction. Names, characters, establishments, places and incidents are either a product of the author's imagination or are used fictitiously. Any resemblance to actual persons, living or dead is entirely coincidental.

Actual places and historical references have been used only in order to place the location and timeline. Any interaction of the fictitious characters in these places or these actual events is pure fantasy.

Table of Contents

Chapter One……………..Graystone Manor …………… 9

Chapter Two……………..Martha's Sea Voyage ……… 16

Chapter Three……………Dust, Dirt and
                         Conestoga Wagons ………… 30

Chapter Four……………..Fort Laramie and the
                         Wyoming Territory ………… 46

Chapter Five……………..Back in London ……………… 58

Chapter Six……………....The Invitation ……………… 64

Chapter Seven…….……..The Search Begins ………… 71

Chapter Eight……….…...Winter Sets In ……………… 79

Chapter Nine……………..Delayed in St. Louis ……… 88

Chapter Ten……………....Spring at Last ……………… 96

Chapter Eleven………....The Search Continues …… 107

Chapter Twelve………....Martha and Jeremy Meet … 115

Chapter Thirteen………..Jeremy and Jebediah ……… 123

Chapter Fourteen………..Decisions to Make ………… 130

Chapter Fifteen………....Return to St. Louis ………… 137

Chapter Sixteen............... St. Louis 145

Chapter Seventeen...........London and Some
                            Surprising News 152

Chapter Eighteen............The Family Settles In 159

Chapter Nineteen….……...The Nuptials 170

Chapter Twenty.............…Abraham and Bo 190

Chapter Twenty-One……....The Christmas Dance…… 201

Chapter Twenty-Two…........ Martha and John 212

Chapter Twenty-Three……… One year Later 219

Chapter Twenty-Four…...…...The Child is Born 228

Chapter Twenty-Five…....…... Six Years Later 237

Chapter Twenty-Six………. Isaac and Annabelle 246

Chapter One

Graystone Manor

A gentle dusting of snow settled on her purple cape as Martha's carriage approached the manor house. She adjusted the wool tartan blanket around her legs, feeling quite warm in spite of the late night chill. The horses' hooves made a steady clopping sound as they contacted the frozen ground. The air was crisp and cold.

"Going to be a cold night, Miss," stuttered Clyde, the hunched, wrinkled coachman, snowflakes alighting on his hat and shoulders. "Reminds me of the night you and that young scallywag, Austin Wells took off when you was twelve to spy on the folks at that fancy ball."

"Oh, Clyde, I'd almost forgotten that night. There we were, peeking in the windows, listening to the wonderful music, totally lost in our own enjoyment. It was a cold, snowy night just like this but Austin and I hardly noticed. Father was very upset, however, it was worth the punishment." Martha smiled as her thoughts returned to that night long ago. The entire staff had been out searching for her and Austin. They sat transfixed by the music, the dancing and the beautifully clad guests attending the gala event of the year. She and Austin had been on many exciting adventures together as children, many of them ending with stern punishment.

"Your father has had quite the time with you, Miss, but he always seems to get his way in the end." Clyde gently reined the two large horses in the desired direction. The hot air from their nostrils created a misty fog around their proud equine heads; a blanket of snow covered their dappled backs.

"Yes, he always does but I certainly put up a good fight, don't I, Clyde?" Martha, grinning impishly, reached up and caught several white fluffy snowflakes in her gloved hand.

"Yes, you sure do, Miss, you surely do. Ah, here we are." The carriage slowed in front of the large and stately house. The imposing front of a solid stone mansion with three stories bearing twenty shuttered windows, greeted the carriage as it came to rest. The soft amber glow from the windows promised a warm and cheery welcome.

"It is cold indeed, Clyde, and I'm glad to be home. You know, I have lived in this house all of my eighteen years and I never fail to be impressed at the sight of it. Good night, Clyde."

"Good night, Miss."

Martha bundled herself into her cape as the carriage stopped at the steps leading to the solid oak double doors. Slowly she ascended the stairs taking in the beauty of the ice sparkling like jewels on the trees and the soft white snowflakes blanketing the manicured lawns. Graystone Manor, a majestic home built by Martha's grandfather, William McGuire, fifty years before. The house and grounds had been maintained much the same as her grandmother, Anna, had designed them so many years ago. Large hedges of Holly and Rhododendron lined the drive and majestic trees were spotted throughout the formal gardens. The ice and snow transformed the gardens into a magical, bejeweled world that Martha viewed with childlike appreciation.

Entering the enormous hallway, she deposited her snowy cape and bonnet on the mahogany bench. She shook her long, thick chestnut hair causing tiny droplets of water to fly in every direction, then immediately smoothed her long locks as she stared at her reflection in the gilded mirror. Moving silently with soft ladylike steps, her floor length gown brushed the polished wooden floors as she walked. As she reached the arch to the great room, loud voices could be heard from the study at the end of the hallway. She paused and listened, resting her hand on the polished dark mahogany trim as she cocked her head towards the study.

Martha recognized her father's raised voice and as past experience dictated, decided to go straight to her room. Martha's father, John McGuire was a well-respected and successful businessman. At the moment, he was obviously in a heated argument with one of his business associates. She knew that it was best not to interrupt; she had simply wanted to say good night. As she proceeded up the grand staircase, she overheard her father say that the money would be available in a fortnight and that he would make the other arrangements as soon as possible. Martha thought he sounded strained and wondered, *Who is he talking to?*

"Money, other arrangements? Odd," she spoke aloud while quietly opening the door to her bedchamber.

Martha loved this room. The soft, burgundy velvet chaise, the delicate French lace curtains and her huge canopy bed made a striking impression, that always reminded her of her mother. Lillian McGuire passed away when Martha was twelve. Burgundy had been her mother's favorite color and the room had not been changed in all these years. She automatically picked up her mother's crystal perfume decanter, removing the lid and sniffing deeply. The scent of summer roses filled her nostrils. How she missed her mother and her wonderful sense of humor. Martha could almost hear her tinkling laughter as she envisioned her smiling face. Perpetually happy was the way Martha remembered her. Her eyes moved to the portrait of her mother that hung over her bed. Her father had argued long and hard about moving it from the great room to its present location above her bed. That was one argument Martha had won and the portrait was her most valued possession. People that had known her mother said that she looked very much like her, with her round face, chestnut hair and deep, sky blue eyes. Her stubborn nature and tall stature apparently came from John McGuire. Her father had been very good to her and gave her anything she wanted: excellent tutors, piano lessons and beautiful clothes. There was even a full stable of horses, although she was never fond of riding and could remember several heated arguments with her father about her lack of interest. Father loved the hunt and the horses but Martha had no inclination to learn to jump or any interest in animals of any kind. Yes, her father was good to her, but her need for her mother was intense. How her mother would have loved discussing the upcoming gala ball, the guests and the beautiful gowns they would wear. It was the time of her life when she had many questions of love and desire that only a mother could answer. She appreciated dear Emma, who did her best but it just wasn't the same.

After hanging her clothes carefully in the near-to-overflowing wardrobe and washing her face, she climbed into bed. Clothes were foremost in Martha's mind at the moment. She was looking forward to tomorrow when she would be fitted for her new gown for the upcoming spring gala. She fell asleep with visions of designer gowns dancing in her head.

The next morning Martha entered the dining room after stopping at the mirror to smooth her hair into place. Her father was seated in his usual chair at the head of the long dining table. Emma, the cook, large and rotund, served the tea and greeted Martha with a wide grin. Her gray eyes twinkled at the sight of this impetuous young woman. Emma was as close to a mother as anyone could be to Martha, but she was still a servant, and certain lines could not be crossed. Often, more through sheer boredom than a genuine desire to help or learn, Martha would wander into the warm, cheery kitchen and watch Emma bake the delicious pastries and cakes that she was famous for in Northumberland. Many of the aristocratic ladies of the town would vie for the right to borrow Emma when a large gathering was planned. Although parties, ball gowns and afternoon teas were the prime interests in Martha's life, Emma persisted in tutoring her in the duties of a mistress of the manor. In spite of herself, Martha could produce a decent pie and did learn the basics of running a household. Emma told her she would soon be able to perform her duties as mistress of the house and govern the staff with some degree of authority and skill. Martha did not relish the idea of doing anything so mundane.

"Good morning, Father, you are looking well this morning." She placed a kiss upon his cheek and thought to herself that his gray hair and slim build made him a very handsome man in spite of his sixty years. Martha inhaled deeply; the delicious, sweet scent of apples and cinnamon filled the room. "Good morning, Emma, I see you have made my favorite apple muffins." Martha pecked the cook's chubby red cheek before taking her seat.

The dining room was large and many portraits of the McGuire

ancestors decorated the walls. The portrait of John McGuire, recently finished, hung over the fireplace; replacing the relocated portrait of Lillian. The dining table held many happy memories of the days when Lillian McGuire had hosted her elegant dinner parties, seating as many as twenty guests. The silver tea service glistened thanks to Emma's loving hands. Emma always made sure the table was set with fine bone china and silver cutlery. Crystal water goblets sparkled in the morning sun.

"Martha, good, I have something very important to discuss with you this morning," John replied looking very somber. He stopped eating and placed his fork and knife on the table. Emma, noticing the seriousness of John McGuire's expression, finished serving and left the room. Not being as intuitive as Emma, the immature Martha did not notice her father's somber mood and chattered incessantly.

"Oh, I hope the invitation has arrived for the gala ball. I'm so looking forward to it. As a matter of fact, Charles Worth is arriving today for a final fitting. I just love his gowns and I know mine will be the loveliest at the ball. I have chosen a deep burgundy taffeta that I know Mother would have loved." Martha chattered as she lifted her delicate china teacup, the warm scent of tea and lemons filling her nostrils. She broke a section from her apple muffin with her other hand. "I only wish Austin were here to escort me, he is my best friend in all the world."

"There will be no gala ball for you this year Martha, you are to be married to Jebediah Whitaker in a fortnight." John raised his voice interrupting Martha in mid sentence.

"Father, you are joking. But what kind of a silly thought has entered your head. I have no intention of marrying anyone right now. Besides, Jebediah Whitaker has three children and is much too old for me." Martha stopped sipping her tea and stared over the rim of the cup at her father in disbelief. As an afterthought she added, "Plus, he is a pompous ass!"

"Martha, do not use that stable language in this house and I'm not joking. You are eighteen years old and he has requested your hand in marriage. I have given my word and you will do as I say." Angered by her reaction, John McGuire slammed his fist on the table, sending the cutlery flying in all directions. Water flowed down the side of the teetering crystal goblet.

"No, I won't do it, I won't. I will go to the ball and I'll not marry anyone." Martha screeched at her father, bounding from her chair. She ran from the room as her mother's fine china teacup hit the floor, shattering into a dozen pieces.

She avoided her father for the rest of the day. Martha convinced herself that he would change his mind. She would argue with him until he gave in. The tutor arrived for her piano lessons but her mind was elsewhere. She was angry that her father had cancelled her fitting with Charles Worth, who was becoming a very famous designer in England and it was difficult to reschedule. She played the piano mechanically, an angry pout on her face. Her fingers pounded the keys, the ivory black and whites bearing the brunt of her anger. *I won't do it, I won't.* Sensing her distraction and realizing he was wasting his time, the tutor packed up his things and left. Relieved to be rid of him, Martha stacked up her music sheets and returned them to the cabinet next to the piano. She paused in front of the hall mirror, primping and patting her soft hair into place before attempting to return to her room unnoticed. Ascending the staircase, she found herself face to face with her father. Martha immediately launched into her rehearsed debate but John McGuire was having none of it. "Martha, this time there will be no discussion. You will marry Jebediah Whittaker and that is that." He continued down the stairs, leaving her staring after him in shocked silence.

Later that night, cheeks stained with tears, a fearful Martha plotted to leave the house in the middle of the night and run off to Aunt Phoebe's in London. She had given a note for Phoebe to Clyde who was traveling to London in the next few days. Lying on her bed, the soft velvet of the duvet offering no comfort, Martha stared at the portrait begging her mother for guidance. She had to think, she must plan to leave in the next few days. The very thought of marrying anyone at this wonderful time of parties and grand balls was one thing but Jebediah Whittaker, well, that was out of the question. Having attended several operas and gala balls, always escorted by handsome young gentlemen, her future was just beginning. Even her dear childhood friend, Austin Wells, escorted her on visits home from college and life was blossoming for her. Jebediah Whittaker was more than ten years her senior, with thinning dark hair, deep-set eyes and a long pointy nose on his gaunt face. Her impression of the scowling widower, on the few occasions they had been in the same company was that he was abrupt and a loner. Martha paced the room; frustrated and angry she threw her silver hand mirror against the wall where it shattered into hundreds of pieces.

Shocked at her own unladylike behavior, she settled on the bed. Even in this time of crisis, years of tutoring and instruction won out. She struggled to regain the air of sophistication and refinement that she had been taught. She hugged the pillow to her ample breast, long legs tight to her body and rocked on the bed in frustration. What could her father be thinking? Clyde's remark echoed in her head *"Your father has had quite the time with you, Miss, but he always seems to get his way in the end."* She mustn't let him win this time, she must think of something. She didn't want to marry anyone, let alone such an unappealing stranger. The fact that he had three children made matters even worse. *Imagine me with someone else's three children, preposterous!* She scoffed at the thought, knowing she was fond of neither children nor animals.

Martha's head was spinning with dread and thoughts of escape when hours later, she finally fell asleep. She tossed and turned on her damp pillow. She dreamt that she was running and running, a menacing, faceless figure in close pursuit. The faster she ran, the closer the dark figure followed. Terrified she ran on, her feet felt like lead; fear filled her very soul. Her body thrashed on the bed, blankets scattering with each anxious, frightened movement. The dark, nightmarish figure growing ever closer descending like death itself. She screamed, calling to her mother to help her; but to no avail, in her heart she knew there was no escape.

Chapter Two
Sea Voyage

How naive Martha must have been, plotting to steal away to Aunt Phoebe in the night. Did she really think that her father would not discover her plans and force her to marry Jebediah?

"Dearly beloved, we are gathered together in the presence of God, to join this man and woman in holy matrimony." The somber elderly reverend slowly spoke the words that she dreaded to hear. She saw the bible shaking slightly in his wrinkled hands as she stared at the floor. *Oh, God, don't let this be happening. Let this be a nightmare that I will wake up from.* Her hands clasped tightly in front of her, she squeezed her eyes shut and willed herself to wake up.

The marriage took place in the great room of Graystone with only four sullen people: John McGuire, Martha's determined father; Emma the cook; the smirking widower, Jebediah Whittaker; and a very angry Martha. In spite of all her tantrums, all of her tears, Martha became Mrs. Jebediah Whittaker on that fateful day. After the wedding vows were complete, a greatly distressed Martha ran up to her room where she promptly locked the door and remained until the next day. Jebediah returned to his home, seemingly undisturbed by his new wife's obvious rejection.

Emma sat in the kitchen where she contemplated Martha's bleak future. Emma loved Martha as if she were her own flesh and blood and anyone could see that Jebediah Whittaker was the worst possible match for the impetuous, stubborn young woman. A girl's wedding day was supposed to be something dreams were made of, not the tense angry farce that had just taken place. Emma did not understand why John McGuire would have chosen such a mismatch for his only child. Unfortunately, there was nothing Emma could do about the situation, she picked up her mop and with quick rough strokes, took her frustrations out on the already spotless floor.

Three days later on a dark and rainy morning, the Whittakers boarded a ship for the Americas. The gray clouds hung low in the sky making the morning seem more like late afternoon. Rain pelted the crowd; the dockyard fast becoming a muddy shallow lake that engulfed the stacks of trunks and crates. Open umbrellas battling for space, the crowded passengers made their way through the water, women's skirts raised and children perched on men's shoulders. In her dark, sullen mood, Martha found the name of the ship to be ironic. Freshly painted on the bow were the words, *The Salvation* and although she looked at them with scorn that first day, they soon became her inspiration.

Even as they boarded, Martha plotted her escape. She contemplated running down the gangplank just before the ship sailed. She would get lost in the crowd on the wharf and be free at last. Somehow she would get away from Jebediah.

The ship was loaded to capacity with most of the passengers traveling steerage; only a dozen cabins were available to the small number of wealthier travelers. Martha, dreading the sea voyage, was relieved to hear that they would have one of the cabins. She could not imagine spending weeks crowded together with these tattered commoners, sleeping in hammocks. She tried to avoid the envious glances of the poor women as she proceeded past. The other women's well-worn clothes were soaking wet, tattered children huddled close to stay warm. Her designer gown was out of place on a ship full of immigrants hoping for a new life in the New World. Martha could not understand why they had not taken one of the more modern ships. Surely Jebediah was not without sufficient funds to make them all as comfortable as possible. She kept her eyes fixed straight ahead and her head held high under her umbrella, as Jebediah led them through the maze of bodies and trunks. She had her first glimpse of the children this morning and she was not impressed. They were unnaturally quiet and sullen for young boys. All three of them refused to look at her and not a word passed between them. *Jebediah had better find a nanny quickly*, she thought to herself.

As soon as they located their tiny cabin, Jebediah ushered the three young ones and Martha into the cabin, quickly exiting and locking the door behind him. A surprised Martha heard the lock slam shut. "You won't keep me locked in here forever, Jebediah Whittaker." She shouted through the locked cabin door, frustrated fists pounding on the hard wood.

Fury filled her as the seriousness of the situation began to dawn. She turned and took stock of the sparsely decorated room. She soon realized there were only two narrow bunks and a single straw mat for sleeping. The boys would have to sleep on the floor. A tattered dressing screen stood in one corner, a small table accompanied by a small faded mirror in the other. She wandered over to fix her hair in the tiny mirror. The furniture was rough and basic. Questions whirled around in her head. *Where can I hang my clothes? Do people really sleep on such tiny uncomfortable cots? Does he really expect me to live in such primitive conditions? This is unbelievable. Did my father not check Jebediah's financial situation before marrying me off?* The possible answers to her questions filled her with dread.

Jebediah was worse than she had imagined. He was tall, extremely thin and his face held a perpetual scowl. His black suit was several years old and showed his lack of interest in fashion. She had been relieved to learn he would leave Graystone right after the ceremony and not return for two days. This morning was the first time she had seen Jebediah since their marriage and the only sounds he had uttered had been orders. He was eerily silent and seemed to be surrounded by a dark cloud wherever he went. His dark, heavily browed eyes sent chills of fear down her spine whenever she looked at him. Her body shuttered involuntarily just thinking about him. Her mind drawn back to the tiny cabin, she realized the three boys were sitting on the cot, staring at her as if she were a monster. She glared back, seeing them as a troublesome burden that she would soon be rid of. *Soon you three will be the nanny's responsibility.*

Her days and nights were filled with thoughts of escape. She stood on deck, staring into the vastness of the deep blue ocean. The cold, damp steel pressed against her palms as she gripped the railing. *Who can help me get off of this ship?* Martha was married to a man whom she despised, a man who did not speak even to his children, except to relay orders. She was beginning to think that Jebediah had very little money. He showed no sign of abundance. She now had full responsibility for Jebediah's young sons, which in her opinion was the only conceivable reason for the marriage. She angrily remembered how Jebediah had laughed in her face when she inquired about the nanny. It was now obvious he expected her to look after the children with no help at all. *Why would Father condemn me like this? What did I ever do to deserve this?* "I must not give up, I must think," she reflected aloud with stubborn determination. Her knuckles turned white as she gripped the cold railing. The salty spray from the sea splashed her face; she tasted salt on her tongue as she licked the tiny droplets from her lips. Her body set in a determined stance, she stared at the ocean contemplating her dilemma.

On the deck just beyond her sight, the boys were playing checkers with some of the other children. Back in the cabin, Jebediah sat alone counting the money he had won in the card game. A mere pittance compared to the countless thousands he had in England and hidden away in his luggage on ship. Nonetheless, he admired each coin as if it were his last. He thought back to the earlier confrontation when Martha suggested a nanny be hired to care for the boys. The look on her face was priceless when he told her there would be no nanny. She had a lot of surprises coming to her. A cynical sneer crossed his face as he realized the irony of her statement. Weeks ago, he had wrestled with the possibility of simply hiring a nanny for the boys and making this trip, however, he soon realized that poor homesteaders would not easily identify with a man who could afford a nanny. That would not suit his plan. No, the idea of marrying and traveling as an immigrant family was much better. A wife would have to obey her husband; besides, why pay a nanny when a wife would care for the children and do his bidding for free. He laughed to himself as he placed the coins in his pocket, patting them lovingly with his hand.

The ship continued its voyage, passengers seldom seeing land or other ships. Porpoises followed the ship, playing in the bow waves and providing entertainment for the children. A pod of whales was seen migrating north; the huge creatures broke the surface, terrifying the women and amusing the children.

About a week into the voyage, Martha and some of the other women were on deck, attempting to prepare a meal of porridge and potato soup in two large cauldrons. She had been shocked to learn that she was expected to cook food at all, never mind on deck with the commoners. The first mate handed out provisions to the women, while the steward and cook minded the fires and supervised the cooking. Martha was no help, having never prepared a meal in her young life. Her negative attitude did not win her any friends amongst the weary women. Most of them were traveling to an unknown land as a last resort, frightened and unsure. This upperclass woman represented everything that they would never have or the oppressive masters they were leaving. Martha did what she could, keeping her eyes down to avoid the stares of the other women. *I hate you, Jebediah Whittaker. I will get away from you as soon as I can.* Her shoulders were tense, her movements abrupt, making her suppressed anger evident to everyone. After an hour on deck, the waves were increasing in height and the wind was starting to roar. Boiling food splashed over the deck as water gushed over the side extinguishing the fires. The sea became a rushing monster with the ship lying first on one side and then on the other. It was as if the ship were first on top of a great hill and then down in the valley constantly pitching from side to side. Looking up at the waves, a terrified Martha thought they appeared as high as mountains looming over the ship. Panicking, she grasped at anything that was secured to avoid being washed overboard. Sails were pulled down and the ship was left to the mercy of the waves. The wind howled and the water rushed across the deck, boxes and contents rattling, men and women staggering and falling in all directions. The men quickly gathered the women together and shoved them down into the hold. The body of the ship cracked and groaned with the strain and passengers did their best to stay in their seats or cots. Children and the elderly were tied to their cots or to support posts to prevent them sliding across the floor with every pitch of the ship.

Martha was terrified. The ship's tossing made walking almost impossible. Martha found Jebediah and the boys and was ordered into the cabin by her husband. She grabbed at Jebediah's coat to steady herself as the ship pitched. He pulled his arm away abruptly, instructing her to stop her squealing and keep moving. Her hand dropped to her side in rejection. As soon as they arrived at the tiny cabin, he thrust the door open and ushered her and the boys inside. Slamming the door, he left them alone, ordering her and the three youngsters to remain there for the rest of the squall. The boys seemed unaffected by the storm, playing together on the floor ignoring her as usual. Removing her wet cotton blouse and wool skirt behind the small screen, she changed into dry clothing. Her lips pursed critically as she smoothed the wrinkled garments. Martha inspected the stained wool skirt, wondering if it would ever be right again. Carefully she hung it on the hook and smoothed the wet fabric with her hands. *Ruined, my clothes are ruined.* Thinking she would be happy to get off this ship and give her clothes the attention they deserved, she adjusted the round collar on her blouse in the tiny faded mirror. For the time being she was relieved to be off the deck and away from the chore of cooking. *Who could cook on a pitching rocking ship and those disgusting women smelled foul, what next?* Although the storm was distracting, with items that were not fixed rolling and pitching with the ship, she sat in the only chair contemplating her situation. She tugged at the lace on her sleeve, ignoring the boys completely. Martha thought back to the first night on the ship when she learned that incredibly, it was she that would sleep on the straw mat. Jebediah settled all three boys in one cot and climbed into the second cot himself, leaving her standing openmouthed in the middle of the room. She argued that the boys should be sleeping on the floor instead of her but he would have none of it. He simply gestured to the mat, and then with a cynical grin, nodded to the narrow space beside him. She chose the straw mat. Jebediah was a force to be reckoned with. She could put up a good fight and often win an argument with her father but Jebediah was another story. For now, she simply complied.

The ship's pitching from side to side was causing his stomach to rebel but Jebediah remained calm. Taking this immigrant ship had been a brilliant idea. He had saved hundreds of pounds over the cost of the more luxurious ships and it gave him an opportunity to observe the behavior of the poor peasants. He would blend in very well by the time they arrived in the Americas. It would also take some of the polish off his new wife. He had not realized she was quite so stubborn and troublesome when he chose her for his plan. It just seemed so easy to include her hand in the deal with McGuire, but she would need considerable discipline. He was determined to look the part of the immigrant family, arriving in the new world to seek a better life and she would have to shape up or else. He felt nothing for her one way or the other. She was simply a means to an end and he would not stand for any nonsense. Leaning against the creaking post, he listened, as the men talked of acres and acres of land available for next to nothing to families willing to travel into the unchartered territories of the Americas. Acres and acres of land for next to nothing sounded like just the thing for Jebediah, especially when he had also heard that a railway was being considered through the very land they wanted to settle. There was gold in the west all right and Jebediah intended to get all he could.

Blackness filled the cabin as night fell. Jebediah and the boys were snoring loudly in the cots. The sea continued to toss the ship to and fro. The floorboards were hard and uncomfortable and sleep was impossible. Martha dozed for a few hours out of sheer exhaustion but woke often during the long night. Her nerves were frazzled, not only from lack of sleep but also from this uncomfortable, trying journey. Her mind was overflowing with thoughts. Never in her pampered life had she lived in such primitive, crowded surroundings. Hands, red and chapped from the lye soap pushed her hair from her face. She looked around the dark cabin. Her beautiful dresses hung stained and wrinkled. How desperately she wanted a hot bath. The boys were troublesome and she wanted nothing to do with them, let alone play at being their mother. Although she was obsessed with it, a reasonable plan of escape avoided her. The only thing she was sure of, was that she would escape. She had no intention of staying in this farce of a marriage. This sea voyage was turning out to be more of a nightmare than she had imagined.

The second week of the voyage, a sudden and deadly illness overtook the ship. Many of the passengers and crew were stricken with violent seizures and vomiting. Feverish, weak and ghostly white passengers were confined to the cramped, crew's quarters, which soon became the infirmary. Most of the women, including

Martha were called upon to aid the only doctor onboard. Dr. Wheeler, a kindly gentleman of about fifty years of age, worked long and diligently to thwart the spread of this unknown illness. People were housed in bunks and hammocks and the smell of vomit and urine was thick in the air. The cries of the delirious patients could be heard above the roar of the ocean. The ship was tossed so violently at times, they were sure that it would tear in two. Many dead patients, young and old, were buried at sea in the following dread-filled weeks.

Martha did her best to help but with very little experience in the care of the sick, she really thought that she was of little consequence. However, she was thankful for the distraction. Dr. Wheeler was supportive and encouraging as they labored long into the dark and dreary nights. He showed her how to tie roasted kidneys or raw potatoes to the soles of the patient's feet to break a fever. Camphor cakes secured in flannel bags were tied around the necks of those who were vomiting uncontrollably. A mixture of coal soot and sugar was administered to those with diarrhea and Martha gained a great deal of knowledge from the kindly doctor during those nights.

Dr. Wheeler could not help but think that a beautiful, young woman like Martha should not be condemned to life with a man like Jebediah Whittaker. In his opinion, Whittaker was miserly, ruthless, and perhaps even cruel. The doctor happened to be in the corridor the day the Whittakers arrived on board. He watched as Whittaker locked his family in the cabin, hearing Martha's protest and her fists pummeling the inside of the cabin door. He would never forget the icy stare the man delivered to him as he passed. Whittaker was always pleasant and friendly in the company of the captain or the other men, yet he was rude and demanding with ship's crew. Dr. Wheeler observed, he was ruthless in card games and never hesitated to take a fellow passenger's money in what was supposed to be a pleasant pastime, not a serious game of chance. Whittaker almost seemed oblivious to the fact that he had a wife at all. He had even witnessed the man brutally striking one of his boys for some minor disobedience. Dr. Wheeler could not fathom why Martha was married to such a scoundrel.

Depression was beginning to set in. Sitting in the dimly lit hold, the smell of sickness all around, Martha's spirits sank lower and lower. Every request she had made of her husband was rejected. Even simple things like a request for hot water to bathe in were denied. Try as she might, she could not figure out how to escape. Every day, her situation grew worse. She was unaccustomed to having no control. In the past she had always come up with a plan to get what she wanted. Martha was beginning to realize just how serious this situation was. Her body, unaccustomed to labor, ached from lack of sleep combined with long hours tending the sick. The other women avoided her. She had no one to talk to other than Dr. Wheeler and he was busy with the sick and dying. As she tended to a deathly ill woman not much older than herself, Martha was overcome with a sudden desire to simply leap into the freezing, violent sea. *"I can't endure another day of this miserable existence,"* she thought in desperation, tears running down her cheeks, a terrible throbbing in her chest. Her entire situation seemed hopeless and at that moment she envied the young woman dying in her arms.

Just then Dr. Wheeler, void of color, sweating profusely and looking extremely tired interrupted her thoughts, "Come quickly, Martha, we've many sick children that need attention." It was then that she decided that Dr. Wheeler might be her liberator. Her hand moved to her hair, smoothing the out of control tendrils into place. At this point she knew she was grasping at straws but she could not give up. That night, she discussed her situation with him and she learned that it was his intention to depart the ship at the first stop. The doctor suggested that, perhaps they could fabricate some story that would allow her to accompany him while in port and then execute her escape. Although completely exhausted, she returned to her cabin elated with some tiny glimmer of hope for the first time in weeks. Martha lay on the scratchy straw mattress, the hard floor beneath, oblivious to the rocking of the ship and fell into a deep sleep. She dreamt of freedom. She was back in Graystone, dancing the Viennese waltz with Austin, dressed in her most beautiful gown. Music played and champagne flowed.

Upon waking and finding herself alone, Martha allowed herself a few minutes lying on the hard straw mat, to compose her plan of escape. *Freedom, what a glorious unappreciated thing it is.* Never did she think she would be in such a position where her every action was filled with her obsession to escape. Her life in England had been one of privilege and contentment. *How could my life have changed into such a horrible, nightmare?* Her heart was beating rapidly with anticipation. Doctor Wheeler had been very sympathetic and kind. Jebediah could rot in hell for all she cared; she was leaving for good. For the first time in weeks she felt like her old self again. She almost smiled as she left the cabin.

As she entered the infirmary, the smell was overpowering, more bodies were being carried to the side of the ship and a horrible premonition of doom descended over her. Two shipmen almost knocked her over as they carried yet another dead man from the room. As they passed, Martha looked at the body and there she saw the white, lifeless face of Dr. Wheeler. "Nooo … God, noo …" she screamed, every ounce of strength draining from her, as her body and her dreams, crumbled to the filthy, wooden deck.

Jebediah spoke to her more that evening, than in the entire time they had been married.

"I'm deeply disappointed at your show of weakness. Fainting like a commoner, you have caused me great embarrassment. I was not happy about being called from my card game because my wife fainted. I'm telling you now that I'll not tolerate such displays. You will perform as my dutiful wife and from now on you will control that impulsive behavior." He paced as he shouted, a frown permanently etched on his face. He ran his hand through his thinning, dark hair; his dark, piercing eyes staring right through her. Martha faced him, crying that the doctor was dead and did he not have an ounce of pity. Her stance, hands on hips, was one of defiance. But Jebediah leaned close, his face inches from hers, he shouted at her, "Silence, woman, you will speak only when spoken to. I am tired of your constant arguing." Feeling his spittle on her face, she backed up, her arms moving protectively, hugging tightly to her bosom. He advanced, backing her into the corner. She was frightened for her safety, cowering in the corner of the cabin, she started to tremble. "Starting now, you will care for the boys first and go to the sickroom only after they have been tended to. I know you are up to something. I am no fool." She watched as he clenched and unclenched his fists; the veins on his neck straining as he shouted. "You will speak to no one and you will do as you are told. I suggest you heed my warning." The look in his eyes turned her blood to ice. Jebediah had never been physically violent towards Martha thus far, but his words were like razors slicing to her very soul. "Your days of fancy dresses and dances are over. You are a soft, pampered, spoiled child. Life will be hard from now on so you had better toughen up." He glared at her; the look in his eyes could only be described as hateful. "I'm your master and you will do as I say without voicing your objections. From this day forward, you are a simple, obedient wife and stepmother." He took another step towards her, his raised hand balled into a fist. "Do you understand? Do you?" Martha could not reply. Words stuck in her throat as she stared terrified at his fist. She crouched down making her shaking body as small as possible, hands over her head. Her muscles tensed for the blows she expected to fall. "You are a pitiful creature." With that, he marched from the cabin, slamming the door behind him. A terrified, heartsick Martha crumbled to the floor with relief where she stayed until her husband and his sons returned hours later.

That night Martha cried silently all through the night. She cried for the deceased Dr. Wheeler; she cried for her foiled efforts and most of all, she cried for her desperate inescapable situation. After this evening, she knew that not only her freedom, but also her life, was in jeopardy.

In the days that followed, the illness seemed to subside and ship life started to return to normal. The weather calmed and the sea was flat and eerie. A thick mist settled over the water, giving it a surreal appearance. It was as if the slower ship, now without the wind, was being swallowed by the mist and the sea. Martha filled her days with the endless needs of the children and walked around in an emotionless fog. She thought of writing to Aunt Phoebe for help but knew that there was no way for the letter to be sent until they reached the Americas. It would then be put on another ship and would not arrive in England for another three months. Besides, she would be on the other side of the world by then and what could Aunt Phoebe or even her dear friend, Austin, do to help her. She now believed escape was impossible. Jebediah had terrified her that night in the cabin. She knew it was only a matter of time before he would resort to violence. Depression and resignation were beginning to take over. The spark in her had been smothered and she was sinking deeper and deeper into darkness. One night as she stared blankly at the endless sea from the deck, she thought she heard her mother's voice. *"Martha, remember the emerald necklace."* Startled, she looked around but found she was alone. She repeated the words over and over in her mind. *Remember the emerald necklace.* Suddenly the thought dawned, the necklace, the one she had sewn into the hem of one of her gowns just before leaving. Her intention had been to bring just a small memento of her mother. Now, perhaps it was to be her *Salvation*. She silently thanked her mother for giving her some hope. As she turned to leave, the lifesaver ring, painted with the ship's name hanging from the rail caught her eye. The words *The Salvation* jumped out at her. She smiled.

Plan in mind, Martha waited until she found just the right seaman, someone whom she thought would be reliable. Her energy returned and she focused all of it on her plan. After several conversations and many observations, all out of sight of Jebediah, she made her choice.

The scenery was never changing with only the occasional ship in the distance and miles and miles of water with little else to focus on. Passengers were growing weary of the never-ending sea. Sensing their boredom and distress, the crew attempted to provide some much needed entertainment. One evening several of the men appeared topside with fiddles, pipes and drums. People danced and sang on deck and the mood was lighter than it had been in weeks. The distraction gave Martha her chance to seek him out. The seaman, Richard, whose handsome but rugged appearance appealed to her, had been considerate and helpful during the epidemic on ship. On the many occasions they had been in the same sickroom, he appeared sincere in caring for the welfare of the passengers. She was beginning to feel confident again. That evening, clean dress, long chestnut hair hanging loose to enhance her appearance; she broached the subject of needing some assistance. Martha was sure to include the fact that she was willing to pay as long as she could trust him completely. Richard observed the shapely, vivacious woman before him hungrily, thinking he would certainly like a night with her. He admired her ample bosom, peeking above the neckline of her bodice. Her waist was narrow and he could only imagine what she would look like without the gown. He eagerly agreed to provide whatever assistance she required. Once she was sure he was willing to help her, she produced the necklace. While Richard appraised the shimmering emerald greedily, she offered up a prayer of thanks. In her heart she knew it was her mother that had given her the idea. Richard, realizing the emerald's value and hoping for more on a personal level, was more than willing and eager to help her and put together a most ingenious plan of escape.

At the first port, they would meet in the dark of night, just before the ship received permission to dock. Permission could take days because the ship had experienced a mysterious illness and would be kept offshore until granted docking privileges. Richard would take her ashore in the small dinghy and then return to the ship to avoid suspicion. Later that morning he would say that he observed her by the handrail during the night while he prepared the dinghy for fishing. Hopefully, this would lead everyone to believe that she had fallen or perhaps jumped, to her death.

Anticipation filled her days and nights. She didn't see much of Jebediah who spent his time playing cards and conversing with the other men on board. How critical and unfeeling he was; even with his own sons. She would be glad to get as far away from him as possible. The ocean stretched before her. Only the occasional ship could be seen on the vacant sea. Soon they would be close to port and Richard would help her to finally be free. She had only seen Richard a few times, carefully steering clear of him to avoid suspicion. Her only concern was the lecherous look in Richard's eyes every time he looked at her. Hopefully he would be satisfied with the emerald necklace and not expect more than she was prepared to give. Refusing to acknowledge any negative thoughts, she concentrated on her freedom. She could barely contain her excitement. Once she was free, she would hideout on shore and then return to England never to see Jebediah Whittaker again.

The night of the escape came in a blanket of fog. Darkness descended over the anchored ship and the taste of salt was heavy in the air. As she crept out on the deck, her small bag containing only a few possessions in hand, she took her position behind the post as arranged. She thanked God for bringing this heavy fog to hide her escape. Jebediah and the boys had been sound asleep when she crept from the dark cabin. Martha was to wait until Richard signaled her from the dinghy, then they would lower the boat and escape into the night. She pulled her cloak tightly around her to ward off the damp night air. Her body shivered with anticipation. After what seemed like hours, but was, in fact, only minutes, a small flicker of light appeared. Her heart was pounding; her palms wet with nervous perspiration. She pulled the cloak over her head and advanced quickly to the small boat that would be her *Salvation*. *At last, I will be free,* she thought as her feet connected with the wooden deck; each step moving her closer to freedom. Coming from behind, she could see that Richard was swinging the brilliant necklace back and forth. This was no time to be admiring his newfound wealth; perhaps she should not have given it to him until she reached the shore.

As Richard turned towards her, Martha gasped in horror. There, in front of her, holding her mother's necklace was Jebediah Whittaker, looking like the devil himself.

"Going somewhere, Martha?" he sneered. "You know, when your father agreed to include your hand in marriage for the land that he wanted desperately, he warned me you were high-spirited. I'm afraid we'll have to break that spirit, my dear Martha." She lunged for her mother's necklace, but Jebediah just laughed, putting it in his waistcoat. He threw the seaman's hat he had been wearing to the deck. "Come along, Mrs. Whittaker," he snarled as he roughly gripped her arm and propelled her forward. "There will be no escape for you. You will not embarrass me or cause me any further problems. After this night, Martha, you will know who is in charge here."

Four weeks later, Mr. and Mrs. Jebediah Whittaker and the three young Whittaker boys, arrived in the colonies.

Chapter Three
Dirt, dust and Conestoga Wagons

The sea voyage had been the worse time of Martha's entire life. She was barely conscious of where she was, having arrived in a crowded city port and immediately loaded on a stagecoach traveling east. Nothing was familiar. The terrain, the people and the weather were all foreign to her. Her life spark had been extinguished, leaving only anger and resentment. Now tired, browbeaten and resigned to her life with Jebediah, she stood looking at what was to be her home for the next few months.

"All five of us are to live in that wagon, preposterous!" Martha cried out, casting her eyes over the wagon that Jebediah was inspecting. "We had better wagons to move our grain in England and you expect me to live in this?" The words were out before she thought about what she was saying, her anger emerging from just below the surface, where it now resided. The other homesteaders stared at her disapprovingly.

"I have learned to expect nothing from you, Martha, but yes, you will live in this wagon with the boys and myself until we arrive in Wyoming territory." His tone was firm but a smile graced his lips as he looked towards the other homesteaders. It was apparent they sided with him in this family squabble. Entirely for their benefit, he added, "It will be fine, my dear."

She saw not much more than a rectangular box with four wheels made of ash, twenty spokes, with a metal outer wheel. The body of the wagon was slightly curved in the center. A stovepipe stuck out of the canvas top leading inside to a small stove that was to provide warmth for the family. The canvas itself was pulled over seven wooden hoops that would keep out the rain, wind and hot sunshine. It had been rubbed with oil to keep the water out. A pair of malodorous oxen stood in wait, soon to be hitched to this atrocity. Dust swirling around her feet, Martha stood horrified at the thought of having to live in such a confined space, never mind traveling to some unknown barren land. She felt furious but completely helpless.

Two oaken casks of water hung on the sides of the wagon. The wagon master or captain as they were sometimes called, explained to the men that silver and copper coins would be added to the casks once they were full. As the wagons rolled over the prairies, the water would slosh and move in the casks. This action would release silver ions, which killed bacteria and prevented further growth. The copper coins, which produced copper ions killed and prevented the buildup of algae. In spite of herself, Martha overhearing, found this information fascinating. However, she soon responded in her newly acquired abrupt manner, her bitterness apparent to everyone.

"Wonderful, not only do we have to live like savages, we could be poisoned by our drinking water," she stated, thinking this was going to make the sea voyage seem like a lark. "You boys come over here and start loading this wagon," she barked, turning up her nose at the smell of the cattle and horse manure that blanketed the corral floor.

Seven-year-old Abraham and the youngest boy, Ezekiel scurried out of the barn where they had been attentively watching the blacksmith at work. It seemed this was all just a great adventure to them.

"We have had our riding lessons, Father. The saddle is different from the ones we used back in England but I think Abraham and I are used to them now. Ezekiel will have to ride in the wagon though since his feet will not reach the stirrups." Isaac, the oldest, sullen-faced, appeared from the side of the barn leading two large stallions. He spoke directly to his father, ignoring Martha completely.

"Fine, fine. Now get busy loading this wagon and I'll make arrangements for the cattle. Martha, supervise the boys and wait for me here." He gave her a look that defied argument. Jebediah moved off towards the cattle drivers to discuss the moving of his herd along with hundreds of others belonging to the rest of the homesteaders. Martha stood by the wagon miserable, dejected and feeling very alone. She surveyed the crowd of homesteaders, thinking to herself that it was quite a diverse mix of nationalities and social classes. There were a dozen or so rugged traders; most of the men were employees of the Hudson Bay Company. Dressed in buckskin and furs, rifles over their shoulders they reminded her of a portrait she had seen in the gallery at home. Several different languages could be heard mingling through the crowd. She recognized a few of the French phrases but many others eluded her. Although most of the travelers were men, there were several women and children in the group. No one looked her way.

On a bright and sunny June morning, thirty-five wagons, 140 people, several horses and almost 1000 head of cattle headed west. Martha had neither the strength nor the inclination to resist. The trail used by Indians, missionaries and fur traders would lead them to their new home. Jebediah, stern-faced and determined, was seated up front on the left side of the wagon, Martha and young Ezekiel sat to the right, both staring ahead as if they were heading into the fires of hell. Isaac and Abraham rode alongside, anxious for whatever this new adventure would bring.

Some days the wagon train traveled only ten or fifteen miles. If the weather was bad, even fewer miles were covered. Martha sat in silence, her hurt and anger festering in her heart. Ezekiel, in spite of his age, was aware of the tension in the wagon. He did his best to run off and play at every opportunity. Riding alongside, the older boys, like sponges were absorbing information on every inch of rugged landscape and each new task of pioneer life. Jebediah silently plotted his course of action methodically, mile after treacherous mile.

Martha feeling she had nothing in common with them and sensing their disapproval avoided the other women. Standing a few yards away, she overheard some of the women talking while preparing lunch at one of the wagon train stops. "That one thinks she is better than the rest of us. I don't know where she thinks she is headed but it certainly isn't Buckingham Palace." The woman shook her head in disgust. She handed the salt pork to Mrs. Brown and walked away. Margaret Brown looked over to Martha, when she realized Martha had overheard, she turned her head in embarrassment. Margaret did not make rash judgments. She empathized with Martha's unfamiliarity with her surroundings, since she was feeling it herself. Deciding to take the initiative, she walked over and invited Martha to help her prepare the lunch. Taken aback at the woman's invitation, Martha reacted stiffly, confusion apparent on her face but Margaret was persistent. Nervously Martha stroked her dusty locks, pushing her hair behind her ear. Recovering quickly, the insult echoing in her head, Martha agreed more as a show of defiance, than any recognition of a kindness on Margaret's part. Keeping her attention on the chore at hand, she purposely avoided the stares of the other women. *Shrews and commoners, how dare they talk about me like that?* Margaret chattered casually and Martha slowly began to relax. She soon began to like this young woman, who, like herself was in an alien land. Margaret had come to America from England just as she had. They were close in age and Margaret seemed to understand her distress. *This is the first friendly person I have seen in months.* Her attitude softened and she watched Margaret chatting, her face animated and happy. This was the first pleasant conversation she had since she left England; she was almost enjoying herself. The rest of the women watched and waited.

Often when it rained, it seemed to come down in torrents. Wagon wheels stopped turning in the thick mud. People pushed and pulled to free them, muscles straining and mud sticking to their clothing. Instead of relief, the heavy rain represented another trial for this adventuresome group. Sometimes, the rain fell in gentle droplets greeted with appreciation by the homesteaders. Martha was more contented when the rain fell because at least it provided a break from the dust and oppressive heat. She passed the hours with daydreams. *How lovely and cool the days in England were. No dust, no oxen, no children, just pretty dresses and tea parties.* She envisioned the rose garden at Graystone. It would be in full bloom now, the bushes heavy with the huge fragrant flowers. It all seemed like a long lost dream to her now. Violently shaken from her reverie, Martha felt herself being pitched to the side with great force. She soon realized that the front wheel had come off and grabbing the sleeping Ezekiel as she fell, Martha screamed in fright. Both of them were thrown to the ground as the sound of Jebediah's cursing filled their ears. Unhurt but shaken, Martha stumbled to her feet and with a certain amount of detachment in her eyes, pulled the frightened Ezekiel to her.

"Stop that hollering and get the grease bucket from the wagon," Jebediah ordered. The large bucket of grease hung behind the rear wheels on the axle and she reluctantly reached for it. "Hurry up, woman, we must get this wheel repaired and get to the river before dark." Perspiring, and smelling of axle grease, Martha stood aside and watched the men repair and replace the wheel. She looked down at the blob of grease permeating the cotton of her skirt with disgust. Taking her handkerchief from her pocket she tried to clean the stain but only managed to make it worse. *How was a woman supposed to keep her clothes clean in this Godforsaken place? Why would anyone want to come here?* Five-year-old Ezekiel, now completely recovered, took advantage of this time to run and play with the other children.

When one wagon had a problem, the entire wagon train would stop and wait. The wagon master, Arthur Langley, rode back to see what the problem was and just how long it would take to fix. He had sent scouts ahead to determine how far they were from the North Platte River and their destined stop for the night. The cattle drovers had gone on ahead with the cattle and would be somewhere in the vicinity of the river by nightfall.

"You men going to be long, Jebediah?" Arthur was in his mid-forties and loved his work. He was based in St. Louis but spent more than half his life on the trail. Many of the wagon trains started their journey in the east from New York, Ohio or Virginia as this one had, and traveled across the entire country to California. He watched the men replace the wheel. Looking in Martha's direction, he noticed the look of disgust on her face as she rubbed the stain. Arthur Langley had seen many immigrants. Women like Martha Whittaker did not survive in the wild west of the Americas.

"Just a few minutes and we'll have the axle greased and the wheel back in place, Arthur." Jebediah forced a grin at the leather-faced, wagon master knowing that he must portray himself as a simple homesteader in order to blend in. Jebediah's plan was coming together. He thought back to the day on the ship when he watched the crew throwing the dead bodies into the sea. The passenger's belongings were piled on the deck as the crew disposed of those that had been overtaken by the disease. Jebediah noticed a shiny gold watch and a bible amongst the belongings. When the crew was looking the other way, he slipped them into his pocket, convinced the person that owned them would not be needing them again. The watch he took because it was gold, the bible was the foundation for his plan. He patted the bible reassuringly, now stored in his coat pocket as he thought to himself, *Thousands of acres of land offered for next to nothing, to families moving west. Martha made the family picture complete; we're just simple immigrants from England, anxious to start a new life in the west. It will all be mine—acres and acres of land and large sums of money.* He grinned at Arthur and directed his attention back to the wagon.

Martha wandered over to converse with some of the other women. Her anger was subsiding and slowly replaced with resignation. Margaret's coaching had been instrumental in her newly acquired tolerance. Realizing they were all in this together, she had put her bitterness aside and tried to blend in. Her class distinctions were slowly disappearing. Many were new immigrants like her, longing for their homes far away and frightened of the uncertain future. Friendships were made amongst the women, all feeling very alone in this new land. During one of the stops, arrangements had been made to start a quilt; with each woman sewing her section as the wagon train progressed. Sewing was something that Martha knew how to do, having been tutored in the craft as she grew up in the Manor. She actually enjoyed matching colors and sewing the tiny stitches that held the beautiful quilts together. Each wagon would have a beautiful, cooperative quilt by the time the group arrived at their destination. Quilts were the obvious choice, because small pieces could be used and old clothing and blankets were quickly turned into useable quilts. Nothing went to waste and even Martha was begrudgingly learning how to make a petticoat last long after it should have been discarded. Wagon travel provided limited space and only absolute necessities were taken. Her trunks and most of her clothing had been left back east. Jebediah told her the trunks would follow on a freight wagon at a later date. She focused with anticipation on their arrival, using it as a way to cope with her current limited wardrobe.

Margaret Brown, who she learned was the wife of one of the

scouts, became Martha's closest acquaintance on the wagon train. Auburn-haired, with a heart-shaped face, Margaret came from England to join her husband who had been in the Americas for two years. She told Martha, it was quite a shock for her to see him, dressed in buckskin and furs, complete with full beard and long hair. James had always been impeccably dressed and clean-shaven back home in England. The two women grew close during the long days and nights on the trail. Martha taught the grateful Margaret how to improve her sewing skills. Margaret was adjusting to her new life as well as could be expected, but she was different from Martha in one very important way. She loved her husband with all her heart and would follow him to the end of the earth to be near him. Martha envied the loving, respectful relationship that Margaret and James had and often enviously watched them together. Martha was simply thankful Jebediah and the two older boys slept outside under the wagon and that she was not required to fulfill her wifely duties. The sleeping conditions of the wagon train had become a blessing in disguise for the humbled Martha. She enjoyed talking with Margaret but there were certain things that she kept to herself.

Each morning, the travelers were up before daylight. Men gathered the livestock and women cooked breakfast. Many times they also prepared lunch for the trail since they did not always stop during the day's ride. Oxen were hitched up, bedding packed away and they started to move out. To Martha, it seemed that day after day, each one was essentially like the last. Rise before dawn, cook and eat, gather the stock, hitch the wagons, head out, choke on the dust all day, and then stop, cook, eat and settle again for the night. The scenery scarcely changed day-to-day, week-to-week just flat grassy plains covered with clouds of dust.

Passengers preferred to walk well off the trail much of the time, since all but the lead wagon were always choked in dust. The wagons were bumpy and uncomfortable and walking, although tiring, was a relief. Martha noticed that she had lost weight, her body appearing more muscular since starting on this trip.

"I'll look more like a boy than a woman by the time we arrive and my feet are killing me," she grumbled to Margaret who was slightly overweight and not noticeably losing any of her womanly curves. Margaret just laughed, having become accustomed to Martha's constant complaining. Margaret looked passed the crusty exterior to the pleasant person she saw beneath.

"Walking is good for you, young woman, you should try walking with these old bones," Olga Mueller added in her broken English. Martha liked Olga. The German woman was in her late forties but as strong as an ox. She wore her blonde braids tied on top of her head, her muscular arms swinging by her side as she walked. Olga told them how she and her husband, Fritz, had moved to England from Germany to take over Olga's father's shop. Her family had been shopkeepers in Germany for generations and Olga came by her shop expertise naturally. They lived above the shop, made a decent living and were happy with their life. Martha asked her why anyone would leave London to come to this Godforsaken place. "We ran the shop for Papa but after he died, my eldest brother inherited everything. He sold it out from under us. We offered to buy it but there was big money to be had from a developer. So there we were, no livelihood, no home, no future just our small savings." The women strained to understand her strong accent. Olga's "w" sounded more like a "v" when she spoke causing the women to listen carefully so as not to misunderstand. "Fritz had been wanting to travel to the Americas and since we needed a new start, here we are." The sad look on Olga's face, told Martha there was more to the story than she was telling. The women walked on silently, each with their own thoughts. Martha felt sorry for Olga. Her own situation in this desolate place was bad enough but Olga was twice her age. At a time in her life when she should have had it all, she had been forced to leave her settled and happy life, to travel halfway around the world to this dusty, dry no man's land. What Martha didn't understand was how Olga could be so accepting of the situation. She didn't appear bitter or angry, just resigned, almost optimistic. *I just don't understand these people or what drives them on.* Her legs were aching and she had blisters on her feet by the time they stopped. Rubbing her calves, she kept her complaints to herself for once. As the sun set, the wagons formed a circle for protection. The children ran and played in the center. Pent up energy was released as the women prepared the evening meal. The men tended the livestock and checked the wagons for needed repairs. After supper, they would all gather around the fire and listen to the scouts and traders tell stories of the places they would soon call home.

Some of the men would play cards, which appealed immensely to Jebediah. In his new role as homesteader, Jebediah reinvented himself. He took to carrying the bible around and quoting scriptures on occasion, but explained that the Lord would forgive a man for seeking some pleasure in a friendly game of cards. This contradiction surprised some of the men, but they still invited the pious Jebediah to play. The stakes were never high since most of the homesteaders were stretching their meager holdings just to make this trip. "You're not betting that watch, are you, Jebediah, it is a beauty." Arthur Langley admired Jebediah's gold watch when he pulled it from his coat and checked the time during a card game.

"Couldn't part with this no matter how broke I was—belonged to my dead father, I am never without it. Only thing I have to remember him by." Jebediah watched their reactions as he put the watch back in his pocket. He was a convincing liar. The others nodded in sympathy, remembering their own dead parents. They understood the importance of memories and family heirlooms. Jebediah looked at them and smiled, thinking to himself, *If they only knew. The fellow that owned this watch is lying at the bottom of the sea.* Unbeknownst to the others, Jebediah had a very large amount of money, gold and jewels hidden away, the rewards of his land sale before leaving England. In fact, he hadn't even owned the land. It was Jebediah's brother, Jeremy, who was the real landowner. The buyers had paid Jebediah thousands of pounds for hundreds of acres that he had convinced them he owned. He wondered how they were feeling now after being parted from their gold and having nothing to show for it. *I wonder how long it will be before they discover that the land wasn't mine to sell. I pulled the wool over their eyes and made a fortune in the process. It served them right for being so greedy.* A smirk crossed his face as he thought about how easy it had been to defraud them. *John McGuire was probably feeling very foolish at having been parted from his daughter as well. It had been a brilliant idea to make Martha a condition to the sale. Saved me a lot of time looking for a wife.* He laughed to himself. Guilt was one emotion that Jebediah never allowed himself. Nothing would stand between Jebediah and his plans to amass a huge fortune. As his hand patted the stolen watch nestled in his pocket, the other men looked at him in sympathy.

The flaming campfire surrounded by black star-studded night sky inspired many stories. One evening, Pat and Dan O'Brien, two Irish emigrants relayed their story to the others.

"We have our local priest to thank for our being here tonight. Although the church relied strongly on the contributions of its parishioners back in Ireland, the priests were very supportive of those who wanted to emigrate. After the great potato famine, life grew more difficult as time passed. People were starving, jobs scarce. Many people wanted to leave our beloved Isle of Green. The local priest provided Dan and I and a few others with enough money to travel to Cork where we could board the ship." Pat paused and nodded to his brother to continue.

"We traveled by train and ere long found ourselves upon the road to Cork. We were in the midst of 200 to 300 men, women and children varying in age from five to fifty." Dan's Irish lilt made him sound more like he was singing than talking. "Upon our arrival in the city, we were obliged to stay in a lodging house. It was not unusual for twenty to forty persons to be crammed in a room four yards by six yards square with nothing but filthy straw on the floor for a bed, on top of which we were charged three pence a night. Breakfast was standing room for a few pieces of dry toast. The sad part is that this turned out to be the best part of the journey." Pat took up the story where Dan left off, many of the homesteaders nodded in empathy, reflecting back on their own journeys.

"Conditions on the ship out of Cork were horrible. Bodies packed in like sardines, sanitary conditions were almost nonexistent and disease ran rampant. We were two of the lucky ones that actually made it to the shore of the colonies. Many of our ship mates died at sea." Pat stopped, looking into the night sky to regain his composure. "I know some of you think this wagon train is a rugged go, but I assure you, there are worse conditions." Martha felt a twinge of guilt at the comment, self-consciously thinking that it was meant for her. Her hand moved to her hair, now dusty, dry and pulled back in a ribbon. Since she was a little girl, she always reached for her hair in times of distress. The soft feel of her hair usually comforted her. Now it felt harsh and dry like her life.

Mick O'Rourke, another Irishman, confirmed the story from his own experience. "I left Ireland when the crops disappeared and traveled to England to work in the fields, but that didn't last long either. I boarded an immigrant ship in Liverpool and conditions were not much better than you describe. Our emerald isle will soon be barren, people are leaving like rats deserting the ship." His voice reflected the sadness in his heart. Everyone on the wagon train seemed to have a story of suffering, persecution and escape. Martha felt ashamed for some of the trivial complaints she had expressed in the beginning of the trip. Compared to these people, her life had been one of privilege and wealth before she left England. Her situation with Jebediah had nothing to do with these determined people. They didn't deserve to listen to her complaints; she would keep them to herself.

Sitting on the opposite side of the fire, Jebediah took something entirely different from the O'Brien's story. People trusted the clergy. This story had reconfirmed that. Fitting in perfectly with his plan, he knew he could turn this to his advantage. Sensing the mood of the crowd, several people obviously offering up a silent prayer, he took his bible out of his pocket. He opened the book and began to read from the scriptures. Several people nodded in appreciation.

Evening fire stories became the only form of entertainment for the travelers and people began to look forward to them. One evening as they gathered around the fire, the air was pierced by a loud scream. Seconds later Abraham ran between the wagons shouting, "Ezekiel has been bitten by a rattlesnake. Help someone help. " Several men ran to where the tiny boy was writhing in pain. A gunshot was heard and the screaming Ezekiel was carried into the circle.

"Shot the bastard, a big one too," one of the scouts informed the terrified women. "Snake soup for supper tomorrow night, ladies." The scout dropped a four-foot long rattler, its head blown off, in front of the terrified women.

People gathered around the blond-haired child, observing that his leg was already swollen to twice its size. Martha pushed through the crowd and cradled the shaking Ezekiel in her lap. Holding him as firmly as she could, one of the fur traders cut the skin around the bite. Martha feared the repercussions. Moments later, blood, and hopefully, venom poured from the cut. All they could do was give the child some Willow Bark tea to ease his pain and wait. Jebediah arrived shortly afterward and carried Ezekiel back to their wagon, with Martha following sheepishly behind.

Back at the wagon, Jebediah berated Martha severely for letting Ezekiel run off unattended. "You are supposed to be taking care of the boys, you stupid woman. I didn't bring you halfway around the world so that I would have to be responsible for these children. Nothing better happen to him or you will pay for it." Martha tried to back away but was soon up against the wagon with Jebediah shouting in her face. Trembling with fear, she could feel his hot breath on her skin. "Oh yes, you will be very sorry for your lack of attention to his whereabouts." The blow came from nowhere. With ringing in her left ear and her vision blurring, Martha's body crumbled to the ground. Half-conscious, faintly somewhere in the distance she could hear Jebediah repeating over and over, "You will pay, oh yes, you will pay." She lay there alone and frightened for what seemed like hours, her world swirling around her as if she were in a drunken haze.

Minutes later, Jebediah stomped away to join the others leaving Martha; her throbbing face soaked with tears to tend to five-year-old Ezekiel. His fever seemed to escalate by the minute. Martha had thus far merely tolerated all three of the boys. Even though Ezekiel spent more time with her than the others, she had not allowed herself to feel anything for him but conscientious concern for his welfare. She had been too consumed with her own desperation to give a thought to anyone else. His feverish condition reminded her of the nights in the sickroom aboard the ship. She felt as useless now as she had then. Overcome with emotion she started to pray.

"Oh, Lord, why is this happening to me? Why did Father do this to me? God, what more must I bear? This is so unfair, God, so unfair." Feeling trapped, downtrodden and very sorry for herself, Martha looked down upon the sweaty, pale angelic face of the tiny boy. His face was flushed; beads of sweat covered his face. His eyes were closed and his breathing shallow. For several minutes she stared at him, not moving. Suddenly realizing that he may die, she was filled with unfamiliar compassion and concern. A strange feeling of warmth filled her body. It was at that moment; consumed with guilt, she shed her childish selfishness. She prayed again, only this time it was Ezekiel and not herself that was to be the recipient of God's *Salvation*. "Please, Lord, don't let him die. He is just a child and not responsible for the situation I'm in. Oh, God, he is so tiny and innocent. Please watch over him and let him live." Martha sobbed from deep within her soul. "I have been a selfish, self-centered woman. Please forgive me. Oh, Lord, how vain and selfish I have been. Others have suffered, as much if not more than I, yet they do not complain. I am not worthy of your help. But this innocent boy is. I'll try harder, God, I promise, just help Ezekiel, please." Her body wracked with sobs, Martha bathed the fevered boy with cool cloths and administered Willow bark tincture through the long night. She prayed like she had never prayed before. For the first time in her life, she was more concerned for the welfare of someone else than she was for herself.

The next morning the fever was down and the child's condition had improved. Ezekiel opened his eyes and actually smiled at her. Her heart leapt into her throat. She pushed back the tears as she stroked his forehead, gently almost a caress. Martha was exhausted but different somehow. Her emotions were in turmoil, fear mixed with compassion, anger mixed with guilt.

Isaac came to see his brother. As he left the wagon, he turned on Martha viciously. The confining space offered only a few feet between them. "This is all your fault. Why did you have to come along and ruin our lives? We were fine before you came. You're not our mother and you never will be. Our mother is dead. I'll never forgive you if my brother dies, never. I hate you! I wish you were dead!" Martha watched him leave, a new fear beginning to grow in her.

Disheveled, exhausted and crushed by the viciousness of both Jebediah's blow and Isaac's biting words, Martha went to find Jebediah and let him know Ezekiel's condition had improved. She pulled her bonnet low to hide the purple and red bruise that was starting to blossom on the side of her face. Her eye was swollen shut. If anyone noticed, they said nothing.

A few brief scriptures from Jebediah over the boy in the presence of the other homesteaders and the wagon train moved out. Life was hard for these new pioneers and they had almost lost one of their own to this new land that they hoped to call home. They began to wonder what other hardships awaited them.

More dusty oppressive miles were covered and Jebediah quickly learned the vocabulary of the homesteaders. "Yes, Jonah, the family and I are anxious to arrive in Wyoming and begin our new life as farmers and homesteaders. Nothing like owning your own piece of God's green earth, I always say," repeated Jebediah to anyone who would listen. At the same time, thinking that he was becoming very convincing in this new role, he offered his assistance to the others to gain their confidence. "We all have to pull together and help build our new homes and barns. Do unto others as you would have them do unto you, saith the Lord." He raised his eyes to the heavens before he continued. "It's going to be a great life for all of us in Wyoming."

Martha found Jebediah's newly acquired love of the land and the scriptures hard to swallow and her bitterness and hatred for him grew like a cancer inside of her. *How could he be so pleasant and friendly to strangers, yet treat his own family with cruelty?* Her confidence and sense of self, eroded away like the wind stripped earth of the prairie. Weeks turned to months as the wagon train, resembling a ship sailing across the Great Plains progressed on its journey. Several head of cattle had been lost to the oppressive heat and the dust was affecting everyone's breathing. Women and men alike wore handkerchiefs tied across their faces most of the day in an effort to breathe easily. Olga's husband, Fritz, had developed a wheezing in his chest, causing Olga great concern. Children grew restless and tempers flared. Fights broke out amongst the men over little things, women barked at their children and spirits were sagging.

Martha noticed that Jebediah never showed the least amount of irritation with the circumstances or any emotion at all. *This so-called husband of mine is a strange creature*, she thought to herself. Although they never said so, she knew that some of the other women pitied her for the relationship she had with him. She often wished she had jumped from the ship that night during the crossing and put an end to this existence once and for all. Those days when plans of escape filled her every waking moment had been replaced by thoughts of resignation, bitterness and basic survival. Food was growing scarce and the men did not always return with food when hunting for supper. Empty stomachs gurgled and faces grew gaunt. Meals often consisted of small portions of cracked wheat porridge, bread and jerky. Flour, sugar and yeast were rationed and meals of boiled rabbit or grouse with little else were not uncommon. Martha willingly passed food to Ezekiel, his young eyes hungrily resting on her plate. She noticed that Jebediah always devoured his food without a thought for the boys. Martha had lost more weight and her prediction of looking more like a boy than a woman was coming true. The few dresses she had been allowed to bring were repaired and made smaller and she was becoming quite proficient at sewing.

"Margaret, just look at these dresses we are wearing." Martha commented to Margaret one evening by the fire. "I have worn the same dress for over a week. Why I remember changing dresses three or four times a day back in England." Margaret had noticed that Martha complained less and less with each passing day. She also noticed that any sign of gaiety and spunkiness seemed to be slowly draining from her. She tried to cheer her friend.

"Yes, we had dresses for taking tea, dresses for garden parties and gowns for operas and balls. Now we have one dress for everything and it's falling to bits," she joked. "Soon we will all be marching stark naked across the plains."

Martha smiled at the thought of it. "We spent more time changing clothes in a day than we spent partaking of the activities. Having no clothes would certainly alleviate that." Martha and Margaret laughed. Laughing was something she rarely did these days and it felt good to forget the troubles of the trail if only for a few minutes. She cherished these moments with her friend.

"When we arrive in Wyoming, we'll be able to make new clothes once we are settled." Margaret looked down wistfully at her dusty cotton dress and apron and then smiled at Martha. Martha was always impressed with Margaret's ability to see the good in every situation. She was having a very difficult time adjusting to this new way of life and admired Margaret's positive attitude. Martha would attempt a little optimism herself from now on, remembering her promise to God.

Early one morning, Margaret's husband, James, announced that the fort was within a day's ride and that the wagon train would be welcomed there. Great jubilation filled the homesteaders, especially the women. Martha raised her face to the sky and thanked God.

"Food, a soft bed and a hot bath!" One of the women exclaimed.

"No dust, no more bumping along in the wagon," cried another. The fort was just what the people needed to rejuvenate their spirits. Even Jebediah looked pleased that the fort was within a day's ride. He led the group in a prayer of thanks.

"Some of us should ride ahead and prepare the fort for our arrival," Jebediah suggested, thinking that if there was any advantage to being there first, he wanted to be the one to benefit.

"Yes, I think that would be a good idea," Arthur shouted over the excitement. "Your wife or Isaac can drive your wagon. You would be a good representative of this wagon train. Take a couple of men and head out this morning." Arthur had always liked Jebediah and thought him a God fearing and friendly man. *Curious relationship with his wife, though,* he mused, *must be a hard woman to get along with.* The poor man never voiced his complaints but it was clear that his wife was not very demonstrative towards him. Sometimes the other men wondered what a fine chap like Jebediah was doing with such a cold, hardhearted woman. A real looker all right but she didn't even appear to be fond of her own stepchildren for heaven's sake. Nursed the boy after the snake bite all right, but she should have been watching him in the first place. Arthur had heard rumors that she had angered Jebediah with her carelessness and the man had been driven to uncharacteristic violence, but as wagon master he tried to mind his own business and leave the rumors for the womenfolk. He allowed himself just a minute to think of his own wife and daughter back in St. Louis. Isabel was the love of his life but embroiled in the society life of the city. When he was home, he was attentive and loving and she, in turn, spent every waking minute in his company. Their marriage was a success because of the separate lives they led. Right now, Arthur had to move a wagon train and thoughts of anything else were quickly replaced with making sure all went well for a swift and safe arrival at their destination.

Chapter Four
Fort Laramie and the Wyoming Territory

Fort Laramie rose like a beacon in a storm on the horizon. It had been months since the travelers had seen more than the occasional supply depot or another wagon train. At last life would return to some semblance of order and the women especially looked forward to a soft straw bed and a bath.

Jebediah arrived at the fort and was greeted by Colonel Watson, commander of Fort Laramie, recently converted to a military outpost. Being sure to begin as he meant to go on, Jebediah introduced himself as Pastor Whittaker. "Fort Laramie was created in 1834 as a trading post for the Cheyenne and Arapaho. It rests in a location that proves to be the path of least resistance for those crossing the continent. Many wagon trains rest and restock here bound for Oregon, California and Utah." The colonel informed Jebediah, who noticed the fort was not an enclosure surrounded by a stockade but an open fort that depended on its location and its garrisons for security.

"Our wagon train is full of homesteaders bound and determined to make Wyoming their home." Jebediah informed the colonel. He wasted no time in inquiring how the homesteaders were to go about filing claims for land and where the best place to settle might be. By the time the wagon train arrived, he had all the information the homesteaders needed and was immediately placed in a position of authority with the group.

"It is my suggestion that we stay in the fort for a few days and then some of us will ride out and look at the land available to us. We'll need water and grazing land and I have all of the information on the paperwork required to become landowners in this part of the country." The men were very impressed with his organization and most of them were happy to let Jebediah handle the details. A trust that they would come to regret.

The reality of the fort soon dispelled the euphoria the women had felt at arriving, leaving the women less than pleased at the state of Fort Laramie. Converted to a military post in an attempt to control the Indian populations in the area, the fort was not the ideal place for tired women and children. Sanitary conditions were lacking. As anxious to be rid of the wagon as she was, Martha soon realized that the wagon was the only refuge.

Military personnel lived in barracks, where tightly packed rows of cots gave another dimension to togetherness. The officer's quarters were known as "Old Bedlam," famous for its raucous parties. At one end of the fort was the guardhouse, whose basement jail lacked water, toilet facilities and even light. Discipline at the fort was strict and many of the soldiers spent time in the basement jail. The men, seeing few white females, leered at the women and made obscene gestures. The women learned to travel in groups and never into the area of Old Bedlam.

The river and the wagons they had traveled in, quickly replaced the decent bed and bath they had longed for. The quick moving, frigid river was used for bathing and it was difficult to find a calm, secluded area in which to bathe. Many of the women crowded together and took turns in the center of the circle. It was the only way to bathe in privacy and to avoid the calls and leers of the nearby soldiers. Several squaws were kept in the fort as servants and nightly entertainment for the soldiers and the women were quick to avoid all contact with them. In fact, most of these women and children had never seen an Indian. They were deathly afraid of the savages.

Martha returned to her wagon after a quick icy dip in the river. Her cheeks were pink, her skin still tingling from the cold water. She ran her fingers through her damp hair, stooping to retrieve her dropped comb before climbing into the wagon. A young soldier approached. "Morning, Miss, lovely day." He tipped his hat flashing his brightest smile. Hesitant to speak to a stranger, Martha nodded to returned his greeting. "Sergeant John Dwyer at your service, Miss." She liked the musical twang to his speech and the way he wrinkled his nose when he spoke. He was young and handsome, making a striking impression in his uniform. He watched her eyes as he spoke to her. Her hand pushed back the damp hair from her face; she looked at him from under her lashes. It was pleasurable to have a polite interchange with a gentleman. She smiled, enjoying herself for the first time in months. John Dwyer was very taken with Martha and hoping to know her better.

"It's Martha McGuire, I mean Whittaker, Mrs. Martha Whittaker, sir. I am happy to make your acquaintance." John, fascinated with Martha's British accent was disappointed to learn she was married. The two chatted for several minutes, discussing the weather, the fort and Wyoming in general before he moved off, leaving Martha staring wistfully after him. She had been battling depression for months. This interchange provided her with the positive interaction that had been sorely lacking. She felt strangely uplifted.

"Whatever it is you are thinking, forget it." Jebediah appeared from the corner of the wagon, startling her. The icy stare turned her blood to ice. She scampered into the wagon as quickly as her legs would carry her. Jebediah stood staring at the soldier's back for several minutes before moving away. Martha's held breath escaped her lungs in relief when she heard him walk away. *I hate you, Jebediah Whittaker.*

Jebediah gathered the homesteaders together. The new title of pastor seemed to become the norm, with no one even questioning how or when Jebediah had become the pastor. Enjoying his new leadership position, he explained to the men that they could acquire land under the Homesteader's Act. "The Act allows anyone to file for a quarter-section of free land (160 acres). The land is yours at the end of five years if you build a house on it, dig a well, plow ten acres, fence a specified amount, and actually live there. There is another way to get more acres, you can claim a quarter-section of land by "tree claim," as long as you plant and successfully cultivate ten acres of timber." Jebediah slyly, watched the reaction of the homesteaders.

"How much is this land going to cost us, Jebediah?" Pat O'Brien asked from the back of the group.

"Well, let me explain. A filing fee of $10 to claim the land, and then there is a $2 commission fee for the land agent. After that you have to Prove Up as I already explained, build a house, grow crops and live on the land. You will need two people who can vouch for you and who are willing to sign a Proof document. Then once you have completed the Proving Up, after about four or five years, you pay a final fee of $6 and you receive the patent for the land."

"So you're telling us that we'll own our land after we build a house and plant crops, and survive for four years. Well, that is going to cost money and some of us will have a hard time making it through the winter until we have crops to sell."

"Not to worry, Jake, there are people who can help you with finances if you get in trouble. Remember, we're all in this together. Now, men, I suggest we go out and pick our acreages and file our claims for our new homes." Jebediah led the men in a cheer and surveyed the crowd for his first victims. Many of the homesteaders were going to need money to survive the winter and Jebediah was the man to lend it to them, with a small lien arrangement, of course. Within the year, he would hold titles to several of the prime acreages.

After a week in the fort, an area had been chosen for homesteading and the wagon train moved off. Supplies had been purchased at the fort so at least the settlers could eat a decent meal and look forward to finally ending this torturous trek across the nation. The women were anxious to finally be able to settle down and at this point anywhere would do. Martha walked beside the wagons with her two friends. "It will be nice to have a home of our own again, no matter how primitive." Margaret said, a longing look on her face. The trip was beginning to wear down even the optimistic Margaret.

"Fritz and I plan to build a store as soon as we are able. We will start with living quarters and then expand for a General Store. The colonel said that he would arrange for the shipment of supplies and stock." Excitement was evident in her voice. "I can't wait to have my own store again. I feel lost unless I am behind a counter." Olga's broken English was becoming more familiar to Margaret and Martha. Martha was only half listening, her eyes combing the fort for a glimpse of Sergeant Dwyer. She had come across him only once more since that first meeting but couldn't seem to get him off her mind. He was so kind; his compliments making her feel alive once more. She remembered finding him loading a wagon near the fort entrance a few days after their first encounter. Not wanting to admit she had been looking for him, she feigned surprise at seeing him. "Why, Sergeant Dwyer, how nice to see you again. It is a hot day to be working so hard." She remembered how he had smiled, wiping perspiration from his brow with the back of his muscular forearm. Dust mingled with perspiration, making trails on his handsome face.

"Mrs. Whittaker, you are looking lovely today." The sergeant thought that Martha would be lovely no matter what she was wearing. Her faded dress did not detract from her appearance in his eyes. Martha felt attractive and interesting again. Before setting out to find him, she had turned her attention to her personal appearance, spending extra time with her hair, brushing it until it shone. She wanted to stay and talk to him for hours trying to prolong this positive feeling. He made her feel like her old self again. She was desperate for any time she could spend with him, but her days with Jebediah had taught her well. Knowing that was an unadvisable situation, they conversed for only a few minutes before she reluctantly moved off to find the boys.

"What do you think of Wyoming so far, Martha?" Mrs. Mueller noticed the faraway look in Martha's eyes. *This one will have problems with this desolate place*, she thought.

Brought back to the present by Mrs. Mueller's question, she stored her memory of the handsome sergeant away for later. "I am reserving judgment until I see where we end up, Olga."

"This will be a hard life. I feel very unsettled with all of these Indians in the area. I know they are under control right now, but what if they decide to rise up against us?" Margaret interjected.

"Let's hope that doesn't happen. I suppose we will be living on a powder keg for some time. " Martha returned her thoughts to the present conversation but continued scanning the area as the fort started to disappear. There were several soldiers working outside the fort and she carefully took in each face, hoping desperately for a last glimpse of the handsome sergeant.

"Did you hear those soldiers when we were loading the wagons, talking about the young sergeant who was found dead outside the fort? Someone slit his throat." Margaret added, shaking her head. "They found him yesterday. Horrible, I am sure it was those savages." Martha turned abruptly and looked at her, a sick feeling growing in the pit of her stomach.

"Which sergeant was it? Do you know his name?" she asked but she already knew the answer.

"Dwayne or Dwyer, something like that. Why did you know him? Martha, you look like you are going to be sick. Are you all right?"

Martha's face lost all color. She felt as if she were tumbling into a deep dark well. The two women supported her, each one taking her by the elbow. They held her for a few minutes until the color came back to her cheeks. Regaining her composure and seeing the worried looks on the faces of her friends, she made the excuse that it must be the heat and the excitement. Satisfied, they walked along in silence. She held back the tears, remembering the handsome young man. She tried to deny it but she knew what had happened. *Sergeant Dwyer was dead. His throat slit. It was a savage all right, but not the kind they are thinking of.* Goose bumps rose on her arms as the cold fear filled her very soul.

Jebediah, Martha, Isaac, Abraham and Ezekiel arrived at their chosen acreage early in the morning. The walking had helped her stow Sergeant Dwyer's memory safely in the back of her mind along with the fear for her own life. She convinced herself that she must accept the situation and do her best not to aggravate Jebediah. By the time they arrived, she had herself under control. The boys were elated with the open plains. Martha, making a conscious effort to be positive, noticed the beauty and serenity of the area. She was almost relieved to be here. Green grasses moved in the wind like waves on the ocean. The cloudless sky was bright blue. Jebediah had chosen well and the river flowed through their property and then on to the other homesteaders. She did not realize that Jebediah had chosen this land as another form of control. Being in control of the water source put him at a definite advantage. Acres of green prairie grass spread out before them as far as the eye could see; a faint sweet scent of wildflowers blew on the wind. Foothills could be seen in the distance and the vastness of it put Martha in awe. Everything she had encountered in the Americas was foreign to her. Because the properties were large, no neighbors could be seen from the location of their homestead. Martha realized that this was going to be a lonely life.

"You realize that we'll be living in the wagon for a few more weeks until our sod home is finished. We'll all have to pitch in to build this home and that means you, Martha." Jebediah grasped her arm, turning her to face him. "You may not want to hear this but your fancy lifestyle is over. You will work side by side with the boys and me until this home is finished." Jebediah's tone as always was sharp and abrupt. She avoided his gaze, fearfully gulping down the bile that rose in her throat. His grip tightened on her arm. He was sending her a silent message and she understood completely. She was alone. There was no escape.

"Fine, I just want to have a home to sleep in and a place to take a bath in privacy. Ezekiel, come back here. There are snakes and savages and who knows what out there." Jerking her arm from Jebediah, Martha started off after Ezekiel. She moved in his direction, distancing herself from Jebediah as much as she could. She knew that this was going to be another trial in her life and suddenly wished for the camaraderie of the wagon train. *Sergeant Dwyer was dead*, she was sure that it was because of her. Tears pooled in her eyes as she made her way through the long grass. *He just talked to me—that was all. He didn't deserve to die. What kind of a man am I married to?* She offered up a prayer of apology to the dead soldier. She rubbed her arm where the red welts left by Jebediah's fingers were beginning to appear. The thought of living all alone with Jebediah, with no distractions or company loomed like a nightmare.

The next morning, the men gathered together to discuss the building of the sod homes. "First thing we have to do is cut bricks out of the ground. Then turn the grass side down and stack the bricks up to make walls. The roof will be made from thin logs and sod and we can put a layer of straw on top to help keep the water out. I have built a few of these and they work quite well. Nothing fancy but after living in a wagon, even the women should be happy with their new homes." James Brown led the conversation since he had lived in the west the longest and the men were soon planning to get together and build all of the homes over the next few weeks.

Women, children and men all worked together gathering sod for the homes and soon the new community was taking shape. Greased paper was used for windows and dirt floors were the norm. Martha was surprised at her endurance as she worked cutting and carrying sod. At night she fell into an exhausted sleep and dreamt of Graystone. Often she dreamt that she was waltzing with Sergeant Dwyer, around and around they would whirl. The harmonious music lifted her up like the comforting arms of a lover. His handsome face smiling at her, she looked deep into his eyes. Suddenly his head would fall to the side, a huge gash across his throat. Blood poured from the gash over her gown like a river of red death. A silent scream exploded in her ears. Night after night she awoke, perspiring and terrified.

Within a fortnight, their sod home was built and they had shelter from the wind and dust. Martha thought that the home was not much better than the root cellars back in England but she didn't express her opinions out loud for fear of angering her husband. She had overheard Jebediah say that they would build a log home once the timber was available from the nearby logging mill and he calculated the state of their finances. Jebediah was determined to blend in with the other homesteaders and most of them had little or no funds. The ones that survived the winter would live in sod houses for years to come. Martha, not knowing the state of Jebediah's finances, simply hoped that building the log house would be soon. She clung to the thought that the log house would provide some comfort. Fighting the darkness of depression, she convinced herself that once the log house was built, things would improve. She needed something positive to cling to. Sitting in the tiny sod hut she looked around at her surroundings; walls made of sod and mud, rough-cut lumber and planks made up what little furniture they had. The house smelled damp and earthy. The smell brought back early childhood memories. She and Austin, hiding in the root cellar back in England not a care in the world. It was their medieval fort and she was the princess with her prince beside her. Childish laughter echoed in the recesses of her mind. How long ago and far away it all seemed now. *Stop it, Martha, think of something positive.* She told herself, first her trunks would arrive with decent clothing and then they would build a log house to live in. Everything else about the situation was negative and frightening. Her foot caught on her torn petticoat when she rose from the chair. Sitting back down she tore the bottom three inches off the soft silk garment. Martha lifted the torn silk to her face. Tenderly she pressed it to her cheek as tears formed in her eyes. *Tearing to shreds, just like my life. Thread after thread, my very self is wearing away.* She put the crumpled silk in her pocket. Sadly, she left the sod house and went in search of the boys.

To Martha, the sod house seemed to disappear into the landscape when you walked away from it, maintaining the impression of vacant, uninhabited plains. She thought of how lovely her home was in England and no matter how hard she tried to be positive like Margaret, her depression and feelings of separation continued.

Pioneers' days were spent digging wells; building fences for cattle, planting crops and helping the other homesteaders build their homes. It was hard, tiring work, taking every ounce of strength and determination. Soon the homesteaders were settled and a celebratory party was planned.

"Now don't be late getting in from the fields, you know the party is this afternoon. I have waited all week for this and I'll not be late." Martha, now inured to drudgery and distress, instructed the two younger boys as they left for their chores. She was looking forward to seeing Margaret and sharing some female conversation and companionship. "I wish my trunks would arrive from the east, I'm almost out of clothes to wear." She looked down at her skirt. The grass stains permanently etched into the faded fabric.

"Don't be waiting for those trunks, they aren't coming." Jebediah sneered as he left the house.

"What do you mean, they aren't coming, you told me you made arrangements to send everything before we joined the wagon train. All of my dresses and personal belongings were in those trunks." Martha, hands covered in flour, left her pie crust and followed Jebediah who turned and glared at her as he stopped in the doorway. She quickly realized her mistake in taking that tone by the glaring look on Jebediah's face. She swallowed the lump that was forming in her throat.

"Cost too much to send them so I just left them with the hotel manager. I'm sure they have disposed of them by now. No place to wear fancy ball gowns here, anyways." He stepped towards her and she quickly retreated. "Now try and make a good job on those pies for the party, I don't want to be embarrassed." With that, Jebediah abruptly turned and climbed on his horse. Isaac, on his own mount stared at Martha with distaste. Jebediah's words stung like a slap.

Tears pooled in her eyes as she prepared the food for the party. *How could he have done that to me? What does he want from me?* She recalled how he watched her day after day, looking desperately for any sign of the wagon that would deliver her things. He never said one word about them not coming until now. *No trunks, no clothes, no shoes or petticoats, what am I to do?* Even the books that she hoped to read to Ezekiel were lost. Jebediah had books for the boy's lessons but she wanted Ezekiel to hear wonderful stories of England. The small, blond boy had grown much closer since his accident and although her feeling for the other boys remained neutral, she could honestly say she loved little Ezekiel. The thought of receiving her belongings was the only thing that kept her going. She waited each morning for the wagon to pull up in front of the sod house and deliver her trunks. Patiently she waited. *For nothing—I have been waiting for nothing and Jebediah knew all along. He probably enjoyed watching me waiting and waiting. Is there no end to his cruelty?* Suddenly she realized that her mother's portrait was amongst the lost belongings. Her body shook. She sobbed uncontrollably. After all she had endured thus far, this was the final blow. She wore the same three dresses for months, patching, sewing and washing them over and over. Martha realized that her ball gowns would have no place in this environment but her day dresses would have suited her perfectly. With her newly honed sewing skills, she could have converted the material from the gowns into wearable clothing. Now even this was taken from her. *Why bother?* she thought to herself. *I tried to be positive. I tried to look forward, believing things would be better when the trunks arrived, where did it get me? Things just keep getting worse.* In desperation, she took out a letter she had been composing to Austin from its hiding place and read her last entry:

> At last we have arrived at our destination. The words "we are finally here," have a hollow ring, when "here" is the same vast uninhabited wasteland that we have traveled for the past months. The spirits of myself and the other women spiraled downward when we came to the realization that our trials had just begun now that we are finally "here."

Several days ago the men returned from the buffalo hunt. After witnessing the devastation, I cannot believe my eyes. Such a wanton destruction of buffalo, the main source of food and pelts for the Indians, is reprehensible. The men cannot suppress the desire of engaging at least once in the buffalo chase. Even Isaac longs to go with Jebediah and the other men to partake in the senseless slaughter. So much like his father is Isaac, serious, silent, lacking in emotion.

Taking pen in hand, tears staining the paper, she added:

I have just learned that my belongings have been left behind in the east, including my mother's portrait. How I have waited for those trunks. Anticipating their arrival was the only thing that kept me sane. I'm devastated, Austin, my life is a shambles. I'm here in the desolate Wyoming Territory with a man I despise, rags for clothing and no hope for the future. I have honestly tried to be optimistic but one thing after another drags me back to my sense of hopelessness. Oh, Austin, what is to become of me?

Although, Martha knew that Austin would not receive this letter for at least six to nine months, if she could get it to the Pony Express rider at all, it made her feel closer just to write to him. Perhaps she would include this letter in a letter for Aunt Phoebe and was very careful to keep her letters well hidden. Jebediah forbade her to contact anyone. She folded the paper and returned it to its hiding place.

Trying to shake off her feelings of desperation, Martha regained her composure and set herself to the tasks at hand. The dough was soft against her kneading fingers and the smell of cooked apples filled the tiny cabin. Thank goodness Emma taught her to make a decent pie. After receiving the last blow on the trail, angering Jebediah was something she learned to avoid. Martha came to realize that Jebediah's expectations were for her to portray the simple, supportive wife in public. Any animosity that existed was not to be revealed to others. She learned quickly to repress both her urge to argue and her emotions if she wanted any contact with the outside world. The demise of Sergeant Dwyer loomed like a dark shadow in the back of her mind. *If Jebediah is capable of that, what else will he do?* She shivered as fear ran down her spine turning her cold. Rubbing the goose bumps that were forming on her arms, she knew she would have to be very careful around Jebediah. Refusing to give in to the terror that was starting to envelope her, she set the pies on the table and took out her sewing box. She would have to sew the tear in the dress she was wearing and patch the others that she wore on the trail. Oh, Lord, is this torture never going to end?

Chapter Five
Back in London

"Don't you walk away from me, John McGuire. I demand to know why you have condemned your only child to a life of hell with that horrible Jebediah Whittaker." Aunt Phoebe screamed in the face of her surprised brother-in-law, John.

"Come in and stop that screeching. The servants will hear you." John stepped back to allow the furious, tiny creature to enter the manor house.

Phoebe Hunter, at only five feet tall, was in spirit, much larger than most men. She swept into the room with her finger pointing towards John's face and her demeanor reminded John of an angry wet hen.

"Have a seat and tell me what has gotten you all worked up, Phoebe. I'll have Emma bring in some tea and pastries." John reached for the cord that hung by the fireplace, which would summon Emma from the kitchen.

"Never mind your pastries, Mr. McGuire, I demand to know what you have done to my sister's daughter and I'm not leaving until I find out." Phoebe stomped her tiny foot and glared at John McGuire with a face so like his dead wife's that he shook his head in disbelief. Although smaller in stature and two years younger than Lillian, the two sisters bore a startling resemblance.

"I have not done anything to Martha. She simply married Jebediah Whittaker and traveled with her new husband and his three sons to the Americas." John was starting to recover from Phoebe's irate entrance. Not wanting to give Phoebe any more information than was necessary, he tried to skirt around the facts. He paced the room, avoiding eye contact. Choosing his words carefully, he kept the tiny tyrant from asking too many questions. The entire group of investors was meeting this afternoon to discuss the development of the huge parcels of land they had purchased from Jebediah. He had no intention of letting Phoebe in on any of that information. It was important that he satisfy her curiosity and get her settled before he could go to his meeting.

"Young ladies do get married, you know, Phoebe. I really do not understand your attitude. Oh good, Emma you can set the tray by Phoebe, she likes to pour herself." The silver tea service was placed on the small table in front of Phoebe. The astute Emma, once again sensing trouble quickly exited. "Besides, you know what a handful Martha can be. I really think this is for the best."

"My niece sent a message that she was coming to stay with me in London and next thing I hear is that you have married her off and she is gone. I think I'm entitled to some answers and I'm not leaving until I get them." Slowly and carefully she poured the steaming tea into the china teacups. "Austin Wells called on me last week and he had no idea that any of this had happened. We both know that Martha and Austin never make a move without the other one knowing about it and he and I both demand some answers."

John McGuire spent the rest of the morning assuring Phoebe that all was well and that Martha simply didn't have time to let everyone know of her plans before leaving on the ship with Jebediah. He did admit that he had arranged the marriage but that was not uncommon in the aristocracy and even Phoebe had to accept the fact that arranged marriages happened often. Finally he excused himself from the unconvinced Phoebe, and set off to meet the rest of the investors.

"Gentlemen, the land we have purchased is the most desirable parcel in the area. We are very lucky that we acquired it from Jebediah Whittaker. The price may have been higher than we had hoped but we are going to make a huge profit when the mine opens." John paused to sip his water.

One of the other investors added, "With all the miners needing homes, many tiny bungalows could be built in the less desirable sections and rented to the miners." They had already agreed that the higher, more desirable sections of land would hold large manor homes for the mine owners and even some of the investors themselves were interested in living on the scenic hilltop.

"My construction company will handle most of the building," John quickly added, thinking it was setting him up for a large profit. As the rest of the investors discussed the location of the actual coal mine at the far west side of the original parcel of land and agreed on a huge amount of money for the sale of that section alone, John's thoughts turned to Martha. *It was a stroke of luck that Whittaker was planning to dispose of his inheritance and travel to the Americas. The fact that he requested Martha's hand as part of the deal seemed most reasonable. After all, the girl is eighteen and Jebediah is a very wealthy man now that he has sold his inheritance.* He did not feel that he had made such a bad marriage arrangement for the stubborn Martha who was in need of a strong-willed man.

"Geologists are currently surveying the coal site. The land for the small bungalows is being cleared, with the building scheduled to start within a fortnight." His companions continued. *This was the business deal of a lifetime and all thanks to Jebediah Whittaker.* Yes, John McGuire felt that the arrangement had suited everyone very well. A great deal of money would be made in the next year.

While the partners met in the large conference room of the hotel, a tall, handsome, well-dressed young man walked into the pub on the main floor. His light fawn Tweedside jacket was loose, single breasted and reached mid thigh. The collar was small with short lapels and patch pockets were sewn at the waist. As he approached, the barman thought him to be familiar. "My but you look like my dear old friend, Jonas Whittaker but he has been dead these past six years. Would you be one of his lads?"

"Yes, sir, I'm Jeremy Whittaker. I've been in India for five years and have just returned to settle some family business. I'll have a pint of your finest ale if you please, sir." Jeremy Whittaker looked around the small pub, thinking about how long he had been away. The cool ale quenched his thirst and the smell of pipe tobacco filled the room. India was very different from England. He found he had missed the small pubs and local atmosphere. Jeremy was dissimilar to his younger brother Jebediah, both in appearance and ambition. After traveling Europe, he settled in India, establishing a very successful import/export business there. Where Jebediah had always taken the quick, easy and sometimes unsavory approach; Jeremy was more conscientious, particular and compassionate in his actions.

Jeremy contacted the barrister, Max Smithson and arranged to meet with him later that day. It was time to dispose of the family land. He reached into his waistcoat for his pocket watch inherited from his father. His fingers rubbed the gold case affectionately. More than five years since his father's death, he now felt more in control of his emotions. Jeremy had been overwrought after the funeral. Not a day went by that he would not remember the wonderful relationship the two had shared. His plan was to dispose of the land, organize his finances, visit his younger brother in the family home and then return to India. The brothers were never close despite the fact that only twelve months separated them in age; but since Jebediah and his sons had moved back to the family home, Jeremy could not really avoid seeing him. He looked down at his gold watch and checked the time. Constantly checking the watch several times during the day was a habit. He found the watch reassuring and comfortable like an old friend. After his meeting with Smithson, he would spend the night in the hotel and then he would travel to see his brother.

Max Smithson's office was in a prestigious building in the commercial district. Jeremy arrived ten minutes early but was ushered into the barrister's office immediately. Pleasantries were exchanged before Jeremy relayed his instructions to Max Smithson.

"But, my dear Jeremy, I have the signed paperwork here in front of me and you have already sold all of the vacant land that your father left you. I prepared the land sale myself over six months ago. You will notice all of the paperwork contains your signature." The barrister handed the pile of papers to the shocked and confused Jeremy. There at the bottom of each page was the signature of J. Whittaker but it was not his own.

"This is not my signature and I assure you that I have not sold anything. I want to know exactly what is going on here. Who signed these papers and why would you transfer land without my say so? Start talking, sir, and it had better be good." Obviously distressed, his face had become scarlet. Anger boiled in his veins as he waited for the now confused and a little frightened, barrister's answer.

"But, Jeremy, your brother assured me that you had signed everything when he visited you in India and I was instructed that you were most anxious to have the transfers done as quickly as possible. He handled the entire sale with the buyers and Jebediah himself delivered the papers to my office just before leaving on his wedding trip." The barrister had begun to sweat profusely and his hands were shaking as he took his handkerchief from his waistcoat. Was it possible that he'd been tricked by one of Jonas Whittaker's sons? This could have very dire consequences indeed.

"My brother did not visit me in India. In fact, I have not seen him in several years. I did not sign anything and I know nothing of a land transfer or a wedding trip. I suggest, Mr. Smithson, you contact these buyers and inform then that this transfer is not legal and that I demand a meeting with them immediately. I'll be staying at Pheasant Run, unless you have sold it as well." The barrister wiped his brow, then rose as the irate Jeremy stomped out of the office.

Max sat shaking for several minutes after Jeremy departed and could not believe what had just happened. Max knew he was lax in his treatment of the land sale because Jonas had been his friend and he trusted Jebediah. The man was so organized and confident. Aware that Jeremy had been in India for years, he just assumed that he was not interested in retaining title to the acres of farmland his father left to him. Jebediah was living at the manor house, Pheasant Run and it now occurred to him that it was the only land that had not been sold. In hindsight, he didn't even question the fact that Jebediah delivered all of the paperwork and never called a meeting with the barristers present. What was to become of him when this was exposed? Most of the buyers were business associates of his. His reputation would be in shambles. How could he have been so stupid?

The meeting of the land developers was going well and the papers to transfer the land to the mine owners were ready to sign, once the geologist survey was complete. Yes, these businessmen had been shrewd in dealing with Jebediah Whittaker. Some of them even felt a little guilty since they had heard the rumor of the existence of coal on this land before Whittaker approached them. Little did they know that it was Jebediah himself that had started the rumors. The coal was where the profits lay. Just as the brandy was poured, the door opened and Max Smithson walked into the room.

"Smithson, what are you doing here? We are in the middle of a meeting at the moment," one of the developers barked.

"I'm afraid I have some very bad news for you, gentlemen." Wiping his forehead with his handkerchief, the barrister relayed the information. The shocked and enraged businessmen stared in confused silence until Smithson was finished.

"But Whittaker took our money for the land and we demand that his brother honor this land transfer," shouted the men in unison. " We are not going to take this lying down. We paid a large sum of money for this land and we intend to keep it. Why, clearing is going on as we speak. Get this Jeremy Whittaker in here now, we need to talk."

Several hours later, John McGuire returned to his home. White, shaken and bewildered he sank into his favorite chair. This couldn't be happening. Jeremy Whittaker was the owner of the land that Jebediah sold them. This was unbelievable. Jebediah assured them that he was the heir and his barristers had handled all the paperwork. Now Jebediah was gone with thousands of pounds of their money and his brother, Jeremy who had not been in England since his father died, was demanding either payment or his land returned. Legally the land still belonged to Jeremy Whittaker and John and his overly anxious partners had been defrauded of their money. Their only recourse if they wished to continue, was to pay for the land again. They had reported the fraud to Scotland Yard and at least Jeremy Whittaker was willing to negotiate. The sheriff had informed them that the likelihood of finding Jebediah Whittaker was slim and even if they did locate him, he would have to return to England before he could be charged.

Suddenly John McGuire bolted upright in his chair. "Martha, oh my God, what have I done?" Phoebe entered the room just at that moment, and seeing the state of her brother-in-law, rushed to his side.

"John, what is it? John speak to me." Phoebe ran to find Emma as John McGuire slumped, unconscious in his favorite chair.

Chapter Six
The Invitation

Austin Wells, preoccupied with his own thoughts, sat in the railway station waiting for his train to Northumberland. The smell of coal hung in the air. The station bustled with passengers and noisy conversations. A handsome young man with brown wavy hair, dark coffee eyes and a small mustache, he hardly noticed the many ladies in the station, vying for his attention. The lounge suit he wore was very flattering with trousers, waistcoat and jacket all made from the same fine tweed. His reefer, a double-breasted overcoat, sat neatly folded beside him on the bench. The message from Phoebe had been urgent. He worried about Phoebe and Martha. He still did not understand why Martha left the country without so much as a word to him. They were true and faithful friends since the age of five and there was not an event in either of their lives that they did not share with each other. Something was definitely wrong and he hoped that Phoebe would have some answers for him. He rolled the words of Phoebe's message over in his mind.

Your company is requested to discuss an urgent matter. Please come at once.

Jeremy Whittaker, seated in the large leather chair was most comfortable in his smoking jacket of cashmere as he stared at the invitation in his hand. *Why is John McGuire's sister-in-law inviting him to the manor house?* The barristers were handling the fiasco of his brother's fraudulent actions; his curiosity was peaked by the invitation. Jeremy decided to stay in the family home until the land matter resolved. Pheasant Run was all he really needed and had it not been located on the other side of the county, it may have been sold as well. He certainly understood the land developers concern over this matter and was anxious to get it settled. Although he sympathized with their situation, he insisted on being paid for his land and the transfer, about three quarters of the original sale price, was going through in a few days. Jebediah really pulled the wool over everyone's eyes. Jeremy was shocked at the lengths Jebediah had gone to. The brothers were born strangers and remained that way. Jeremy was very angry and disappointed with his brother but had no idea where he was and resolution was unlikely.

Very curious indeed, his thoughts returned to the invitation in his hand. The black ink on the embossed invitation seemed to jump off the paper.

Your company is requested to discuss an urgent matter. Please come at once.

He heard that McGuire had taken ill but was not sure how that situation would concern him. Well, he would just have to go and find out what this was all about. He leaned back into the soft plush chair and sipped his brandy, the strong liquid warming his body.

"I tell you, John, this is the only answer." Phoebe paced back and forth in the great room. John McGuire, looking pale and much thinner, sat in his favorite chair in front of the fireplace with a blanket over his knees. "The doctor said that you had to take it easy for the next few months and someone has to do something. You paid that horrible man and then handed him your daughter as well. Who knows what terrible things he has done to Martha." Phoebe rung her hands together as she paced in front of the two large mullioned windows. Heavy blue draperies hung on either side making a solid backdrop for Phoebe's agitated motions. Her tiny figure was taut with tension and excess energy.

"Phoebe, please, I know I have made two terrible mistakes and I do not need to be constantly reminded that my daughter may be in grave danger." John could still not believe the events that had taken place over the past few weeks. The land partners decided to go ahead and buy the land from Jeremy Whittaker, in spite of the fact that more money was to be paid. Hopefully, they would recover some of the money when the mine was sold but the profit margin was definitely shrinking by the day. Martha was another matter altogether. He sent his daughter off to the Americas with a criminal and now they didn't even know where she was. He was stricken with this illness and not able to go and search for her. Phoebe was right; something had to be done.

"Mr. Austin Wells is here to see you, sir," Emma announced as Austin followed her into the great room. "Shall I bring in the brandy now, sir, or will you wait for the rest of the guests?"

"We'll wait, Emma, thank you. Austin how good to see you, however serious the circumstances." John McGuire remained seated but offered his hand to young Austin.

"I'm curious as to exactly what the circumstances are, Mr. McGuire." Austin was surprised to find the usually vibrant John McGuire, seated and pale. Austin gave Phoebe a serious look as he kissed her hand in greeting.

"All in good time, Austin. We are expecting another guest and we shall discuss this matter when he arrives." Phoebe, returning Austin's concerned glance, continued her pacing.

Jeremy arrived within minutes of Austin and was shown into the elegant great room. Phoebe took in Jeremy's physical features and confident air. His hair reminded her of the color of toffee and his green eyes were gentle and full of wisdom. Phoebe Hunter appreciated handsome men and this one was worthy of her appraisal. After introductions were made, the two young male visitors stared at each other with obvious curiosity and confusion. Emma returned with brandy and the young men waited to learn why they had been summoned.

"Unfortunately, I find myself in need of assistance and although I have been taken ill, I must find my daughter. There has been a serious miscarriage of justice here and Martha should not be married to Jebediah Whittaker. The man is a trickster and a thief. I have asked you both here to request your help." John McGuire coughed as he tried to retain his composure. Even John's voice was weak as he relayed his needs to the guests.

"But I do not see what possible assistance I can be in this matter, sir. I do not even know your daughter and although I would indeed like to find Jebediah, the sheriff has informed us of the unlikelihood of that." Jeremy was watching Austin with increased curiosity. Was this the rejected lover of Martha McGuire, and what was this to do with either of them?

"Please, let me finish, sir. I'm looking for a competent man to travel to the Americas to find Martha and bring her home. I realize that Jebediah would not return willingly and would escape our attempts to bring him back to England, but I want my daughter back here as quickly as possible. I'm not asking either of you to go to the Americas, but I'm asking if you could recommend someone for this delicate position. Jeremy, you are a world traveler and a businessman and I'm sure you have many business contacts." John covered his mouth with his fist as he coughed before continuing. "Austin, you have known Martha all of your life and if you can think of anyone that will help me with this, I would be very grateful. I'll pay all of the expenses for this person as well as a tidy sum of money upon the return of my daughter. I'll leave this with you, gentlemen, and appreciate any help and information you can give me as soon as possible." Once again John stopped to cough. "Now if you will excuse me, I must lie down. Phoebe will provide you with further information." Wheezing, a ghostly pale, John McGuire rose slowly and, with Austin's assistance, left the room.

Austin returned to find Jeremy and Phoebe involved in an intense discussion of the arranged marriage of Jebediah and Martha and the ill health of John McGuire. Austin wondered what possible help Jeremy could be, obviously wanting to be left out of this family business. It was his brother Jebediah that had caused this problem, however, and perhaps Phoebe expected Jeremy's help as restitution for his brother's sins. Jeremy did seem to be genuinely concerned about the situation. Reluctantly Austin admitted that the fellow impressed him. Jeremy was self-confident, straightforward and appeared genuine. Perhaps he would provide them with the right person to find Martha. Austin knowing Phoebe since he was a child knew that what Phoebe wanted, Phoebe usually got. Personally, he was considering taking the job on himself. Martha was not only his best friend but the sister he had never had and he loved her with all of his heart. If she needed him, then he must go to her. But where was she?

"Leave this with me and I'll return in a few days with any information I can provide." Jeremy rose, realizing he was becoming involved with the McGuires in spite of himself. Phoebe was charming and very convincing. He was sad to see the vibrant John McGuire, deteriorating with guilt before their eyes and Austin Wells had definitely peaked his curiosity. The young man seemed very concerned with Martha's welfare; perhaps he was right in his assumption that Austin and Martha were romantically involved. He admitted to himself that the idea of revenge against Jebediah was an appealing one. His brother brought great shame to the Whittaker family and Jeremy knew that it would be up to him to uphold the family name. Jeremy was very much like his father, considering respectability and honesty to be important qualities. Jebediah always preferred deceit and trickery and as a boy, he was a bully and a troublemaker. Yes, it was his duty to see that Jebediah did not escape unpunished. He owed his father that much.

Phoebe watched the two young men like a cat scrutinizing two mice. Both of them were deep in thought, each one questioning the presence of the other. Both men were young, strong and honest. If anyone could help find Martha, these two were Phoebe's choice. Now she would stay quiet and wait. Give them time to think about it and pray that she made the right choice.

"Thank you for coming, Mr. Whittaker, I shall expect to hear from you soon. Austin, you will stay for tea before going home to your mother." Smiling demurely, Phoebe escorted Jeremy to the door.

Sitting in his father's study, Jeremy was contemplating the day's events. The fireplace warmed the room, glow from the flames reflecting on the books that filled the shelves. From floor to ceiling, Jonas Whittaker's books remained just as they had been when Jonas was alive. Jeremy questioned getting involved in the McGuire business but something was pushing him towards Jebediah. His thoughts went back many years to the day he almost drowned. The boys were swimming in the pond located at the back of Pheasant Run. Jebediah started screaming and flailing the water in panic. Jeremy immediately swam to his rescue but when he reached Jebediah, his brother dragged him under. At first Jeremy thought that Jebediah was reacting in panic, but soon realized his brother was intentionally holding him under. As his lungs begged for air, Jeremy fought his brother with all of his strength. Jebediah was relentless in his attempts to drown Jeremy. Finally his survival instinct took over and Jeremy broke free from Jebediah; he surfaced gulping and gasping in huge quantities of air. His brother, realizing that his attempts failed, immediately started laughing and swam away. Although Jebediah insisted he was just fooling around, Jeremy knew better. He never trusted his brother from that day on. Too many times, Jebediah let his dark side show. Jeremy wasn't convinced that Alicia, Jebediah's first wife, had died accidentally. The facts just didn't add up and although he had no proof, he always believed that Jebediah had something to do with it. If so, the McGuire girl could be in serious danger.

His company was in the hands of a capable manager in India, his land transfer would be complete in a few days and there was a certain excitement growing in him. Jeremy loved his travels through Europe and Asia. The thrill of the unknown was what kept Jeremy traveling. He'd almost forgotten the rush of adrenaline traveling had given him. Perhaps he was too settled in his ways in India and this little diversion could do him the world of good. He'd considered expanding his import/export business. The Americas were an unclaimed market. Combine business with adventure; find his brother and bring him to justice and perhaps rescue a damsel in distress. Yes, this definitely had possibilities. He would sleep on it and then call on McGuire in the morning. He tipped his glass slowly, allowing the last of his brandy to warm his throat as he swallowed.

Austin explained the situation to his mother, Minnie, who had known the McGuires since before he was born. Austin, whose father died when he was a boy, always discussed his decisions with his mother. They were very close and he welcomed her sound advice.

"You know I love Martha as if she were my own daughter and just thinking of what that monster may be doing to her makes me weep. I remember the rumors about poor Alicia Whittaker years ago. I never did believe she fell down the stairs. No, I never liked that fellow and now he is Martha's husband." Minnie passed the tray of cookies to Austin. "It would certainly help if you knew where they were going. I understand the Americas are very large and vast and I do not know how anyone would find Martha. Austin, perhaps you should go to John McGuire and offer your services. Your schooling will wait until you return, and hopefully, you would be back within the year." Minnie Wells lifted her bulky form from the rocker that sat in front of the fireplace. "You know I'll respect your decision, son." She brushed her gray hair off her face and kissed her son good night. "Now I'm off to bed. I'm sure you will make the right decision."

Austin sat in the warm, sweet-smelling kitchen long into the night. Any excuses were quickly replaced with the feeling that Martha needed him and he could not desert her. Austin must have been a young teen when Alicia Whittaker died and he could not recall ever hearing of her death. He'd only seen Jebediah Whittaker once or twice but his mother's intuition was very good when it came to assessing people. Visions of a laughing pigtailed Martha up in the apple tree throwing apples at him while he ducked behind the closest tree for protection flashed in his mind. Chasing her through the moors or dancing with her at the ball, she was his constant companion. Austin could never afford to travel to the Americas with his meager inheritance but Mr. McGuire was willing to pay his expenses. Austin realized he was clenching his jaw and shook his head to release some of the tension in his shoulders. If that monster Jebediah Whittaker, did anything to hurt Martha, he would kill him. As he stared into the flames, Martha's lovely young face appeared and Austin knew that he could never turn his back on the woman he'd loved all of his life.

Chapter Seven
The Search Begins

"Boarding passes, please, gentlemen. Whittaker and Wells, you may proceed to your cabin, next please." The bearded second mate processed the passengers as they boarded. He had been with Cunard and Collins since he was a boy and even he was surprised with the swiftness that these new steamships could now cross the Atlantic. Three weeks instead of months was a great improvement and the passenger ships were booked well in advance.

Jeremy and Austin found their cabin and settled their bags before returning to the deck. The two had become better acquainted over the past few weeks while planning their trip and each was equally impressed with their new companion. Phoebe had been correct in her choice. Jeremy and Austin were very compatible. Phoebe was both pleased and relieved that they had agreed to search for her niece. John McGuire was guilt-ridden and this had given them both some hope of seeing Martha again.

Jeremy pulled his brown wool overcoat over his shoulders as the cool moist wind blew across the crowded deck of the ship. Unlike the *Salvation*, most of the passengers on this ship were wealthy travelers who would eat in the dining room on board and sleep in comfortable well-appointed cabins. "I always love watching the dockyard disappear in the distance. You've never sailed before, Wells?"

"Never. Trains have been my transport of choice and I honestly hope I'll not become seasick and spend this voyage in the cabin."

Austin had to admit that he was more than a little apprehensive at the prospect of spending weeks at sea but Jeremy did his best to reassure him. Austin's hands were white as he gripped the ship's rail. The smell of fish mixed with the salty air wafted towards the deck, making Austin's stomach flutter.

"Nothing to it really, old chap. Just stay focused on the horizon until it is out of sight and then keep your eyes focused on some part of the ship and you will be fine. I have some excellent herb tea with ginger if you do feel a little queasy. These new passenger liners are a huge improvement over the wooden sailing ships of the past. Why, they even have a full dining room and a dance hall aboard." Jeremy looked at his nervous companion sympathetically. " It was a stroke of luck that we were able to find the ship's list for the *Salvation* and determine that it docked in Boston. At least we have a starting place. I hope you are a better sleuth than sailor, my dear friend, because we are going to need all our wits about us if we hope to locate Jebediah, especially if he doesn't want to be found."

Jeremy stared pensively at the dockyard as the ship moved out of the port. He like this intelligent and likeable young man. He was impressed that he was not impulsive and had given a great deal of thought to making this voyage. He understood that the lad was driven by concern for Martha McGuire. Austin referred to Martha as a lifelong friend, but Jeremy thought he noticed more than friendship in Austin's eyes when her name was mentioned. Odd travel partners, he thought to himself, one on a mission of love and the other a mission of revenge and justice. "Well success to us both and may God be with us." Jeremy muttered under his breath.

Austin wrote in his journal as the ship made its more than three-thousand-mile journey across the Atlantic Ocean.

A rough night indeed, the sea is running at what the captain termed "mountains high" and it is bitterly cold on deck. A ship traveling to Liverpool was seen from our ship's deck today, with her main and topsails running before the wind; she was a beautiful sight to behold. A grand concert and dress ball on the quarterdeck had been planned for this evening, however, due to the size of the waves and the colder temperatures, was moved indoors. Dinner was a perfect commotion with the occasional unfortunate dish sliding across the floor. Many soiled dinner clothes and soup flowing like a waterfall from the dining table were the result. A degree of effort was necessary just to stay seated at the table.

Today I observed porpoises for the first time. Most interesting creatures, they can be seen following the ship and playing in the bow waves. On several occasions we have passed mail and freight ships during the evenings. Rockets are fired from our deck and returned by the other ship. The sight of the red rockets against the black sky, reflected in the dark ocean is truly indescribable – a most breathtaking sight.

Austin managed to make the three-week crossing with only minor bouts of seasickness and was relieved to be standing on solid earth once again. "Thank God for solid ground. I'm definitely a land lover. What now, Whittaker?" Austin stomped his feet on the dry earth as if he could not believe it was there.

"A hotel and then we begin our search with many questions to many people." Jeremy was thoroughly enjoying this adventure and his eyes took in every detail of the Boston harbor.

There were several large ships docked in the harbor and piles of trunks, crates and boxes covered the docks. People milled around looking for their belongings and several family reunions were taking place. Boston was a thriving city port and Jeremy knew that they had a very difficult task at hand. Finding Jebediah would be like finding a needle in a haystack unless they could find someone that knew where he was. Austin stooped to retrieve a dropped bag for an elderly woman. The woman smiled, thanking him for his kindness.

The evening of their arrival, settled in their hotel room, Austin continued his journal entries:

Jeremy and I have taken up quarters at the Brookside Hotel and today toured the city. Boston is a most impressive place with *splendid buildings; lovely green parks and the ladies of Boston do surpass anything I have seen in weeks for beauty and dress. I'm truly relieved to find the Americas more civilized than I had expected.*

At dinner, a few days after their arrival, Jeremy and Austin were enjoying the last of the delicious roast beef. The taste of the succulent beef remained on his tongue as Austin reached for his brandy. He could not help but notice the lovely blonde seated across the room that was smiling in his direction. His dinner partner seemed distracted by another table. Ever observant, Jeremy was listening to a conversation by two seamen seated behind them.

"Glad to be off the *Salvation* and signing on with *Cunard*," one of the swarthy seaman told the other. "*Salvation* was an old ship used mostly for immigrants and homesteaders, broke and more trouble than they were worth. At least the *Cunard* ships have wealthy travelers and businessmen who might be good for a few bob now and then in a game of chance."

Jeremy could not believe his luck. He turned to face the two seamen. "Excuse me, sir, did you say you were with the *Salvation*?"

"Yep, was until yesterday. What's it to you?" the suspicious seaman eyed Jeremy cautiously.

"I was curious as to whether you remember a family named Whittaker that traveled on the *Salvation* about six or seven months ago? Man and woman with three young boys? Tall, dark-haired fellow about thirty years old?" Because the ship took almost six months to make a return, Jeremy knew that would have been the last trip from Liverpool to Boston that this seaman had been on.

"Nope, can't say as I do remember them. Lots of families on the *Salvation*." The seaman turned his back and returned to his conversation.

Austin passed Jeremy a few pound notes and intimated that perhaps they would revive the seaman's memory. Pound notes in hand the seaman did seem to think harder.

"Well, I do remember one guy named Whittaker. Hell of a gambler, took a lot of money off of several of the passengers in one game onboard. Rest of the crew thought he might have been cheating.

Of course, he didn't have any fans amongst the crew; mean son of a bitch, always complaining. Can't say if he had any kids or a wife, though."

"Do you know where he went once he arrived in Boston?" Jeremy was hoping this was the lead they needed.

"Nope, but probably the same place as the other homesteaders. Wagon trains west, that's where they all go. Thanks for the money, sire." The smiling seaman took his newfound money and returned to his ale and steak pie.

Days of questions led Austin and Jeremy further inland to an outpost where most of the immigrants traveling to the west began their journeys. They checked into a hotel, finding it lacking in all but the bare necessities.

"We don't even know if this is the place or if indeed they did go on a wagon train. Your brother certainly doesn't sound like a homesteader and the idea of Martha traveling west on a wagon train is laughable. She wouldn't even ride a horse and her father owns a stable full of them." Austin was beginning to think they were on a hopeless mission and he doubted that they would ever find Martha.

He found the rural Americas a huge contrast to Boston. Everywhere they went appeared to be primitive, dirty and crude and he wasn't at all sure he wanted to continue. Horses, wagons and people filled the dusty streets. Horses hooves pounded the dirt and manure-covered ground and dusty, smelly particles of the mixture filled the air and the lungs of the pedestrians. Primitive wooden buildings lined the main thoroughfare and items of every description were being sold. Food, tools, clothing, oxen, horses, just about anything a homesteader would want or need was available in these filthy, crowded commercial hubs. Saloons and brothels provided lonely men with anything they might desire and many drunken brawls broke out in the streets. This was definitely not the environment for Austin but Jeremy seemed to be taking it in his stride.

"We have to follow all the leads, Wells. Now start asking around and see if you can find out if they were here." Jeremy headed for the local saloon to make some inquiries.

Tired, dusty and discouraged, Austin returned to the hotel hours later. He held the door open for a young woman and entered the small dining room for some supper. Fragrant smells of beef, herbs and sweet butter filled his nostrils and began to lift his spirits. Austin found a quiet table in the corner. As he looked up from his book while the waiter served his meal, a stunned Austin stared at the wall of the dining room. There, staring at him like a face from the grave was Lillian McGuire. Trembling he grabbed the waiter by the sleeve and demanded to see the manager. The startled waiter ran off to find his boss.

"Yes, sir, what seems to be the problem? Is something wrong with your soup?" The manager appeared full of concern and anxious to satisfy his customer's every need.

"That portrait, where did you get it?" Austin's eyes had not left the portrait that had appeared like an omen in front of him. Blood had drained from his face and his hands were shaking as if he had seen a ghost.

"Oh, she is a beautiful woman, no? It is most unfortunate that her husband could not afford to send the trunks to their final destination."

"What destination, where did they go? What husband? Her husband is in England," questioned a dazed Austin, who then realized that the manager was mistaking the woman in the portrait for Martha not Lillian. "Where did they go, how long ago were they here? What are you doing with that portrait? Where are the trunks now?"

"Slow down, sir. The gentleman and his family left for St. Louis to join Arthur Langley's wagon train several months ago and I assure you the gentleman gave me the trunks and their contents. I remember the details because the gowns made a big impression on the ladies at the Bordello and I have been treated very well ever since; if you know what I mean." The manager winked at Austin. " I thought the portrait added a measure of class to the dining room and that is why I kept it. I assure you there was no foul play here, sir."

Martha had been in this very hotel; he must find Jeremy and give him the news. Austin ran from the dining room leaving the bewildered manager standing at the table with the overturned potato soup dripping onto his shoes.

Jeremy was asking questions in the saloon and getting nowhere. He decided it was time to return to the hotel and find Austin. As he walked along the dusty boardwalk, two filthy, drunken men from the saloon followed. When he turned down the alley, they pounced. One leaped on Jeremy's back while the other knocked his legs out from under him. Punches and kicks were delivered to a shocked and unsuspecting victim, who attempted to fight back without success. The thought that he was about to die loomed large in Jeremy's mind. He swung at the men but was overpowered by the two assailants. A fist buried itself in his abdomen.

"Get his money and take that pocket watch." One of the men reached for Jeremy's watch as his partner held the arms of a bloodied and barely conscious Jeremy behind his back.

Suddenly, a loud ear-piercing crack was heard behind the struggling trio. The men turned to see a smoking gun pointed at the head of the taller assailant. The man released his grip on Jeremy who crumbled to the ground.

"I suggest you back away from the gentleman before I blow your pal's head clean off," the gunman sneered as the first terrified drunk moved back. Being inches taller than the second scruffy thief, the gunman grabbed him by the arm and shoved him against the wall. The first man began to run and the other was roughly shoved in his direction. "Now away with you both and remember the next time you will be face down in the dirt." The would-be thieves quickly disappeared through the alleyway. A dazed, bloodied Jeremy rolled over and stared into the face of his rescuer. His gold watch lay in the dirt, its face cracked. Jeremy picked it up and put it in his pocket.

"Austin, old boy good to see you. When, pray tell, did you purchase that gun?" Jeremy, smiling and still dazed, staggered to his feet, attempting to walk. Austin quickly put his arm around Jeremy's shoulders, brushed the dirt from his friend's clothes and returned the wide grin. The two well-dressed, aristocratic English gentlemen had experienced their first down and dirty, western skirmish unscathed and returned to the hotel.

"Well, I guess I'm beholden to you forever now that you have saved my life, Austin." Back in their room, Jeremy had cleaned the gash on his face and was inspecting the bruises that were beginning to appear on his arms and chest. The broken watch tick-tocked on the dresser, a reminder of just how close he had come. He was very grateful that Austin had arrived when he did. "I do believe we should purchase different attire in order to blend in. We stand out like peacocks in a hen house in these suits. Now, where did you get that gun?"

"I picked it up in Boston. I decided that since we may be traveling into unchartered territory, we may need one and now I'm glad that I put it in my waistcoat before I went to look for you." Austin was still reeling from the experience and although he had appeared calm and in control during the altercation, he had, in fact, been petrified. "Luckily I've done some shooting and I do know how to use the gun if necessary. Why, just the sight of it was enough today. Now let me tell you why I was searching for you." Putting on a false bravado so that his friend did not know how frightened he was, he told Jeremy of the portrait that hung in the dining room. The men talked into the night and decided on the best plan of action.

"So that is what our Martha looks like. I see why you are enamored, Wells. She looks a little like Miss Hunter." Jeremy was taking in every detail of Lillian McGuire as they drank their tea the next morning. Martha must be quite the beauty indeed; no wonder Jebediah wanted her for his wife and Austin was so stricken with her. Well, where was Martha McGuire now? He stared, hypnotized by the portrait.

Austin hardly noticed the hot tea and lemon as he rehashed the events of the preceding day. His fingers stroked his mustache and he stared blankly, deep in thought. He'd actually saved Jeremy's life and now they were about to travel further into the interior of a land that was filled with men like the two he had confronted. Was he up to this adventure? The attack on Jeremy had frightened him. Austin was wrestling with self-doubt and fear of the unknown as the undeterred Jeremy was being drawn deep into the sky blue eyes of Lillian and Martha McGuire.

Chapter Eight
Winter Sets in

Snow blew across the land like a wave in the ocean. Vision was limited to a few feet and the temperatures were dropping fast. The small sod house, buried on three sides with snow with only a narrow dugout path existing between the cabin and the outbuildings disappeared in the landscape. The inside consisted of one room with two sets of bunks and one single cot, where Martha slept. An iron wood stove sat in one corner behind a small table and chairs. Coats and clothing hung from hooks on the walls and stacked wooden crates held most of their possessions. The entire building was smaller than Martha's bedchamber at Graystone.

Martha huddled under her buffalo skin trying to keep from shivering. Her feet felt like ice inside her woolen stockings, her breath settling like fog around her face in spite of the flames in the wood stove. She had never experienced such cold and was sure she would never survive six months of this. Darkness filled the room except for the glimmer of orange light escaping through the vents in the door of the stove. In the dim orange light, she could see the occupants of the other four cots asleep under layers of blankets. Isaac slept in the bunk above Jebediah, the two younger boys in the other bunk bed. Abraham's voice broke the silence. He was talking in his sleep. Martha listened for any signs of alarm but had no desire to leave her bed in the chill of the night. Abraham was indeed the most handsome of the three boys, with his blond hair, large blue eyes and round face.

A kindhearted boy, who loved animals, he could always be found near the goats, cattle or chickens.

"He's buried, hurry, he's buried," mumbled Abraham. Martha wrapped the buffalo robe around her shivering body and reluctantly left her bed, rushing to the sleeping child's side. Gently, she shook him until he awoke. Abraham slept in the bottom bunk with Ezekiel overhead. She ducked her head as she sat beside the small boy on the narrow cot.

"It's just a dream, Abraham. You're fine and no one is buried," Martha whispered as she looked into the angelic face of Jebediah's second son. She turned her head to be sure Jebediah was not awake.

"Martha, John is buried in the snow. He can't breathe, hurry we have to save him." Martha knew he referred to the Tucker boy, John who was Abraham's only friend and lived in the next homestead. The two boys spent a great deal of time together with the cattle and tending to the animals on both farms. Tiny beads of sweat appeared on his forehead. He seemed almost delirious.

"Abraham, it's only a dream. Now back to sleep before you wake your father." Due to Jebediah's harsh disciplinarian nature, Martha constantly tried to keep the boys from disturbing him. "Now go back to sleep, I'll stay with you." Martha settled herself on the side of the narrow cot and brushed the light blond hair from his face. She arranged the buffalo skin over them both.

"It's real, Martha, but no one ever believes me when I tell them these things. No one ever believes me." Abraham slowly drifted off to sleep. Martha returned to her cot but the dream disturbed her and it was hours before she fell asleep.

The dim morning light filtered into the cabin; a loud pounding was heard just as the family was rising. Jebediah opened the door and found John Tucker's father covered in snow and looking panic stricken.

"Jebediah, come quickly, my boy was out checking on the animals and the snow fell off the roof of the shed burying him; by the time we found him, he was dead. Oh, God, oh, God. He needs the last rites, Jebediah, we need you to come right away." Tucker was distraught, wringing his hat in his hands as the never-ending snow settled on his heavy coat. Jebediah quickly tucked his shirt into his trousers, raising his suspenders over his shoulders. He grabbed his bible, coat and hat and followed Tucker out into the blizzard like conditions. Icy air permeated the small abode and snow covered the doorway making it hard for Martha to slam the door shut.

Abraham, still in his bunk, stared at Martha with wide, frightened, tear-filled eyes.

"I told you, Martha, I told you," he mouthed without a sound.

Abraham's premonition frightened Martha. She had heard of people with second sight but had never met one. Martha also knew that Jebediah was not going to be happy knowing one of his children was gifted with it. She went to Abraham and took the frightened seven-year-old in her arms. She whispered as she pulled him to her.

"I think it is best we keep this between us, Abraham. I don't want you to discuss this with anyone. I'm sorry I didn't believe you last night but I will in future." Abraham moved into her arms like the tiny frightened boy he was. "Please, do not say anything to anyone about your dream. I'm sorry about your dear friend, John." Martha sat rocking the now weeping child and trying to absorb what had happened. The other two bunks creaked as the boys rolled over and Martha knew that Isaac was never going to keep silent about this conversation.

Early the next morning, Jebediah dragged Abraham into the shed and slammed the door behind him. A terrified Martha followed them treading through the deep snow, shouting at Jebediah to leave the boy alone. It took all of her courage to open that door but she knew she had to intervene. It was one thing for Jebediah to beat her, but Abraham was a tiny boy. Martha took a deep breath, summoned all of her strength and yanked the door open. The sight that greeted her made her cringe. Jebediah drew the strap back and administered another heavy blow to the boy's back. The horrified Abraham crumbled under the blow.

"Jebediah, stop, you'll kill the boy." Martha screamed at her husband and ran to Abraham's side, crouching over the whimpering boy. The cold wind swirled in the shed from the open door. Abraham's fearful face turned towards her with pleading in his eyes.

"Move, woman, or you will take the blows for him. This is none of your concern. The demon sight must be beaten out of him before anyone finds out about this. Now out of the way." Jebediah raised the strap once again.

"Isaac told you, didn't he. He is the devil himself, that one. Abraham just had a dream, please, Jebediah, leave him be. I beg you. He is bleeding." Martha reached for Abraham.

The strap fell across Martha's extended arm, stinging her flesh through her heavy coat. The smart of the strap was intense. Another blow and this time she raised her arm to defend herself. The strap caught her wrist making a snapping sound. A sharp pain shooting up her arm confirmed her suspicions that her wrist had been broken. She recoiled instantly and again the strap struck Abraham's back. The boy screamed.

"Isaac did what was right. We'll have no secrets in this house and no son of mine will do the devil's bidding." Jebediah showed no concern at having broken Martha's wrist. Once again, the strap fell. "Now the two of you can stay here and pray to the Lord for forgiveness." Crimson with anger, Jebediah turned and left the shed, locking it behind him. The shed grew deathly silent. She stared after him—hate consuming her soul.

In the hours that followed, Martha and Abraham huddled together as the light grew dim. Martha searched the shed for cobwebs and packing them tightly to the wounds on Abraham's back, managed to stop the bleeding. She wiped the blood from the large welts and wrapped him in his overcoat in an attempt to keep him warm. The tracks of her tears were coated with grain dust mixed with dirt from the shed floor. Her hair fell loose from the tight bun on the back of her head. She pushed the hair from her face. Her wrist was throbbing. A most grateful Abraham tried to reset it for her. The pain was excruciating but it felt a little better after he pulled it back in place. Unselfishly, forgetting his own pain, he made a splint out of some old rags and pieces of wood to hold it firm. He tore a strip from her petticoat for a sling, tying it behind her neck to cradle her arm. He looked at her with eyes that seemed to hold the wisdom of the ages as he tended her wrist. There was something mystical about Abraham. She was amazed at how much this seven-year-old knew about joints and breaks but he had tended to the animals and learned from the men in the fields. She was thankful for his skill, however inexperienced and primitive. Finally beginning to know this child, she was finding that, like Ezekiel, he was loving and gentle and needed her for comfort and protection. She reached up with her good arm and pulled down a large fur pelt that had been hung to dry in the shed. Their survival depended on staying warm. The walls of the shed had many narrow cracks between the boards where the faintest light filtered in. Tiny piles of snow appeared at the bottom of each space in the boards, stacked like tiny anthills by the increasing wind. Abraham piled the crates in the center of the shed, making a windbreak. Hours passed and the two were growing hungry. She found some wilted carrots and radishes that had been stored there for the animals, which the two prisoners munched on greedily. Finally total darkness enveloped them. There was no telling how long Jebediah would leave them here. A rat ran across the floor in front of them. The scratching sound as it clawed at the crates constantly reminded them that they were not alone. Martha screamed when she felt something on her leg. It turned out to be Abraham's foot but the terror was real, nonetheless. The beaten and dejected pair huddled together shivering under the thick, foul-smelling fur as the blackness of the night like the blackness of Jebediah's heart, seeped forever into their memories.

Several days later, Martha was hanging the wet laundry inside the cabin to dry. Her wrist throbbed and her shoulder was aching but the chores had to be done and there was no time for self- pity. It was impossible to dry laundry outside and she hoped that the heat from the iron wood stove would be sufficient. She thought of Abraham who was tending to the animals alone, now that John was dead. The thirty-six-hour ordeal in the shed had ended late the preceding day but not before she and Abraham had bonded as only terror and pain can bind two souls.

Isaac approached her. Martha was growing more and more nervous of Isaac. She shuttered when she saw the evil look in his eyes whenever he looked at her. Isaac resembled his father both physically and emotionally, dark in color and countenance. She continued her task waiting nervously for him to speak. Rubbing her arm, still encased in the sling she draped another shirt over the makeshift clothesline.

"Don't think you can win the boys over to your side. I'll be watching you and Father will know everything that goes on in this house. You are only here to clean and cook and nothing more. I'm glad Father locked you both in the shed overnight. I hope you were frightened and cold. It is just unfortunate that you survived." Isaac sneered at Martha and she felt a shiver of fear go down her back. Yes, Isaac was definitely Jebediah's son and both of them filled her with apprehension. Isaac picked up his rifle, gave Martha one last look and left the cabin.

Ezekiel stayed close to Martha. He had not spoken of the banishment to the shed. The young boy helped her with the chores, waiting anxiously for her to read the dog-eared and worn books. Ezekiel could hear the same story over and over and never tire of Martha's voice. "Martha, I heard Mrs. Mueller tell Father that you made the best pies in the west. She even said that she wanted you to supply the General Store with pies. You should be very proud." He smiled his angelic smile that reached right to her heart. She was not surprised that Jebediah had not mentioned this conversation to her. Even the news that Mrs. Mueller thought her pies were the best in the west did nothing for her ego. It was as if she was an empty shell, her ego and her old self, lost somewhere between England and Wyoming. Ezekiel approached her, placing his arms around her waist and hugging her. "I like your pies too, Martha." This boy was the only small joy in her life. She reached down, hugging him with her good arm. She had to be very careful when she acted out of love for Ezekiel. Only if they were alone would she respond to him. Sometimes she saw the confusion on his young face and it broke her heart. One night he crawled into her cot with her, but she insisted he go back to his own bed for fear Jebediah would beat them both. Life was very trying for them all in this tiny sod house, snow-covered and isolated. Winter was very long indeed.

Jebediah visited all of the homesteaders and was carefully gauging their progress. When one or the other was almost down to his last few coins, Jebediah would generously give them a small hand out. Naturally, he was very popular with the homesteaders and all thought him to be a fine, trustworthy gentleman. He was fast becoming the community pastor and was called upon for funerals, weddings and baptisms. Of course, this was all part of Jebediah's plan and planting the seeds of trust was necessary to fulfill his desire to own all of this land within a year or two. He took his new pastoral duties one step further and began holding services in one of the larger outbuildings on Sundays and many of the homesteaders traveled through mounds of snow and icy cold to attend.

He sat bundled in furs in his buckboard. Making his way back to the homestead, Jebediah spent his time alone, thinking. He knew that his mama would be proud of all he had accomplished. His father may have given all of their land to Jeremy, but Jedediah had outsmarted them. He would be the successful landowner now, just like he and Mama planned. It was pure genius starting the rumor that there was coal on the property back in England. He had no idea whether there was or not and it didn't matter to his plans. The gullible developers had believed the rumors and almost begged him to take their money. Now halfway around the world, these gullible sheep were walking blindly into his trap. Mama would be proud. Martha was becoming a burden but Isaac would keep a close eye on her and he still needed her to take care of the house and the two younger boys. He felt that she was making them soft, but things would change once she was gone for good. That would be some time though since his plan was going better than he had expected and he still needed her to maintain his façade.

Power was physically arousing to Jebediah. He was seriously considering going to the fort to satisfy his sexual need for a woman but decided that it was a long trip. He saw no sense since he had a wife at home. Jebediah felt no sexual desire for Martha or any other woman; he simply had to satisfy his physical needs. There was only one woman that Jebediah Whittaker loved and that was his mother. He knew that he was the only one Mama loved too because she told him often. Even after they sent her to that horrible place, he would go to her and she would always say she loved her Jebediah. Father and Jeremy would pay for taking Mama away from him; yes they would pay. Jebediah closed his eyes and imagined the sound of his mother's soft lullaby in his ears as snow began to fall.

That night when the boys were asleep, Jebediah went to Martha's cot and shook her awake. Startled by the dark silhouette standing over her, she gasped and pulled the blankets to her face. *Oh, Lord, no not again.* Jebediah forcefully threw back the blankets, grasped the bottom of her gown tearing it as he forced it up and proceeded to lie on top of her. Martha, knowing better than to struggle; clenched her jaw, closed her eyes and allowed him to have his way. Her body rigid, her arms pinned to her sides, she endured his weight. She could feel his foul, hot breath on her face. His rough and animal like rutting reminded her of the buffalo that she had seen in the fields, filled only with their need to mate. Tears filled her eyes but she refused to cry out. She would not give him the satisfaction. *I hate you, how I hate you. I wish you were dead.* She filled her head with thoughts of hatred in an effort to block out what was happening to her. When he was finished, he returned to his own cot without a word.

Jebediah had only demanded his husbandly rights a few times but he was always callous and cruel. Martha was a virgin the first time he took her on the ship and never dreamed that the physical act of coupling could be so violent and painful. Each time was the same and she dreaded it with every fiber of her being. She remembered, as a young girl, how she had envisioned her wedding night married to a handsome, attractive man. She dreamt of his loving embrace and how wonderful it would be to be united in love. But reality was a cruel taskmaster and her life and her marriage were anything but wonderful and loving. Jebediah's sickening smell lingered on her bed covers and she could still feel his calloused rough hands on her body. Resigned, sore and soiled, she rolled over and fell asleep.

Outside the coyotes howled and the wind continued to blow. The monotony of life wore away at her spirit. She would do the chores, tend to the boys, and stay out of Jebediah's way. When the weather was damp, her wrist ached, sending pain down through her fingers and up her arm. Once a vibrant, beautiful young woman, Martha no longer resembled the carefree girl from Graystone Manor. Her thick chestnut hair was now tied tightly in a bun on the back of her head. She lost weight and her girlish curves were replaced by long lean muscle. Drab, patched cotton dresses made up her wardrobe; making her look and feel she had aged ten years. The Mueller's store was up and operating, with Martha's pies on sale. Apparently they were very popular with the soldiers from the fort and brought increased sales. Naturally, she didn't see any compensation for her work. Jebediah arranged for Mrs. Mueller to apply the money against their store account. Only her time with Ezekiel and Abraham gave her a small amount of joy as she taught them to read and write. Isaac was taught by his father and stayed clear of Martha as much as possible.

In private moments, Martha continued her letter to Austin. She wrote:

> My mental state could only be described as dark and depressed. All the love, laughter and joy have been replaced by endless toil, sadness and defeat. I'm mortified to say that I sometimes wish Jebediah were dead. The situation is hopeless and my life has become a nightmare. I feel my own heart filling with evil thoughts and I'm ashamed. Only the young boys keep me going. I realize that they need me for protection from their own father and I must be strong for them. My feelings for Abraham and Ezekiel can only be described as love. They make me laugh and give me purpose. Isaac terrifies me and I find him staring at me from the other side of the room. He has such a vacant evil look in his eyes and I'm worried that he will act upon it. Jebediah is cruel and heartless. Austin, oh my dearest friend, how did I come to this?

While her days were full of trepidation, Martha's nights were full of dreams of England, beautiful gowns and Austin. One night she dreamt that she was sewing beautiful ball gowns for designer Charles Worth in Paris. Colorful, silken gowns hung all around her like a giant rainbow. Women filed by smiling and nodding their approval. She herself was dressed in one of the glorious gowns and a brilliant smile lit up her face. Martha's dreams were her only escape.

Chapter Nine
Delayed in St. Louis

Austin and Jeremy waited weeks for Arthur Langley, the wagon master to return to St. Louis. St. Louis was a booming city with factories and foundry industries producing tons of pig iron. Many of the grand homes were elaborately appointed with wrought iron decoration. Steamboats, sometimes, anchored three deep for more than a mile in the Mississippi, carried supplies of iron and were the major form of transportation. St. Louis was one of the busiest ports in the Americas.

Although St. Louis provided the two young men with comfortable lodgings and the amenities of a large city, they were anxious to meet with Arthur Langley to discover Jebediah's final destination. When he finally did return, Arthur was hesitant to give them any information until he learned that Jeremy was Jebediah's brother. Naturally, he assumed that Jeremy was searching for his brother for family reasons and was happy to give the two young men as much information as he could.

"I left the Whittakers at Fort Laramie in the Wyoming Territory several months ago. I was most impressed with Jebediah and I wish you luck with the search." Jeremy inquired as to the welfare of his nephews and was happy to hear that they were well. Langley mentioned the snakebite incident but was quick to assure them that Mrs. Whittaker had nursed the boy back to health. Austin could not resist asking about Martha and Langley acknowledged that she had been well when he last saw her. Austin picked up on Langley's obvious dislike of Martha and decided it best to leave it at that. Something was definitely going on with the Whittakers. Martha was outgoing and friendly and Austin could not understand why anyone would have a bad impression of her. Of course, with everything he knew about Jebediah, he could never imagine anyone being fond of him. Even the seaman from the *Salvation* had referred to Jebediah as a mean son of a bitch. Perhaps he had underestimated Jebediah's powers of persuasion. All he could think of was that Martha was somewhere in the west and living with this monster. He must find her before anything happened to her. Although he was a gentle man, Austin knew he would kill Jebediah Whittaker if Martha had been harmed. Austin was uncomfortable with this malevolence for the brother of his dear friend, but in his heart, hate was growing for Jebediah.

Unfortunately, now the winter weather had taken a turn for the worst and travel was difficult if not impossible. Jeremy spent his time making business contacts and arranging for shipments to and from India. The Hudson's Bay Company was the largest company in the Americas and Jeremy was pleased to be associated with them. Beaver fur top hats were the fashion craze in London. Fur trappers were abundant in the west fortunately demand for pelts was high. The pelts and skins available for export were of the highest quality. Jeremy, pleased he had decided to travel to the Americas, was excited with his new business prospects. He visited the telegraph office. A telegraph was sent to London and John McGuire was advised of their current situation. Nothing they could do but wait until the weather improved.

Austin's journal entries for St. Louis:

> We traveled by stagecoach to Portson as the water was too low to allow boats passage. There we boarded the *Olympic Bell* steamboat and traveled to St. Louis, after learning of Martha's departure with a wagon master from that city.
>
> Unfortunately, winter is close and navigation is near closed on

the upper river. We have taken quarters in the St. Louis City Hotel and here we'll await a break in the weather. I'm learning a great deal about the export and import business and I hope that I'm a help to Jeremy. He has become like a brother to me and we rely on each other for support and companionship. This trip will prove difficult and I pray for Martha's safety.

Austin was becoming more relaxed with the colonies and actually enjoyed the camaraderie of the locals. Many of them were German and Irish immigrants that settled in St. Louis. He enjoyed the conversations, learning a great deal about the west. One night in the saloon, Austin learned that an Irish immigrant named Joseph Murphy built a wagon, now called a Murphy wagon, which could hold 5000 pounds of freight and was used on the Santa Fe and Oregon Trail. Murphy was also the builder of the "Prairie Schooners," the covered wagons that took the homesteaders west. Fur traders had opened the west over the past fifty years, and it was now ready for the homesteaders. Apparently land was offered for next to nothing in the western territories and Austin surmised that this had been the enticement for the materialistic Jebediah.

On several occasions, Austin, who had been studying business and law when he met Jeremy, assisted with a sale or two and was learning more and more of the import and export business. The Hudson's Bay Company intrigued him. The export of furs, whale oil, wood and ore was big business. The work provided a needed distraction.

Austin, who had never witnessed snow of such depths or freezing cold that chilled to the bone, was anxious to leave. He wanted to find Martha but as he watched the snow growing deeper and deeper, realized that it was impossible until the weather changed.

Austin and Jeremy now dressed in denim, buckskin and Stetsons and more than one lady had her eye on these handsome young men. Never lacking for dance partners or dinner invitations, the two were very popular with the female population of St. Louis. Even Arthur Langley's seventeen-year-old daughter, Loretta, thought Austin to be the most attractive man she had ever seen. Tall, handsome and a real gentleman, he was a definite contrast to the brash and bawdry cowboys or the crass and dirty ironworkers of St. Louis. The sassy Loretta went out of her way to be in the same place as Austin whenever she could.

One afternoon the two young men sat in the hotel lobby enjoying a brandy. Jeremy took his gold watch from his pocket checking the time. The broken face was a constant reminder of the possible dangers this new land held. "Still early yet, Wells, I believe your new friend is coming this way," teased Jeremy The young men watched the curvaceous, golden-haired young woman approach and even Jeremy thought that she was most attractive in a down home sort of way. Innocent of face and with a body that any man would love to get his hands on, Loretta Langley was definitely a good catch. The only problem, Jeremy could see, was that it was Loretta that was doing the hunting and Austin had become the quarry. Still unsure of the relationship between Austin and Martha, he wondered just what Miss Martha McGuire would think about this turn of events, even if she was a married woman?

"Why, Austin, Jeremy, what a nice surprise. I was just dropping off some papers for Daddy and here you are." Loretta, coquettishly arranging her long crinoline dress as she sat, immediately took her place next to Austin on the Gold settee. Although Loretta's mother always dressed her in the most up-to-date fashions, styles in the Americas lagged behind Britain and France by about two years. Miss Langley's dress and fur-trimmed overcoat however, were definitely stylish and very flattering.

"Nice to see you, Loretta. Jeremy and I were just catching up on some news while we wait for dinner. Would you care to join us?" Austin was not unaware of Loretta's interest, besides, he enjoyed her company and any diversion was a good one in this frozen environment. In any man's opinion, she was an extremely attractive young woman. The three enjoyed several evenings together over the course of the next few months. Austin found Loretta to be sparkling and bright and looked forward to seeing her whenever he could. She was like a twinkling star in a dark night sky. Even Jeremy was becoming smitten by the innocent charms of Miss Langley. As the frost remained on the windowpanes and the snow continued to fall on St. Louis, the dull days were brighter because of the sunny Loretta Langley.

In England, the telegram arrived and Phoebe and John were relieved to know that at least there was some progress in the search. John's health had greatly improved and although he was constantly worried about his daughter; he returned to his construction business and dealings with his land partners. The land on which the mine was located was sold and the coal mine was operational. The small miners' cottages that had been built by John's construction firm were now occupied. The developers were feeling much better about the entire land transfer. All of them were experiencing some guilt and embarrassment at having allowed Jebediah to cheat them but they all realized that it was their own greed that was the real culprit. In future, these men would be more careful and less self-serving. All had learned a good lesson, but John McGuire suffered the most.

John spent many hours sitting in Martha's bedchamber longing for their old life together. If only Lillian had lived. Phoebe's presence in the house had only reminded him of how much he still loved and missed his wife. Now, with Martha gone, the house was very lonely indeed. Even Lillian's portrait was gone from the wall; it was as if Lillian's spirit had left with Martha and neither of them was ever coming back. Tears flowed down his cheeks onto the burgundy velvet and his heart ached for his lost family. Those two young men were his only hope in recovering his daughter but his worst fear was that she would refuse to come home to him. He had made a terrible mistake and had allowed greed to cloud his judgment. He prayed that Martha would forgive him and be returned safely to his side, even though he would never forgive himself.

Phoebe remained with John until his recovery and then returned to her home in London. Emma could take care of Graystone and Phoebe missed the London social lifestyle that she was used to. It was good to be home. She wrote a letter to Minnie Wells to reassure her of her son's welfare and the current situation with the search. Phoebe was not the most patient woman, but in this instance there was nothing to do but wait. She prayed they would find Martha before something dreadful happened to her.

Max Smithson left Northumberland and moved to London. He and Phoebe became acquainted at the McGuires' and frequently dined together at Graystone. During one of their dinner parties, John and Max discussed the fact that married women could not be landowners and any land inherited by a woman immediately became the property of her husband. Therefore, if anything were to happen to John, it would be Jebediah and not Martha that would be heir to Graystone. This bothered John immensely and gave more reason for him to pray for Martha's safe return and an immediate annulment of this marriage.

Phoebe was very distraught over this whole business and was glad that Max Smithson had become a friend to her and John. One night she and the distinguished, gray-haired, Max dined alone. Max told her of a long forgotten conversation he had with Jonas Whittaker. Over his second glass of French champagne, Max told Phoebe, "Jonas was depressed after having to commit his wife to the asylum. He loved his wife dearly and had coped with her illness for years but finally, there was no choice. She didn't recognize Jonas or her sons and was becoming a threat to herself and possibly to others. Jeremy agreed with his father's decision but Jebediah fought to keep his mother home. Apparently Jebediah went to the asylum on several occasions to see her and always returned claiming that she was cured. It was a difficult time for all of the Whittakers."

"My God, Max, you don't mean he put that poor woman in a workhouse?" Phoebe was aghast. Workhouses were horrible places occupied by lunatic paupers and criminals.

"Phoebe, let me explain about lunatic asylums. Workhouses are exclusively for paupers. Licenses Houses do take both paupers and non-paupers and Hospitals receive few poor lunatics. There are single houses that are exclusively for the rich. The process of making someone a Chancery lunatic is very expensive. It offers confinement for a considerable sum but allows a certain element of privacy and usually a patient is given his or her own room. Where as the workhouses and madhouses simply house the lunatics together, the criminally violent are chained and the others simply put together in large rooms. Conditions are deplorable at best and there is really no regulation. Commissioners could visit a single lunatic confined for profit, by obtaining the authority of the Lord Chancellor or Home Secretary but it is seldom done. Jonas tried to find a Single House that would care for his wife in the best possible way." Max gave Phoebe a reassuring pat on the shoulder and apologizing for being a bit long winded on certain topics, continued.

"Now back to my original thought of the conversation between myself and Jonas."

"It was the night of Jebediah and Alicia's wedding and Jonas told me of his concerns regarding Jebediah's motive for marrying the girl. Apparently Jebediah showed no interest in her at all until he heard that Alicia's father, Ezekiel Barstow, was ill. Barstow owned the mill in Northumberland where Jebediah was employed. Shortly after learning of Barstow's illness, Jebediah proposed to Alicia. Jonas told me that he was concerned that Jebediah was marrying her under false pretenses." Max continued filling in the gaps for Phoebe.

Three years and two sons later, Jebediah became the owner of Barstow Mills and the Barstow family home, upon Ezekiel Barstow's death. Shortly after the birth of her third son, Alicia Barstow Whittaker mysteriously fell to her death. Jebediah disposed of the mill and the Barstow family home saying that he was too distraught at the loss of his wife and moved back to Pheasant Run. Max offered to set up trust funds for the boys with the money from the sale, but Jebediah said he would take care of it when the mourning period was over. Max now realized the trusts had never been set up and the entire inheritance had gone to Jebediah. This new information made Phoebe worry even more about Martha's safety. Was it possible that Jebediah Whittaker killed his own wife? Was he a lunatic like his mother? Phoebe could not allow herself to think of the possibilities. She just prayed harder for Austin and Jeremy to find her niece.

Max was enjoying his new office in London. He stood looking out the window at Piccadilly Square. London was where the action was and a successful lawyer could make a lot of money in this busy metropolis. Thinking back to a few months before, he still could not believe how his life had changed. Fortunately the Whittaker business had not destroyed his reputation, however, Max felt that it was best to leave Northumberland and start fresh in London. When he had unexpectedly been offered a partnership in a very prestigious London firm, he accepted immediately. The firm even helped with his relocation to a lovely new home in the upscale side of London. The idea of being closer to the alluring Phoebe had been a definite influence on his decision. He pictured her pale smooth complexion and her lovely chestnut hair with hardly a sign of gray. For a fifty-year-old widow, Phoebe Hunter was most attractive. It was a definite plus that she enjoyed his company. Something good had definitely come out of a bad situation. What a brilliant stroke of luck this London partnership had been for him.

Phoebe, who was very influential in London society, was very fond of Max Smithson. Unbeknownst to him, she had made a few inquiries with a law firm with whom she was a long-standing client. With Phoebe's prodding, they arranged for Max's partnership offer with an associate firm in London. The firm had even found a most suitable Tudor style home for Max to live in on the upper east side of London, at Phoebe's request. It had all worked out wonderfully and now Phoebe and the successful barrister enjoyed each other's company on a regular basis. Operas, gala balls, dinner parties, and charitable events were the entertainment of London society and one definitely wanted a suitable, distinguished escort. She and Max appeared on the social pages often. The two were making quite a hit with London society. Yes, what Phoebe Hunter wanted, Phoebe Hunter usually got.

Chapter Ten
Spring at Last

Although clumps of snow and ice could still be seen, most of the landscape was covered in green sprouts of grass. Martha stood in front of the cabin, the sun's rays bringing warmth to her face. A wagon approached from the east. Martha shielded her eyes, waving to the people approaching. "Morning, Arnold, Ethel, where are you off to this fine day?" As the words left her lips, she realized that the Swartz's wagon was piled high with furniture and crates.

"We came to say goodbye, Martha. The winter has taken its toll on our finances. We can't survive another month. This land has taken our dreams and our money. Nothing to do but move on." Arnold Swartz sadly shook his head as he extended his hand to Martha in farewell. "We are going to California."

"But, Arnold, is there nothing that can be done. Perhaps you could get a loan or we could take up a collection. Everyone has suffered the long winter, but I know they would all try to help." Martha could not bear the dejected look on the pair. "How are you going to make it all the way over the mountains to California?" Ethel sat shoulders hunched in the wagon. She lifted her sad eyes in Martha's direction but didn't say a word. Tears were pooling in her eyes. Martha was speechless. She noticed Arnold look past her, his eyes full of disgust and anger to the doorway, where Jebediah stood. He quickly averted his gaze and nodded to Martha. She turned in time to see Jebediah return to the cabin, shutting the door. Martha was curious as to the look that Arnold had given him. There was definitely a sign of anger in the man's face but Martha had no idea why Arnold would be angry with Jebediah. The people loved Jebediah. The Swartz's wagon disappeared in the distance as she pondered the strange look. It was sad to see one of the townspeople leaving, when hopes had been so high. These people were strong and courageous, battling almost insurmountable odds to settle in this barren land. As she stared in the direction of the disappearing wagon, in the back of her mind, she wished she were going with them. A single tear trickled down her face.

The temperature had risen and the homesteaders had been busy with the building of the new parish church. Everyone contributed time and energy and finally the tiny church was ready for the opening presentation. The sky was bright blue with only a few wispy clouds.

"Ladies and gentleman, it gives me great pleasure to present the key to our new church to Pastor Jebediah Whittaker. Jebediah, could you come up front, please?" Jake extended his large, calloused hand to invite Jebediah to join him. All of the homesteaders crowded around the front of the new church building. A loud applause was heard as Jebediah walked up the steps of the church. The homesteaders were very proud of their new building and sincerely believed no one deserved the applause like Jebediah. He had been kind enough to loan most of them money over the course of the winter and they considered him a Godsend. The Swartzes were the unfortunate ones. They had the parcel directly next to Jebediah's and were his first victim. After lending them money early in the winter, he recalled the loan as the snow started to melt. Arnold Swartz had no choice but to leave, increasing the size of Jebediah's holding by double. Defeated and too embarrassed to say anything, they simply packed up and left. The rest of the homesteaders remained in the dark to the serious fate that awaited them. Totally unaware of Jebediah's sinister plot, they praised him as a Godfearing, generous man. Taking time from their chores to complete the church building. Jebediah was a Godsend. They simply accepted him as the church pastor, rejoicing in his presence in their lives.

"Words can not express my appreciation. We have taken the vast barren plains and built a community to be proud of. Soon we'll have more shops, log homes and a town of our own. Thank you, my friends, for your continued faith in God and in me as your pastor. Praise the Lord!" Jebediah accepted the key from Jake and smiled as he opened the door to his future.

Martha, Abraham and Ezekiel sat on the knoll opposite the church. It felt good just to be outside once again and Ezekiel ran off to chase a prairie dog or rabbit. Martha and Abraham sat in silence taking in the scent of fresh grass mixed with the smell of pies and fried chicken from the large wooden tables. Just the warmth in the air was enough to lift Martha's spirits. Clad in her simple blue gingham dress with lace trimmed white apron, she felt renewed. Jebediah had uncharacteristically, allowed her to take the material in trade for some of the pies she had baked. Mrs. Mueller had been pleased to barter with Martha, selling the pies was good for business. The newly built General Store was very successful under the constant care of Olga. Fritz's wheezing had grown worse over the winter, but he did what he could to help out. More and more supplies became available in the tiny town, thanks to the Muellers. It had taken some convincing to get the small roll of material, but Jebediah had finally given in. Of course, he had done it so that she would look presentable to his parishioners, but at this point she didn't really care why, grateful for anything he would give her. Her hair now dull and lackluster was tightly knotted on the back of her head. She had cut several inches of dead ends off during the winter hoping to restore it but it seemed hopeless. At this point in her life it was no longer important. It had been a long and torturous winter; maybe things would improve now that spring was here. Perhaps now she would not have to force herself to get out of bed in the morning, actually wanting to see another day. People were getting reacquainted and there was much merriment and laughter. Children played, food was consumed and the sound of fiddles and guitars filled the air. This was an important day in the life of this growing western town.

Once Ezekiel was out of range, Abraham began to tell Martha of his latest dream. They had agreed that they would never discuss Abraham's dreams unless they were alone. Even an innocent comment by Ezekiel could put them both in grave jeopardy.

"I think I know who the man in the dreams is, Martha." Abraham had several dreams over the winter of a man that seemed familiar to him but whom he did not know. "I think he is my Uncle Jeremy." Abraham pensively twirled a blade of grass in his fingers, his foot tapping involuntarily to the sound of the fiddle.

"Your uncle, but hasn't he been away for years? Why would you dream of him?" Martha had learned to pay close attention to Abraham's dreams as most of them came true. "Why do you think it is your uncle?"

"When I was very small, I remember Uncle Jeremy used to take me to the stables to see the horses and the dogs. Once he let me sit with the new puppies. I still remember how round and soft they were. One of them licked my face with his little pink tongue. We loved Uncle Jeremy. He was very kind to us. Then he went away after Grandfather died and we never saw him again. I haven't thought of him for years. Last night when I woke up I realized that the man in the dream was him."

"So the man you saw on a ship in the dream was your uncle. What about the man you saw riding in the stage coach, was that your uncle too?" Martha was very patient with Abraham because his dreams were very intense and she did not want to upset him.

"Both times I saw Uncle Jeremy he was with the same stranger. On a ship and in a stagecoach but I don't know what the dream means. I just think he is angry with Father for some reason. That is just a feeling I get when I dream of him." Abraham kept his eyes on the church door for any sign of his father. He had learned never to speak of his dreams within earshot of Jebediah or Isaac. Abraham knew that Martha was the only person he could trust with his strange ability. Jebediah believed in harsh discipline and beatings were common for all of the boys but none were as severe as the one in the shed, when Martha had intervened. Abraham had learned that he could trust her that day and he never forgot what she had done for him. He loved her with all of his heart. He remembered the time he had picked flowers for her from the back of the church. She had been so happy and given him her best smile. Martha set them in a jar of water on the kitchen table and gave him a big hug. Then his father came home and made him take the flowers back to the church. They remained on the table at the front of the tiny church during the Sunday service; Abraham's anger festered as he sat in the front pew. Reminded of his father's cruelty every time he looked at them. She deserved a few moments' happiness. What harm did the flowers do sitting on her kitchen table? His father was cruel and heartless; sometimes Abraham thought he hated his father.

Moments later, Ezekiel ran back to Martha with tears in his eyes. "Ezekiel what is the matter? Why are you crying?" Martha pulled the weeping boy into her arms and tried to soothe him.

"Isaac killed the rabbit. I was chasing it and Isaac shot it with his bow. I just wanted to see it. I didn't want it to die." The sobbing youngster gasped for breath. "Isaac is mean, Martha. He laughed when he shot it. I hate him." Ezekiel sobbed and rested his head on Martha's lap as she tried to console him, convincing him that he should love his brother no matter what he did.

Martha however, agreed with Ezekiel; Isaac was meanspirited and probably killed the rabbit just because Ezekiel was enjoying it. Anger boiled up inside of her, *how could Isaac be so cruel to his little brother. What drove the boy to such lengths?* She would like to shout at Isaac and admonish him for the cruel thoughtless things that he did. Unfortunately, she knew that any anger against Isaac or his father would have to be suppressed. Ezekiel soon became distracted and ran off. She stood, fists clenched and stomped her feet in an effort to dispel some of the pent-up anger she felt. She wanted to walk into the field and just scream as loud as she could. Scream for Isaac's cruelty, scream for the beatings that the boys and she had endured, and scream for someone to come and help her. Abraham watched her silently from his perch in the nearby tree.

Instead, Martha looked to the sky and prayed for some sign of hope. She prayed to a different God than Jebediah claimed to represent because no God of hers would ever condone Jebediah Whittaker as community pastor. This entire church ceremony made her sick to her stomach. *Are they all so gullible to think that Jebediah was a wonderful Godfearing man? Do they not see how cruel and unfeeling he really was?* Martha was beginning to believe she was living with the Devil himself and Isaac was the Devil's own seed. She found it difficult to maintain the pretense forced upon her by Jebediah.

Unfortunately her feelings were distancing her from the only people she now had contact with. Jebediah kept his family separate from the others as much as possible. Even during church services, they sat in the front pew and were instructed to return to the cabin as soon as the service was over. An occasional quick conversation with Margaret after church and the off chance that Jebediah allowed her to deliver the pies to Olga, were the only communication Martha had with the outside world. Needing some of that communication, Martha moved towards the church in an effort to find someone to talk to before Jebediah came and instructed her to go back to the cabin. Abraham stayed in the tree and watched her go, disheartened by the sad look in her eyes.

The next time Abraham and Martha discussed one of Abraham's dreams, it was very disconcerting to Martha. She could see the toll, the confusion and distress the dreams were having on Abraham. He was so young and innocent to have to deal with such a gift. She often wondered whether it was a gift or a curse. It was weeks after the church ceremony and almost dusk. The days were getting longer and drier now and their life seemed to have moved outside.

"I think God is angry, Martha." Abraham whispered as he and Martha fed the goats. Jebediah was at the church where he spent most of his time and Isaac was delivering his supper to him. Ezekiel had fallen asleep so the two were alone.

"Why do you think God is angry, Abraham?" Martha was not sure what to expect next. She spread the straw in the pen where the new mother goat and her kids were housed. A low bleating sound was coming from the goat.

"Because I saw the church burning." Abraham reached out to stroke the back of the newborn kid. "It burned and burned and I heard someone laughing," relayed Abraham. "Yes, I think God is very angry that Father is the pastor."

Martha did not know how to respond. She assured Abraham that perhaps this time his dream would not come true but asked him to be very careful around the church. He was to keep a very close eye on Ezekiel as well. Fires were one of the worst nightmares for the homesteaders. Earlier in the week she noticed with apprehension the dryness of the land. She had stooped to pluck a blade of prairie grass and found it dry, almost to the point of brittleness. When she felt the rising wind, her glance at the fresh stocks of wheat and the foot high cornfield was uneasy. A fire would start readily, and drying fields were excellent tinder. She remembered thinking of the one precautionary measure against prairie fires taken by all of the homesteaders. A broad strip of bare stamped earth circled their cabins and the outbuildings as well as the church. There was reasonable safety within that line, for this path of grassless earth would hopefully form a magic ring of protection for the families and the stock. However, fire was known to leap narrow streams and even the fact that their property was surrounded on two sides by the river did not ensure that they would be safe. Martha pushed her anxiety to the back of her mind and finished her chores. Hopefully, this time Abraham's dream was just a dream. The young boy stayed with the goats, stroking the young kid gently and scratching the goat on the head. The animals were very comfortable with Abraham and he with them.

She fed the stock, collected the eggs, and watered the horses then returned to the cabin. Although she still had no great love of animals she had learned to accept them as part of her life. The log home was built and she was relieved to have a proper house. Unfortunately it did not improve her situation as much as she had hoped. It proved to be more work for her being larger than the sod house. She had now been given the responsibility for cleaning the church as well; but, now grateful for any small improvement, she was glad to have a decent place for herself and the boys. Having accepted the fact that there was no escape from Jebediah, she knew that she had to make the best of the situation. At least they had more room and she put up a privacy curtain for her baths. She shuddered every time she remembered that in the sod house the tub was set up and filled in the middle of the room. Everyone was required to leave the house so she could bathe, but she had been subjected to Jebediah's unwanted presence on several occasions. Now the privacy curtain provided her a certain amount of privacy, no matter how small. The log house had a large fireplace and would be much warmer next winter. She stacked the wood near the fire and carried the basket of vegetables to the table. As she prepared the evening meal of boiled rabbit, vegetables and bannock bread, Abraham's dream kept returning to her mind. *Will there be a fire?* The dreams about his uncle troubled her as well. *If Jeremy Whittaker is anything like his brother, he is the last person I want to see.* What could it all mean?

She prepared the meal and waited while the boys washed for

dinner. Around the table the five ate in their usual silence. Ezekiel reached for his glass of milk and it tumbled over sending a river of white in Jebediah's direction.

"You stupid boy, I have told you to be more careful." Jebediah barked at the boy. Ezekiel's eyes were downcast as he blinked back the tears. "Enough of that crying. Martha is making a baby out of you, now away from the table with no supper. You can go and finish cleaning the last of those rabbits before you go to bed. Now go." Jebediah reached out and struck Ezekiel across the face. He roughly pushed the small boy from his chair in the direction of the door. Then as quickly as it had happened, Jebediah turned his attention back to his food as Ezekiel, hand to his red tear-stained face, left the cabin. Abraham and Martha exchanged a concerned glance but not a word was spoken. Isaac ignored the entire situation, continuing to consume his food. Hours later, Ezekiel returned to the cabin and without a word climbed into his cot, Martha was sympathetic but knew better than to approach the boy. She prepared for bed and that night she dreamt of flames engulfing her new log home.

Days later while cleaning the small church building, she entered the office area where Jebediah spent his time. The space was small containing only a wooden desk, chair and a small bookshelf but it was adequate and fast becoming the Pastor's sanctuary. Relieved to see the room was empty, she pushed the door open, noticing a large leather bound ledger book on his desk. Making sure she was alone, she curiously flipped open the pages. There she found the names of most of the people in the community and a sum of money beside each name. Even the Muellers, who were expanding the much-awaited General Store, were indebted to Jebediah. She found lien notes made out to Jebediah for almost all of the properties in the community. The lien from the long departed Swartz family was marked: Plot now transferred. *So this is what he is up to.* Jebediah was worse than she thought. These people had put him on the highest pedestal. It was all a sham, a trick to take their land from them. Angered at the tyranny towards these trusting souls, she felt sick. She took a deep breath, but started feeling weak in the knees. *What can I do with this information?* Suddenly she was aware of someone approaching the office. Slamming the book shut, she moved nervously towards her bucket and mop. Isaac appeared in the doorway.

"What are you doing in here? You know you are to stay out of my father's office. Get back to your cleaning." Isaac raised his hand as if he were about to strike her. The boy of eleven was almost as tall as Martha but it was the look in his eye and not the raised hand that frightened her most.

"I simply came in here to mop the floor, now I'll be going, if you will get out of my way." Pushing past him her shoulder brushing his, she returned to the church. Isaac stood staring at her for a few minutes before leaving by the back door. Unsure if he had seen her, Martha grew more and more nervous as the day progressed. The sick feeling in her stomach would not go away. Jebediah would kill her if he knew that she had seen the ledger.

Supper of venison, fresh baked bread and garden vegetables took place without incident but Isaac's glare never left her. Perhaps he had not seen her with the ledger, perhaps he had already told Jebediah or perhaps for reasons of his own, he had decided not to tell his father yet. She was unsure how the final scenario would play out. The food caught in her throat as she nervously tried to finish her meal. She rose to move her half-eaten plate from the table, but Jebediah ordered her to sit down. "Finish that food before you leave the table. The Lord provides and we will gratefully consume all we are given. Now sit down and eat." He barked at her as if she was a child. Eyes down, she returned to her chair and picked at her food.

The evening progressed and it soon became obvious that Jebediah did not know, but what could she do with this information? No one would believe her. The homesteaders worshipped Jebediah and there was nothing she could do that would convince them he was trying to take their land. If Isaac had seen her, when would he tell? Well one thing was for sure, Martha knew what her husband was up to and she would find a way to use it to her best advantage. She sat mending the boy's shirts, her mind filled with possibilities. Finally a small glimmer of hope, a tiny flame of empowerment was growing in her soul. She also knew she could trust no one but herself, remembering the deception of both her father and the seaman Richard. The cruel beating on the ship that resulted had taught her a very grave lesson. Never trust anyone. Perhaps God had given her a long awaited sign today in the church.

Jebediah sat in his office enjoying the solitude, being pastor was certainly more than he could have asked for. The simple sheep had fallen into his trap and then made him the leader of the flock. Amazing how really trusting and gullible they were. Now he didn't even have to use his own money for the loans, but would simply use the church funds, of which he had full control. He would put all of the liens in his name and that way when it came time to foreclose, the properties would be his. The west was definitely the land of gold and Jebediah Whittaker had struck pay dirt with these homesteaders.

Isaac appeared at the door. "Isaac, my boy, come and sit by me." Jebediah was very proud of Isaac. Physically similar to himself, the boy was tall and thin with dark hair and sharp features. Characteristics inherited from Jebediah's maternal grandfather, which he and Isaac shared. The boy kept a close eye on Martha and the young ones and could be counted on to tell him everything that went on in the house. Jebediah had great plans for Isaac, shaping him in his own mold. Isaac was becoming an able marksman and this western life seemed to suit him. Mama would love Isaac, like she loved him. Too bad she wasn't here to see him for herself but that was Father's fault. Jebediah scowled and returned his thoughts to his eldest son. "Are you looking forward to your first buffalo kill, Isaac?" He and Isaac chatted about the upcoming buffalo hunt and the shops that were springing up in the new town. As the sun set, father and son, locked the church and left for home. The church had been built close to the Whittaker's home, so the walk took no time at all.

The storm started just after midnight. Ear splitting thunder shook the walls of the log cabin and lightning turned night into day. Martha rose from her bed and went to check on the boys; a deafening crack of thunder startled her as she covered Ezekiel. From the window a bright orange glow appeared. Martha rushed to the door, looking in the direction of the golden brilliance. Over the treetops, flames leaped from the corner of the church roof. Abraham's dream instantly came to her mind.

"Jebediah, the church is on fire! Hurry," she screamed. Jebediah leapt from his bed and still clad only in his long underwear, ran from the house followed by Isaac. Abraham and Ezekiel crawled from their beds and stood with Martha, staring wide-eyed at the burning church. Abraham and Martha exchanged a frightened knowing look, pulled on some clothes and then ran for the water buckets. Ezekiel followed with a shovel and blanket to smother the small fire bursts on the ground. People appeared from everywhere at the first sign of fire. The community sprang into action. Rakes and shovels pounded the burning earth and buckets of water were toted from the river. The wood shed beside the church had been hit by lightning, quickly turning into a blazing inferno. Flames leaped onto the church roof. The searing heat from the blaze was unbearable. Black smoke filled their noses and stung their eyes but they did not quit. Luckily, torrents of rain fell that night, helping to extinguish the flames and soaking the tired and dirty fire brigade. Thanks to the rain, the fire was extinguished before much damage to the actual church was done. A new roof would be built and the community would return to normal but Martha and Abraham would never be the same. After that night as they stood with the flames of hell reflecting on their sweaty faces, they both believed that God was angry.

Chapter Eleven
The Search Continues

Finally the weather had improved enough for the stagecoach to leave St. Louis. Jeremy and Austin found the trip to be back breaking. The ride was bumpy and erratic. The coach was either filled with dust or bogged down in the mud and once they left St. Louis all signs of civilization disappeared. The only stops were tiny, shack-like buildings where passengers could get a cool drink and the horses were changed. Whenever a small town with a hotel appeared they were thankful. Hotels were primitive to say the least and bar room brawls, dirt and tiny rooms coated in dust were the most they could hope for. Both of them were beginning to wonder just what on earth they were doing here. Austin found that he missed Loretta's funny giggle. Often he would be reminded of her by the scent of her Lily of the Valley perfume, which hung on his clothing. She was a charming creature, full of life. Hopefully he would see her again someday, but now he had to go and find Martha.

Jeremy, although an adventure lover at heart, thought that the western territories were most primitive and even he wished he were back in London or at least St. Louis.

"Fort Laramie will be weeks away. I hope we'll make it in one piece," stated Jeremy. What they would do then, neither of them knew.

"All I know is we must find Martha and Jebediah. Hopefully we'll have a plan before we do." Austin wrote in his journal of a particularly interesting site they witnessed from the stage:

> As we traveled in the stage today, a long band of red light was observed against the distant horizon. It appeared to be moving towards us. Awed by the spectacle of it, we were not aware of its sinister significance. Jeremy commented that the dull red glow in the distance was brightening and widening. Stage driver and shotgun stopped the stage and the four of us stood mesmerized. The burning prairie grass crackled, and the wind sweeping the fire made a roaring noise, still faint in the distance but unmistakably menacing. My first impressions of the grandiose beauty of the towering wall of fire were mingled with a sense of terror at the fire's uncontrolled destruction. We watched the fire for hours, unable to travel ahead until the wind carried it from our path. The air was thick with the smell of smoke. Afterwards, the prairie's deep carpet of luscious green grass was only a black and barren wasteland, as far as the eye could see. I had heard the pioneers in St. Louis talk of prairie fires but nothing could have prepared me for this.

As the stagecoach traveled mile after dusty mile, Austin and Jeremy tried to decide exactly what they were walking into. Jebediah was not the kind of person who would take kindly to an intrusion and he definitely would not release Martha to Austin without a fight. What were Martha's feelings for Jebediah? They had to consider that although she obviously would have fought the idea of the marriage, she might have been taken in by Jebediah. She may actually be fond of him. Austin thought this idea to be utterly absurd, but the two were taking nothing for granted. Plans were discussed and plots were laid out but nothing would be settled until they arrived and found out what they were dealing with.

Stops were made, horses changed and the journey continued mile after tedious mile. Meals were eaten at the stage stops and many nights were spent on cots in tiny shacks. Primitive outdoor toilet facilities were the norm and baths were nonexistent.

"Well, we are beginning to smell like we belong in the west." Austin turned up his nose at the strong body odors emanating from them both.

"I never want to see bear meat again and a good glass of brandy would certainly be welcome, although right now even a glass of gut-rot whisky would suffice." Jeremy replied. He took his watch from his pocket, checking the time more from habit than any real need.

"Why don't you get that watch face fixed, man?" Austin laughed as Jeremy stuffed the broken watch back in his pocket.

"Because I don't want to forget the day you saved my life," Jeremy patted Austin on the back. "No, seriously, this broken face keeps me on guard. This is not England and there are dangers around every corner." Austin just laughed at Jeremy. He knew the watch had been Jeremy's fathers, but why he insisted on looking at it through a cracked face, he could not imagine.

The day was uneventful until the afternoon. Austin and Jeremy watched the landscape for interesting sites as the miles continued on. All of a sudden, gunshots were heard and the horses increased speed. The stage bumped and thrashed feeling as if it would break in two. The sound of the speeding horses' hooves was like thunder pounding the earth. More shots filled the air around the coach and dust choked the two young passengers.

"Stage robbers, start shooting." The coach driver shouted as he tried to control the runaway horses. Jeremy and Austin gave each other an alarmed, confused look and started shooting out the windows of the coach. Two riders with scarves over their faces were following the stage, firing on the driver and his guard. Austin shot towards one of the men and thought he hit him but the two kept coming. Jeremy, who was not as good with a gun as young Wells, did his best to aim at the robbers but to no avail. His shots flew haphazardly into the air. Finally his gun was empty and he had to reload. The stage driver, Austin and the fellow, riding shotgun, fired on the two robbers as the stage careened across the plains. Shot after shot pierced the dusty air. One of the robbers finally fell. The second robber's horse was abruptly pulled to a halt, the rider veering to the right and back towards the fallen rider. The relieved passengers holstered their guns and held on for dear life as the runaway stage continued to bounce and jolt them from their seats. The harness leather strained as the four powerful horses ran out of control. The driver yelled, "Halt, Ho," over and over but to no avail. Equine muscles strained, their breath coming in gasps as their hooves continued to pound the earth. After several tense minutes the tiring horses were pulled back under the control of the driver. Finally the sweat covered and exhausted horses were hauled to a stop, the driver jumped down and opened the doors to the stagecoach. The two rumpled male passengers stared shocked and dismayed at the driver.

"What the hell is going on?" Jeremy shouted. "Is this normal for the stagecoach to be chased by robbers and paying passengers required to shoot for their lives?" The usually calm and cool Jeremy had finally reached the breaking point. He leapt from the stage as if he expected the horses to bolt any minute.

"Yep, sure is." The driver replied sarcastically. "You fellers OK?" The grizzly stage driver and the fellow, riding shotgun seemed to be taking this all in his stride but Austin and Jeremy had enough for one day. The harness and horses were thoroughly checked while the shotgun rider stood on guard. He scanned the horizon for any movement.

"How far is the next town? We need a night in a hotel and a good stiff drink." The shaken Jeremy waited while the driver scratched his head and thought a bit. He was enjoying the agony on their faces and tried to prolong the moment. Laughing, he finally said they would reach a town by nightfall, then he informed them triumphantly that Fort Laramie was only a day or two away. Relieved and anxious to get going, Jeremy and Austin returned to the dust-filled stage. The stage driver expelled a spit of tobacco, chuckled to himself and climbed aboard the stage.

The town was small but Jeremy was able to find a washerwoman to take care of their neglected laundry and for an extra half dollar, they both had a long hot bath in the back of the woman's cabin. Clean and feeling more civilized they returned to the hotel. The facilities were acceptable and Jeremy and Austin were relaxing in the lobby. The shoot out with the stage robbers was almost laughable now that it was over and the whisky warmed their spirits.

"Tell me a little about your nephews, Jeremy. They will be affected by whatever we do and I would like to know a little about them. I guess Martha is their stepmother now and if Jebediah goes to jail, she will be responsible for the boys." Austin swirled the cheap whiskey in the glass and tried to picture the impulsive, pampered Martha as anyone's mother.

"I think you are getting ahead of yourself, Austin. Jebediah is going to be our biggest problem and he certainly can't be charged with any crime here. He would have to go back to England to be convicted and that is highly unlikely. Getting Martha away from him will be a challenge in itself, but that has to be our first priority. After all, that is what John McGuire hired us to do, Jebediah is secondary." Jeremy reached for the decanter and poured himself another whisky. In his mind, revenge on Jebediah was first and foremost but he would have to handle that himself.

"The boys, how old are they?" inquired Austin, attempting to bring the conversation back to his original question.

"Isaac is eleven, Abraham eight and little Ezekiel would be about six. I haven't seen them for years, not since my father died and I left for India. I remember trying to spend time with them after their mother died, at least the middle boy. The youngest was only a babe and Isaac had some serious problems."

"What kind of problems, he must have been a small child. Was he ill?"

"After his mother fell to her death, Isaac didn't speak for months. He sat silent and pensive, staring out the window. Doctors said he was in shock and although he had been asleep when his mother fell, he did see her lying at the bottom of the stairs before they took her body away." Jeremy stopped to sip his whiskey. "He had been such a happy bubbly child but after Alicia died, his entire personality changed. He eventually started to talk again but he was spiteful and angry. Jebediah was no help at all and my father and I tried to amuse and care for the boys. The younger ones were too young to realize what had happened. Then Father died, I left and I don't know whatever happened to Isaac. Hopefully he recovered."

Austin remembered the terrible grief when he was very young after the loss of his father and it saddened him to know that these young boys had lost their mother. He could not imagine what role Martha might now play in their lives. Although Jebediah had been the cause of their troubles, the boys were innocent victims. If it came to it, could he kill the father of these motherless boys?

"Our first course of action when we arrive in Fort Laramie will be to locate Jebediah and since I'm his brother, we should receive some cooperation. Once we locate them, we'll have to devise a plan to inform Martha of your presence without raising alarm. We'll look the situation over and ensure that her safety is not being threatened first. Then we'll decide on a plan of action. I must warn you that Jebediah is very dangerous, so don't get any ideas about taking him on yourself. Leave him to me. Martha will be your responsibility but we must be very careful." Jeremy lowered his voice as several people passed the settee where they were enjoying their whisky. "Remember, we trust no one."

"Tomorrow, you and I'll practice our marksmanship while the stage is serviced. I don't think you would be much good if we ran into a band of savage Indians and after today, I'm beginning to believe anything is possible." Austin punched his friend's arm jokingly. "Now, pass the decanter and let's enjoy this soft settee and soothing chamber music." Austin facetiously referred to the sound of an out-of-tune piano and the warbling off key voice of the saloon singer pounding in their ears. The two travelers sat back and laughed while the noise engulfed them and the whisky helped soothe their travel weary nerves.

Fort Laramie was bustling with activity when the stagecoach arrived. Military personnel, homesteaders, fur traders and Indians crowded the large fort. Austin and Jeremy stood surveying their new destination. Fort Laramie's main purpose was to maintain peace between the Indians and the settlers and at the moment, seemed successful.

Colonel Watson was happy to meet with them and gave them directions to the new town where Jebediah and Martha lived. Jeremy introduced himself but Austin's identity remained secret. The last thing they wanted was for Austin's name to reach Martha's ears before they were ready. "You just missed Pastor Whittaker. He was here yesterday for supplies. He's not expected to return for several weeks so you had best go and find him. The town is about a half day's ride." The colonel turned and walked away leaving the two confused men staring after him. Jeremy found it strange that Colonel Watson referred to Jebediah as Pastor Whittaker. Religion and his brother were strange bedfellows indeed. Austin's curiosity was definitely aroused now. Was there no end to Jebediah's trickery? A haggard man appeared from the shadows and approached the pair.

"Did I hear you say you were looking for Pastor Whittaker?" The man's clothes were tattered and his face bore a long scar on one cheek. "Why you looking for him? Did he steal your land too, rotten bastard?" The man was obviously agitated but his words peeked the curiosity of the two young men. Austin saw a window of opportunity present itself.

"My good man, you look like you could use a stiff drink. Please come with us to the mess tent and let us buy you an ale." Austin reluctantly put his hand on the dirty man's shoulder and urged him towards the tent on the far side of the fort, away from prying eyes and ears. The three men walked in silence. Ale was ordered and Jeremy led the others to a table at the back of the room. "I didn't catch your name, sir."

"Name's Swartz—Arnold Swartz. I don't think you answered my question either. Did that bastard steal something from you too?" Swartz tipped his glass back and savored the cool liquid. Jeremy knew they had to handle this situation carefully.

"As a matter of fact, we have traveled all the way from England to find Jebediah Whittaker. Does that tell you how badly we want him?" Jeremy looked at Austin, signaling that they should give nothing away. Ordering another ale for the thirsty, trail-weary Swartz, they waited until he finished his second glass before prodding him further. "So the bastard stole from you, eh? Tell us, how did he do that?" The second glass seemed to loosen the man's tongue.

"That son of a bitch tricked me out of my land. Pretended to be so generous and caring. Kept lending us money after he got us to sign that piece of paper. Then he comes and orders us to leave, says it's his land now—we were left homeless. Felt sorry for his wife and kids, seemed like a nice woman that Mrs. Whittaker. My wife and I tried to make it to California. Broke but determined, we headed west, but Indians attacked not forty miles out. We put up a fight. Did no good, though, I was injured and she was killed." Arnold Swartz drew in a deep breath before continuing. He was talking more to himself than to Jeremy and Austin. "That Bastard Whittaker took my wife and my land. I could kill him with my bare hands." He unconsciously reached up and stroked the scar on his face. A look of deep sadness filled his eyes but was quickly replaced with pure hatred. With that, the man rose slowly and walked away. His fists were clenched and his shoulders drooped. Austin and Jeremy just sat and stared after him.

Now armed with more information, but apprehensive about the possible revenge on Jebediah by Swartz, they put their heads together. At least they knew that both Jebediah and Martha were here and now they had to devise a plan of action. Word might reach Jebediah in a few days and Jeremy wanted to arrive unexpected and without Austin.

Chapter Twelve
Martha and Jeremy Meet

Details settled, Jeremy left the fort and headed out to the small town where his brother lived. Austin would travel separately from Jeremy to a location close by. They had learned that the buffalo hunt was in progress and that Jebediah and the rest of the men from the small community would be gone for a few days. Hopefully, Martha would be alone on the homestead and they could approach her with their plan.

It was dusk when Jeremy rode into the small but growing town. A General Store, a blacksmith shop and a few wooden homes made up the main street. A small church sat at the end of the street, which Jeremy surmised was his destination. Stopping in the General Store, he inquired casually of the buffalo hunt.

"All the men left this morning, even the pastor. You know men, can't wait to go out and kill something. If you are looking to join them, you better ride hard to the north." Jeremy enjoyed talking with Mrs. Mueller. He felt comfortable with the sturdy, smiling woman with a German accent. He chatted while she filled the freshly scrubbed shelves.

"No, I think I'll just wait until the hunt is over, thank you for your time, ma'am." He walked out of the small store into the dusty street, which contained only a few children.

Jeremy mounted his horse and rode towards the church. Mrs.

Mueller continued stocking the shelves smiling to herself, thoughts of the handsome young stranger fueling her imagination.

Jeremy watched the log house and yard for some time before approaching. A young boy was tending to the stock. Jeremy thought he would start with him. "Hello, young man, is your mother or father here?" Jeremy approached slowly scrutinizing Abraham who looked up from his chores. The blond angelic face reminded Jeremy immediately of Alicia.

"Martha's in the church, sir, and Father is gone on the buffalo hunt with my brother, Isaac." Shielding his eyes from the sun, Abraham stared at the stranger's silhouette.

"Thank you, son, I'll ride to the church and talk to, who did you say?"

"Martha, she is our stepmother." Abraham was feeling uneasy. A memory prickled at the back of his mind. The stranger rode off towards the church. Intuition made Abraham follow him. Martha was all alone except for Ezekiel and Abraham was the man of the house when his father and Isaac were away.

"Hello, anyone here?" Jeremy entered the little church and looked for signs of life. A small, blond boy was seated on the altar, reading a book. The smell of lye soap filled the air. He looked up when he heard Jeremy and nodded to his left. There on her hands and knees was the long awaited Martha. Beautiful was not the first thing that sprang to Jeremy's mind. He was expecting the woman in the portrait and was met by the scrub woman. The woman rose, brushed a stray hair from her face and turned toward him. As he walked closer, he realized that in spite of the drab clothing and the severe hairstyle this was indeed a magnetically beautiful woman. Taken aback by her appearance, he stood silently.

"Can I help you, sir? The pastor is not in but I'm his wife." Martha was used to strangers arriving in the church for various pastoral reasons. Nothing about this man alarmed her. She dried her hands on her apron as she spoke. She could not help but think the stranger was quite handsome and very polite. Her long forgotten vanity showed itself as she smoothed loose tendrils of her hair back from her face.

"May I speak to you in private, ma'am? Perhaps the boy could leave us alone for just a minute?" Jeremy removed his Stetson and ran his fingers through his hair.

Unsure of what to do, Martha was growing nervous. *Why does this stranger want Ezekiel to leave? What does he want?* Just then Abraham arrived, panting and out of breath.

"Martha, it's him, the man in the dream, it's him." Forgetting that Ezekiel and the stranger were present, Abraham blurted out his realization with no thought of consequences.

Jeremy turned and looked at Abraham, then back at the now shocked and paralyzed face of Martha Whittaker. Abraham ran past him towards Martha and Ezekiel.

"Ezekiel, Abraham come here. Who are you, sir, and what do you want?" Martha gathered the boys to her and began to back away but Jeremy's words stopped her.

"I'm Jeremy Whittaker and I must speak to you on an important family matter. Please ask the boys to wait outside, I assure you, I mean you no harm." Jeremy did his best to assure Martha that his intentions were honorable and he needed to speak to her in private. Still frightened, Martha assessed this stranger but trusted her intuition that she was not in danger. Her curiosity raised; the appearance of Jebediah's brother after Abraham's dream was more than coincidental. Her first priority was not to upset the boys and she was anxious to remove them from harm's way.

"Abraham and Ezekiel, go to the cabin and stay there until I come for you. I'll not be long, now do as I say. This is your Uncle Jeremy and there is no need for concern."

Martha was not sure why, but she was not afraid of this man. Something in the back of her mind told her he meant no harm to her or the boys. Perhaps God was giving her direction.

"But Martha, I …" Martha raised her palm and stopped Abraham in mid-sentence. Abraham stared at his uncle nervously. Ezekiel picked up his book and started towards the door.

"Abraham, please take Ezekiel and go now." Abraham and Ezekiel walked slowly, looking over their shoulders several times. Martha watched from the door as they returned to the cabin. She took a deep breath and turned slowly to stare into the green eyes of Jeremy Whitaker.

"Now sir, what do you want?" Martha sat in the pew, fear mixed with curiosity, inviting Jeremy to sit beside her but maintaining a safe distance between them.

"I was sent by your father to help you. My brother has committed a terrible injustice upon your family and I want you to know I'm traveling with Austin Wells." Jeremy wanted to give Martha as much information as possible to ease her mind and let her understand the urgency of this conversation. He noticed the shocked look on her face at the mention of her father and Austin. He also noticed the mistrust in her blue eyes.

"My father sent you? How do you know my father? Austin is here, where is he?" Martha was stunned. Austin was here with Jebediah's brother? Her father had sent him? This man wanted to help her? What was going on? Was this someone's idea of a cruel joke?

"I'll take you to him shortly. Let me explain but first, our meeting must be kept confidential. Is it correct that Jebediah will not be back for two or three days?" Jeremy was very cautious with this woman. He really did not know the situation between her and his brother and wanted to be very careful.

"Yes at least two days, possibly four, but why don't you want anyone to know you are here?" Martha's head was spinning. She was starting to feel some glimmer of hope that perhaps this ordeal was finally over. Emotions wrestling, her lack of trust was winning out.

"Just listen, I'll start at the beginning. Your father and some of his business partners bought some land from Jebediah. Your father gave Jebediah your hand in marriage as part of that land transfer. Please do not interrupt." Jeremy raised his hand to silence her. The involuntary flinch as his hand raised spoke volumes of how this woman had been treated. "Once they discovered that I was the real owner of the land, your father contacted Austin Wells and myself and requested our help." Jeremy continued the tale as Martha sat openmouthed but listening.

She watched Jeremy as he told her of how Jebediah had defrauded her father and his associates. As the words fell on her ears, she could not help but take in Jeremy's appearance. How different from his brother he seemed. They were like opposite sides of a coin. Where Jebediah's essence was dark and full of dread, Jeremy's was light and airy, even physically they were different. Jeremy was a handsome man and very unlike his dark, sharp-featured, plain brother. He instilled trust and confidence as he spoke.

"So you and Austin have come to take me home, well, anything would be better than life with your brother, sir. But I don't think I want to go home to my father, who you say, sold me in a land deal." Martha was regaining her composure and anger was replacing confusion. If this man was telling the truth, she would never forgive her father for this, but right now she wanted to see Austin. She desperately wanted to believe this stranger but prayed that she was not being tricked again. She clenched her hands firmly together as she waited for Jeremy to finish.

"Let's go and see Wells and I'll talk with the boys while you and he meet in private. We must not let the boys know he's here. That is most important and another thing, we must not trust anyone." Jeremy stressed the last point.

"Trust is something I no longer give, even to you, sir." Martha rose and followed Jeremy out the door, taking in the length of his stride and the tilt of his broad shoulders.

After brief introductions and instruction from Martha for the boys, Jeremy directed her to Austin's location at the edge of the property and went back into the cabin to talk to his nephews. She was hesitant to leave the children with this stranger but her desire to see Austin was driving her on. She faltered for just a minute as she wrestled with the thought that this could be a trap. If Austin was here, then she must go, pushing her doubts aside she climbed into the wagon.

Excitedly driving to her destination she could not believe she was actually going to see Austin. For the first time in almost a year, Martha actually thought about her appearance. If only she had stopped and fixed herself up. What would Austin think seeing her like this? *Oh, what did it matter? Austin, dear Austin was waiting. Thank you, God, thank you.* She pulled her hair from the tight bun on the back of her head and shook it loose. She looked down sadly at her patched gray dress and dirty apron as she slowed the wagon to a stop. Climbing down, she looked around assessing the situation. Cautiously, she approached the storage shed; her footsteps silent on the earth but feeling like her feet were made of lead. Her heart was in her throat. Her hands were shaking.

"Austin, are you here?" Martha called out, her voice trembling uncontrollably. Tenuously she entered the shed hoping and praying she was not walking into a trap, her eyes scanning the dimly lit enclosure.

"Martha, over here." Austin appeared just to her left and approached with arms open. Thankful and relieved, the breath she had been holding escaped from her lips, she ran into his arms, sobbing uncontrollably. Austin's arms felt like a warm tender security blanket, the first embrace she had experienced in a year. She drew strength from him like a sponge. Tears rolled down her face. Unable to move away, she tried to memorize everything her senses were feeling. The smell of Austin's body, sweet with perspiration, the soft but secure feel of his arms, his gentle reassurances whispered in her ear, the touch of his hand on her hair, she would never forget this moment as long as she lived. She wasn't dreaming. Total relief poured through her veins. Her ordeal was over, it was really over. Austin, too, was experiencing the sensual pleasures of holding Martha. The smell of soap lingered on her clothing, her hair was soft against his skin, her thin but hard body against his, all recorded in his memory. At last he had found her and she was alive.

After several minutes she regained her composure and leaning back, looked into Austin's teary, deep brown eyes. She still could not believe she wasn't dreaming. Austin looked at her shabby clothes and realized that Martha, no longer innocent and carefree, had changed considerably in the course of a year. He hated Jebediah Whittaker even more for what he had done to her. Martha held his hand in her rough, calloused palm and eagerly told him everything that she had endured. The more she talked, the deeper the pain and the greater the hate for Jebediah grew in his heart.

In the cabin, Jeremy sat at the wooden table and looked at his two blond nephews. He realized they were very much like their mother, Alicia. Abraham seemed to have calmed down and Jeremy was curious about his comment about a dream. He decided to leave that for later, keeping the conversation light.

"So how do you boys like the west? Tell me about your lives as cowboys."

The boys giggled at Jeremy's reference to being cowboys and both of them were drawn to this newfound uncle. Stories were exchanged and Jeremy inquired as to Isaac's well being.

"He is a big meanie and a spy." Ezekiel offered. "I don't like him, he does bad things and he is a tattle tale."

"Isaac is fine, Uncle Jeremy, Ezekiel is just a little boy and doesn't mean what he says." Abraham, only two years older than Ezekiel reassured his uncle, giving his brother a silencing look. "Father took him on the buffalo hunt. Isaac likes to shoot and hunt. I don't like to kill animals; I love animals." Abraham looked deeply into Jeremy's face. "Why did you come, Uncle Jeremy, and how did you get here? Did you take a ship like we did and then a wagon train?" Abraham was still thinking of his dream where he saw Jeremy on a ship and was trying to find out as much as he could about this virtual stranger. He also wondered about the other strange man in the dream.

"Yes, I came on a ship but then I took a stagecoach. We even got shot at by robbers." He continued telling the spellbound boys of the robbers and the runaway stagecoach. They were fascinated by the story and wanted to hear more of his adventures. Ezekiel even crawled in his lap and Abraham was very surprised. Their father never allowed contact and was not demonstrative in any way. In fact, Jebediah never engaged in conversation with the younger boys. Abraham understood Ezekiel's feeling of comfort with Jeremy, however, because he, too, felt very safe and relaxed.

The three adults had one day to devise a plan and Martha was very nervous. At first she just wanted to take the boys and leave immediately. This place held nothing but misery for her. She wanted to be gone. After learning that the next stagecoach wouldn't leave for a week and being reminded they were in the middle of nowhere, she calmed down and listened to her champions. She refused to leave Abraham and Ezekiel with Jebediah, even though she knew they were in for a battle. At least she had reserves on her side now and perhaps a solution could be reached. Martha was holding on to her secret of Jebediah's liens until she needed them and had not told either Austin or Jeremy what she knew. Jeremy was going to try and use the legal charges to convince his brother to let her and the younger boys go. Somehow she doubted it would work. Both Jeremy and Austin had issues with Jebediah and would not leave until they were settled. Some of her old resolve returning, Martha began to plan for her future.

Jeremy and Austin returned to the fort, Austin's identity remaining a secret. Martha and the silenced boys, who were told Uncle Jeremy wanted to surprise Father, were left to wait for Jebediah and Isaac to return. Vegetables were picked and stored in the root cellar and the stock was cared for. She put her house in order and crawled into her cot spiritually hopeful for the first time in ages. She was unsure of Jeremy but Austin had assured her that he was sincere. Before laying down she brushed her hair slowly and carefully counting the strokes, something she had not done in many months. Martha lay in her bed reliving the reunion with Austin and the secure feel of his arms around her. *Could it be true? Am I really going to escape this time? Do I dare hope for a future away from Jebediah?* Just as she drifted off to sleep, Abraham let out a bloodcurdling scream.

"Father, Father."

Martha rushed to Abraham's cot. *Please, God, not again. Let me escape this torture once and for all.* Shaking the small boy she prayed that he was not having another premonition. Jeremy's arrival had given more credence to Abraham's ability to see the future and right now, she didn't want to know what was coming next.

"Martha, someone shot him. Someone shot Father," cried the shaking Abraham, who had just shattered Martha's momentary serenity with another unwanted prophecy.

Chapter Thirteen
Jeremy and Jebediah

The women were gathered in the main street of their small town, anxiously awaiting the arrival of their husbands and sons. Conversations on cooking, gardening and child rearing filled the street and the air was alive with their enthusiasm. Children played in the dust and food had been prepared and set up in the Church. Martha milled around the street, trying to maintain a casual appearance. She stopped to talk with Margaret Brown, who she had seen little of since winter set in. Margaret was pregnant and absolutely glowing with health.

"Here comes James, Margaret." Olga Mueller hollered, her arms waving. Martha and Margaret turned towards the rider that was approaching the group.

"Ladies, good afternoon. I'm afraid the men have been delayed because of an accident during the hunt. They should be here tomorrow about this time." James announced in a loud voice, as he climbed from his sweating mare. The women rushed to him all speaking at once. The word accident hung like a dark curtain over their heads. Martha turned pale, immediately remembering Abraham's dream. *Was it possible Jebediah had been shot during the hunt?* Hunting accidents and even men trampled by the stampeding buffalo were common.

"I don't have any details, ladies, I just received a message that there had been an accident and the hunters were delayed. Please understand you will have to wait until the men arrive. I'm truly sorry but I do not know anymore than I have already told you." James put his arm around Margaret and they slowly walked towards their wagon. Most of the women gathered their children and walked to the church where they would pray for their husbands. Martha followed the others but she would not be praying for Jebediah's safety. *If he is dead, it would save us all a lot of trouble.* Guilt filled her heart for these dark thoughts but she could not bring herself to ask God to bring her husband home alive.

The next morning the women gathered again in the street and waited for the hunters to return. Many looked as if they had not slept and even the children were more sullen and subdued than the day before. A cloud of dust rose in the distance and the women knew that one of them was about to receive the dreaded news. The men returned to the street, each one greeted with large hugs and great relief. Fritz climbed off his horse and into the waiting arms of Olga. An injured man was being unloaded from a wagon in front of the General Store. Martha hesitantly walked to the wagon and slowly and fearfully looked down. There was Jake, a great deal of blood on his arm and shoulder, eyes closed. Air was sucked into Martha's lungs involuntarily as she looked at Jake's face. It had not been Jebediah but Jake that had been hurt. She could not describe her feelings, disappointment or relief. Expressionless she surveyed the large crowd for her husband.

Isaac found them first, busting with news of the hunt and how he had shot a buffalo himself. The three boys wandered off with Isaac expounding the joys of the hunt. Martha saw Jebediah talking to Jake's wife and waited for him to notice her. When he did, he simply turned and continued his conversation. *How am I going to act normal with Austin and Jeremy a few miles away?* Abraham's dream echoing in her ears over and over; *Someone shot Father. Martha, someone shot Father* made the hair on the back of her neck stand up. She stood still trying not to tremble.

Finally Jebediah approached Martha and handed her his saddlebags. He spoke to her in a quiet whisper, the false smile never leaving his face, "Carry these and put a smile on that miserable face. You are supposed to be happy that I'm home from the hunt." He reached for her hand, but instead of a caress, he crushed her fingers causing her to wince in pain. "Now everyone to the church to thank the Lord for the successful hunt." Jebediah turned, pulling her along, still keeping the pressure on her hand and led the faithful procession to his church. How she hated this man. With every fiber of her being, she wanted to be as far away from him as possible.

Jeremy learned from those that returned to the fort when the hunt had ended. Now he had to decide when to come face to face with his brother. He was not looking forward to the confrontation. Austin relayed Martha's horrors to him and his brother was like an evil stranger that needed to be eliminated. He knew Austin was more than capable of killing Jebediah and he questioned his own reactions. The man at the fort, Swartz, was definitely a threat to Jebediah. Jeremy had his own feelings of revenge. His brother had tried to kill him once and if he were faced with it again, would he be able to kill his brother to save himself or the others? Austin had taught him to shoot but in his heart he doubted he could pull the trigger on his own kin. Hopefully, it would not come to that. Maybe Jebediah would realize that allowing the woman and the two younger boys to leave was his best option. Jeremy was counting on Jebediah's love of money to be the deciding factor in any confrontation. He was upset to learn that Isaac had become so like his father and was still uneasy with Martha's decision to leave the oldest boy here. Jeremy would have to assess that situation when he came face to face with Isaac.

Austin was feeling much lighter than he had in months. At last they had located Martha and although she had faced almost unbearable hardships, she was alive and well. How they would travel back to England with her and the boys was something he would think about later. Right now he wanted to find Jebediah Whittaker and put a bullet in his head. Austin had long buried any feelings of remorse or guilt where Jebediah was concerned and was convinced death was the only solution. He would give Jeremy his chance to appeal to Jebediah's greed, he owed his friend that much. If it didn't work, however, Austin would provide the only solution.

Early the next morning in the forest just outside the village, Isaac crawled on all fours behind the boulders, rifle in hand. He was sure to stay down wind of the deer and as silent as a dead man, he moved through the brush. The smell of earth and rotting leaves filled his nostrils and the dampness of the moss soaked his knees and elbows.

This was Isaac's environment. He loved the smell of the earth and the thrill of the hunt. He raised his head just enough to take aim and fired. The deer collapsed a few feet from the river. He waited the required five minutes to be sure the doe was dead. Just as he was about to come out of hiding and claim his kill, a rider appeared to be crossing the river several yards down stream.

Isaac remained hidden and watched the man dismount and water his horse. Something familiar prickled in the recesses of his memory, who was this stranger and why was Isaac feeling such unease? The man removed his hat, splashing his face with water. As he turned towards Isaac's hiding place, his face came into focus. Isaac stared at that face. Paralyzing shock settled over the young boy's body. A dull pain started at the back of his head and increased in intensity as it moved toward Isaac's forehead. He clutched his head in his hands and collapsed on the ground unconscious. The man, not having seen Isaac or the deer, mounted his horse and continued across the river and into the town.

Jebediah sat in his church office, looking over his notes. Some of them were coming due and he would have to make his move soon. He must be very careful how he did the foreclosures so as not to raise suspicion amongst the rest of the homesteaders. Perhaps he would call in the liens and then tell the homesteaders they could stay on as tenants, unbeknownst to the rest of the community. He would appeal to their pride and assure them that the rent would be reasonable and no one would have to know of their failure. Eventually he would run them off and sell all of the land himself but for now he must go slowly. Something was going on with Martha but he was not sure what it was. She was acting very nervous and edgy. He spoke with Mrs. Mueller and some of the other women, who were not aware of anything happening while he was away and even suggested she might be with child. Another mouth to feed was just what he didn't need but he would wait and see. He had been thinking of a way to be rid of her without raising suspicion but so far had been unsuccessful. In the next few months, many of his plans would come to fruition and Martha, with child or not, would be disposed of in a most convincing way. For now he would concentrate on the land acquisitions and the talk of the railway that was coming to the west. The railway would mean huge increases in land value and Jebediah smiled at the thought of the abundance that was soon to be his.

Austin, careful to remain unseen, ducked into the storage shed beside the church. He was to wait here until he saw Jeremy enter the church and then go for Martha who was to be waiting in the cabin. The storage shed smelled of manure and grain and Austin tried not to sneeze or cough. His revolver was loaded and ready and his mind was made up. Any sign of trouble and Jebediah was going to be shot. Austin had not traveled halfway around the world to find Martha, only to be shot by her husband. He would protect himself and Martha no matter what the consequences. The only other alternative was Jeremy's powers of persuasion and Austin hoped for all their sakes, they were good.

Martha sat in the cabin sewing Abraham's shirt as she waited. Sweat ran between her breasts and her blood was pounding through her veins. *What if Jeremy can't talk Jebediah into letting us go? Should I bring up the liens and threaten to expose Jebediah?* She was frightened of him and could only imagine to what lengths he would go to protect his secret. *What if something happens to Austin and Jeremy?* She remembered Sergeant Dwyer. Jebediah would kill her for sure. Time seemed to stand still as she sewed and waited. The boys were feeding the livestock and Isaac had gone off somewhere with his rifle. After a year of torment, her fate was about to be decided. She felt a jumble of nerves.

Jeremy rode towards the church, his revolver tucked under his coat. He prayed he wouldn't need it but he knew his brother and wouldn't be so gullible to leave anything to chance. He rehearsed his speech in his head. God give me strength and the wisdom to say the right thing. Jeremy hoped the fact that he was going to confront his brother in a church was a good sign. He saw the boys as he passed the cabin, signaling for them to be quiet so as not to give away his surprise.

Jebediah heard the church door open and rose to meet his parishioner. As he stood, a strange premonition overtook him and uncharacteristically, he lifted his revolver from the desk and slipped it in his coat. Leaving the office placed Jebediah directly behind the pulpit and gave him a good view of who had entered.

"Welcome to God's house, sir. What can I do for you today?" Jebediah walked to the center of the altar.

"Hello, Jebediah. It has been a long time." Jeremy approached his brother with confidence and caution. He removed his hat, allowing Jebediah a good look at his face.

"Jeremy, what the ..." Jebediah was shocked. What was his brother doing here? How had he found him? Instinctively, he stroked the revolver in his pocket.

"Surprised to see me, Jebediah? I guess you thought you were pretty safe way out here with the Indians. Of course, money is not an object since you sold all of my land." Jeremy was keeping his distance and watching his brother for any quick moves.

"So you know about that, do you? I thought it was rather clever myself and what the hell do you think you can do about it? You are on my turf now, dear brother, and coming here was a big mistake." Jebediah had regained his composure quickly and realized that there was nothing to fear from Jeremy. No one knew him and he could be quickly and easily disposed of as an outlaw who had tried to rob the church.

Austin left the shack and headed for the cabin. Martha met him outside after securing the two younger boys with some chores. The two of them approached the church from the back door. The back door led directly into Jebediah's office and was usually locked, but Martha had slipped in this morning and unlocked it. The two silently slipped in unnoticed. Voices could be heard from the church and they strained to hear what was being said. Austin's hand never left his revolver, ever ready when trouble struck. Martha's hand was shaking as she held Austin's arm. Both of their bodies pressed against the wall to avoid being seen they edged their way closer to the door.

"So what do you want, brother dear?" Jebediah spat the words in Jeremy's face.

"I have a proposition for you, Jebediah. You already have a great deal of money and prosecuting you would be impossible out here. I'm asking you to release the woman and the boys to my care and I'll forget where you are. You will be free to do whatever you want and as long as you stay out of England you will be free." Jeremy spoke slowly and purposefully.

"Why do I have to release the woman to you? What do you care about her? Why would you think I would release my children to you? I think you've lost your mind. All I have to do is put a bullet in your head and say you came to rob the church. I'm the pastor here after all and my sheep will believe me." With that Jebediah drew his gun.

At almost the same instance, Jeremy pulled his gun and pointed it at Jebediah. The brothers stood facing each other guns drawn, staring into each other's eyes. Austin started to enter the church but Martha pulled him back, signaling that he should wait.

Abruptly, the door to the church opened and a filthy, shell-shocked Isaac appeared. His eyes were wild and sweat glistened on his face. Taken aback, both of the brothers turned to look at him.

"You, I remember now. As soon as I saw your face at the river, it all came back to me. I wasn't asleep that night. I was in the hallway. I saw what happened. I remember all of it now." His voice came in gasps as if he were suffocating. His rifle was in his hand and his body shook. Now he started to shout. The brothers, momentarily forgetting each other, stood staring at the boy in shocked silence. Martha and Austin listened to the angry boy, unable to move from their hiding place.

"You killed my mother. I remember, it was you. I trusted you. I loved you. You hit her hard and then you threw her down the stairs. I saw you. You bastard, you killed her." With that eleven-year-old Isaac Whittaker raised his rifle and shot his mother's killer right between the eyes.

Martha and Austin rushed from the office. Abraham and Ezekiel charged in, bumping into their shocked and zombie-like brother. The rifle fell to the ground and Isaac collapsed in a heap. His brothers immediately tried to revive him, not having noticed the dead man lying in the church pew.

Chapter Fourteen
Decisions to Make

Martha returned the boys to the cabin and instructed the younger boys to watch their brother. Dazed and delirious, Isaac was put to bed. Abraham and Ezekiel held cool cloths to his head and sat beside his cot in case he woke up. Traumatized, Martha returned to the church where Austin was waiting.

Some serious decisions had to be made and this entire episode had shocked all of them. A grave must be dug and a story invented. Martha met up with Jeremy outside the church. He was badly shaken and had put the horses in the corral, more for a diversion than out of necessity. His brother was dead, shot by his own son. The adults had some serious thinking to do.

Martha and Jeremy entered the church and locked the door behind them. Austin had wrapped Jebediah's body in a blanket and cleaned most of the blood from the church.

No one spoke. Jeremy dropped into a pew, dropping his head into his hands. Zombie-like, Martha took the scrub brush from Austin and finished cleaning the pew and the floor. Keeping busy seemed to help but all of them were in shock. Austin walked over to his friend and put an arm around his shoulder. The repetitious scratching of the brush against the floor was the only sound.

Finally after what seemed like hours, Jeremy whispered that they would have to bury Jebediah but would need a good story before the community found out he was dead. Isaac could not be blamed for his father's death and something convincing had to be decided upon.

"I think the best plan of action is either to say that Isaac's rifle discharged by accident or that someone broke in the church and shot Jebediah just before we arrived." Austin's mind was racing. He knew that the boys had not seen what happened but they did know that their brother and their uncle were in the church. Then there was Isaac himself. Would he know he killed his father and what state would he be in when he woke up?

"I think for the sake of this community we need to protect Jebediah's reputation. Not for him, but for the homesteaders that live here and that trusted him. Isaac may remember shooting his father and he could make liars out of all of us if we are not careful." Martha was thinking first of the younger boys and then of the people that had been her friends for the past year. Her hand never stopped moving the brush, back and forth over and over. She also knew that Jebediah had been trying to take their land from them without a second thought for any of them. She felt nothing but relief at Jebediah's death. At last her ordeal was over. "Isaac has been through enough. First seeing his father kill his mother and now shooting his own father. The poor child, what a horrible situation. The younger boys must not know what happened here." Martha now realized why Isaac had been the way he was. Now he had her complete sympathy and concern.

"Martha is right. We must protect the family first and the good people that live here. What about the robber theory? We could say we arrived to find Jebediah dead and the cash box empty. Or perhaps we should wait until Isaac wakes up and see just what he remembers. We can put Jebediah's body in the shed for now and make an announcement in the morning." Jeremy needed to regain control and was fast realizing that his brother was dead and he had three nephews that would be depending on him. "Martha, please go and see if Isaac is awake."

Austin approached Martha and helped her to her feet. He pried the brush from her stiff fingers, pulling her close to him. She looked in his eyes with no emotion and walked from the church. Jeremy and Austin watched her go, both with deep concern.

Isaac, wide-eyed, lay staring blankly at the ceiling. Abraham said that they had been talking to him but he would not answer them. Seeing Isaac in this state, Jeremy was reminded of the months of silence after Alicia's death. Now he knew why. The boy had seen the whole thing and had been traumatized.

"Let me try. Please leave us alone." Jeremy sat with Isaac and waited. Martha moved mechanically, gathering the two younger boys. Martha and Austin took the boys out to do the chores and to try to find out what, if anything, they had heard. Abraham kept staring at Austin, knowing he was the stranger in the dreams.

"Isaac, this is Uncle Jeremy. Will you talk to me, please? I understand why you did what you did and I want you to know that no one will blame you. We must talk about this, Isaac." Jeremy was gentle but insistent, hoping to penetrate the zombie-like state of his nephew. Somewhere in the back of his mind, he saw his own mother staring blankly in much the same way. He mustn't let his nephew slip away into that lost world. He continued encouraging Isaac to talk to him. He spoke of Pheasant Run and of Alicia. "Come on, Isaac, come back to me. I know you can hear me." He repeated over and over. Finally after quite some time Isaac spoke.

"It's over. It's finally over. Many nights I would see my mother in my dreams but I could never see what happened to her. Now I remember everything. He killed her, Uncle Jeremy, my father hit her and then he threw her down the stairs and killed her. I hate him." Isaac started to cry and Jeremy held him until he was spent.

"Try to listen to me, Isaac. You will have a long time to deal with this, but right now we have to come up with a story for the fine people of this community. I want to tell them that a robber killed Jebediah and we found him after the robbery. You fainted because you saw your father dead. Will you be all right with that, Isaac? We are leaving it up to you. In some cases, a lie is better than the truth. " Jeremy tried to console the boy.

"Whatever you say, Uncle Jeremy, just leave me be. I need some time to think about this. Now my mother can finally rest in peace. Tell everyone Father was robbed and I'll not say any different. Abraham and Ezekiel do not need to know what happened. I would never want them to feel the way I do. We need to bury him now. It's over." Isaac spoke with such conviction for one so young and turned towards the wall. Jeremy felt uneasy with the finality that Isaac seemed to put on

OF DREAMS AND NIGHTMARES

the situation. Perhaps he was just in shock and would be better in the morning. The cry had done him good but Jeremy was sure he was crying for his mother and not his father.

Jebediah Whittaker was buried beside the church with all the community present. Mr. Mueller read from the bible and said a few kind words. Wildflowers of all kind and color were laid on the casket. Many tears were shed for the pastor and Jebediah was returned to the earth. Eyes were dried and many somber comments made.

"Terrible situation for that woman and those boys. Imagine someone robbing a church, disgusting heathen."

"Just before his brother arrived for a surprise visit too. Damn shame. Jebediah would have been thrilled to see his kin. Yep, damn shame. Good man, Jebediah Whittaker, none better."

Martha clad in black, with Jeremy and the boys by her side received the mourners. The three boys stood silently while people spoke highly of their father and all the good work he had done. Isaac, eerily silent, his eyes downcast, didn't look at his father's grave or speak to anyone. The other two boys followed Jeremy to the graveside and added their final handful of dirt just before the wooden box was lowered into the ground. Martha's hand remained steadfast on Isaac's shoulder; an unseen energy running between them.

Finally, everyone left the family alone to mourn and Martha felt great relief. She stared at the grave where her torturer lay and felt only relief. *Good riddance, you bastard.* All of the hate, fear and anguish she felt for Jebediah would be buried with him. No tears would ever be shed for Jebediah; but she pulled her black veil over her face and composed herself like a mourning widow should. Who would have thought that it would be Isaac that would save her from her tormentor? She looked at the boy with a new understanding, as Isaac wandered off alone into the woods.

She and Jeremy, who she trusted despite her fears, discussed the liens later that week. Jeremy agreed to take each one to the homesteader and tell them that their debt was forgiven. Martha insisted that Jeremy say that he was sure this was what his brother would want. She was determined to leave this town and never look back and guilt over Jebediah's evil ways was not going to haunt her. She would settle all the accounts before she left and he would remain a hero for the sake of the homesteaders and his sons. Jeremy admired Martha's strength and the manner in which she settled his brother's affairs. Jebediah did not deserve to be a hero in anyone's eyes, but Jeremy knew that Martha was being totally unselfish in her motives and he respected her for it. Jonas Whittaker would have one reason to be proud of his youngest son and that reason was the widow Whittaker. Quite a woman indeed, this Martha McGuire Whittaker. Jeremy could not help but wonder what Austin's intentions were and what his own role would be in the lives of his three nephews.

"Jeremy, I think you should have this." Martha held out her open palm. Jebediah's gold watch sparkled there. Jeremy gave her a quizzical look. "It was your father's after all. It is only fitting that you have it."

"I don't know where Jebediah got that watch, Martha, but I assure you it was not my father's." He lifted his own watch from his pocket. "This was our father's watch." Martha stared at him in disbelief. *Was there no end to Jebediah's lies and deceit?* "Put it away for one of the boys." Jeremy could see the disgust and disappointment on her face. He wanted to console her. The more Jeremy saw of Martha, the more enamored he became. She had suffered unbelievably at the hands of Jebediah, but she showed an almost superhuman inner strength and determination. Even her physical appearance seemed different. She reminded him of a butterfly emerging from its cocoon.

Austin helped her pack up what few belongings they had. He felt great relief, knowing Martha's nightmare was over and that they would all return to England. Martha was a widowed mother now and would have three boys to care for. The last year had added great maturity and responsibility to his dearest friend and he loved her even more for the courageous way she had endured. Austin thought back to the vain, innocent girl he had last seen and this strong, brave woman before him held no similarity to that person. What would their relationship be like now? Where did he fit into this scenario? Was he man enough for a woman like Martha or would she always be simply his best friend? Martha would need a man in her life to help with the boys but Jeremy was their uncle and Austin knew that he would never turn his back on them. Austin had also noticed the new look of interest in Jeremy's eyes whenever he looked at Martha and was unsure if it was jealousy or relief he was feeling.

Jeremy visited each homesteader personally. Isaac remained subdued and silent and spent most of his time alone in the woods where he felt comfortable. The young boy wondered what the future held for them. Martha had told them that she would take care of them, but Isaac had been terrible to her. Why should she want to take care of him? He would make out fine as long as the other boys were taken care of. He could survive on his own. Abraham gave each of the animals to a different homesteader and Ezekiel said goodbye to his little friends. Martha was surprised when the church safe was opened by Isaac, who ironically, was the only one Jebediah had trusted with the combination. In the safe she and Isaac, found thousands of pound notes, jewelry including her mother's emerald necklace and several gold bars. Jebediah had indeed been a dark horse, but this money would help her and the boys establish themselves back in England. Martha assured Isaac that she intended to care for all three of them and this money would ensure their future. Isaac slowly began to trust Martha and Jeremy. A new pastor had been found and would live in the Whittaker home on the church property. Martha had transferred the land to the town in Jebediah's memory. She handled herself regally and everyone showed great respect for Jebediah's widow. Abraham and Ezekiel seemed upset about losing their father but grew closer to Jeremy with each passing day.

Austin went hunting with Isaac, much to everyone's surprise. Martha thought that Isaac would never want to hold a rifle again. But he surprised them all when he announced he was going hunting and would give the deer to the Muellers. Austin asked permission to accompany him and Isaac seemed glad for the company. Isaac even smiled at Martha as they rode off and she found his new attitude very unsettling. She experienced an unwanted fear that something would happen to Austin while in Isaac's company. However, the hunting trip went off without a hitch and Austin complimented Isaac on his marksmanship and skill with a knife upon their return. The two seemed to be forming a bond and the vicious and angry Isaac seemed to be emerging from his shell as a content and almost normal boy.

Isaac found Martha alone one evening and sat at the large wooden table where she was folding clean laundry. He hesitated for several minutes before speaking. "Martha, when I went hunting with Austin, he told me a little about your life before you came to live with us. He said that you lived with your father. Austin told me that your mother died when you were young. Is that true?"

Martha was a little surprised that Isaac was speaking to her at all, never mind in a courteous and almost interested manner. The two had seemed to find an amiable silence over the past weeks. "Yes, all of that is true, Isaac. My mother died of an illness when I was just a little older than you are now. I loved her with all my heart and I still miss her every day."

"I miss my mother too. She was very pretty. Not like you, but a different kind of pretty. She had blonde hair and blue eyes and she smelled like roses. Abraham and Ezekiel look a little like her. Sometimes when I look at them, I see her face." Isaac seemed to stare off, his gaze upon a long forgotten face. Martha was unsure whether she should mention Jebediah and what had happened. Isaac had not spoken of his father since that fateful day; she decided to let Isaac lead the conversation.

"I'm sorry that your mother died, Martha. My mother fell down the stairs to her death. It was a long time ago and now it is finally over." With that, he rose from the chair and walked out of the cabin. Martha sat staring at the chair Isaac had vacated for a long time. *Is he trying to reassure me that the story of Jebediah's death is safe with him, or is something much deeper going on with Isaac? Only time will tell.*

Weeks later the wagon was loaded with trunks and the Whittakers were ready to leave town. A small gathering in the town square to say goodbye and Mr. Mueller announced that the town would be named Whittakerville after the most honest, generous man they had ever known. Martha smiled, thanked them all and told the boys this town would be their heritage. She embraced Margaret and Olga, wishing them well and promising to write. Then she rode away, straight backed and looking forward with Isaac, Abraham and Ezekiel, accompanied by Jeremy and Austin on horseback. Although the younger boys turned and waved to their friends, Martha and Isaac never looked back.

Chapter Fifteen
Back to St. Louis

The five travelers waited at Fort Laramie for the stage to arrive. Austin accompanied the boys while they walked around the fort getting their final look at the fur traders, Indians and soldiers. Jeremy and Martha sat together and waited, both lost in their own thoughts.

Although she was relieved that her ordeal was over, she was very confused and frightened about the future. *What is waiting for me back in England? Will I live in Father's house with the boys or stay at Pheasant Run as Jeremy has offered?* She knew that he had lived in India and it was possible he intended to return there. Pheasant Run had been the boy's home and as Jebediah's widow, she now belonged there. *And what about Father? Can I forgive him for giving me to Jebediah? Could I bear another ocean crossing after the last ill-fated trip? Can I take care of the boys and myself?* Her head was spinning with questions and any answers were avoiding her at the moment.

Jeremy, too, was thinking of Pheasant Run. Would he stay in England to be near his nephews? What would Martha do once she returned? Where did Austin fit in the scenario? Many questions ran through his head as he sat next to Martha. He felt the heat of her body next to his and the scent of rosemary from her hair filled his nostrils. Was he falling in love with his brother's widow?

Upon their arrival at the fort, Jeremy had gone in search of Arnold

Swartz. He found the man packing a horse, ready to leave the fort. He was surprised the man recognized him and spoke to him immediately. "Howdy, stranger. I never did thank you for the ale. Sorry I got so depressing but I do appreciate your kindness." Arnold extended his hand to Jeremy. Jeremy reached into his pocket and handed Arnold an envelope. The surprised Swartz opened the envelope slowly and gasped when he saw the money there. "What is this for?"

"Jebediah Whittaker is dead. This money is from his estate and you deserve your share. Use it wisely, my good man. Good luck to you." He shook the man's hand, and then he turned and walked away, leaving Arnold Swartz staring openmouthed with tears in his eyes.

The boys wandered around the fort. As they stopped to watch some Indians unload pelts and furs, they overheard two scouts discussing a stage that had traveled through a few weeks ago.

"I tell you the Sioux attacked travelers and stage stops from Platte to the Little Blue. About forty whites were killed, scalped and cut to pieces, the buildings and stages were burned and all the stock was run off." One of the scouts stopped talking to expel some tobacco as the boys turned their heads in alarm. Austin wanted to leave but the boys were glued to the spot. "A stage arrived out of Nebraska and found the road lined with butchered whites and burned wagons. Passengers almost panicked but the driver managed to bring them through safely."

"Come on, boys, let's go and find Uncle Jeremy." Austin pulled the three brothers along as their faces turned white with fear. Upon reaching Martha and Jeremy, all of them spoke at once.

"Uncle Jeremy, there are Indians killing everyone on the stages." Isaac directed his statement at Jeremy. "We better get the rifles from the wagon."

"Bodies lined the road and there was blood and guts and burned wagons everywhere," Abraham added, his voice trembling.

"I'm not going on any stagecoach, Martha. I'm staying here where there are lots of soldiers." Ezekiel looked at Martha with his eyes wide and his hands trembling. Martha immediately turned her face towards Austin with a stern, questioning look.

"We overheard some scouts telling tall tales that is all, Martha.

OF DREAMS AND NIGHTMARES

Jeremy, tell the boys how the scouts like to exaggerate." Austin knew he should not have let the boys hear the scouts' stories and he expected Martha to chastise him for it.

Jeremy immediately calmed the situation by laughing. "Don't tell me you believe such tall yarns. Haven't you boys lived in the west long enough to know how those men like to take a small story and let it grow beyond belief? Now let's all sit down and wait for the stage. You have had enough excitement for one day."

The boys obeyed but kept their eyes glued to the Indians that walked past and now seemed to be everywhere in the fort. Abraham pulled his hat down over his hair, thinking that the Indians might prefer blond scalps. Martha looked at the boys and her heart was filled with fear that she could not protect them. She prayed for strength and guidance.

Austin returned to the scouts to find out just how much of the tale was true and was unhappy to learn that the incident had really happened and no exaggeration had been made. Now he was not looking forward to traveling back to St. Louis. It was one thing for he and Jeremy to travel all those dusty dangerous miles but now they had Martha and the boys to consider. Austin prayed that they would make the trip safely. He had not traveled all this way for Martha, to lose her to a band of savages.

The weary and dusty travelers managed an uneventful stagecoach trip all the way to St. Louis. Martha was pensive and quiet for most of the trip. *What do I do now? Oh, Lord, help me find myself again.* Not one Indian was seen and no robbers tried to hold up the stage; the boys were almost disappointed as they arrived tired but safe in St. Louis.

Once they were settled in the St. Louis City Hotel, Austin went to see Loretta Langley. Even he was surprised with his urgency to see her again.

"Austin, you came back." Loretta threw herself into Austin's arms and covered his face with kisses. Grabbing her around the waist, Austin held Loretta and gazed into her eyes. He had missed this bubbly, blonde woman and he immediately pulled her back into his arms and returned her kisses. How he had missed her.

"Come to the hotel this evening, there is someone I want you to meet, Loretta." Austin kissed Loretta once more and left her standing on the porch of her father's house. A smiling, swooning Loretta leaned against the porch post and watched her whistling beloved walk away.

Back at the hotel, Martha waited patiently for Jeremy at the top of the stairs where he had asked her to meet him. She leaned against the brightly papered wall with her eyes closed, listening to the sounds of the people milling below. A lively melody drifted up the stairs from the piano bar just off the lobby. The air was a cacophony of cigars, heavy perfume and cooking odors. *Life, this place is alive with the smell, the sound and the feel of life. How long I have waited to experience life once again.* She opened her eyes just as he turned the corner. He could not help thinking that she looked content, almost peaceful for the first time since he had met her.

Jeremy took Martha to the hotel lobby and instructed her to wait for him. She stood stiffly, curious and cautious at the same time. *What is he up to?* Jeremy was having a strange effect on her. She was wary of him but she found him most attractive. She was drawn to him unwillingly. Just the sound of his voice made her heart beat quicker. She mustn't let herself be taken in by his manly charms. Men had proven that they could not be trusted. Even her father, the only man she had loved and trusted in her entire life, had betrayed her. The pain of that betrayal was still heavy on her heart. *No, I cannot trust any man ever again. It is just the unbelievable pleasure of being back in civilization once again that is making me feel this way.* He disappeared into the back room with the hotel manager and when he reappeared, he was dragging one of her trunks. Stunned, Martha could not believe her eyes. One of the missing trunks she had brought with her from England was now placed at her feet. She looked into Jeremy's green eyes as tears welled in her own. He nodded to her to open it. She knelt slowly, her hand reaching out to stroke the top of the trunk as if to confirm that it was real. Carefully she lifted the lid, examining the contents one item at a time. Inside she found all of her books, a dress, hat and the portrait of her mother.

"Oh, Jeremy, my mother's portrait. But how did you find it? Jebediah said he left it back east." Martha, overcome with excitement and joy, jumped up and threw her arms around Jeremy's neck. Suddenly shy, she tried to withdraw but Jeremy pulled her to him. His body felt so warm and inviting to her and she reluctantly leaned into his arms. She was starved for affection and the human contact felt so good to her. Jeremy's arms tightened and he looked into her sky blue eyes; the same alluring, hypnotizing sky blue eyes in the portrait. Suddenly they were kissing. Martha pushed Jeremy away, her face turning crimson. Embarrassment and shame flooded in as she turned away, shocked at her brazen behavior. *Am I so weak as not to heed my own good advice?* Only moments before she was expounding on the dishonesty of men and now, oh, what had she done? She could not look him in the eye.

Recovering from the surprise but most pleasant embrace, Jeremy calmly explained that he and Austin rescued what was left of her belongings back east and then left them here in St. Louis for safekeeping. Jeremy realized that Martha was embarrassed and he tried to put her at ease. He discussed the trunk and apologized for the lack of contents but Martha was happy with what she had. She knelt once again beside the trunk hugging the silky fabric of the dress to her chest. She rubbed the silk against her cheek, inhaling the familiar scent of roses. This was the first time she had felt any happiness in almost a year and she wanted to prolong this moment as long as she could. Embarrassed but glowing, she savored the wonder of the lost trunk and secretly, the warm excitement growing in her chest. Furtively, eyes closed she relived the feeling of the gentle embrace. Jeremy stood aside, allowing her time with her things; he could still feel the softness of her lips on his. A great heat was growing in his loins. He turned away from her.

Jeremy and Martha took the trunk up to her room where Ezekiel squealed with delight when he saw all of the books. "Oh, Mama, look at all the books," he cried, pulling books one after another out of the trunk, unaware of what he had just said. Martha, however, was very aware that this wonderful little boy had just called her Mama. Eyes watering for the second time in one day, overflowing with love, she hugged the small boy to her breast. Tears of joy ran down her face as she began to realize that there was so much to be thankful for. *I will never have to ignore you again, my son. I will fill your life with love and affection.* Ezekiel's tiny arms hugged her tightly; overjoyed at the wonderful gift she had just given him. After that day, Ezekiel called her Mama and Abraham soon followed.

That evening Austin presented Loretta Langley to his dearest friend, Martha Whittaker. Jeremy watched the exchange with mounting interest. Martha, the slim, lovely brunette clad in her recently recovered, resized bright blue gown and the fashionably dressed blonde, curvaceous Loretta in red, eyed each other cautiously. They were most polite in their conversation. Strategic questions were asked and each woman discovered what she wanted to know about the other. Austin and Jeremy sat back and enjoyed their brandy, cigars and the most entertaining interaction between the two beauties. After a few hours, the atmosphere was much more relaxed as each woman found her own place in the scenario. Loretta found Martha to be strong, beautiful and confident. She was impressed with how knowledgeable and mature Martha seemed. Martha, who was only two years older than Loretta, thought that the pert and talkative young Miss Langley was charming, likeable and very sincere. She also realized that Loretta was in love with Austin. Jealousy was not an emotion she felt she deserved to feel with Austin, however, they had been inseparable most of their lives and she loved him deeply. After seeing Austin and Loretta together, Martha knew that Austin had made his choice of a lifetime companion and it was not she. She also knew that, in spite of herself, her own feelings for Jeremy were growing by the day and was unsure what, if anything would happen between them.

As she lay in her bed that night, she pondered the past year. She smiled at her beautiful blue dress hanging on the back of the door. Life was so confusing now. She was finally free of Jebediah but now she had the boys to care for. *Am I up to the challenge?* She doubted her own competence. *Was Isaac really changing for the better or was there more to it?* He seemed so different than the boy she had come to know in Wyoming. She was being returned to England, but did she want to go home to her father? *Can I ever forgive him?* Where did Jeremy fit into her future? Was she so vulnerable to a kind word? She could not put the kiss out of her mind. Could she hope he cared for her and could she trust him? She could not forget that he was Jebediah's brother and although he had been nothing but kind and considerate of her, she knew the Whittakers had a way of fooling people. Jebediah certainly had done a good job of convincing the homesteaders that he was worthy of their respect and loyalty. *Only time will tell what Jeremy's true character is.* Austin, her love, had traveled all this way to save her and now he was in love with someone else. *How long will it be before I can recover from those long arduous months with Jebediah, if ever? Who exactly is Martha McGuire Whittaker?* The fear of her own survival had been replaced with emotional turmoil and an unknown future. It seemed that peace and tranquility were too much to ask for.

Austin, too, was feeling confused. Martha had been the only love of his life and now he was feeling such desire for Loretta. Was it just physical? Was it Martha that he should be planning a future with? Jeremy and Martha seemed to be getting closer and maybe Jeremy was Martha's destiny. His own feelings for Loretta seemed very strong and he was much happier now that he was with her again. Would she be willing to leave St. Louis and travel to England? His mind was muddled as Austin tossed and turned in his hotel bed, just down the street from the totally in love, Loretta Langley.

Isaac knocked on Austin's door, early the next morning. "Can I talk with you, Mr. Wells? I need to ask you some questions about our travel plans." Austin was very impressed with Isaac, who appeared much older than his eleven years. With all he had been through in those few years, it was not a wonder that he was more adult than child.

"Of course, I'm just having some tea, would you like some? Come in and sit down and, please, call me Austin." Austin poured Isaac a cup of tea and the two sat at the small round table, beside the hotel window comfortable in each other's company.

"What is on your mind, Isaac? I suppose this entire situation has you confused and bewildered. I know it does me for reasons of my own."

"I don't know if I want to go back to England, Mr. ... er, Austin. I like it here. The hunting, the horses and this is the most beautiful land I have ever seen. I remember England is nice and green but this is something else, so wild and unchartered. Of course, I won't have much choice because Martha is responsible for us and I'm too young to stay alone. I really don't want to go back to England, Austin." Obviously troubled, Isaac sipped his tea and with furled brow, stared out the window.

"Isaac, we are all in a transition period. None of us knows the future, least of all Martha. I suggest that you return to England and then in a few years, you could return to the Americas and live however you want. Martha will need help with your brothers and you are the man of the house now. I know that you and Martha have not been close but give her a chance, Isaac. She is a kind and loving woman and she truly cares about you and your brothers. She has had a very rough time this past year and she needs time to recover. I believe that England is the best place for her to do that. You're an amazing young man, Isaac, and I know that you could be a big help to her." Austin was most sincere in his assessment of Isaac, who seemed to respect Austin immensely. Isaac seemed to ponder the situation for a few minutes before speaking.

"Thanks, Austin, you're so easy to talk to. I'll think about what you said. Could we go hunting anywhere around St. Louis?" Isaac seemed more relaxed and talking of hunting always brought a smile to his eyes if not his lips.

"I'll arrange it and let you know later today, I would ask Uncle Jeremy to join us but just between you and me, he is a rotten shot." Austin laughed and escorted Isaac to the door. Later that day, he discussed his conversation with Jeremy and expressed his thoughts that Isaac deserved some happiness in his life. Uninvited, Jeremy did not go hunting with the pair but he did think about what Austin had said. Earlier, Martha had expressed a hesitation about returning to England and her father. Jeremy had made several good business deals here in St. Louis and was considering opening an office and hiring a manager. Perhaps none of them should go back to England.

Chapter Sixteen
St. Louis

Martha found St. Louis to be quite a change from Wyoming. A bustling city with a theatre, opera, department stores and beautiful homes, it was a welcome sight for her. She was feeling totally confused about her future. The trials and tribulations of the previous year and a half were finally over. Jebediah was dead. It was very disturbing to learn that he had killed Alicia. Martha wondered when he planned to kill her because she was certain that he would have. She would never forget the horrors Jebediah subjected her to and now that it was over, what should she do? She was responsible for the boys, although she had some money, it would not last forever. She was unsure about England and what she would do there. Women were very limited and could not have professions. The lower classes performed cleaning, sewing and outdoor tasks but the women of society simply entertained themselves with parties, teas and their children. An altered Martha was used to doing her own chores now and didn't really think she could return to the shallow, pampered life of England's aristocracy. She definitely was not ready to rely on her father's financial support. How far she had come. Only little over a year ago, her life was one of parties, dresses and carefree days. It all seemed so long ago and now it seemed so shallow and irresponsible. She thought about her friends in Wyoming, struggling to feed their families and make a life in the unsettled west. Those women were strong and courageous. She admired them a great deal and vowed to do something with her life. Martha knew she would never return to Wyoming and the life of a settler but she could make something of herself here in St. Louis. She must push this lack of confidence aside and convince herself to try something new. Filled with a new optimism and determination, she set out to explore the city and its possibilities.

The boys were finding many interesting things in St. Louis. "I don't think this place is so bad, Abraham. There are lots of surrounding woods full of wild life and this river has lots of different fish. Me and Austin are going fishing this afternoon." Isaac threw a rock into the Mississippi.

Abraham had already visited the stables and blacksmiths and realized that although this was a city, animals were still a big part of the community. "You should see all the horses in the stables outside of town. Mr. Langley keeps some of his wagons and horses corralled just behind the blacksmith shop." Abraham enjoyed talking with this new and more open Isaac. He picked up a rock and threw it, watching the water splash as it skipped the surface.

Ezekiel found the library and when he entered, he was in awe. Thousands of books on hundreds of shelves filled the space. The building was large and spacious with comfortable tables and chairs for reading. The oiled wooden walls shone, heavy fabric drapes hung over the tall windows. Several people searched the shelves for books. Some sat at the long tables with pen and paper in hand researching some project or another. This was heaven to a boy with only three dog-eared books and an insatiable appetite for knowledge.

Martha and Loretta got better acquainted and became close friends. They shopped together and Martha was rebuilding her wardrobe with fabrics purchased in the large department stores. The new clothes supported her in her inner battle against fear and failure.

"The retail shopping center is at the upper end of Fourth Street near Washington Avenue. We have Scruggs and the Barr Dry Goods Company and I'm sure you can get some fine fabrics there." Loretta told Martha. "Afterwards, we can stop at the hotel for lunch and then more shops." Martha was happy to have such a good friend and confidante. She was beginning to feel much better and was enjoying the shopping and city life very much. Traces of her old confidence were returning but now peppered with a maturity and determination she had never known in England.

Jeremy investigated property in St. Louis and considered buying a large building for his business. Even if he decided to return to India, this would be an excellent place for a branch office. His brother was dead and Jeremy felt some responsibility for his nephews. Any money that was left in England by Jebediah would by law, go to he and the boys and not Martha. Jeremy would see that the money was put in trust for the boys and some of it was sent to St. Louis to help Martha get settled. Knowing Jebediah as he did, Jeremy was sure there would be a sizable amount of money to deal with. He was concerned about the way the boys had just stopped talking about their father. He knew that Jebediah had beaten the boys as a form of discipline, however, he found it odd that they chose not to mention him at all. Perhaps they were aware of Martha's feelings and wanted to spare her or perhaps they simply didn't want to deal with it. Jeremy's feelings for Martha were confusing. He was very attracted to her and would like to get to know her better, often reminiscing over their kiss in the hotel. Jeremy could sense reluctance on her part. His brother had beaten her down physically and mentally, leaving her full of mistrust. He understood that Martha would need time to heal. He would have to win her trust and see where their relationship would lead. In the meantime, Jeremy looked at property and arranged for shipments to and from India.

Austin was a big help to him and decided to stay in St. Louis as well. Of course, his motives revolved around Loretta Langley. Her parents were very impressed with Austin and were hoping for a wedding in the near future. Austin felt a responsibility for Martha and wanted to be sure she was settled and the boys were taken care of. Austin tried to spend time with Isaac whenever possible. He felt sorry for the quiet solitary boy and since Isaac seemed to enjoy his company, Austin spent as much time as he could with him. The incident in the church was never mentioned and neither was Jebediah. It was as if he had never existed. Austin also noticed that Jeremy seemed to be very enamored with Martha and was hoping for a development in that relationship. Austin wanted Martha to be loved and happy the way he felt with Loretta. She had suffered over the past year and deserved some happiness, but she was also very stubborn and would have to make her own choices. Austin had watched her grow from a child to a woman and even he would never try to change her mind or influence her in any of her decisions.

"You really should come to the country club, Martha. Mother would be happy to introduce you to several eligible bachelors. Unless of course, a certain brother-in-law has your eye these days." Loretta teased over lunch. She, like Austin, wanted to see Martha and Jeremy together. Martha had confided in her about Wyoming and life with Jebediah and Loretta wanted her to find some happiness as soon as possible.

"I honestly don't want to be involved with any man right now, Loretta. Jebediah was enough to last me a lifetime. That man ruined any hopes I have of a loving relationship and I really don't know if I could bear to have anyone touch me that way, ever again. Besides, men have shown their true colors to me over the last year. First my father, then Jebediah, then the man on the ship, Richard; not one of them can be trusted." Martha shuddered at the thought of her time with Jebediah. "I'm very grateful to Jeremy for helping to rescue me but I'm not ready to have a relationship, let alone marry anyone." Her hand moved to smooth her hair, now softer and more alive under her touch. The softness helped to calm and reassure her.

"You will feel differently in time, I'm sure. My father always says that life has a way of making us forget the bad and only remember the good. There are a lot of good, trustworthy, gentlemen in this world. I know one of them is just for you." Loretta picked up her menu. "Now about that lunch." She decided to order the fresh fish.

"Actually, Loretta, I'm thinking about starting a business of some kind. Do you think I could do it? I want to be independent and self-reliant. What do you think St. Louis society would think about a woman owning a business?" The waiter arrived and took their order smiling at the two lovely women before him. Loretta smiled at him before continuing.

"Now that is a nice looking young man. Perhaps he would like to escort you around town." Sensing Martha's embarrassment at her teasing, she changed the subject once again. "Lots of women have businesses here. A widow owns the boarding house and two sisters own the Walnut Street Tearoom. A woman even owns the bakery; but her husband is the baker because they have ten children and she is busy with them. Women are less restricted here than in England, Martha, and I'm sure you could come up with something. St. Louis is growing all the time. You are very smart. You could be a tutor or even a teacher, to the wealthy children if you wanted."

"I'll look around the city and make a decision. Thank you for all of this information and all of your support, Loretta. You are becoming such a dear friend to me." Martha reached over and squeezed Loretta's hand. "I'm happy for you and Austin. He is my best friend in all the world and I'm glad he has found you." Loretta returned the squeeze and smiled at her friend. "My next plan of action is to find a house. I never thought I would hear myself say this but I'm tired of living in the hotel and it's too hard on the boys. Tomorrow we'll go and look at houses; if you are free, I would like you to come with us." The waiter returned with their lunch. Martha blushed, remembering Loretta's earlier comment. Loretta giggled. Martha tasted her fish, relishing the delicious sauce that covered it. "You cannot know how nice it is to sit in a restaurant once again. This is delicious."

"Enjoy yourself, you don't have to pick up the boys at the stables for another two hours. Are the boys coming with us tomorrow?"

"I want the boys to help with the choices because it will be their home as well. They have been through enough in their young lives. I intend to make them very secure and happy here with me. I just pray that I can do it. Perhaps we can all forget Wyoming."

"Oh, I know just the place. The new homes in Lucas Place are very lovely and spacious. They are so modern with indoor plumbing and wonderful yards. You will love them." Loretta excitedly told Martha of the new residential area being developed in St. Louis for the upper classes. The two women ate, chatted and wiled away the afternoon.

Bright and early the next morning they headed for Lucas Place.

"I like this one the best," Ezekiel proclaimed as he plopped exhausted, on the steps of the newly built house.

"You do not, you just don't want to look at any more houses." Abraham corrected.

"Both of you, come along we have one more to see and then we'll discuss which one we like best." Martha ushered the boys back into the carriage and she and Loretta talked of the many homes they had seen. The boys were becoming restless.

"I want a house with a big yard so we can have lots of pets." Abraham declared.

"I want my own room so no one will bother me when I'm studying. I'm going to get so many books from the library and I want to be alone to read them," Ezekiel piped up.

"I just want a place to sleep that is close to the woods and the river," Isaac added his comments however short and to the point. The carriage stopped in front of another new home.

"Now this is a lovely house. Let's go inside and see if it has everything you want." The boys moaned but jumped down from the carriage and headed towards the house. After looking at the front yard, Martha entered the two-story brick house and headed for the kitchen. The boys scurried upstairs and Isaac checked the backyard.

"This kitchen is perfect and look at the big sitting room." Loretta was impressed with this house. "It even has indoor plumbing, Martha. A lot of the older homes do not."

"I love this front porch and the price is reasonable." Martha agreed with Loretta, this house was just right. Now she just had to convince herself that she was ready to take on the responsibility of a house and a family alone. She took a deep breath and willed herself to be confident. *I can do this, I can.*

"Woods out the back and the river is just down the street. OK with me." Isaac rejoined the others, entering through the back door.

"This is the one, Martha, lots of bedrooms and a big yard." The other two chimed in.

"Looks like we have found a new home for the Whittaker family," Martha proclaimed, hugging two of the boys to her. "I believe we can start our new life together looking forward to a wonderful future." A feeling of contentment filled Martha's heart as she looked down at her boys. Even Isaac smiled at her from the other side of the room. Loretta beamed at the little family, happy that her new friend was staying in St. Louis.

Later that day, Loretta and Martha returned to the house with Jeremy and Austin. Alone in the parlor, Jeremy walked to the window where Martha surveyed the property of her new domain. He stood just a little too close and she moved closer to the window, almost pressing her body into the glass to avoid any contact with him.

He wanted to reach out and take her in his arms, but instead, he moved to the center of the room.

"This is a lovely house, Martha. I am sure you and the boys will be happy here."

Relieved to have some space between them, she turned and smiled. "Yes, a new home and a new life. Jeremy, I want to thank you for all you have done for us. You have been most kind." Taking this compliment as encouragement Jeremy again moved towards her. However, Martha smiled and walked from the room, leaving him frustrated once again.

Chapter Seventeen
London & some surprising news

John McGuire was relieved to know that Martha was safe at last. A telegram from Jeremy had confirmed the death of Jebediah Whittaker and the safe transport of Martha to someplace named St Louis. Further information would be forthcoming in a letter, was all the telegram said. No mention of when Martha would be returning to England or her plans, but John would be patient now that he knew she was safe.

Phoebe was happy to receive John and his wonderful news in London. Phoebe and Max were very compatible and had become much closer over the past months. John had business in London for the next few weeks and would stay with her and partake of some of London's pleasures.

Max and John visited the London Men's Club and enjoy indoor games of whist, cribbage and bridge. If the weather permitted, they partook of tennis, shooting, cricket and/or fishing. While the men were otherwise occupied, Phoebe and the ladies would walk and promenade with the occasional game of croquet for amusement.

"Well, John, actually Mrs. Jonas Whittaker is still alive and incarcerated in the asylum in Northumberland." Max reiterated during a game of cribbage. John was very surprised to hear this as he had been under the impression the woman had died years before from her long-term illness.

"What responsibility is this woman to Martha now that Jebediah was dead?" When confronted by this question, Max confirmed that

Jonas had left a trust fund to take care of his wife until her death, therefore, she was taken care of and should not be a burden but John was not convinced. He pushed this thought away until he could give it more attention.

Evenings in London were spent at the Music Hall, The London Philharmonic or dancing the Viennese waltz or even the polka at Vauxhall or Cremorne Gardens. Often Phoebe would invite one of her widow friends to join herself, Max and John and the four of them would have a wonderful evening full of music and excellent food. Although John McGuire was not looking for a companion, he always enjoyed the company of a beautiful woman.

"Phoebe, I always take pleasure in these trips to London filled with social engagements and business meetings. After a few weeks, however, I'm ready to return to the slower pace of the country and Graystone. I'm slowly becoming accustomed to living alone with only the servants for company but I look forward to Martha's return." John lifted his suitcase and placed it in the carriage. "Jeremy's telegram said that Martha was safe but did not expound on the details of her year away. He did not say if Martha was anxious to come home or unforgiving where I'm concerned." Phoebe tried to reassure him but she too wondered if they would ever see Martha again. John and Phoebe climbed into her carriage and rode to the station in silence. Both of them were curious as to what had happened to Jebediah. All the telegram said was that he was dead. They would have to wait for the letter that was on its way with more details and just be happy that she was safe.

After saying his goodbyes at the train station, John sat in the railcar and pondered his visit. Phoebe and Max made a lovely couple and John was happy for them. Phoebe had been a widow for many years and deserved some happiness. The conversation with Max came back to him. His curiosity was raised by the discovery that Mrs. Jonas Whittaker was confined to the asylum. Perhaps the illness was hereditary, accounting for Jebediah's despicable behavior and what of the children, could they be affected? When he returned to Northumberland, John intended to find out exactly what was wrong with Mrs. Jonas Whittaker. He put his head back on the seat of the rail car and eventually fell asleep to the clickety-clack sound of the wheels on the rail.

"Mrs. Elizabeth Whittaker has not had a visitor in over a year, sir, may I ask what your relationship is to the patient?" The mousy-looking nurse spoke in a monotone that reflected both her appearance and her attitude.

"My daughter is her daughter-in-law, making us family and I would like to see her if possible. Is she lucid? If not, could I speak to her doctor, please?" John was calm and confident on the outside but inside his stomach was doing nervous somersaults.

"The doctor will be happy to discuss her with you, please sit over there." The nurse pointed to a ragged chair and left John alone. The asylum was a huge rambling mansion in great disrepair. The dark gray walls did nothing to make the place upbeat. The smell of lye soap and urine permeated the air and calls and shrieks of all kinds could be heard from beyond the doors. The odor and the unsettling noise were making John feel ill and he hoped the doctor would hurry. A door opened and a large, burly orderly appeared dragging a man with shackles on his legs and hands. The man's eyes stared vacantly and his clothes were filthy. The orderly ignored John as he passed and roughly took the shackled man through another locked door. Finally the doctor appeared and asked John to step into his office.

"What kind of a place is this?" John asked in disgust.

"It is a lunatic asylum, sir. Obviously you have never visited one before or you would realize that this is one of the best. Now what do you want to know about Mrs. Elizabeth Whittaker?" The doctor was obviously in a hurry and wanted this interview over with. He tapped nervously on his desk with his pencil.

"I want to know what is wrong with her and if it is hereditary, as my daughter is married to one of her sons." Sweat appeared on John's brow and his stomach felt as if it was tied in knots. He could not imagine what the lunatics in this place had to endure.

"She is insane, a complete lunatic. Doesn't know who she is or where she is. Not expected to live much longer, anyway. As far as whether it is hereditary, well, your guess is as good as mine. No one knows these things; why? Does anyone in her family display any symptoms?"

"Not that I know of. Why do you say she is not expected to live much longer, is she physically ill as well?" John was sorry he had come. The answers to his heredity questions had not been answered and this place made him extremely upset. "Can I see her?"

"If you want to but she won't know who you are. The nurse will take you."

The mousy nurse appeared at the door and took John down a long hall. All of the doors were closed in this section of the house and finally they stopped at the end of the hall. The nurse unlocked the door and there, lying on the bed, eyes closed, was Elizabeth Whittaker. The woman was extremely thin with stringy, sparse white hair. The yellowish flesh on her face was sunken in and her eyes were ringed with blue-black circles. John asked the nurse if she was still alive, the body looked so still and no sign of breathing could be seen. The room held a foul odor. The nurse impatiently checked the pitiful remnants of a woman and looked at John with a surprised look on her face.

"Well you are right, she is dead. Good thing you came today, or we wouldn't have checked her until tonight. It is Sunday and the staff goes to visit their relatives. We always confine all the patients to bed and feed them after the staff returns on Sunday evenings." The nurse saw nothing wrong with the situation but John was feeling nauseous. He ran from the room, down the hall and out the door. Behind a sparse rose bush he vomited, sweat running off his brow, his heart pounding in his chest. The sight of Elizabeth Whittaker's corpse and the callous attitude of the nurse was more than he could bear. Composing himself, he returned to the nurse's station and inquired what was to be done with the body.

"Says in the file that the lawyer paid for the plot already so we'll have her transported to the churchyard. Apparently the family already made arrangements for the headstone so you don't have to do a thing. Maybe you could let the family know." The nurse walked away, leaving John pale and shaking and about to vomit again.

"I'm telling you, Smithson, something has to be done about that place. People are treated like animals there. You should have seen the filthy state of the patients and the chains. Are they really necessary?" John was beside himself, never having had experience with asylums before and not realizing that some of the patients were violent.

"Unfortunately, there is not much we can do. The government is forming a committee to try to improve the situations but so far not much has been done. Private asylums like the one Elizabeth Whittaker was in are much better than the workhouses and public lunatic asylums that the criminally insane and penniless lunatics are kept in. I understand your concern, John, but there is really nothing we can do. Jonas kept his wife at home as long as he could but there was no alternative. He chose the best place he could for Elizabeth." Max defended Jonas, his lifelong friend. Max had traveled to Northumberland and arranged for the small service at the churchyard for Elizabeth Whittaker. John had joined him feeling an odd responsibility to the poor woman who was not much older than he. The trust fund paid for a nice head stone and being one of only two mourners, John left flowers on the grave. The dead woman and the place where she spent her final days haunted him. As the flowers were laid on the grave, Elizabeth Whittaker was reunited with her husband and her youngest son, Jebediah, at last.

John McGuire, driven by some unknown force, spent the next month investigating the new government committee on asylums and then became very involved for the betterment of facilities for the insane. Some of the information gathered shocked him and made him all the more determined. He was shaken to read the reports:

> The severe whippings were most obvious; they were the favorite method of procuring a ready obedience from the inmates of the madhouses but they were also the first abuse, which it is necessary to lop off; a witness said in her evidence to the Select Committee appointed to consider the provisions being made for the better regulation of Madhouses in England. The whip was used as an engine of punishment; it was considered a most valuable therapeutic agent. In one madhouse, a doctor found a man confined in an oblong trough, chained down not having seen the light of day for weeks … .

The reports went on and on, one abuse after another and John was determined to instigate changes.

As a result, he was an integral part of the 1862 Lunacy Acts

Amendment, which set out conditions and regulations for the establishment, management, and inspection of county asylums. Workhouses were regulated so that the chronically ill were separated from the other inmates and given extra comforts. More changes to the Lunacy Act regulated the care and treatment of lunatics and provided for routine maintenance of asylums. Changes were also made in respect of the proof of insanity and disposal of the property of lunatics. John never understood his driving need to make such changes, other than the fact that he could never get Elizabeth Whittaker off of his mind. It was as if she was directing him from the grave, but the changes were good ones and he was happy to have concentrated his efforts on them. Perhaps it eased his conscience where Martha's arranged marriage was concerned. John also found it took his mind off of the fact that his daughter, now a Whittaker, was not returning.

A telegram was sent to St. Louis informing Jeremy Whittaker of the death of his mother and the arrangements that had been made. That same week a letter arrived from St. Louis:

Father:

I hope this letter finds you in good health. As you have been told, my husband, Jebediah Whittaker, is dead. A robber, in the church where Jebediah was the pastor, shot him to death. I'm now in St. Louis with Austin and Jeremy Whittaker and my three stepsons. My health is good, although the past year was one of extreme trials and tribulation. I do not know at this time if I'll ever forgive you for giving me to such a man as Jebediah. I have endured physical abuse, emotional torture and deception. My future is unsure as of now but I have decided to stay in St. Louis for at least a year or two. I'm unable to face England right now and St. Louis is a bustling city full of interesting prospects. Jeremy has decided to open an office here and will be staying here as well. Austin Wells now Jeremy's partner, has also decided to stay in St. Louis for the time being and is to be married in one month's time to a Miss Loretta Langley. The boys and I have purchased a lovely home on the western outskirts of St. Louis and they are happy to be staying here. It is a small but comfortable house with three bedrooms and a lovely sitting room. We have a small garden area for the boys to play in and there are several lovely parks in the city. I hope you are well, Father, as I wish you no harm. I love you, however, I cannot forget what you have done and I'll need some time to try to forgive you. Give Aunt Phoebe and Emma my love and I'll send another letter soon. I enclose my address in Lucas Place for your return letter.

Your loving daughter,
Martha

Tears stained the paper as John learned of his daughter's unbearable suffering over the last year. Now she would not return to him for at least another year and would she ever forgive him? He had no one to blame but himself but his heart was breaking. He mournfully carried the letter up the stairs to Martha's bedchamber, where he sat and cried for hours.

Chapter Eighteen
The Family Settles in

Austin and Loretta discussed their future and although she was willing to travel to England with him, they decided to settle in St. Louis for the time being.

"Now that Jeremy has opened an office in the city and asked me to join him as his partner, I think it is time for me to ask you an important question." Austin was feeling like a young boy as he dropped to one knee. "My darling, will you be my wife?" He looked at her hopefully.

"Oh yes, Austin, yes yes yes." The blushing young woman beamed from ear to ear. Austin slipped a sparkling diamond ring on her finger and she gushed over it. Her father, Arthur Langley, gave the two his blessing several hours later when they informed him and Isabel, his wife, of their plans. Austin wrote to his mother and told her of his marriage and also that he and Loretta would travel to England sometime in the coming year. Jeremy informed Austin that several trips to England would be necessary and offered to pay the way for Loretta to join him on one of the trips, as a wedding gift.

"I'll take the other trips, as I have to settle some business arrangements for shipments between India, Britain and the colonies. I also want to visit my mother's grave and make arrangements with Max Smithson for the smooth running of Pheasant Run in my absence." He informed Austin as they looked over the new building. He still enjoyed his travels and looked forward to seeing England as well as India again. Jeremy had invited Martha to accompany him on one of the trips but she declined. Perhaps she would change her mind when the time came. "Besides, Wells, you aren't much of a sailor if I remember correctly," Jeremy laughed.

Martha and the boys were settling in their new home in Lucas Place, an upscale section of St. Louis. Their home was newly built and two stories, with three bedrooms and a lovely sitting room. A small kitchen and indoor plumbing completed the picture of the perfect little home for the new family. The boys were enrolled in school and even Isaac seemed to be enjoying St. Louis.

"Martha, I have to tell you that I'm very happy we're staying in St. Louis. I didn't want to go back to England and thank you for asking my opinion," Isaac told her one afternoon. He was slowly becoming more trusting of her and she, in return, was becoming fond of him. They both had come a long way in building self-confidence and trust.

Martha was lighthearted and happy as she decorated her new home and the portrait of Lillian McGuire hung in the place of honor in the sitting room. She whispered a silent prayer to her mother, asking for her help with her new life. Lillian McGuire smiled down on her lovely daughter. Martha paused at the mirror in the entrance hall and smoothed her long chestnut hair. She was pleased with the reflection that looked back, not only her outer appearance but also the new more confident glow from within. *One step at a time, I have my own home and my boys. I must not rely on anyone.*

Martha allowed Jeremy to help her with the arrangements for the house and introductions to the bankers in St. Louis. She was a widow with money and a home of her own. She had come a long way from Wyoming.

"Max Smithson has forwarded a large sum of money that Jebediah left in English bank accounts and that, plus the money and gold in the church safe added up to a considerable sum, Martha. You are secure for the present," Jeremy informed her. But she was concerned about the future. She was firm in her conviction the boys would want for nothing and would have to find a continuing source of income. Plus, she was determined to do something useful with her life. "I suggest that you buy a boarding house and become a landlady," he suggested, but she had other ideas. Business was not open to women in England but things were different in the colonies and a woman could own and operate an enterprise. Martha was determined to make her own decisions, not relying on anyone ever again. She realized that she was becoming very fond of Jeremy, against her better judgment but she had been controlled long enough and would make her own decisions from now on.

Austin and Jeremy looked at several properties. "Many of the older buildings burned to the ground in the Great Fire of 1849 that destroyed most of the city. The new structures in the riverfront district are generally three to five stories in height with heavy brick walls faced with stone or cast iron facades. I'm sure we'll find one of them satisfactory." Jeremy informed Austin as they looked at building after building. He finally purchased a three-story building down by the riverfront. The first floor would be used as his import/export office, with warehousing in back and the second floor was to be Austin's flat.

"I insist that you take the second floor and I'll use the top floor myself." Jeremy showed Austin through the new building and Austin was impressed.

"I just know that Loretta will love this place. The riverfront is right across the street and the park is on the other side of the block. It is perfect, Jeremy, thank you. I'll make you happy that you put your trust in me as a partner and will work very hard to make both of us a great success. I'll have a wife to care for and this job is just what I needed and now we have a home as well." Austin walked to the window and took in the beautiful sunset over the river. Orange and pinks filled the sky and reflected on the water as Austin imagined coming home to the loving arms of Loretta.

The third and top floor Jeremy used for his own living quarters. It was quite large and more than enough room for one man. He especially liked the view of the river and surrounding wooded area. Its location on the riverfront was ideal for shipments in and out of the city. Austin was a most efficient partner and the business was going well. St. Louis was fast becoming a busy commercial hub and Jeremy knew that there would be many business prospects in the future. It was also a pretty city with many green parks, clean streets and attractive buildings. Jeremy was not greedy and obsessive like Jebediah but he was a very good businessman and knew how to make money. He wanted only a secure future and one day a family of his own with whom to share all he had. He wondered if Martha, who was blooming by day in this environment, would be part of that family. Other than the one kiss, they had remained platonic in their relationship.

Jeremy had sought membership in the Businessmen's Association of St. Louis. The secretary of the association was expected any minute. He tidied his desk and finished combing his hair just as the door opened. He was surprised to see a lovely young woman walking towards him. Her hair was black as midnight, her face round with a beguiling smile. Jeremy stammered his greeting. "I was expecting a gentleman, my apologies for appearing startled." He rose from his chair and extended his hand. Clarise Graham fluttered her eyelashes at the handsome Jeremy and extended her hand palm down, hinting at a kiss rather than a handshake. Jeremy lifted her delicate hand to his lips. "Allow me to introduce myself, Jeremy Whittaker."

"Clarise Graham, I am happy to make your acquaintance. I am here about your appointment to the Businessmen's Association." Clarise was besotted with this handsome, sophisticated man. Seating herself gracefully in the large leather chair, she stared at him coquettishly, demurely adjusting her gown to show her best features. Jeremy returned to his chair behind the desk, feeling foolishly nervous in Miss Graham's company. He watched in silence, her hand moving unconsciously to her hair. Wanting to dispel the tension, Clarise turned the conversation to the Businessmen's Association, explaining that her father, Morris Graham, was the president. As the conversation progressed, both occupants of the room were sizing up the other. Clarise thinking that this was a man she could pursue; Jeremy enjoying the sparkle in her eye and the soft tone of her voice. She was very attractive, providing a pleasant distraction.

Not wanting her to rush away, Jeremy offered her a glass of brandy. "I would prefer sherry if you have it." Clarise moved towards the table where Jeremy was pouring the drinks. She moved closer than would be deemed proper, brushing her hand against Jeremy's as she took the crystal glass from his hand. She looked up at him through her lowered lashes as she delicately sipped her sherry. Jeremy watched her full pouty lips on the crystal rim. Feeling the heat rising in his neck, Jeremy did not move away. He admired her features and her curvaceous body. He could not help but think that it had been a long time since he had lain with a woman. Suddenly the door opened and in fluttered Loretta, who stopped dead in her tracks at the cozy scene before her.

"Loretta." Jeremy turned and walked towards his desk, away from Clarise who looked very perturbed at the interruption. "Miss Graham, this is Loretta Langley." Loretta glared at the young woman before nodding her head in acknowledgment.

"Jeremy, Austin asked me to drop off these papers." She gave Jeremy a scowl as she handed the papers to him. It was very obvious that Loretta was not happy with the situation at hand. Jeremy thanked her, missing neither, the look or the tone. Clarise took her cue to leave and slowly walked towards the door, setting the crystal glass on the table as she passed.

"Thank you for your time, Mr. Whittaker, the association will be holding their next meeting on Tuesday, we shall expect you. Nice meeting you, Miss Langley." Jeremy quickly moved to hold the door for Clarise. Loretta waited just long enough to be sure the woman was gone, before bidding Jeremy farewell and heading straight to Martha's.

"I'm telling you, she is after him, the brazen hussy. If you want Jeremy, you had better make your move soon." Loretta fretted and fussed as she paced Martha's kitchen.

"Loretta, Jeremy is a free man. He can see whomever he wants. You know I am not ready to make a commitment." Martha was more disturbed by this news than she was letting on. "Loretta, please stop pacing, you are making me nervous."

Loretta stopped and plopped herself into the kitchen chair. "I know all that but you can't let him start seeing that strumpet. You should have seen the way she was looking at him. Just give him a little encouragement, I know it is you he wants." Martha would not take the bait, but Loretta was not about to give up. She and Austin were both hoping that Jeremy and Martha would get together. Finally exasperated with Martha's unwillingness to make a move, she left for home but this would not be the end of it as far as Loretta was concerned.

"I'm home, Mama." Ezekiel called out as he dropped his schoolbooks on the kitchen table. The kitchen was bright and sunny and the smell of apple pies filled the air. "Abraham went to the blacksmith shop again. Can I have some pie?" Martha appeared in the doorway of the kitchen, a smile forming on her lips as she looked at Ezekiel. She could not help but feel pride and deep affection for this impish and charming boy. He was growing taller every day and his love of books served him well in his studies. She had been preoccupied with the previous conversation with Loretta and welcomed the distraction.

"Abraham might as well move his bed over to the blacksmiths. I'll never understand how he can spend so much time cleaning horses' stalls. When I was a girl, I avoided the horses in Father's stables at every opportunity. Smelly creatures, horses." Martha scrunched up her face as if a bad odor had just wafted past. Ezekiel giggled at Martha's obvious distaste for the horses. Abraham had a part-time job cleaning the stables and although he was paid a half dollar a week, he did it purely for the love of the horses. Knowing the hound dog at the blacksmith shop was expecting pups any day now; Martha was dreading a discussion of all of the benefits of owning a dog. The boys were each settling in and St. Louis seemed to have something for each of them. Isaac spent a great deal of time fishing in the river and hunting with Austin. The two of them were very close and Martha was happy that Isaac was spending time with him. Isaac never mentioned his father and it was as if Jebediah Whittaker had never existed. Ezekiel and Abraham very seldom mentioned him and Martha never did. These were her sons now and Jebediah was no longer of any consequence.

"Fish for dinner tonight, Martha." Isaac appeared on the back porch carrying a large catfish and grinning from ear to ear. "What's in the box?"

"Yes, what was that box I saw on the porch, Mama?" Ezekiel asked, his mouth full of apple pie. Crumbs falling on his shirt as he spoke.

"That is my new sewing machine. I bought it yesterday and I'm waiting for Austin to come and carry it upstairs for me. I'll be able to make my dresses and your shirts much quicker now and Mrs. Langley asked if I would sew Loretta's wedding dress." Martha announced proudly, impressed with her new purchase. Her sewing skills were becoming most proficient and her sense of style cultured by designer, Charles Worth in England, gave her dresses a most flattering look and wide appeal. Jeremy imported all types of fabrics and accessories and was sure to bring her samples of beautiful, materials unknown to the colonies; including silks from the Orient and ostrich feathers from Australia.

"Austin's coming? Good, we have enough fish for all of us so he can stay for supper. I'll help him carry your machine up stairs when he arrives." Isaac wandered into the yard to clean his catch, most confident that Martha would have no problem with his decision to have Austin join them. Isaac was very fond of Austin and could relate to him with ease. Isaac did not relate to many people well but his relationship to Martha had improved considerably since that fateful day in the church. They seemed to have developed an unspoken understanding and a shared desire to forget Jebediah Whittaker. Now when Isaac dreamt of his mother, Alicia, she was smiling and happy, the way he remembered her. Blonde hair blowing in the breeze and the corner of her eyes creased with laughter lines as she and tiny Isaac played on the lawn. He was no longer tortured by nightmares of his mother screaming and of the dark unidentified shadow throwing his mother down the stairs. Isaac had pushed all memory of the incident in the church to the back of his consciousness and considered the matter closed. Although he could not bring himself to call Martha "Mama" as the younger boys did, he was very fond of her and particularly impressed with the way she had set up house for them all. He regretted that he had not been pleasant to her in the past but she seemed to have forgotten those days and treated him the same as the others. Many conversations with Austin allowed him greater insight to her past. Martha was no-nonsense and determined and Isaac admired that. He had seen the way she would appear frightened and unsure one minute and confident and determined the next. He took comfort in her ability to overcome her fears and often copied her, using the technique on himself. Isaac, too, had demons to battle but every passing day seemed to give him hope.

"Mama, I brought some eggs from Mrs. Johnson's." Abraham arrived home, sweaty and smelling of horses. The basket of eggs was deposited on the porch and he went out back to wash up at the well pump. Martha didn't allow him in the house without washing up; he couldn't understand what she found so offensive about the smell of horses. He thought they smelled wonderful. He pondered how he was going to talk her into a puppy, as he pumped the water into the bucket and washed his face and hands.

    Austin finished his ledgers and closed the office for the night. Martha had asked him to stop by. Austin was impressed with Martha's resolve and determination. She had made her decision to stay in St. Louis and had purchased a home for the boys within weeks. She had taken to her role as mother with enthusiasm and purpose. Austin initially felt guilty about his choice of Loretta over Martha but soon realized that Martha had matured during her time with Jebediah and grown away from him in her interests and ambitions. Loretta was much more suited to Austin's desires and dreams and he loved her with all his heart. Perhaps Jeremy and Martha would have a future together, but for now, he knew that his dear friend was determined to do things her way and without interference from anyone. He smiled when he thought of Loretta's anger over finding another woman in Jeremy's office. Upon seeing Miss Clarise Graham, Austin could understand how a man would be attracted to her. Loretta was determined to make sure there would be no relationship between Jeremy and Miss Graham. He laughed to himself, with Loretta as her champion, Martha wouldn't have to worry about Jeremy. He walked the short distance to Martha's house.

    After a delicious catfish supper, Martha carried a letter from Margaret Brown to the table. She unfolded the letter and was about to begin reading aloud when her gaze settled on Isaac. She could read the questions in his rigid face and nodded to assure him that his father was not mentioned in the letter. *You have not recovered either have you, my son? How long will he haunt us?* Isaac's facial features relaxed and she began:

Dearest Martha,

    Motherhood suits me to a tea. I have never been so happy as I am now. The baby, Sarah June is doing well and growing bigger every day. Unfortunately, the Grimeses' baby was not as lucky and passed away last week of pneumonia. The Muellers' store is bringing in more and more items every week and a feed store is now opened on the main street. The sawmill is up and running and most of us have log homes at last. You remember Arnold Swartz. Well, he returned to town and opened the sawmill. It is a shame about his wife's terrible death at the hands of those savages, but he seems to be adjusting. Next we anticipate the opening of the new bank, which will be needed in the coming winter. The pastor and his family are blending in well and life goes on in Whittakerville. It has been a good year and most of us were blessed with large harvests and healthy cattle. The cattle auction is next week and we are hoping for a sizable amount from the sale of our cattle. As you experienced, the past winter was very hard for many of the homesteaders and this good crop and cattle auction will ensure our futures here.

We are most concerned about the unrest with the present Indian Treaties. James says that the Lakota, the branch of Sioux in this area, are no longer happy with the treaty arrangements and he worries about an uprising. Fort Laramie has a large contingent of soldiers but there are many Cheyenne and Sioux in this area and we are concerned for our safety. James is very sympathetic to the Cheyenne, Sioux and the Arapaho. After meeting with Chief Red Cloud, he seems to understand their concerns. The new white settlers traveling the Bozeman Trail, cutting through the buffalo grazing grounds, are determined to run the Sioux off and take all of their hunting territories for homesteads. Many conflicts have exploded south of here and many people both white and Sioux have been killed. The buffalo herds are already showing drastic declines and some of the Indians are finding it difficult to find food, covering for their dwellings and raw materials for many of their tools. James spends much time at Fort Laramie trying to convince the officials that new treaties must be written before it is too late.

I must admit that I'm envious of you being far from this danger. I'm not ashamed to say I fear for our lives and pray that we'll have an uneventful winter. The constant struggle with the snow and freezing cold is enough for any of us without this added burden.

I send you my love and affection and wish you well in your new home. I'm happy to hear that you have decided to stay in the colonies. I hope this letter finds you settled and happy. Give my regards to the boys.
Yours sincerely,
Margaret Brown.

Martha looked up from the letter to find the boys staring wide-eyed with deep concern for their friends. She was more than relieved to be as far away from Whittakerville as possible, but she, too, was most concerned for her friends' safety. *Thank God we escaped before we all died. It was not just the savages that threatened us.* She felt a cold chill down her spine. Austin looked from Martha to the boys and sensed the tension growing.

"Looks like we got you out of there just in time, Martha. Now is there more pie?" Austin promptly changing the subject smiled at the boys and held his plate up for a refill of Martha's delicious apple pie. "Now, Isaac, where did you catch that delicious catfish?" The boys were quickly distracted but Martha continued to worry about her dear friends.

Tuesday evening, Jeremy arrived at the Gentlemen's Club a few minutes early. He hadn't admitted his desire to see Clarise again even to himself, but here he was scanning the room for a glimpse of her. "Why, Mr. Whittaker, how lovely to see you again." Suddenly there she was right in front of him. His eyes were drawn to the plunging neckline of her gown and the ample bosom displayed there. He quickly averted his eyes to her face and bowed to kiss her extended hand. She giggled flirtatiously, as an older gentleman appeared to her right. "Father, this is Jeremy Whittaker. Mr. Whittaker, this is my father, Morris Graham." Graham could not help but see the definite mutual interest in the eyes of the two young people before him. He directed Jeremy to the boardroom where the meeting would soon begin, taking stock of this young man as a possible match for his impetuous daughter. Morris noticed as Clarise's eyes followed the handsome young man. Another business associate of Morris' had asked for Clarise', hand but she put him off, stating she was not ready for marriage. Morris was more than anxious to find her a husband before people considered her an old maid at twenty-three. She had many suitors but always discouraged a permanent alliance. Perhaps this new chap was the one. Taking her arm, he escorted her into the boardroom, seating her next to Jeremy.

Chapter Nineteen
The Nuptials

"Loretta, you have to hold still while I pin this seam. Isabel, talk to your daughter before I stick her with this pin. I have to get this fitting done before dark." Martha was applying the finishing touches to Loretta's wedding gown and Isabel Langley, usually very sophisticated in her appearance and attitude was fussing like a mother hen.

"You know, Daughter, this is the most beautiful dress I have seen in this city. As you know, I have attended most of the high society weddings. You are very lucky to have a friend as talented as Martha." Isabel was admiring all of the detail that had been taken with her daughter's gown. The crinoline domed skirt silhouette had a flattened front and a dramatic sweep to the garment back. The fabric was the softest of silk and a snowy white. Tiny pearls and feathers were sewn strategically over the bodice and the bottom section of the sleeves. The sleeve tops were puffy from the shoulder down to the elbow where they hugged the lower arm tightly.

"This gown will be the talk of the town, Martha. I assure you that the best of St. Louis society will be in attendance and I know that the ladies will be curious as to the creator of such a lovely garment." Isabel was a pleasant woman but very society conscious. Her husband was away a great deal as wagon master and she spent her time embroiled in all things upper class. Martha found her a bit snobbish and often had to bite her tongue when in conversation with Isabel. Loretta was much more friendly and down to earth and Martha truly loved her as a sister.

"Thank you for your compliments, Isabel, but I'm sure the ladies of St. Louis have designers of their own. Now, Loretta, step out of the gown and let me finish it up. Tomorrow we'll finish the veil and headdress." Martha was thoroughly enjoying herself. She found a new sense of pride as the creation took shape.

The day of the wedding was sunny and bright. Jeremy arrived dressed in a tailored navy blue suit to escort Martha and the boys to the wedding. He had considered inviting Clarise, however, Loretta made it very clear that he was to escort Martha and the boys. As best man, he was to be there early and Martha was going to help Loretta with any last minute adjustments to her gown. The boys were most uncomfortable in their fussy suits and were wishing the wedding were over so they could change. Isaac pulled at his tight collar causing his tie to sag. Abraham had unbuttoned the top button of his shirt and then cleverly covered it with his tie.

Jeremy arranged the boys in the coach and turned to see Martha coming down the front stairs. He gasped at the breathtaking sight. She wore her new gown of forest green with a crinoline skirt, a low-cut bodice and at her throat was her mother's emerald necklace. Her shining chestnut hair was gathered on top with several ringlets cascading down the back of her head. Jeremy thought that he had never seen such an enchanting sight in all of his life.

"Wow, Mama, you look like a princess." Ezekiel chirped, followed by loud approval from the other two boys.

"You certainly do, your coach, your highness." Jeremy bowed and kissed Martha's hand. She giggled, pleased with her appearance and the look of desire in Jeremy's eyes. She had taken great pains with her gown and wanted it to be very special. Isabel's comment about the ladies of St. Louis had struck a cord with her and she was determined to make an impression. Perhaps there was a future in dress design for Martha and if so, this was the place to start. She was happy and content while she sewed the wedding gown for Loretta and this starting her thinking that perhaps this was her calling.

"Sit beside me, Mama." Ezekiel was suddenly jealous of Jeremy's attention to Martha and wanted to get the two of them apart as quickly as possible. "Move over, Abraham, Mama will need lots of room with that big skirt."

The Wells' wedding was the social affair of the year in St. Louis. Over one hundred carefully chosen guests were in attendance. The bride and groom made a most handsome couple and the wedding gown was the talk of the town. A pianist and a five-piece band provided the entertainment for the guests. Jeremy danced with Martha holding her tightly in his arms as they floated to a Viennese waltz. Clarise Graham, not having met Martha and wondering just who she was, glared at them from the other side of the room.

"You look absolutely breathtaking this evening, Martha. That gown is stunning and I see the ladies of St. Louis are discussing both you and your dress. I also notice that the gentlemen seem to be taking notice." Several gentlemen asked her to dance, much to his chagrin. He advised the boys to keep their mother busy dancing and thanks to the three boys; any future suitors were chased away.

The wine made Martha relaxed and talkative. She found Jeremy easy to talk to. "I feel like I have woken up from a terrible nightmare and now I'm dreaming of this beautiful wedding. The music is food for my starving soul and this dress makes me feel beautiful again. You could not know how ugly and undesirable I felt in Wyoming. There was only one time I can remember feeling attractive." She got a faraway look on her face. Her memories of Sergeant Dwyer's handsome face began to surface but were quickly replaced with the horror of his death. Martha shook the sadness from her mind and looked at Jeremy. His body was warm against hers; his arms felt comfortable and secure as they danced. Martha found herself physically aroused by his handsome face and his tall masculine build. Could she possibly learn to enjoy the physical side of love with someone like him? *Was Loretta right? Should I make advances towards him, before he is swept away by someone else?* Suddenly, conscious of Jeremy's eyes on her face, her cheeks burned crimson with embarrassment. She smiled demurely and returned her thoughts to the dancing. She was enjoying herself. This reminded her of the gala balls in England. How she had missed the music, the dancing and the beautiful clothes. At last, she felt as if her future was bright. She was amused at the young boys' possessiveness and more than a little flattered at the several dance invitations she received. She laughed several times when a prospective suitor approached only to be interrupted by Isaac, Abraham or Ezekiel. She danced with each of the boys and thoroughly enjoyed the evening.

Later as she spun around the dance floor with Abraham, she caught sight of Jeremy dancing with a beautiful raven-haired woman. The woman was laughing and whispered something in his ear causing him to grin flirtatiously. Martha noticed that Jeremy held her very close. The woman raised her eyes in Martha's direction. Their eyes locked and the woman immediately raised her hand to stroke Jeremy's face possessively. Losing her concentration, Martha almost tripped over Abraham's feet. Loretta danced past with Austin, pointing her finger in Jeremy's direction and mouthing the words "Look at that. I told you so." There was nothing she could do about it at the moment. Destiny would prevail and if she were meant to be with Jeremy, then things would work out for them. She danced to the other side of the room with Abraham, destiny or not, she didn't have to watch him with someone else.

Austin and Loretta were very happy. They would live in Austin's flat and travel to England in three weeks time. Austin was sorry that his mother could not be here for the ceremony but knew that she would love Loretta when they met. Food and drink were plentiful and Arthur and Isabel Langley were very proud of their new son-in-law. Arthur would have preferred someone with a little more interest in the rugged life, but Isabel was thrilled to have a businessman in the family. She was sure to introduce Austin to every influential gentleman at the wedding. She was also telling all of the females who had designed and sewn the bridal gown and pointed out Martha's own lovely dress. Isabel loved to be the center of attention and was determined to be one up on everyone else.

Several days after the wedding, Isabel Langley invited Martha to the country club for lunch. Wanting to make a good impression, Martha wore one of her new gowns in a deep royal blue with lace at the throat and a large blue hat, embellished with a peacock feather. Conversations turned to Martha as she entered the dining room. "Who is that with Isabel?"

"I don't know but that gown is definitely from Europe," Mrs. Carruthers remarked, appreciating the way Martha's presence took command of the room.

"I love that hat," one of the other women added.

Introductions were made. Isabel informing everyone that Martha was newly settled in St. Louis originally from England. Martha noted that she eliminated any mention of Wyoming. *I guess Wyoming isn't socially acceptable, what unbelievable snobbery.* Although it grated on her, she remained silent. Over the course of the luncheon, the women politely made their inquiries as to the design and origin of Martha's gown. Isabel reminded them that Martha had sewn and designed Loretta's wedding gown, being sure to add that Martha was making her dress for the Christmas ball. The other women looked at her with envy, which was the desired effect. Isabel was enjoying herself immensely. What happened next surprised Isabel.

Agatha Carruthers offered to show Martha around the club. Agatha was usually very reserved with newcomers. The tall and stately woman was much respected in St. Louis and the pair drew a great deal of attention as they walked out into the formal gardens.

"I would like you to come for tea tomorrow at four, Martha." Agatha Carruthers was impressed with this young woman.

"Oh, Mrs. Carruthers, I would be honored." Martha treated the older woman with great respect. She found Mrs. Carruthers, who Martha guessed to be about sixty-five years old, to be extremely knowledgeable. Thin, poised and gray-haired, Agatha was interested in everything. It was as if she had found a source of unending amusement in the world around her, making anyone who came in contact with her feel that life was worth living. The two chatted as they continued their promenade through the gardens of the country club.

Isabel Langley was surprised at the attention Agatha Carruthers showed Martha. On the ride home, she reminded Martha just how lucky she was. "The Carruthers come from royalty you know. Her husband's grandfather was a duke," emphasizing the word duke, she continued, "You should be honored that she invited you to her home." Isabel was green with envy, but if Martha were a success in St. Louis society, she would be sure to take the credit. Martha's stomach was full of butterflies as she realized the possibilities.

The next afternoon, a nervous Martha arrived at the imposing mansion on the north side of St. Louis. She had barely slept the night before. Taking extra care with her appearance, the rose silk blouse and navy wool skirt were perfect for afternoon tea. Her curiosity was peaked by the older woman's apparent friendliness towards her.

The visit went well with each sharing amusing stories of England. Martha noticed a piano in the corner and wandered over to it. She allowed her fingers to play a few chords. Mrs. Carruthers watched her with interest. "We bought the piano for Priscilla, our daughter. Unfortunately, she died shortly after it was delivered. She was only twenty." Martha watched as a deep sadness crossed the grieving woman's face before she turned away. "Do you have a piano in your home, Martha?"

"Oh no, we have no room or money for a piano. I have three stepsons to raise. It has been a few years since I last played." Martha played a few more notes before returning to the settee.

Apparently wanting to change the subject, Agatha Carruthers quickly turned the conversation to fashion.

"Martha, my dear. I would like you to design a gown for me. My husband and I are traveling to New York in a month's time and I will need a very special gown for the gala." Mrs. Carruthers paused to sip her tea. She lifted the tiny cucumber sandwich to her lips delicately.

Martha sat in shocked silence. Her teacup began to rattle in its saucer as she nervously set it on the table. Had she heard correctly?

"You are very talented, my dear. I will pay you a sizeable amount for the gown naturally."

"Oh, Mrs. Carruthers, you flatter me. I would be more than happy to make a gown for you. Thank you for your confidence in me." Martha blushed with excitement. Arrangements were made for a fitting and Martha was to draw several design choices for Agatha over the next few days. The butler arrived to clear the dishes and Martha prepared to leave. Agatha Carruthers shook her hand delicately and smiled at the young woman's apparent nervousness.

She left feeling elated and excited. Sitting in the carriage, she offered up a silent prayer. *Thank you, God, help me make this a reality. Give me strength and imagination to design a beautiful gown for her.*

Word spread quickly through the club that Martha Whittaker was designing a gown for Agatha Carruthers. Having observed Martha's own creations, the women were most impressed with the flair and style of her designs and anxiously awaited the completion.

Within a month the gown was complete, ready for delivery. She was surprised to be ushered into the parlor where seven other ladies were seated. "Martha, just give that to William and have a seat." Martha did not expect there to be other women present. She thought she was coming for a final fitting. Confused she took her seat and nodded to the others. She recognized most of the women from the country club. A few minutes of chitchat and a glass of sherry increased rather than diminished, Martha's apprehension.

Mrs. Carruthers and Martha went upstairs for the final fitting. Martha was very nervous. *What if she doesn't like it? I will be so embarrassed in front of everyone. I just don't understand why she invited them today of all days.* The gown was purple velvet, floor length, with clean, sophisticated lines. Martha thought that the color was lovely with Agatha's gray hair and pale skin. She was not a beautiful woman but would be considered handsome. There was a certain quality about the woman that made her appear more attractive than women with perfect features. The dress fit like a glove.

"You have outdone yourself, my dear." Agatha admired her reflection in the mirror. After turning left, then right and admiring the back of the dress, she walked to the dresser and handed Martha an envelope. Martha had given her a tally of the expenses for the gown and added a small amount for her time; the envelope contained three times what she had requested.

"Mrs. Carruthers, you have given me too much." She began to protest but the older woman held up her hand.

"Martha, do not sell yourself short. You and this gown are worth every penny in that envelope. I told the other women that you were delivering my gown today. Curiosity overtook them and they all invited themselves for a viewing. Once they see this gown, you will be swamped with orders." Agatha twirled around like a schoolgirl in her new gown. A huge smile lit up her face. She was obviously pleased. "I told them your prices start at the amount in that envelope and not one of them so much as blinked. I have set the stage, now go and make your debut, my dear, and thank you." With that, she kissed Martha's cheek and shooed her out the door.

Martha stood in the hallway, trying to catch her breath. Mrs. Carruthers was happy and now the cream of St. Louis' society was about to see the finished product. Her hands were sweaty and her heart was pounding. She took a few deep breaths before nervously descending the stairs and returning to the parlor.

Moments later, Agatha Carruthers made a stunning entrance, complete with upswept hair and a diamond tiara. A collective gasp rose up with the women rushing to her side. The room was alive with chatter. They touched the soft velvet, stroked the long skirt and sighed with admiration. Martha was beaming. From across the room, Agatha winked at her, smiling her magical knowing smile.

Over the next seven days, much happened to increase Martha's appreciation of the good fortune that had brought her and Mrs. Carruthers together. Several of the club members, not wanting to be outdone, requested that Martha design gowns for the Christmas Ball. She was in shock at the quick response.

Martha met with Agatha and Isabel for a celebratory glass of wine at the Country Club. Isabel gushed over Martha, constantly repeating, "I told you so." The wine was a deep Merlot with a fine bouquet and a brilliant color. As she raised her glass to her lips, Martha's face reflected her appreciation of the delicate flavor. "You know good wine, Martha. Just as you know fine fabrics and elegant design," Isabel commented, always trying to impress Mrs. Carruthers, and making sure she was included in this celebration, raised her glass to toast Martha's upcoming success. Mrs. Carruthers simply smiled. Martha was in awe of both Isabel and Agatha. Both of them had been instrumental in helping her achieve her dream. It appeared she would be very busy for the next few months. Hopefully she would be up to the task. Smiling self-assuredly, she thanked the women for their confidence in her abilities. She glanced in Isabel's direction thinking, *Thank goodness for Isabel Langley's snobbish society connections. Now, Lord, help me do this well.*

Austin and Loretta left for England and Jeremy was busy with his business. He had invited Miss Graham to dinner and the opera on several occasions and thoroughly enjoyed himself. He did find her to be rather forward, but was finding it harder and harder to resist. He tried to convince himself that Martha was never going to come to him and that perhaps he should move on. He desired Miss Graham physically, but in his heart, it was Martha that he wanted to spend the rest of his life with.

Martha sewed long into the night and the gowns were all original in design and color. This was to be her future. No matter how hard she had to work, she would make a success of it. Martha found a strength and determination she didn't know she possessed in Wyoming and now she would use it to form her destiny. Knowing women like Olga and Margaret had instilled a resolve and strength of character in her and she would not let them down. She decided to pour all of her energies into the work, needing to distract herself from the ever-insistent Loretta, who persisted in telling her that Miss. Graham was wooing Jeremy and Jeremy was weakening.

Martha hired the daughter of the baker, Mike O'Malley, to help with the simple hand stitching. Before the wedding, Martha delivered several of her pies to Mike O'Malley, who agreed to sell them in the bakery. She initially thought that baking pies could somehow be turned into a business. After visiting the bakery and seeing the many younger O'Malleys baking, kneading dough and packaging bread, she knew she did not want to do that for a living. Plus, she felt that Mr. O'Malley did not need any competition with such a large family to feed. She would continue to supply him with pies for extra money but sewing was what gave her the most pleasure, so that is what she would concentrate on. During a conversation with Mike, she mentioned her need for a seamstress. Mike suggested she talk with his daughter who, he claimed, could sew a stitch better than the tailor. Martha asked her to sew some ribbon onto one of the gowns and hired the young girl immediately. The girl, Annabelle, was a tiny sprite with red hair, freckles, large green eyes and a talkative personality. The solitary Isaac was infatuated with her and tried to be in the house whenever she was there. Annabelle, who was Isaac's age, thought he was charming and whenever the two were together, she chatted endlessly, while the quieter Isaac simply looked at her adoringly. Martha found her to be very proficient with a needle and was surprised with how quickly the girl learned. She paid her half a dollar per week and often gave her extra food to take home to her family of twelve. One evening after a long day of sewing, she prepared a basket for Annabelle.

"Oh, Mrs. Whittaker I really couldn't accept all of this food." Annabelle was proud and very humble, but she also knew that with ten children to feed any contributions would be appreciated at the O'Malley home. Martha prepared a basket of meat, fish and fruit adding a dozen chocolate candies for the children.

"Isaac hunts and fishes and we have more than enough food to share. Please let me send this home to your family. We are very lucky Isaac is such a good provider." Martha looked over to Isaac, "Please walk Annabelle home, Isaac. It is almost dark and a young lady should not be on the streets alone." Isaac blushed. Annabelle blushed and the two youngsters left Martha smiling in the doorway. Isaac was showing off his prowess as a hunter and Martha found it charming. She constantly looked for ways to bring a smile to his face. Annabelle's presence seemed to be the most recent. She closed the door, stopped at the mirror to fix her hair and headed for the kitchen.

Isaac and Annabelle walked toward the Kerry Patch where Annabelle lived. Most of the Irish population of St. Louis lived in the large parcel of land north of Carr Square. Both of them were nervous and shy. Annabelle handled her nervousness by talking, Isaac by remaining silent.

Annabelle explained to Isaac, "The area is called the *Kerry Patch* because many of the Irish immigrants came to St. Louis up the Mississippi from New Orleans or across land from Boston or New York. Soon almost half of St. Louis' population was poor Irish. Some of them even lived in the street. An Irish philanthropist, John Mullanphy, donated a large parcel of land for the Irish people to live on and since many were from the Kerry area in Ireland, it became known as the *Kerry Patch*." They passed the picturesque St. Patrick's church on the corner of Sixth and Biddle. Isaac took Annabelle's basket, kicking a stone as they walked. The stone rolled ahead, leading the way to the *Patch*. Isaac listened attentively and Annabelle continued her chattering, taking her turn at kicking the rock when it crossed her path. "My family has been here for ten years. We moved into the *Patch* shortly after it was opened." Isaac noticed that most of the houses in the neighborhood were clapboard—small frame houses and built close to the sidewalk. From the number of children on each doorstep, it appeared that most of the families were large. It was obvious that the streets in this part of town were dirt and often flooded. A water line was visible on the side of many of the houses where the water level had risen above the doorways. Isaac looked down at the drunken man lying in the street; the smell of alcohol permeated the air. Annabelle didn't seem to take any notice of him.

"Maybe we should help him; he looks bad." Isaac was concerned but Annabelle quickly moved away pulling Isaac with her, explaining that the man usually woke up and went home on his own.

"There are lots of drunks and lots of fights in this neighborhood, Isaac. Mother says to 'just keep on walking.'" Sensing his discomfort, she added, "You get used to it." Isaac didn't like the idea of Annabelle living in such a place. He was happy that Martha had asked him to walk her home. Isaac delivered Annabelle safely to her doorway and then ran all the way back to Lucas Place. After experiencing the *Kerry Patch*, he now had another reason to be thankful for Martha's stubborn determination.

Agatha Carruthers watched Martha's progress with interest. While dining with her husband Phillip, the conversation turned to Martha, as it often did. "I tell you, Phillip, this woman has breeding. The tiny house, the three stepsons and the sewing are all negated by her speech and voice, which are so obviously those of a lady. There is a story there and I intend to find out what it is." Phillip stared at his wife. If anyone would get to the bottom of this, it would be his ever-curious wife. He reached across the table and squeezed her hand. "First I need to see her alone without that irritating Isabel. That woman is too much, always trying to ingratiate herself."

"You seem fascinated with this young woman, Aggie. Now, don't be so hard on Isabel. I give that woman a lot of credit. After she married that cowboy years ago, she has had to fight to keep her social standing in this city. I think she has done a very good job of it."

"Oh, Phillip, I know all of that, but sometimes she doesn't know when to leave well enough alone. Martha is different. She so reminds me of our Priscilla. I had the piano tuned today and I intend to invite Martha and her family for dinner next week. It is time you met this lovely young woman." Surprised that she mentioned the piano, Phillip's curiosity was peaked by his wife's interest in this newcomer. He looked forward to meeting the family, always keen to have youngsters in the house.

"Wonderful, my dear. Make the arrangements and I shall be there." Phillip was pleased to hear the piano would finally be played.

It had sat silent for over twenty years. Perhaps Martha was just what Agatha needed.

One evening Jeremy arrived with some bright red silk that just arrived by ship. He knew Martha would love it. "Martha, Martha, are you here?" Jeremy pushed the door open when no one responded to his knock. Entering the sitting room, he found Martha asleep in a sitting position with a blue gown spread over her knees. Several beads were spilled on the rug and a spool of thread had rolled onto the floor. He approached silently so as not to startle her. He was not pleased with the dark circles under her eyes. "Martha, wake up." He shook her lightly. She awoke with a start.

"Oh, Jeremy, I must have dozed off. I've had a few late nights trying to finish these gowns." Even her voice sounded exhausted. She reached for the thread. *O God, I must look a mess.*

"Perhaps it is time to take a few days off. You look exhausted." Jeremy began picking up the tiny beads and set them on the table beside her.

"No, I must get these dresses finished on time. My entire future and the future of my boys depend on it. I will not quit until every dress is finished and delivered." The near panic in her voice disturbed Jeremy, but it also spoke volumes of just how desperately she needed to prove herself. Her confident air sometimes fooled him into believing she was secure, but now he was reminded of just how lacking in confidence and fearful she was.

" I think it is time to employ another assistant. That little elfin girl is hardly enough help for St. Louis' famous fashion designer." Jeremy joked with her but he was concerned at the dark circles under her eyes. He knew her stubborn determination would not allow her to take the time she needed for the good of her health.

"I just don't have room in my bedroom for any more people, Jeremy, but I could use some help. This sewing business is growing in leaps and bounds and as much as I hate to admit it, I'm afraid it is a little too much for me." Her distress was evident.

"Well, I have just the answer then. The building next to mine is for sale and it would be more than enough room for you and your assistants. You could rent the flats upstairs and that would help you with the finances until you get going. There is much more space for your sewing machine and perhaps you could get another one. You could even open a shop in the front of the building to sell your creations." Jeremy, always enterprising, was enthusiastically thinking ahead of himself. He rambled on and on coming up with some excellent suggestions. He watched the uncertainty shadow her face but there was a hint of excitement as well. He continued to encourage her.

"Oh, Jeremy, do you really think I could do it?" Martha was caught up in Jeremy's enthusiasm and she desperately wanted a business of her own. "Would the bank lend me the money for the building?" *A building and a business of my very own, could it really be possible?* Silently she prayed for this to work.

"I don't see why not; I'll speak to the manager tomorrow on your behalf if you like. If he won't lend the money to you, I'll sign the loan and lend you the money myself. I have great faith in your ability, Martha, and if you can create gowns like the one you wore to the wedding, then you will be a huge success." Jeremy lifted Martha's hand and kissed her palm. She didn't pull away, wanting to move into his arms and embraced her champion. Jeremy always supported and encouraged her in everything she wanted to do. He was generous, considerate and gentle; everything that his brother had lacked. She looked up and felt as if she were drowning in the green of his eyes. Jeremy wanted her more than ever at that moment and kissed her gently on the lips. She returned his kiss and moved into his arms. He knew he would have to tread lightly with this independent, gentle woman after what his brother had done to her. The fact that she remained in his arms was definitely encouraging. After a few minutes, feeling the relaxed weight of her body, he realized that she had fallen asleep. He settled her on the chair with a woolen afghan over her, and left the house, whistling to himself.

After canceling several times, Martha and the boys were finally going to visit the Carruthers. Agatha, who, much to Phillip's amusement, had been impatiently watching out of the window, opened the door herself. "Martha, how wonderful to see you again. Come in."

Martha ushered the three boys into the magnificent mansion coming face to face with Phillip for the first time. The man before her looked much older than Agatha, his face lined and sallow. He was an attractive man nonetheless with a bright smile that reached his twinkling eyes.

"Martha, let me present my husband, Sir Phillip Carruthers. Phillip, this is Martha Whittaker." Before Martha could take Phillip's outstretched hand, Ezekiel spoke out loud.

"Did you say 'Sir', like Sir Galahad or Sir Lancelot kind of Sir?" The young boy stared at Phillip with admiration.

"Yes, young man, Phillip was knighted by Queen Victoria and his grandfather was a duke. He is Sir Phillip Carruthers, my knight in shining armour." Agatha knelt beside Ezekiel, placing her hand on his shoulder. "And what is your name, young man?"

"Ezekiel, Ma'am. I read about knights in one of my books but I never thought I would meet one. Wow did you really meet Queen Victoria, Sir?" Sir Phillip nodded in the affirmative a broad smile graced his face. He was not one for pomp and pageantry but he knew that Agatha was intentionally making things interesting for the child.

"My brother talks too much. Please forgive his outburst. My name is Abraham, I am happy to make your acquaintance, Sir." Abraham bowed low and then extended his small hand in Phillip's direction. Martha beamed with pride.

Phillip turned to Isaac. "Well that leaves you, young man, what do we call you?"

"Isaac, Sir." Always short and to the point, Isaac shook Phillip's hand and stood quietly surveying the huge entrance hall.

"So you like books, do you, Ezekiel? How about you two, do you like books as well?"

"No, Sir, I like fishing and hunting and Abraham likes animals, all kinds of animals." Isaac spoke while his eyes remained fixed on the huge stag head that hung above the doorway. Abraham, too, was staring at the stag.

"Wonderful, I have just the room for all of you to see. Come along." Phillip held out his hand to Ezekiel who reached up and placed his own smaller one in it. "Men only." The older man winked at the boys, causing Ezekiel to giggle and led them off towards the west wing.

"My, but your husband is wonderful with the children. I have never seen the three boys so taken with anyone before." Martha watched as the boys followed Phillip without looking back.

"He truly is a knight in shining armour. I have loved that man for over forty years. Come, Martha, let us relax in the great room while the boys play with Phillip." She chuckled at the thought of Phillip playing. "I am sorry your husband could not join us."

"My husband is dead." Martha did not explain. Agatha sensed that something was amiss and quickly directed Martha to the piano.

"I have had the piano tuned, my dear. Would you play for me?"

The boys were in awe of the Carruther's study and trophy room. Stuffed lions, antelope and even a large Musk Ox head mounted on the wall, amazed them. A glass case filled with all types of guns and weapons mesmerized Isaac. Ezekiel sat in the study, pulling book after book off of the shelves. "Mr. Carruthers, Sir Phillip, your highness, Sir, are these books really all yours? You have more books than the library almost." Ezekiel was most impressed.

"Why don't you call me Grandpap Phillip. It is much easier than all of that Sir business, don't you think? I hope we will be seeing a lot of each other and if your mother doesn't have any objections I would be honored to be Grandpap to you boys."

Isaac turned and looked at Phillip in surprise. He was still suspicious of strangers and this man seemed too good to be true.

Abraham studied the paintings of horses and dogs that lined one wall, inquiring about their significance. Mr. Carruthers, or Grandpap as they all agreed, told the boys he would take them to the stables after dinner and Abraham could hardly wait. All four were thoroughly enjoying the interchange.

Back in the great room, Martha's playing took her back to Graystone and her life before Jebediah. Agatha did not miss the longing on the young woman's face.

"Mama, you should see Grandpap's study. It is amazing." The boys bounced into the room. Martha turned and gaped at them.

"Abraham! What did you call Sir Phillip? I am so sorry, Mr. Carruthers."

"But, Mama, Grandpap Phillip said to call him that because we don't like all of that pompous stuff, do we, Grandpap." Agatha chuckled and winked at Phillip. She could see that Phillip was enjoying the boys and the feeling was obviously mutual.

Dinner was a succulent roast of beef, with Yorkshire pudding, candied carrots and mashed potatoes. Everyone ate until they were sated, the delicious food keeping even the talkative Ezekiel quiet.

As promised, Mr. Carruthers took the youngsters to see the stables and Martha and Agatha retired to the conservatory. Plants of all size and description surrounded them as they sat on the wicker chairs. The atmosphere was moist and tropical and Martha found the room very relaxing.

"I am so sorry for your loss, my dear. You must miss your husband terribly. I don't know what I would do without Phillip." Mrs. Carruthers reached over and took Martha's hand.

"I would rather not discuss my husband's death, if you don't mind, Agatha. It is a time I would rather forget." Martha stood and caressed the green and white leaves of a large fern. "What lovely plants you have." Agatha did not push but she could see by Martha's reaction that something terrible must have happened to her. Just then, the boys returned full of stories of horses and African lion safaris.

"Oh good, let me get the cookies. You must be hungry again." Agatha walked towards the door to retrieve the treats for the boys. "Come along, boys, and give me a hand. I guess this makes me Grandmam. Wonderful, I have waited years for someone to call me that." Martha and Phillip exchanged a look of mutual appreciation. She could see why Agatha was so fond of this gentle man. By the time the family was ready to leave, Martha knew that her family had grown by two and she and the boys would be seeing more of the Carruthers. Agatha and Phillip were truly lovely people and the boys were growing fond of them already. She hugged them both affectionately.

"Goodbye, Grandmam and Grandpap, thanks for everything." Ezekiel was beaming, holding the books that Grandpap had insisted he borrow. Isaac clutched the journal of Phillip's African adventures to his chest and Abraham carefully carried the framed picture of the horse that Phillip had given him. Agatha and Phillip glowed with happiness at their newly acquired family.

After much trepidation on Martha's part, the building purchase was settled and Martha and Annabelle moved into the new facility. Martha stood in the empty building envisioning her new business. *I cannot believe I am standing on the threshold of my dream.* With renewed confidence, she began her planning and soon the building came alive. Painters and carpenters soon transformed the empty building into a viable shop.

Phillip and Jeremy stopped by on their way to lunch. They looked for Martha in her back office. Papers and account books were spread on the desk. Samples of fabrics, strips of ribbon and spools of thread were piled high on the side table. Martha was nowhere to be found.

"How on earth is she going to handle all of this, Jeremy?" Phillip was astounded at the progress of construction and the chaos everywhere in the building.

"Don't you worry about Martha. She is excellent with figures and there is a certain organization to this tangled mess. She knows exactly where everything is." Jeremy was impressed at rate of Martha's progress. Finally the elusive entrepreneur appeared carrying boxes of fabric samples from the backroom. She was surprised to find visitors.

"Gentlemen, welcome. Please excuse the mess." She was in her element and appeared perfectly at ease. Both men were awed.

Martha and Annabelle worked long hours stopping only to eat and grab a few hours' sleep. Several of the gowns were finished. Over the next few months the business grew once more. Another sewing machine was added and Annabelle was soon turning out pieces of the garments almost as quickly as Martha. Two more assistants were hired, one was Annabelle's older sister, Ellen and May, who was the daughter of Jeremy's warehouse manager, completed the staff. Both were excellent and enthusiastic seamstresses. Money was tight in their families and the wages were greatly appreciated. Martha was surprised with her own organizational skills. She found that business came almost naturally to her and she handled difficult management decisions with ease. The ladies of "St. Louis Couture Designs" hung their sign with great pride. Christmas was going to be a busy time for Martha and her new staff. Looking up from her paperwork, Martha beamed with pride and elation as she surveyed her business. *A shop of her own*, she could hardly believe it was true. It was hard work but worth every minute. Orders continued to flood in, thanks to her benefactor, Agatha Carruthers.

Down the block, Jeremy's business was also doing well. It was his habit to take care of his paperwork and mail early in the morning before going to the docks to supervise his shipments. His office faced the east and the river but the large windows allowed the daylight to fill the office most of the day. A long table by the window was laden with samples of materials, sundries and various dried herbs. He loved his work spending long hours in his office. It was decorated to provide him with a soothing atmosphere. Deep brown leather chairs and settee blended with the forest green and rust brown carpet to compliment the rich wood paneling. A small antique table bore a silver tray with silver tea service and a crystal brandy decanter. Several delicate crystal glasses and china teacups sat conveniently on a small shelf above the table. The room was manly and professional. Jeremy sat at his large oak desk and opened the mail. A letter from Austin and Loretta was amongst this week's delivery.

Dear Jeremy,

Loretta and I made the crossing without crisis. I was surprised that Loretta, unlike myself, showed no signs of seasickness and quite enjoyed the shipboard activities. Mother met us at the harbor in Liverpool with John McGuire and the two ladies immediately became friends. John looks well and inquired about his daughter and her plans to return. I was troubled to have to tell him that it was unlikely that she would return any time soon, however, he took it in his stride and gave a sum of money as payment for the rescue mission. I'll bring it with me upon my return. I did try to refuse my half but he would not have it. I intend to give some of it to my mother and then put the rest in a trust for the boys.

We had dinner with John, Phoebe and Max Smithson, who it now appears, is Phoebe's beau. Loretta, Mother and I accompanied John to the churchyard and put fresh flowers on your mother's grave. It appears that John visits the graveyard weekly, bringing flowers not only to his own wife, Lillian's grave but to your mother's as well. John has been very active in reforms to the Asylum Acts in England. He seems to have been affected deeply by your mother's situation prior to her death.

We'll be returning before the weather gets too cold and the seas too rough and want to be in St. Louis for Christmas. Mother has loaded us down with gifts and I'm sure we'll need another trunk for the ship. I delivered your instructions to Max about Pheasant Run and it will be taken care of.

Tell Martha that Loretta is getting all kinds of information on current fashion trends in England and France from Phoebe and will return full of news for her. Apparently, Martha's old designer, Charles Worth, is now in France and most famous. John sends his love to Martha and his great appreciation to you. We look forward to our return. It is strange but St. Louis feels more like home to me now.

Your friend and partner,
Austin Wells

Jeremy was happy to know that Austin would be home soon. Business was brisk and he could use the help. He, too, would put the money from John McGuire into a trust for the boys. He was fascinated to hear that John McGuire had taken such an interest in the lunatic asylums since visiting his mother there. Perhaps it was his way of making restitution for marrying Martha off against her wishes to Jebediah. Well, whatever the reason, he was happy to know that changes had been made. It was a sorry day when his father had committed their mother but she was a danger to herself and did not even recognize them. Jonas Whittaker was devastated and never really recovered from it. Jeremy remembered that Jebediah had never come to terms with his father's decision to commit her. He just didn't seem to believe that she was ill; perhaps Jebediah's denial was a sign of his own illness.

Jeremy rose from his desk and walked to the window. His hand rested on the dark wood frame as he scanned the street below basked in early morning light. Martha was crossing the street and approaching her new shop. His heart began to beat quickly and his mind filled with intimate thoughts of her. How he loved that woman. Telling himself to go slowly, he was very careful not to overstep in helping her, knowing that she had to do things herself. Looking forward to the day they could be together, he believed it would happen with all of his heart. He thought back to the night at the county club just before the Wells had left on their honeymoon. Clarise danced several dances with him and she seemed to be enjoying his company as much as he was hers. Later, as he stood in conversation with some of the Business Association members, Clarise, without warning, approached him and slapped his face. She marched angrily from the club without a word, leaving him dumbfounded. Days later he heard that she was engaged to some business associate of her father. The whole incident was very confusing. He still didn't know why she slapped him. Even her father seemed cool towards him after that night. Well, it did not matter now because he knew where his heart belonged. He checked his watch and locked the door. Jeremy left his building and rushed out to meet Martha for an early morning breakfast.

Chapter Twenty
Abraham and Bo

Abraham returned from the blacksmith shop early one evening carrying a large parcel. As he entered the kitchen, Martha turned and inquired what he was carrying.

"Well, Mama, it's like this. The hound dog at the blacksmith had puppies about three months ago and all of them were given away to fine homes. Good thing too 'cause the Smitty was going to drown any of them that didn't get a home." Abraham shuffled his foot on the floor and stared down at his shoe. Martha had a hard time keeping a straight face at the comical sight he made. "So this here parcel is, uh, for your birthday, Mama." Abraham held the parcel out to Martha and she reached for it cautiously with both hands.

"Well, thank you very much but my birthday is not for months." She held the parcel in her hands and felt it move. As she peered into the sack, a pair of big, brown, sad eyes looked back at her. "This present seems to be alive, Abraham."

"Happy Birthday, Mama, his name is Bo." Abraham beamed from ear to ear and lifted the already large, puppy from the sack. "I just knew you would love him. I already made a house for him at the blacksmith shop and I'll go now and get it." Without giving her a chance to reject the idea, he started for the door. "I just knew you would love him." With that, he turned and ran across the porch and down the street. Leaving a laughing Martha holding a squirming fat three-month-old puppy. She had known this was coming and had joked with Jeremy as to how Abraham would broach the subject. Neither of them had considered the birthday angle. She had already decided that a puppy would be a good idea for the boys and a dog was good protection for the family, but she wanted to see how inventive Abraham would be. *And so my family grows by one.* She carried the soft brown ball of fur out in the yard and put it on the grass. The brown pup immediately started sniffing the ground and marking his territory.

"Just remember one thing, Bo, I'm the boss around here and all of the men listen to me." Martha smiled and watched Bo make himself at home. She lifted Isaac's fishing pole and moved it out of harm's way. Isaac had been fishing with Grandpap Phillip in Austin's absence and Martha was pleased to include the two older people in her family circle. *Life just keeps getting better and now we even have a dog.* Abraham returned with Bo's new home and the two of them set it up in the back corner of the yard. Bo immediately settled into the straw that Abraham had put in his new doghouse and Martha returned to the kitchen, leaving boy and dog alone. She had received a letter from Wyoming, delivered by Arthur Langley that morning and sat down with her cup of tea to read it.

    Dearest Martha,

    Please forgive my poor English. I am not good at writing letters.

    I know you are surprised to receive a letter from me, Martha. Mr. Mueller and I are sorry to have to tell you that Margaret Brown and her young child have been killed in an Indian raid. It happened just two weeks ago. Indians rode north of the town raiding and burning several of the homesteader's farms. The Johnsons, the Edwards, and Margaret and the child were all killed in a savage attack during the night. James Brown was off on a scouting mission and is devastated. The poor, poor man has lost not only his wife but his child as well and him trying to keep the peace between the Indians and the settlers. The entire town is in shock and fear for their lives.

Martha, her hands trembling, dropped the letter to the floor as tears for her dear friend filled her eyes. Abraham found her sobbing with her head on her arms. Although she never expected to see her again, she still felt a certain closeness to Margaret. Her heart was aching. She felt that an important part of her had died.

"Mama, what is wrong?" He put his arms around her and she lifted the letter and handed it to him. "Oh, Mama, our friends are dead. This is terrible. Don't cry, Mama, don't cry." The boy did not know what to do. Isaac arrived home a few minutes later and went to fetch Jeremy. Martha was put to bed and Jeremy stayed with the worried boys.

"Thank God we got you out of there before this happened. It's a terrible thing that has happened to your friends but I just thank God it wasn't Martha and you." He reassured them that Martha would be fine in a few days and tried to answer their questions to put their minds at ease. His heart went out to James Brown, who he knew had done his best to bring peace to the unsettled land. It was a wild and unsettled country. Jeremy and the boys were thankful to be living in St. Louis and not Wyoming. Upstairs Martha lay in her bed, sobbing. Memories of her time in Wyoming came flooding back. She took the folded worn letters from her drawer. A torn piece of silk from an old petticoat fell to the floor. Picking it up, she caressed it with her fingertips as she began to read:

My dearest Austin,

My mental state could only be described as dark and depressed. All the love, laughter and joy have been replaced by endless toil, sadness and defeat. I'm mortified to say that I sometimes wish Jebediah were dead. The situation is hopeless and my life has become a nightmare. I feel my own heart filling with evil thoughts and I'm ashamed. Only the young boys keep me going. I realize that they need me for protection from their own father and I must be strong for them.

She had resolved never to destroy the letters that she had written during her time in Wyoming. The letters, never mailed, that kept her sane. Holding the worn paper in her hand, her wrist began to ache and her whole body shuddered as she remembered how it had been broken. Tenderly she replaced the torn silk and folded letters to their hiding place. That night her nightmares were filled with the blood curdling screams of her friends and the face of her tormentor.

The following week, Martha wrote to the Muellers to thank them for letting her know and sent her condolences to all of the people of Whittakerville. She was glad to be away from Wyoming and all of the troubles but she felt sorry for those that remained.

Vowing never to forget, she planted a pink rose bush in her garden as a remembrance to Margaret and her baby. She thanked God for bringing Jeremy and Austin to her rescue before it was too late. *Every time I look at this rose, I will think of you, my friend.* Almost as an afterthought, she planted another rose bush beside the first for Sergeant Dwyer. As her fingers held the tiny white rose growing on the thin stem, she sent up a silent thank you to the man who had given her those precious moments of feeling beautiful and special in Wyoming. *Thank you, John Dwyer, for giving me a few moments pleasure in a time of misery.* With tears in her eyes, she dusted the soil from her apron and swore that she would never forget them.

Bo, who grew quickly, soon became a permanent member of the family. Isaac was impressed with the hound. "A good hound dog is the only dog for hunting. We'll take him out and see what he's got next week, Abraham. You can come with me and control the dog and I'll do the hunting." Abraham was thrilled to be included in Isaac's plans.

The following week, Isaac and Abraham went off to the woods alone with Bo. Isaac much preferred hunting alone or with Austin. Abraham didn't like to kill any creatures and he really was out of his element in the woods. Isaac loved the tranquility and solitude of the woods. He actually preferred animals to people and had few friends.

"We are big game hunters, just like Grandpap. Aren't we, Isaac?"

"You just watch the dog and do what I say, Abe." Isaac was beginning to think he had made a mistake bringing his brother along.

The three headed deep into the thick hardwood forest. The dog took the scent and started running. Isaac took off after the dog and

Abraham tried to keep up. Not long into the chase, the dog disappeared and neither of the boys could see him. Isaac told Abraham to stay where he was and he would go and find the dog. Moments later, concerned about his pet, Abraham's alarm grew and throwing caution to the wind, he ran deeper into the woods to find Bo. Soon Isaac could not find either Bo or Abraham and was beginning to get worried. He searched the woods for over an hour but there was no sign of his brother. He felt both anger and concern for Abraham as he continued his search.

Abraham wandered through the forest aimlessly. He was frightened, shouting for his pet. He finally spotted Bo down in a gully. He scrambled down the bank after the dog, catching his clothing on branches and brambles as he went. As he reached the bottom of the gully, he heard a loud low growl. The dog was nowhere to be seen but the bushes shook and a huge black bear appeared, with teeth flashing and angry eyes fixed on Abraham. The small boy started to run but tripped over a log and tumbled down the ravine with the bear close behind. A few feet from the terrified Abraham, the bear stopped and turned, distracted by something behind it. Bo appeared out of nowhere and leaped on the bear's back. The two creatures rolled over and over on the ground and loud growls, grunts and yelps permeated the air. The infuriated bear turned side to side as the determined Bo attacked, lip curled, teeth bare, first from one side then the other, always avoiding the bear's head. Abraham covered his head with his hands and rolled into a ball under the closest shrub. His heart pounded and his body trembled with fear. Clumps of fur and blood flew through the air and the two animals were embroiled in a vicious battle. Abruptly, the sound of a gunshot cracked above Abraham's head startling both he and the two battling animals. He looked up and watched as the bear fell to the side. The snarling dog, torn and bleeding, immediately went for the bear's throat. Isaac slid down the side of the ravine to where his brother was crouched and shaking. He called Bo off the bear and fired two more shots into the bear's hide. The dog crawled to Abraham and licked his face. The frightened, shaken boy sobbed at the bloody sight of his dog.

"Come on, Abraham, we have to get Bo back home as soon as we can. Are you hurt?" Isaac took charge of the situation and prayed that neither his brother nor the dog were badly hurt. He could see that the dog needed immediate attention and took off his shirt and tore it into strips. Abraham crawled out from his hiding place and started to wrap the dog's wounds with the pieces of fabric. Tears rolled down his cheeks as he patted and consoled his poor pet. The dog had saved his life and now might lose his own.

"He saved me, Isaac, Bo saved me. We can't let him die." Abraham looked at his older brother with pleading in his tear filled eyes.

"Nobody going to die but that big old bear. Now let's find some big sticks to make a travois so we can pull Bo home." Isaac went off to find two long sturdy sticks and when he returned, they tied Abraham's jacket over the sticks and made a stretcher for the dog. They lifted the dog onto the stretcher and Isaac covered the bear carcass with twigs and branches. It was a good-sized bear and he intended to come back and get it when he could get someone to help him retrieve it. "Now stop that crying and start pulling."

Martha was beside herself when she saw the blood soaked boys and their dog returning to the house. She trembled as Isaac carried the dog onto the porch and Abraham ran to her arms. *Oh, dear God, what now? Thank you for watching over my boys.* Pushing her own fear away, she quickly set herself to the job at hand.

First she cleaned and bandaged the dog's wounds and a salve that Abraham got from the blacksmith was applied. Then the boys were bathed and fed and Bo was put in the warm kitchen for the night. Abraham brought a blanket and pillow and fell asleep on the kitchen floor beside his beloved pet. His hand was resting on the dog's head as if he were willing the dog to live. Ezekiel was sent to bring Jeremy.

Jeremy arrived within the hour and listened patiently as Isaac told him how he had found Abraham and shot the bear but the dog was the real hero of the day. "I can't wait to tell Grandpap and Austin about this. They will be so excited." Isaac was wrapped up in his story. Seated in the sitting room with Isaac and Ezekiel, Jeremy felt very at home in this cozy house. His nephew was telling him quite a story. Jeremy shook his head in amazement at this young man's nonchalant attitude to the events. Not being a hunter himself, he was very impressed with Isaac's quick thinking and shooting abilities. Austin and Phillip would be very proud of him. Ezekiel thought it was most exciting and asked Isaac to repeat the story again.

Listening from the kitchen, Martha was concerned at the danger the boys had been in and shuttered to think what may have happened. After hearing of Margaret's death, she was even more aware of how precious life could be. As she watched Abraham sleeping, the big dog cuddled in his arms, she realized that the boy had not had any premonitions or dreams since they had left Wyoming. Perhaps that part of his life was over. *Please let them all grow to be strong, confident men, dear Lord. Keep them safe.*

Smiling, she looked upon the scene in the sitting room, Jeremy and the two boys together, huddled in conversation and her heart filled with love. Her sons were safe and their uncle was becoming an important part of their lives. *Yes, life is precious and each day has to be lived as if it is the last.* She stroked her hair unconsciously as she absorbed the contentment and peace of the scene before her. As she continued her chores, she toyed with the idea of an intimate relationship with Jeremy. She was attracted to him but still frightened of anything sexual. *Could I love you, Jeremy?*

Abraham willed his pet back to health, never leaving his side. Soon the dog was up and running once more with the grateful boy following in his tracks. Bo and Abraham traveled to the Carrutherses' stables often, always welcomed by Phillip and Agatha. Ezekiel often tagged along still fascinated by Philip's stories of African safaris and English knights.

Isaac and some of the boys that worked in Jeremy's warehouse retrieved the bear carcass from the woods. The meat was distributed to several families in the *Patch* including the very impressed O'Malleys, and the bear hide hung on the back porch to dry. The story of the great bear hunt was circulated through the school over the next few weeks and Isaac, the loner became very popular. Martha was surprised to see Isaac with two other boys, sitting on the porch together when she returned from her shop. Isaac was relating his story of the buffalo hunt in Wyoming and the two city boys were fascinated. Bo, now recovered, sat beside Isaac completing the perfect picture. Her heart swelled with pride. *Perhaps there is hope for Isaac's future after all.*

Austin and Loretta arrived home the following week. Austin patted Isaac on the back and congratulated him on his kill. Knowing the danger involved, Austin also suggested that Abraham or Ezekiel not be included in any more hunting expeditions. Isaac rolled his eyes, assuring him that he had no intention of doing that again.

Martha and Loretta sat in the kitchen sipping tea. "Mother tells me your new shop is very impressive. I am happy to hear that Mrs. Carruthers has taken you under her wing. Mother and Priscilla Carruthers were very good friends. After Priscilla died, Mrs. Carruthers distanced herself from Mother because she reminded her of Priscilla."

"I hadn't realized that Agatha and your mother had a history." Martha picked up her cup and sipped her tea. She found the connection between Agatha and Isabel very interesting since they didn't appear close at all.

"Oh yes. It was Priscilla that convinced Mother to marry Father, in spite of the upper crust of St. Louis. Mother's family was embroiled in society and marrying a cowboy didn't sit well with the Country Club set. It took years before they accepted her back in the social circle. Sometimes Mother tries too hard, but she really is harmless."

"Oh, Loretta, I am sure people just love your mother. She certainly helped me."

"So what news of the strumpet? Is she still sniffing around Jeremy?" Loretta laughed as she watched Martha's reaction. Martha quickly put her finger to her lips, not wanting Jeremy to overhear. *Oh, Loretta, how I have missed you.*

"You won't believe it, but I heard that she became engaged to some business associate of Mr. Grahams and they left for Europe. I have no idea what happened, she left shortly after you and Austin left on your honeymoon." Martha could not help but smile. She reached for the china teapot, refilling their cups.

"I'll tell you what happened. That night at the club before we left for England, I went over to have a little chat with Mr. Graham. I casually pointed you out and asked if he had met Mrs. Whittaker. Then I casually pointed to Jeremy with Ezekiel and said, 'Why there is one of the Whittaker boys now with Mr. Whittaker.' You should have seen his face. He looked at you and then at Jeremy and Ezekiel. Naturally he made an unfortunate assumption, however, I am not responsible if he misunderstood." Loretta grinned sheepishly. Martha stared at her with disbelief. She could not believe Loretta had done such a thing.

"But you made it sound like Jeremy and I were married with children. He had no way of knowing we were in-laws. I'm sure he rushed over to tell Clarise that Jeremy was married. Loretta, you are too much." Martha reached over and gently smacked Loretta's hand.

"Well, it worked, didn't it? Minutes later, Clarise slapped Jeremy across the face and ran away with her fiancé. Bye, bye, strumpet." Loretta's musical laughter brought the men into the kitchen. Martha tried to suppress her own laughter but it was impossible.

"What's so funny, you two?" Austin quizzed the blushing pair. Jeremy was right behind him. Martha looked like a schoolgirl caught by the schoolmarm. Red-faced she jumped from her chair and turned her back towards the men pretending to make more tea.

"Oh, Loretta was just telling me a funny story. Anyone for more pie?" quickly changing the subject, Martha chuckled to herself at Loretta's brazen behavior. *Loretta, dear Loretta.* In her heart she was very thankful for such a dear friend.

Loretta returned to the shop with pictures and descriptions of the latest English fashions. She also brought a letter from the now famous French designer, Charles Worth. "Martha, did you know that Charles Worth was awarded the First Class medal at the International Exhibition in Paris. His new design has a train, falling not from the waist but from the shoulders. The silhouette is stunning. You really must sew one for the shop; I brought you the drawings." Loretta wandered around the showroom admiring the décor. "His shop is called 'Furnisher of the Court' and he is commissioned by all of the royal families of Europe. This is too wonderful, having a personal letter of congratulations from one so famous." The letter to Martha wished her well in her new dress design enterprise. Martha proudly framed and displayed the letter in her showroom. *It seems that I dreamt of this a long, long time ago; perhaps Abraham is not the only one whose dreams do come true.*

Loretta was astonished at the way the dress business had moved from Martha's bedroom to this new facility. The showroom was decorated in pinks and burgundy velvet and a few designer gowns hung on a small rack. A settee and several soft plush chairs filled the space. A teacart held tea and fresh pastries baked by Annabelle's father, which sat in the corner. The entire atmosphere was one of prosperity and luxury. The gowns were all original designs. Each dress was made to measure for the individual in her choice of color and design. Several books of designs drawn by Martha rested on a low table. Ezekiel, the bookworm, had gone to the library and brought several books of costumes and dresses, which she had used to practice her drawing skills. She was surprised at how well she could draw. Jeremy had suggested the book of designs after seeing the original sketch of the gown for Mrs. Carruthers and it had been an excellent idea. Yes, Isabel had been right in her earlier description of Martha's shop, it was very professional and elegant. Loretta was very impressed. Martha was explaining how the ladies would arrive, sit, sip tea and look over the book of designs. They could make any changes they wanted to a specific design and she would draw the final product. Her self-confidence was growing daily.

Agatha arrived early one morning to pick up a gown she had ordered. Loretta called Martha from the showroom, then she went to retrieve the order.

"Martha, the shop looks lovely. You are a great success, my dear. Now we need to find you a man." Agatha laughed, admiring the samples hanging in the shop while she waited.

"Amen to that," Loretta added upon returning to the room. "We definitely need to find her a man. There is a certain brother-in-law that would jump at a chance to take her out." Martha blushed and Agatha and Loretta joked and giggled at her expense.

"I will never understand why women who have wonderful husbands want the whole world to be married," Martha scoffed. How she loved these two women.

The shop was a big success with the ladies of St. Louis society as well as the surrounding cities. Isabel Langley naturally took all of the credit.

Annabelle, May and Ellen all worked very well together and Martha paid them a decent wage. She had experienced the dressmaking sweatshops in England and was determined to treat her employees well. Some of the seamstresses in England worked twelve to fourteen hours a day for not much more than room and board. The facilities were small and cramped and the air was thick with sawdust and fabric particles. Many of the girls that worked in the sweatshops were only eight or nine years old. Ellen, May and Annabelle had excellent facilities, the most modern equipment and only worked eight hours a day. If they were exceptionally busy, Loretta would work the front room and Martha would join the girls in back at the machines. Loretta was a good saleswoman and although Isabel Langley was aghast to see her daughter engaged in employment of any kind, the designer shop was a different matter. Martha soon came to rely on her more and more as business grew. The two grew very close and it was Martha that was first to learn of Loretta's pregnancy.

"Oh, how wonderful, you must tell Austin right away." Martha beamed at the lovely young woman. She was happy for Austin, who would make a wonderful father.

"I'm going to tell him this evening, after supper at the club with Mother and Father. I'm so happy, Martha, my life is like a dream come true." Loretta already glowing with happiness hugged her friend and employer. As she embraced Loretta, Martha could not help but think of her own teenage dreams of love and marriage and marvel at where life had taken her. *Will I ever experience the joy of having a child of my own?*

Chapter Twenty-One
The Christmas Dance

"Oh, Miss Martha, I really can't accept it. It is too much really." Annabelle held the lovely blue dress in her arms as if it was made of glass.

"You certainly can accept it and you are going to accompany my sons and me to the Christmas Dance. Now go and try it on and I'll make the alterations." Martha had wanted to give Annabelle something special. The girl was an excellent worker for one so young and Martha knew that with ten children, there would be little under the Christmas tree at the baker's house. Annabelle stepped from the dressing room and twirled around the room like a fairy princess. The dress fit perfectly and the color complimented her red hair and freckled pixie face.

"Oh but what about the others, Miss Martha? I really couldn't accept if they were not getting something as well." Annabelle was so happy with her dress but was totally unselfish stemming from having so many siblings.

"I have something for May and Ellen as well, now enjoy your dress and you can leave it here until the dance. Oh, that is the bell, I'll be right back." Martha went through to the front showroom in time to see Isaac coming through the door. "Oh wait, Annabelle, there is someone here that would love to see your new dress." Annabelle shyly walked into the showroom. Isaac's eyes lit up like stars in the heavens.

"Boy, Annabelle, you sure do look pretty. Good enough to dance with." Isaac stared at the little pixie girl as she curtsied to him.

"Well, looks like you will get your chance because your mama invited me to the Christmas dance." Annabelle fluttered her eyelashes in Isaac's direction and the boy's face turned crimson. "I'll go and take this off now, Miss Martha, and thank you so much." Annabelle ran and threw her arms around Martha's waist. Immediately realizing her impropriety, she quickly released her hold on Martha and ran from the room. Isaac gave Martha an appreciative smile and wandered over pretending to look at some of the new designs.

"Isaac, was there something you needed? I was just getting ready to come home and make supper. You can wait and walk with me." Martha closed the oil lamps and lowered the shades. Annabelle appeared from the back room looking more like herself in her simple skirt and blouse. She thanked Martha again and skipped out of the store, but not without giving Isaac a huge smile and a quick flutter of her long lashes.

"I was wondering if you could take me Christmas shopping, Martha. I would like to buy a new rifle for Austin and I would need some money. I'll be glad to do some sweeping up in here for you or some chores at the house to earn enough." Isaac never assumed that Martha owed him a living; he wanted to make his own way much like she did.

"Well, I tell you what. You go out and shoot us a big turkey for Christmas dinner and that will be your contribution. I'll pay for the rifle but you can pick it out. Austin is a wonderful friend to you and he deserves something nice. What are you getting your Uncle Jeremy?" Isaac and Martha strolled down the street and into the business district of St. Louis. Several of the shop windows were decorated with garlands and huge evergreen wreaths. There was a wintry chill in the air and large white flakes were beginning to fall.

"I already bought him some brandy glasses at the shop on Walnut Street. He likes his brandy and they are nice crystal glasses, Grandmam helped me pick them. I used the money that I got from the butcher for the bear meat. I bought your gift and Ezekiel's and Abraham's as well. I just have one more gift to buy other than Austin." Martha was impressed with Isaac's resourcefulness and was sure the last gift would be for Annabelle. She had purchased a few of her gifts as well and was looking forward to a wonderful Christmas, much different than the year before. She and Isaac strolled through the city streets enjoying the festive decorations and the sound of carolers in the square.

The dance was held at the Country Club with a large orchestra playing music of the day for the guests. Gentlemen were dressed in tails made of fine black cloth with silk or velvet collars. The ladies blended like the colors of the rainbow in taffeta, silk, satin and velvet for the more mature. Many of Martha's creations bearing the new overskirt, which was fastened in front at the waist providing a great deal of ornamentation. Music drifted through the rooms from the dance hall and people mingled and laughed in the spirit of the season. Waiters with trays overflowing with wine and champagne threaded through the crowd like salmon swimming upstream. Holly and pine branches decorated the walls and a huge tree stood in one corner. Several of the children peeked anxiously at the gifts hidden in its branches. The scent of Pine boughs filled the air contributing to the feeling of Christmas. Outside a light dusting of snow blanketed the ground.

Loretta was beginning to show and Martha had altered a few of her dresses for her. She beamed with the glow of motherhood and Austin, her proud husband, was never far from her side. Isaac purchased a small gold locket for Annabelle with Martha's help and the tiny girl was ecstatic. She bought Isaac a hunting knife, which he had been admiring in the hunting shop. The two were lost in a world of their own and danced several dances during the evening. Martha and Jeremy smiled watching the two youngsters dance past. Phillip and Agatha Carruthers joined them and Phillip commented that Isaac was smitten with the little Irish lass. The evening was a huge success and everyone enjoyed the merriment of the season and each other's company. Isabel Langley was beaming with the possibility of being a grandmother and fussed over Loretta constantly. Martha enjoyed seeing many of her creations on the dance floor. Jeremy noticed she was exhibiting a new self-confidence and pride. The more Martha matured and grew, the more Jeremy loved her.

Morris Graham spotted Jeremy and Martha on the dance floor. Thinking this was the perfect opportunity to embarrass the scallywag that had toyed with his daughter, he approached them as they danced. Jeremy was surprised at the greeting since Morris Graham had been avoiding him of late. "Mr. Whittaker, all the best of the season, I have not had the pleasure of meeting your good wife." He emphasized the word *wife* and waited for the reaction. Jeremy and Martha turned to face him, their confusion evident on their faces.

"May I present, Mrs. Martha Whittaker, my sister-in-law, the widow of my brother. Martha, this is Mr. Morris Graham." Jeremy stressed the words *sister-in-law* and watched Graham's shocked reaction. Finally realizing why Clarise had slapped him and why her father had been cool towards him, Jeremy was enjoying the obvious embarrassment on Graham's face. Now that things were clear, he politely inquired as to Clarise' well being. " How is your lovely daughter, Morris?"

Morris Graham was shocked to learn Martha was Jeremy's sister-in-law. He had been a fool not to check his facts before telling Clarise. She had been very distraught over the news that Jeremy was married. Well, it all turned out all right in the long run. "Fine, she and her fiancé are in Paris. Lovely to meet you, Mrs. Whittaker." Slightly embarrassed, he shook Martha's hand and quickly walked away. Martha and Jeremy looked at each other and laughed out loud. Martha turned her head away as she remembered what Loretta had done. *Loretta, you are a scallywag.* She offered up a silent thank you to Loretta. Jeremy twirled her around the floor, thoroughly enjoying the festive mood of the season, chuckling to himself at Morris Graham's obvious misunderstanding.

Later as the youngsters sang Christmas carols, Jeremy and Martha stood together, his arm around her waist, listening to "Silent Night." Phillip held Agatha's hand as they swayed to the music. Ezekiel stood in the front of the group, singing at the top of his lungs. Jeremy watched the pride glowing on Martha's face as she listened. He hesitated asking her the question that nagged at him all evening.

"Martha, I'll be traveling to England after the holidays and I would like you to come with me." Jeremy had been avoiding the question but he really wanted her to accompany him. "I know you are busy but Loretta will be fine; she is not expecting until spring and more than capable of handling the shop and the girls." Seeing the excuses mounting in her face, he added. "Your father needs to see you and know that you are well. It is time to face your demons in England, Martha, and I would be honored to have you accompany me." Martha looked at Jeremy and heard the pleading in his voice. "Austin said that he and Loretta would take care of the boys, Martha, please say yes." His request caught her completely off guard. She was unsure about the trip but didn't want to say anything to hurt him.

"Let me think about it, Jeremy. I have to ask the boys and check on business after the holidays. I can't decide right now but I'm not saying no. Come, let's dance." She whisked him off to the dance floor and hoped that he would be satisfied with her answer for now. Jeremy was part of her life and never pressured her, although she realized he wanted more from her; she was not sure what she wanted. It was important that she do things her own way with no interference and she was not sure she was ready for a relationship. Jebediah soured her on anything physical and she wondered if she could ever physically love anyone. She was frightened of the answer. *What if I am destined to spend the rest of my life alone? How long would Jeremy wait for me without getting impatient? Can I love him completely?* She knew she was fond of him and growing more reliant on his advice and opinions. *Oh, why couldn't I meet Jeremy first and never married that awful creature Jebediah? Do I forgive Father for what he did? Should I go and face him?* Thoughts circled in her mind as Jeremy whirled her around the dance floor.

Christmas day was a wonderful day for all of them. Gifts of all kinds filled the room, the tree sparkled in the corner and good food and drink were plentiful. Martha never saw the boys laugh and smile as much and she was grateful. This was her greatest gift. Jeremy, Austin and Loretta were with her and life was wonderful. Phillip and Agatha joined them for the evening and completed the family picture. Martha remembered the somber and sullen Christmas of the year before. Jebediah reading scriptures and the boys holding their gift, a bound bible, in their disappointed hands. Jebediah had not given her anything but she didn't expect him too. She was sad for the boys. Jebediah never thought of their emotional well-being and she was sure that the bibles were just for show. She was not convinced even then that he was sincere in his religious beliefs. She had knitted each of the boys a scarf and mittens, having saved wool from the sweaters she had made them earlier in the winter. Jedebiah gave her

205

a suspicious look when she produced the gifts on Christmas morning. *You were a monster, Jebediah Whittaker.* Yes, this year was different. Martha raised her hand to adjust one of the ornaments on the tree, admiring the lovely sapphire bracelet on her wrist, which Jeremy gave her. Everything was definitely different now and she would make sure her family never wanted for anything again. She thanked God for this wonderful family and for bringing her through the past two years. Much had happened to her since she left England and she was questioning whether Jeremy was right. *Is it time to return and face my demons? Perhaps I need to go back and get closure with Father before I can move on.* She wanted to see Aunt Phoebe, Emma and Clyde again. She wandered to the window and watched the moon's reflection on the white snow. Ice sparkled on the trees and it reminded her of another magical winter evening when her life was so simple.

The holidays ended and life returned to normal in St. Louis. Martha was visiting with Agatha when the older woman asked her a very personal question. "Martha, my dear, I know that you don't like to talk about your husband but Ezekiel told Phillip some very disturbing things and I really want you to talk to me. You know I will respect your confidence. I love you like my own daughter, please let me help." She took Martha's hand and looked lovingly into her eyes.

Martha was shaken to her very core.

"What did Ezekiel say?" her voice trembled as she stared at the older woman.

"He told Phillip that your husband locked you and Abraham in a shed and that he beat you both very badly. Please, Martha, what happened to you?" Agatha was near tears and Martha knew that if there was anyone she could tell about her past, it was Agatha. After all she had done for her, Martha decided her friend deserved to know the truth. The death of Margaret and the others had brought her memories of Wyoming to the forefront and perhaps talking about that time would help ease the pain.

"I will tell you from the beginning, but it is not a pretty story." Taking a deep breath, Martha began with England and the arranged marriage. She told Agatha of the sea voyage, the wagon train and Wyoming. Agatha sat listening, quietly holding Martha's hand. She reached up to stroke Martha's hair and Martha paused in her story. She leaned her head into Agatha's hand and her mind was filled with a flood of remembrance of another time and another gentle hand on her hair. Her mother had always stroked her hair when she was upset. How comfortable, safe and loved she felt at that moment. Martha looked lovingly at Agatha and continued. When the story was done, the older woman's eyes were filled with tears.

"Oh my dear, I had no idea. Now I understand why you do not want a man in your life. Go back to England and put the ghosts to bed, my dear. Thank you for telling me."

"I really don't think I could ever love any man completely after what Jebediah did to me. It is not that I don't want someone to love me." Martha feeling as if some of the weight had been lifted, just by speaking the words out loud, hugged her friend. She was very grateful to Agatha.

Agatha looked at her with such understanding as a sudden sadness fell over her face. "I understand better than you could know, my dear. One day I will tell you my story."

The talk with Agatha helped her put things in perspective. Martha, after many anxious nights, made her decision.

"Now remember to listen to Austin and Loretta and keep that dog in check, Abraham. Isaac, no guns in the house while they are staying here and, Ezekiel, do not track snow all over the floor. Loretta is expecting a baby and won't be able to mop the floor all the time." Martha looked at her family, how tall they were, how proud she was of them. "Oh, come here and let me hug you. I'm going to miss you terribly." Tears rolled down her cheeks as she thought of being away from them for two months. The trip would take three weeks each way because of the winter weather and she and Jeremy would be staying in England for two weeks. Now that it was time to leave, she didn't want to go. Jeremy looked at his watch and announced they must be going.

"Oh, Mama, stop crying. We are all grown up now and we'll be fine. You know we'll take care of Loretta and Austin and Grandmam and Grandpap for you." Ezekiel, always the little man, squeezed Martha's hand and gave her a reassuring look.

" Now, Martha, don't forget to bring all of those new design ideas back from Paris. We'll all be fine here. Now off you go." Loretta straightened Martha's hat and gave her a big hug. The other boys embraced her and shook Jeremy's hand.

After the tearful goodbyes, Jeremy and Martha departed for England. Martha had decided to travel to Paris to see Charles Worth, while she was away. She could see the new designs for herself and Jeremy had business in England that would keep him busy. Now that they were on the way, she was excited about the prospects. The time away with Jeremy would give her a chance to assess her feelings without the boys or the business to distract her.

They boarded the ship and found their adjoining cabins. Martha was surprised to find this cabin fully equipped with fine furnishings and a very comfortable bed. Just the interior of the cabin seemed to assure her that this trip would be much different than the first one. Cases were unpacked and they went to the dining room for dinner. She did her best not to think of the other fateful crossing. Martha and Jeremy had not spent many hours totally alone and both of them were a little uncomfortable at the new arrangement. Talking helped her overcome her nervousness. She told Jeremy of the frightening experience she had while cooking on the deck of the *Salvation*. He assured her that this ship could handle any inclement weather with ease. Martha felt like a shy schoolgirl and giggled when her wine glass was empty. The glass was refilled immediately and the evening progressed well. An excellent meal of poached salmon and new potatoes with a Cherries Jubilee for desert was followed by several glasses of wine and dancing. Unaccustomed to drinking more that one glass, Martha started to relax after the third glass of wine and Jeremy was thoroughly enjoying himself. They returned to their cabins and Jeremy kissed Martha good night. Slightly inebriated, she clung to him wantonly as he opened her cabin door. This was not the way Jeremy wanted Martha for the first time. She could barely stand on her own. She giggled uncontrollably as he helped her to her bed. Jeremy's last words echoed like an unintelligible murmur as the walls of the cabin seemed to swirl. Fully clothed, she rolled over and fell fast asleep. Back in his cabin, Jeremy lay awake for several hours. Physically he wanted Martha more than he could bear, but he wanted her to come to him willingly and sober. He felt the heat in his body as he thought of her next to him. He knew some of what she had been through with Jebediah and wanted their first coupling to be loving and gentle. He loved her and wanted her to love him in every way. He would wait.

Sunlight streamed into the cabin, finding Martha with an aching head and an unquenchable thirst. She was surprised to find herself fully dressed and not remembering much of the previous evening. The fact that she was alone and dressed reassured her that she had not done anything inappropriate. She would restrict herself to one glass of wine from now on. She picked up her brush and removed the pins from her hair. After drinking insatiably from the pitcher beside the bed, she continued her routine of one hundred strokes of the hairbrush before changing her clothes and leaving cabin.

Finding Jeremy on deck and seeing his welcoming smile, she forgot her embarrassment immediately. The rest of the voyage was uneventful. Several nights the temperatures dropped and it was impossible to go on deck. The crew entertained the passengers with dances, games and talent shows. Martha and Jeremy arrived relaxed and happy in Liverpool.

Martha did not notify her father of her travel plans. It was her intention to see Aunt Phoebe first. Jeremy and Martha traveled to London where Jeremy's business contacts were. The city felt familiar and comfortable to Martha. She had not realized how much she had missed England. Leaving Jeremy in town, Martha traveled by coach and arrived at Phoebe's unannounced.

"Miss McGuire, how lovely to see you. I'll tell Mrs. Hunter that you are here." The reserved butler admitted Martha and went to find Phoebe. Martha had spent many happy times here as a child and the butler did not seem surprised to see her. He announced her arrival to a very surprised Phoebe. Martha stood in the hallway, admiring the lovely antiques that decorated the entrance hall. Phoebe's home was not a large as Graystone but was most impressively decorated. Martha had always felt very comfortable here.

"I don't believe my eyes. Martha, at last." Phoebe rushed to Martha and took her niece in her arms. "Thank God, you are back, does your father know?"

"No, he doesn't but I'll see him soon. How are you, dearest Auntie?" Martha clung to Phoebe, happy to be back. Phoebe ushered Martha into the elegantly decorated parlor and tea was summoned. Martha started to feel like her old self again. It was good to be here with her aunt. The two sat on the settee, holding hands and chatting. Getting reacquainted, Martha told of her life over the past two years.

Phoebe was shocked at some of the things Martha told her. She felt such pity for what her niece had endured. However, Martha looked lovely and happy now. Phoebe was glad that Martha had friends like Loretta and Agatha. She was overjoyed to hear that things had improved greatly in Martha's life and was curious if there was a man in the picture. Phoebe knew better than to ask too many questions. She would wait for Martha to offer the information. Arrangements were made for Max, Phoebe, Jeremy and Martha to go out for dinner and the theater. The every observant Phoebe could see that Jeremy was more than a little enamored with her niece. Martha was a little harder to read, however. Considering what that monster had put her through, it was no wonder she was being cautious. Max and Jeremy caught up on business news and the evening was most enjoyable. Phoebe agreed to accompany Martha to Paris in a few days to see the French couturier. When they returned, Jeremy and Martha would travel to Northumberland to see John McGuire and visit Jeremy's home, Pheasant Run.

The two women traveled to Paris accompanied by Phoebe's maid. She felt like her old self again; surrounded by the things she was familiar with. Martha was in awe with the beauty of the French city. She loved everything about it-the buildings, the food, the people and especially the fashions.

On the third day of their trip, Martha wrote a letter to her family from Paris:

> Paris is the city of dreams, my darlings. The Musee du Louvre is a most impressive structure with the Tuileries Gardens at the far end. The city is like the spokes of a wheel, all streets running off of the center hub. The museums and art galleries are marvelous and you, Ezekiel, must come here one day. One of my favorite sights is the iron bridge, The Pont des Arts, which offers a magnificent view of the Paris riverfront and the Seine River. I have met with my former designer, Mr. Charles Worth, and gained a great deal of knowledge on designs and fabrics. The fashion industry is booming in Paris and I feel that the visit was a good one. Phoebe and I are enjoying the French culture, delicious wines and the rich and

creamy food; we eat in quaint sidewalk cafes. I am happy to be returning to England although I hesitate to return to Northumberland. However, I must see my father, your step-grandfather and settle some issues with him. Your Uncle Jeremy is conducting his business in London and sends his love to all of you. I'll be home soon; I trust you are behaving for Austin and Loretta. I miss you terribly and I send you my love.

Martha, your loving mother.

The visit to Paris confirmed to her the necessity of this trip. She returned revived, inspired and braced to meet her father once again. After tearful goodbyes, Jeremy and Martha left London by rail and headed north. Martha was nervous about meeting her father. She desperately hoped she had forgiven him in her heart as well as her mind.

Chapter Twenty-Two
Martha and John

Jeremy and Martha arrived at Graystone just before dusk. The gray cloudy sky cast a dark foreboding over the mansion. She found it strange that it no longer felt like home to her as it once did. As they reached the bottom of the stairs, Martha hesitated, her feet wanting to turn and walk away. Jeremy knew that Martha was nervous and gave her hand a reassuring squeeze, urging her up the stairs. She gave him a quick nervous glance, took a deep breath and opened the door. The rotund Emma was cleaning the hall and gasped at the sight of Martha. Martha rushed to her arms and felt instantly at home. John McGuire walked unaware from his study and stared in shock at his daughter and housekeeper locked in an affectionate embrace.

"Martha, so you have come home after all." John approached cautiously unsure of the reception his daughter would give him. "Jeremy, nice to see you again."

Jeremy shook hands with John and walked into the great room followed by Emma. "Would you like brandy, sir?" Without waiting for an answer, Emma scurried off, leaving Jeremy to seat himself. John and Martha stood alone in the hall. The two stood, staring at each other, neither of them wanting to speak first. Martha removed her cape and stiffly dropped it on the bench. She wandered over to the mirror and smoothed her hair more for comfort than necessity.

"I'm here for a short visit, Father, I intend to return to my home in St. Louis. You are looking well." Martha chose her words carefully, still unsure of her feelings. She adjusted her skirt nervously.

"Please come and sit and we can talk. It is so wonderful to see you again. You will never know what I have gone through while you were away." John turned to walk away but stopped dead in his tracks at Martha's next words.

"What you have gone through!" shouted Martha, becoming very irate. "Do you have any idea what you and your arranged marriage did to me? Do you, Father?" Martha paused to take a breath and resumed her shouting; all of the past tensions coming to the surface. The pent-up anger of the past escaped from her like a caged animal. "I was dragged across the ocean, beaten, raped and belittled. Then stuck in a bumpy, dirty wagon and taken over hundreds of tortuous dusty miles to a Godforsaken place of ice and snow and more abuse. My belongings were intentionally left behind in the East and I had nothing but patched rags to wear. I lived in fear for my life; my dearest friend and her baby killed by savage Indians. I'm so sorry that you suffered, Father, so very sorry." Sarcastically, she spat her words in his face. Martha started to cry and all of the repressed emotions surfaced. Jeremy overhead the conversation and wanting desperately to go to her, held his place. She needed to do this on her own. John remained silent, knowing he deserved every harsh word she spoke. His eyes were downcast and his shoulders hunched as he waited like an accused man for his sentence. "My sadistic husband was shot to death and he deserved it. Do you know why, Father, because Jebediah killed his first wife. He beat her and threw her down the stairs and I was next Father, oh yes, I was next. You sold me in a land deal, you bloody, selfish, old fool, you traded me for land and I'm supposed to feel sorry for you. I don't know why I let Jeremy talk me into coming back." With that, Martha, red-faced and shaking, lost all of her strength and crumbled to her knees. John ran to her side. Face wet with tears, he put his arms around her and begged her forgiveness over and over. The sobbing pair stayed that way for a long time. Father rocking his daughter in his arms.

"Please, Martha, come into the great room and let us have some tea and talk. I'm so sorry for what happened to you, I pray every day that you could forgive me. Please, Martha, please, I had no idea what kind of a man he was." John helped Martha to her feet and walked slowly into the great room with his shattered daughter on his arm. She ran to Jeremy, weeping against his shoulder. John sank into his chair and rested his head in his hands. Jeremy tried to console Martha; his heart was breaking for father and daughter. He knew that this confrontation had taken a lot out of both of them but it was necessary. Now perhaps they could start fresh.

Eventually, over the next few days, Martha and John came to terms with their situation and John asked for forgiveness one more time. This time Martha forgave him and told him she loved him. It was a relief for both of them and their relationship although still strained, was back on track. Martha spent time with Emma, telling her how she had sold her pies in Wyoming. She told Emma how she loved St. Louis and the dress designing. Emma could see that Martha had matured greatly since she left Graystone. She was happy that everything had turned out so well for this wonderful woman that she had raised as if she were her own. Clyde was fascinated with stories of the wagon train and life in Wyoming. Martha was careful to leave out the more disturbing personal details. John agreed to travel to St. Louis within the year and visit the family in their new home.

For the next week Jeremy traveled between Pheasant Run and Graystone and settled most of his business. He visited his mother's grave and found fresh roses there. John was taking good care of the deceased Elizabeth Whittaker.

He arrived early one afternoon for Martha and took her back to Pheasant Run for supper. They traveled past the mining town that had sprung up on Jeremy's land, the land that Jebediah had sold. Tiny bungalows strung together like a strand of black pearls filled the lowlands. A few shops intermingled with the houses; the streets were rut-lined and muddy. The finer homes were built up on the ridge. Huge mansions loomed over the shantytown below like sentries. Fortunately, Pheasant Run was a considerable distance from the miner's homes. The carriage turned down a long tree lined laneway. Fields of crops gave way to formal gardens as they approached the mansion. She had been there a couple of times but this time he wanted her to see the entire house and have a tour of the grounds. Pheasant Run was part of who Jeremy was. He wanted to share it with her. They walked the large manicured grounds across the dew-dappled grass. The formal rose garden was just beginning to bud and a mild scent of Wallflowers filled the air. As they approached the pond, Jeremy told Martha of the drowning incident with Jebediah. "We were only boys but Jebediah was cruel and spiteful even then. I never trusted him again."

"Nothing you could say about your brother would surprise me. The man was a cruel, greedy and sadistic bastard." Martha rarely spoke of Jebediah but her feelings of distaste and victimization were obvious in her tone as well as her words.

"Oh, Martha, I'm so sorry that he put you through such tortures. I promise no one will ever hurt you like that again." Jeremy took her in his arms and kissed her forehead. She felt safe in his arms. Jeremy took her hand and the walk continued around the perimeter of the pond.

"I have to wonder if perhaps he had suffered from the same illness that your mother had but in a different way. Father and I talked of his recent involvement with the insane. It gave me a better understanding. I still harbor a great hatred for Jebediah, but I now understand that it was nothing I did to cause it." She stopped to pluck a small bloom from the garden, placing it in her buttonhole. "Lunatics have many types of illness and can react in different ways. Father was concerned that it may be hereditary but could find no proof. I just pray that none of my boys will ever be affected." Concern reflected on her face when she referred to the boys. She couldn't bear to have anything happen to one of them. Jeremy had often wondered if Jebediah was stricken with the illness as well but had never considered it might pass to the boys. He sent up a silent prayer that they would be spared. The evening grew cool as they returned to the mansion.

She loved Pheasant Run. It was large and elegantly decorated very similar in style to Graystone. The predominant colors were green, orange and brown and although she found it masculine in décor it was most inviting and comfortable. Large overstuffed sofas and chairs and warm inviting rugs filled the rooms. It was odd but Pheasant Run seemed to be decorated with the colors of the male pheasant. Martha wondered if the Whittakers had done that intentionally. When she saw the study with its walls of books, she knew that Ezekiel would love this place. Perhaps somewhere in his memory he remembered of all of these books from when he lived here as a youngster. She commented to Jeremy that they must bring the boys back one day.

Martha and Jeremy enjoyed a delicious dinner of lamb with mint sauce prepared by Jeremy's staff and then relaxed in the parlor. They sat together on the settee in front of the fireplace and both were very comfortable in each other's company. Flames flickered casting a warm orange glow over the room. Jeremy turned to Martha and kissed her lips tenderly. She smiled, put her hand to his cheek and returned his kiss.

"Jeremy, I want to thank you for talking me into coming on this trip. It was what I needed to do and I could not have done it without you." Martha wanted Jeremy to know how much she appreciated his company. This trip lifted a huge burden from her shoulders and she was looking forward to a bright future. Jeremy looked deeply into her eyes.

"Martha, you must know how I feel about you. I love you very much and I want you to be my bride." Martha was taken aback by Jeremy's proposal. She knew that he had feelings for her but she did not expect him to propose to her now. "Please take all the time you need, I'll be patient, Martha." Jeremy looked into those sky blue eyes and knew he saw love there, but he also saw hesitation.

"I have feelings for you, Jeremy, and any woman would be proud to be your wife, but I'm not ready for marriage. I'm flattered and I can only say that I need more time before I could be any man's wife." She was stammering. " I hope you understand, my dearest, for I would not hurt you for the world." Martha looked at Jeremy and knew he was the man she loved. But the feeling of anxiety over a physical relationship still haunted her, preventing her from moving on.

"Take your time, just promise me you will say yes one day." Jeremy was not going to let this woman go. "I'll give you all the time you need. I love you, Martha."

Could I take the chance? He loves me and I love him. "Oh, Jeremy, I promise one day I'll be your wife. I love you, Jeremy, please be patient with me." Martha, wishing she could conquer this sexual fear, leaned into her beloved's arms where she felt safe and secure. *How long would he wait?*

"Will you wear my ring, Martha?" Jeremy asked the question as he reached into his waistcoat and withdrew a small jewel box. He opened the box to reveal a brilliant pear-shaped diamond surrounded with sapphires.

Martha gasped at the beauty of the ring. "Oh, Jeremy, oh my yes, that is so beautiful." Jeremy, his eyes moist with tears, slipped it on her finger and kissed her. *Am I dreaming? Could this really be happening after all I have been through?*

"Sapphires are the blue of your eyes and the diamond sparkles like the light in your heart, Martha, this ring was made for you, my darling." Jeremy was a patient man and this was the woman of his dreams. He was ready to battle her memories of another man. Not a man that she had loved, but a man that she had hated. A man that caused her so much pain and heartache, she was afraid to enjoy the pleasures of love. Jeremy understood what Martha was dealing with and he was prepared to wait. Martha looked at the ring shining on her finger and silently prayed that one day she would be able to love him completely.

Martha and Jeremy returned to Liverpool within the week and waited to board the ship. Martha never dreamed she could feel such love for anyone other than her sons or her parents.

They sailed from Liverpool to Boston in three weeks and the time was a happy, love-filled blur for both of them. From Boston to St. Louis they held hands and talked of England, France and St. Louis. Both of them discussed their businesses, the boys and of their future together. Martha needed time and with Jeremy she had love and all the time in the world.

The boys ran into their mother's arms when the coach dropped her at the door.

"Mama, we missed you so much. Oh, Mama, tell us everything." Abraham wanted to carry Martha's bag and Ezekiel wanted to know what she brought for him. Isaac, being a teenager and more reserved, simply hugged her quickly and pecked her cheek. He was taller than she was now. Martha was so happy to see them all. She rushed into her cozy little house, happy to be home at last. Jeremy left the happy foursome, but not before kissing Martha goodbye. Loretta jabbed Austin in the ribs. He headed for his own flat with Austin and Loretta who were glad to be returning to their own home at last.

Once they were back home, Loretta bubbled over with excitement.

"Did you see the size of that ring on her finger? They got engaged, I'm telling you, Austin. Oh, what wonderful news." Loretta, now growing large with child, lumbered around the flat. "And that kiss, well, that gave it all away."

"I think they would have said something if they were engaged. Perhaps she bought the ring in France for herself. Why wouldn't they tell us if there was a wedding in the future?" Austin was not convinced that Jeremy and Martha were engaged and was more content to wait and see. Loretta, on the other hand, was excited and chattering away about how wonderful it was. "Come here, little mother, we are finally alone and your husband wants some of that attention." Austin turned down the oil lamps for the night and pulled Loretta to him.

"Oh a wedding, how exciting. Oh, Austin …" Austin silenced her chattering with his hungry lips on hers and his hands unbuttoning her dress.

Chapter Twenty-Three
One year later

Abigail Wells was a chubby, blonde one-year-old with sparkling brown eyes and a happy disposition. Her favorite person other than her mother and father was Ezekiel.

"Come on, Abby, you can walk. Just hold my hand." Ezekiel stood over the baby and held her hands in his as he walked her around the showroom. The child laughed and cooed at Ezekiel and attempted to keep her balance.

"Ezekiel is the best babysitter a woman could want. Abby adores him and he seems to be content to spend time with her. Perhaps I could take him home with me for good, Martha." Loretta, ever attentive, watched the eight-year-old and her angelic baby together.

"No, I don't think so Loretta, you would have to pry that boy away from me with a crowbar. He is such a great help around the house and he is always bringing me books on design and costumes. I'm a lucky woman to have such wonderful boys. Speaking of which, have you seen Isaac, he was supposed to come in today and move some boxes up to the top floor for me." Martha finished packing the boxes of fabric samples and bolts of cloth.

"Now where do you think he is? Wherever Miss Annabelle is, there you will find Isaac." Loretta laughed and pointed to the sewing room. Martha peered into the back room to see Isaac sitting beside Annabelle while she put the finishing touches on a bright yellow gown. She chattered endlessly as she sewed. Isaac just sat and looked at her silently and adoringly.

"They remind me of Austin and me except we were always getting into some mischief or other when we were their age. Austin was never that quiet either and we had some great arguments and discussions." She turned towards Isaac. "Could you take these up to the second floor for me now, Isaac?" The shop and sewing room were now too small for the growing business and the second floor was being renovated for a new sewing room with the top floor for storage. The existing sewing room would become part of the showroom and more dressing rooms would be added. Martha was also borrowing an idea from Charles Worth and installing an outdoor runway in the rear courtyard for May and Ellen to model the various gown designs. Spring, summer and fall, she would send out invitations to her best customers and have a fashion show for the upcoming season. Loretta and Martha had devised the idea after she visited Worth's and learned of his use of models in France. Ellen and May were both shapely and tall young women and would be perfect models. Both were excited about the opportunity and the extra money it would pay. The society ladies of St. Louis were most impressed.

"Just these boxes or the ones over here as well, Martha?" Isaac tore himself away from Annabelle and began carrying boxes up the narrow stairway. Ezekiel and Abby giggled and played on the Persian Rug on the showroom floor. Jeremy appeared in the doorway and smiled at the two children. He chucked Abby under the chin and tussled Ezekiel's hair. Both women turned and smiled as he approached. Martha kissed him on the cheek and Loretta, never missing an opportunity, casually asked if he was here to look at wedding gowns. Martha gave her friend a silencing look and Jeremy laughed out loud at the brazen suggestion.

"I have come to ask my fiancée out for dinner, if you must know. Martha, can I pick you up around seven?" Jeremy was taking Martha to the grand opening of the opera in St. Louis and wanted to take her to dinner first.

"Seven will be fine. Isaac will watch the boys, if he ever gets finished moving all these boxes. See you then." Martha picked up a small box and headed up the stairs to hurry Isaac along. Loretta fluttered her eyelashes at Jeremy teasingly and followed Martha.

Before going home, Martha dropped in on Agatha. Her friend was happy to see her as always. "The day I told you my story, you said you had a story of your own, Agatha. I would like to hear it now." For some reason Martha felt compelled to hear the older woman's story today. Something she had said had haunted Martha and it had been rolling over in her mind all day. *I understand better than you know, my dear.*

"Sit down, my dear. It was a long time ago." Agatha had been waiting for Martha to ask her about her past. The older woman made herself comfortable. She paused, clasping her hands together in her lap. "I was sixteen when it happened. I had been to a dance with some friends. The driver dropped everyone off, my home being the farthest away." She paused to compose herself. "On the way home, the coach driver attacked me. We were in a deserted area and he threw me down and brutally raped me. He left me lying on the muddy ground, where some shepherds found me the next morning." She raised her hand to silence Martha, wanting to finish. Martha could see it was very difficult for her to talk about. *No wonder she understood. The same thing happened to her.* "I won't bore you with the details. I was shut away in shame as if it were my fault. I became pregnant and was sent to a convent. Luckily I had a miscarriage at five months but the memory of that attack kept me away from men for a very long time. I was forced to move away from my family and make a life on my own. It was only when I met Phillip years later that I gained the courage to try to have a real relationship with someone. He was so gentle and patient. I understand exactly how you feel, my dear, but Jeremy is a good man. He loves you with all of his heart."

"I am so sorry. I never should have made you tell me. How horrible for you." Martha felt terrible for making her friend remember such a horrible incident. She reached for Agatha's hand.

"Don't feel badly, my dear. It helps to talk about these things and I have been married to a wonderful man for over forty years. You deserve some happiness in your life, Martha." The two friends embraced, their relationship bonded by a mutual tragedy. Martha's respect for Agatha grew even greater that afternoon. She realized how difficult it was for her friend to tell the story but she knew that Agatha was unselfishly sending her a message.

Martha headed home with mixed emotions. She felt pity for

Agatha but she also found strength that the older woman had overcome her fears and found real happiness. *Could I do the same? Thank you, God, for sending Agatha to me.*

After the opera, Martha and Jeremy returned to his flat for brandy. While they were relaxing in the sitting room, Martha surprised Jeremy with a suggestion.

"Jeremy, would you make love to me, please?" A slight blush appeared on her face and her voice was barely a whisper. Jeremy was shocked. *Let this be the right time, please let me do this.*

"Martha, are you sure? I will, of course, I would like nothing better but you must be sure." How long he had waited for this moment.

"I want you to, Jeremy, but if for any reason I ask you to stop, promise me you will. I hate feeling this way but there is nothing I can do about it." She paused and took a deep breath. "I know we said we could wait until we were married but I can't set a wedding date until I know what will happen." Martha's hand shook as she held her glass. She was a bundle of nerves. "I would like to try now, please, Jeremy." Jeremy's hand caressed her cheek. She looked in his eyes and saw love and compassion. *Lord, let me go through with this. Help me to forget. Help me be strong like Agatha.*

"Right this way, my darling." Jeremy took Martha's glass from her hand and led her into the bedroom. She asked him to turn off the lamp and the two nervous lovers undressed, slipping under the covers. She was trembling like a virgin on her wedding night. The dusky light from the full moon filled the room with a smoky romantic hue.

Jeremy was slow and gentle with her. He felt her stiffen a few times and slowly caressed her and kissed her. Although he was burning with desire, his entire future depended on his control and patience. Martha eventually relaxed and actually began to enjoy Jeremy's hands on her body. Hesitantly, she caressed his naked body and explored her lover. This was a new sensation for her, to be touching and exploring a man's body. Her fingers tingled as she moved them over his skin. Her body was quivering with pleasure at his gentle touch. When he finally rolled on top of her, she froze, every part of her went stiff and rigid. Uncontrollably her breathing increased its pace and fear began to take over. Jeremy, feeling her stiffness, did not stop; he kissed her and whispered reassuringly in her ear. He kissed her neck, feeling her body relax slowly, muscle by muscle. After several minutes, Martha started to relax at the sound of his voice and realized that this was lovemaking. This was Jeremy, the man of her dreams and this was love, she had nothing to fear. When he felt confident she was ready; slowly, very slowly, he entered her. They moved together like the instruments of a symphony and together, they made beautiful, soft and loving music. At last she felt fulfilled and loved completely and absolutely. She was drowning in the pleasure of the man she loved. Now she could take the next step and become his wife.

A week later as Martha finished cleaning the kitchen and headed up the stairs to her bed, she heard Abraham call out. She rushed to his room to find him in the throws of a nightmare. Gently waking the tossing boy, she held him close and thinking, *no God not again*, she waited.

"The woman is dead, Mama, the baby was born and then she died." Abraham was white and shaking. Beads of perspiration covered his forehead.

"What woman, Abraham, who was it?" Martha stroked his hair.

"I couldn't see her face, I just saw the baby being born and then she was pale and white and lying very still as if she were dead. What does it mean, Mama?" Abraham looked to Martha for answers. She had none; only the future would tell who the condemned woman would be. *Why are these dreams starting again? Why now when the future looks so bright?*

Loretta and Martha had set the new sewing machines up on the second floor and hired three more seamstresses. Ellen and May would still sew but would also model when required. Annabel was specializing in trims and accessories since her hand skills were impeccable. Martha was about to share her news of the wedding with Loretta when her friend made an announcement of her own.

"Martha, I think I'm pregnant again." Loretta revealed to her as they worked.

"What wonderful news, Loretta, does Austin know?" Martha was happy for her friend. Suddenly remembering Abraham's dream, a frightened look came over her face.

"Not yet, I want to wait another few weeks to be sure. Martha, what's wrong? You look like you've seen a ghost."

Martha recovered quickly and laughed with her friend. "No, silly,

I just realized that if I want you to be my matron of honor, I had better hurry and set a date before you are too fat to walk down the aisle." Loretta looked at her friend and excitedly hugged her tightly.

"Finally, a date, finally; oh, Martha, I'm so happy for you and Jeremy. Yes, let's do it soon so that I'll not be fat and rolly-polly. Wait until I tell Austin, he will be delighted." Loretta spun her friend around and around the sewing room, laughing and giggling like schoolgirls. "Two wonderful announcements in one day."

A date was set for two months' time and just before the wonderful day, Martha realized that she had not had her monthly period for more than a month and with jubilation and excitement went to tell Jeremy he was about to become a father. Before she reached his office, Abraham's forgotten dream crushed her happiness and replaced it with dread. She froze with her hand on the door. *This time Abraham will be wrong, nothing will happen to me or Loretta*, she told herself. Refusing to think of it, letting denial overcome her fears, she rushed excitedly into her lover's office. "Darling, I have wonderful news." Martha looked at him with such love, he rose from his chair and took her in his arms.

"What news do you have, my love? Lately everything seems like wonderful news to me."

" I believe I am carrying our child, Jeremy." She looked into his eyes and felt her heart fill with his love. Jeremy was ecstatic. The woman of his dreams and a child of his own, what more could a man want? The two elated lovers decided to keep the pregnancy a secret, as it was socially unacceptable for an unmarried woman to be with child. She was happier than she had ever been.

The day of the wedding arrived in a flurry of activity. Finally, it was time for the ceremony. Austin and Jeremy waited at the front of the church with Isaac, Abraham and Ezekiel all dressed in black suits and matching vests. Pink roses in their lapels and most of St. Louis society seated in the pews. Phoebe, Max Smithson and Minnie Wells were in attendance from England. Phillip and Agatha sat in the second row dressed in their finest. Isabel was seated to their right looking around the church to make sure everyone noticed that she was seated in a place of importance. Agatha sniffled into her handkerchief.

Loretta and Martha were preparing to walk down the aisle. John

McGuire stood outside the dressing room, waiting for his daughter. He said a silent prayer to God thanking him for bringing his daughter back to him. He smiled as he pictured Lillian's face watching from Heaven as their lovely daughter married the man of her dreams.

Alone in the dressing room, Martha told Loretta of her pregnancy and swore her friend to secrecy.

"I can't believe it, both of us pregnant at the same time. This is wonderful; I'm so excited. The babies will be just like siblings or twins only a few months apart." Loretta babbled, "Oh, this is so exciting, I will have trouble keeping this a secret." Martha, who wanted only to enjoy every moment of this dream wedding, walked towards the door, her finger on her lips to hush her excited friend. One final stroke of her hair and she opened the door. Loretta stepped out, dressed in full length lilac and lace, preceded down the aisle by the tiny Annabelle in a paler lilac creation. Martha's gown was a new design without the hoop skirt. It was a thinner silhouette with a bustle in back and a long train flowing from the back of the bustle. The color was ivory, in silk with small pearls decorating the sleeves, high neckline and bodice. Her bouquet was made of pink and white roses, chosen from her garden to ensure Margaret shared this day. There were strands of pearls falling softly from the flowers. Martha's face shone with happiness. This time she was truly marrying the man she had waited her entire life for. John took his daughter's arm and together they walked down the aisle. Both of them chose to think of this as Martha's first and only wedding and her bright future with Jeremy. *Lord, at last, I will have the marriage I have always wanted and a child of my own. Thank you.*

Isaac had eyes only for Annabelle, smiling adoringly as she approached the front of the church. Abraham and Ezekiel smiled admiringly as their mother came into view. Austin watched his wife coming down the aisle and was filled with feelings of adoration and love for her and the child she carried. Agatha reached over and squeezed Phillip's hand; he kissed her cheek lovingly. Jeremy was happy beyond belief that he was about to become Martha's husband and not only father to the three boys but to his own child as well. No church had ever been as full of love as the parish in St. Louis on that day. As Martha stared into Jeremy's eyes, she knew that her dreams were coming true. This was the man she was meant to be with, the man she loved with all of her heart. Martha became Mrs. Whittaker for the second time, but this time she had the man and the life that dreams are made of.

A magnificent party followed the wedding and all congratulated the bride and groom. The boys practiced calling Uncle Jeremy, "Papa" because "Father" reminded them of Jebediah, whom they just wanted to forget. John got to know his grandsons and was a big hit with all of them. John invited Isaac and the boys to Graystone to ride the horses and go with him on the foxhunt. Abraham just wanted to go and see the horses and Ezekiel informed him emphatically, that Austin told him ships make you sick so he would stay here, thank you. John laughed and laughed and was very happy to be here with these wonderful youngsters. The Carruthers enjoyed meeting John and Phoebe and the four exchanged stories of Martha and the boys.

Phoebe, Max and Minnie decided that Martha had done a wonderful job of raising the boys. Everyone agreed that Jeremy and Martha made a stunning couple. Minnie, holding Abby, was staying in St. Louis until her second grandchild was born, however, the other three were returning to England the following week. Martha and Jeremy were going on a short honeymoon to Chicago where they could both combine business with pleasure. Martha kissed Agatha and whispered a thank you as she left the party for her honeymoon. Her friend was crying and smiling all at the same time. She was so happy for Martha and Jeremy.

Train travel had become much more desirable since the invention of the Pullman car. Jeremy and Martha boarded the train and entered the Pullman Palace car. Lamps with silk shades, leather seating and chandeliers with electric lighting gave the car the feel of a luxury hotel. Fresh gourmet meals were prepared and served making the trip most enjoyable.

"Oh, Jeremy, this is so beautiful. Have I told you how happy I am?"

"Only five times in the past hour but tell me again my darling. I want you to have the world." Jeremy kissed his bride, he was so proud of her. After they finished a wonderful meal, they returned to their private compartment to relax. Jeremy noticed that Martha was deep in thought. "Martha, is something on your mind? Please share it with me."

Martha was hesitant to discuss Abraham's dream with Jeremy but it was nagging away at her and she wanted to clear her mind for her honeymoon. "You will think it silly, but Abraham had a very disturbing dream." Jeremy was reminded of Abraham's reference to his being the man in the dream back in Wyoming. That mystery had never been cleared up and now Martha had his full attention.

"Nothing you say is silly. Now what is this about?"

"Abraham has dreams that seem to come true. He dreamt of you before you arrived in Wyoming. He dreamt of a fire at the church and he dreamt of Jebediah's shooting. He never gets exact details but his dreams are like premonitions and very disturbing." Martha looked at Jeremy and hesitated to tell him of the latest premonition.

"That explains his referring to me as 'the man in the dream.' I wondered what he meant at the time but there were other things to think about then. What has this to do with us? What did he dream?" The concerned look on Martha's face told him that this was not something trivial.

"He dreamt of a woman giving birth, only the child was born and the woman died. Oh, Jeremy, he couldn't see her face and now both Loretta and I are pregnant. What if something happens to one of us? I'm so frightened." Martha cuddled into Jeremy for support. She shuddered to think of either herself or her friend in jeopardy.

"He didn't see her face, that means it could be someone else. Let us not look for trouble, my darling. I searched for you for years and I'll not let anything happen to you now. Austin feels the same way about Loretta; now don't worry about this. You'll just upset yourself. This could be nothing more than a dream." But Jeremy was worried too now, the boy seemed to be able to predict the future and Jeremy prayed that it was not Martha or Loretta that he dreamt of. Jeremy prayed for the safety of his new family and his friends as he held his new bride in his arms. He wanted only beautiful dreams for Martha; she had experienced enough nightmares to last a lifetime.

Chapter Twenty-Four
The Child Is Born

"Austin, go for the midwife and stop fidgeting." Minnie took charge of her daughter-in-law, who was obviously in labor. "Take Abigail to Martha's and tell her to come right away." Minnie started the water boiling and tried to make Loretta as comfortable as possible. The woman was huge with child and Minnie was worried about the size of this baby. She prayed as she made the preparations that Loretta would come through this without difficulties. Minnie was very fond of Loretta and the two were closer than ever now that they had spent several months together. Isabel Langley was in New York visiting some friends and Martha was the only other person Loretta wanted in attendance at the birth. Martha, pale with worry, arrived after the midwife and held her friend's hand. Loretta was sweating and writhing in labor. Martha prayed like she never prayed before for her friend and herself. *Let the baby be born healthy and let Loretta come through this with no difficulties, please, Lord, spare my dearest friend.*

The birth was taking longer than it should and the midwife was growing anxious. Jeremy and Austin paced the sitting room as the hours dragged on. Screams of pain could be heard from the bedroom and both men were worried. Jeremy could not push Abraham's dream from his mind. The boy had asked to come with him but Jeremy told the boys to look after Abby and he would come for them when the baby was born. Finally after what seemed like hours, a baby's cry was heard from the other room. Minnie carried her new grandson out into the sitting room and presented Austin with his son.

"How is Loretta?" the proud father inquired as he held his son in his arms.

"I have to get back in there, now keep the little fellow warm. Congratulations, Son." Minnie kissed Austin's cheek and returned to the labor room. Loretta was losing blood and the midwife was doing everything she could to stop it. Martha, who felt useless, was crying. Minnie was praying. Loretta was lying white and still on the bed and Martha was afraid, very afraid.

Austin wanted to see his wife but was kept out of the room for several more hours. Minnie emerged and prepared a meal for the men and the children who were now in the flat. Martha walked into the sitting room and gave Jeremy a mournful, worried look. He rushed to her side at the sight of her pallor and made her sit and drink some tea. No one noticed Abraham as he slipped into the bedroom. The startled midwife looked at the boy and was about to gesture for him to leave, but the look on his face stopped her. She nodded for him to approach the bed and Abraham walked slowly towards the deathly pale Loretta. He sat in the chair vacated by Martha and took her hand in his. The midwife watched as the young boy seemed to will the woman to open her eyes. His look was distant. The midwife was sure she was hallucinating, as a bright glow seemed to surround the pair. She crossed herself, muttering under her breath. She watched stunned for several minutes as the boy concentrated with all his might on the ashen woman, who the midwife knew, was slipping away.

Loretta lay very still but the look on her face was calm and almost peaceful. Abraham, after several minutes, kissed her forehead, rose silently and slowly walked from the room. The midwife stood speechless and immobilized at what she had just seen. She watched this mysterious boy leave while she prayed to the Heavens convinced she had just witnessed a visit by an angel. Loretta let out a low moan. The stunned woman went to her and checked the bleeding. It appeared to have stopped and Loretta slowly opened her eyes. A thankful, but mystified midwife wiped Loretta's face with a cool cloth, then raised a glass of water to her parched lips.

"My baby?" Loretta smiled and although she was very weak, inquired in a quiet whisper.

"I'll bring him to you and you have an anxious father waiting to see you as well." The confused but elated midwife left Loretta and summoned Austin.

Austin carried David to his mother and was devastated by the pale, lifeless figure lying on the bed.

"Here is David, our beautiful son, my dearest." Austin supported the baby as Loretta fed him. She fell asleep very quickly but Austin, with a tear-stained face, sat and looked at his wife, his heart full of fear. The midwife told him of the large loss of blood and that only time would tell if his wife would recover. She did not tell him of the mysterious visit. Austin held his son; his other hand on Loretta's and prayed for his wife with all his might. Loretta was his life; he could not bear to lose her. He looked at his son and tears trickled down his face as he considered raising his son and daughter alone.

Over the next week, Minnie cared for young David and Abby and Jeremy, Martha and Austin took turns sitting with Loretta who seemed to drift in and out of consciousness. Even Annabelle came and sat with her for a few hours each day. Martha reassured the boys that all would be well, praying that she was right. Martha was getting close to her own delivery date and she did not want the boys to be apprehensive about her delivery. Only Abraham seemed unconcerned. This made Martha feel more confident with the situation. She was so worried about Loretta that it was affecting her health. After trying to keep up the façade, she finally told Jeremy that she was not feeling well. He insisted that she stay home and rest and he and Austin took over her times with Loretta. Agatha sat with Martha and together they prayed for Loretta. Abraham arrived at the Wells' flat one afternoon with flowers for Loretta.

"Can I sit with her for a while?" Abraham looked very concerned and Austin, who was exhausted with worry and lack of sleep, needed a break.

"Of course, Abraham, just call me if she needs anything. She sleeps most of the time, thank you, son." With that Austin left Abraham and Loretta alone. The young boy took Loretta's hand and again, tried to use all of his will to make her well. He had used this technique with the animals on the homestead and knew that if he concentrated, he could send healing energy to the ailing beasts. It had worked on Bo. Perhaps he could do it with people and he loved Loretta. He sat with her for over an hour and Austin smiled when he found him slumped over exhausted and asleep, his head on Loretta's shoulder. But Austin was more surprised by something else he saw in that room. His wife was awake and smiling at him with the most beautiful smile he had seen in weeks. Her color was much better and she looked radiant. He rushed to her side, and without disturbing the sleeping boy, Austin kissed his wife and thanked the Lord for this miracle. Loretta smiled down at Abraham unsure of why he was there but feeling thankful and strangely, spiritually connected to the boy somehow. Within days, Loretta was walking around the flat and Austin and everyone else were extremely thankful. Abraham was jubilant but remained humbly silent.

"The food looks wonderful, Mother Minnie what would we do without you?" Loretta was grateful for her mother-in-law and looking forward to this party. Her health was improving by the day and she was almost back to her bright, and chatty self. Minnie assured her that everything was under control and not to overdo it.

Austin was playing with Abby on the floor, waiting for the guests to arrive. The baby slept in his cradle by the window. Austin looked at his wife and said a silent prayer of thanks. The past few weeks had been torture for him, never knowing if Loretta would survive the night. Now his family was on the mend and he had two wonderful children. He was very grateful.

A small gathering took place to celebrate Loretta's recovery and David's birth. Food, drink and good music provided the family with a renewed hope for the future. Martha was very relieved and felt her health improve immediately upon Loretta's recovery. Now she had her own delivery to think about.

Baby David was six weeks old when his future best friend, Anna Lillian Whittaker was born. She was a healthy and bubbly seven-pound baby with chestnut hair and green eyes. Mother and baby were doing well and Jeremy, the proud Papa, handed out cigars to everyone he met. Anna's brothers were most impressed with their new sister and happy that their mama had come through the delivery with no problems.

Martha sat rocking her daughter. She stroked the tiny head

covered in dark-brown fuzz and took in every feature on the sleeping baby's face. "You will never want for anything, my love. Your father and I will protect you and love you for your entire life. I promise, I'll make sure that all of your dreams come true." Her heart was filled with more love and contentment than she thought she was capable of. *How far I have come since that dreadful day that I boarded* The Salvation. Her child had been born surrounded by love and her family and friends were safe. Tears of happiness pooled in her eyes. Jeremy appeared in the doorway and smiled lovingly at his wife and child. The baby screeched, breaking the serenity of the moment. Anna Whittaker was demanding attention and would continue to do so for years to come.

Minnie Wells decided to stay in St. Louis. The weather was milder in St. Louis than England and her arthritis didn't bother her as much. There were three babies to care for and she had no one in England to rush home to. Loretta and Martha were thankful for Minnie who took complete charge of the babies and left the women to return to the dress shop. Minnie would arrive at feeding time and the babies were fed, cuddled and returned to Minnie. She was happy to have the responsibility and was the perfect nanny. Isabel Langley visited her grandchildren once a week and although the two women had nothing in common but baby David and Abby, they spent many pleasant hours together.

Austin gave his flat to Minnie, who was thankful to have her own place. Austin and Loretta moved into Martha's small house and Jeremy and Martha moved to a larger home. A new section of St. Louis was being built and they found a perfect place in the upscale Vandeventer Place. The brick house was much larger than Martha's cozy two-story, with six bedrooms upstairs, a lovely sitting room, great room, kitchen and good-sized dining room and a large two-acre lot. Jeremy was becoming very successful in St. Louis and wanted to have many business dinner parties. Thanks to the Carruthers, Martha's fashions were now being sold in a shop in New York. Agatha had made the arrangements on one of her many trips. The woman never failed to amaze her. Martha intended to have several dinner dances in her new home to promote her growing business and the house suited both of their purposes. A woman was hired to cook and clean and the six Whittakers began their life in their new home.

Martha's first day in her new home was spent transplanting the white and pink roses that she moved from Lucas Place. She knelt in the grass, soiled garden gloves on her lap and sent up a silent prayer for Margaret and John Dwyer. She would not forget them.

Isaac and Annabelle sat on the riverbank, fishing rods in hand. Annabelle enjoyed fishing and Isaac was pleased. Now he could partake of his favorite pastime with his best friend. "How long will you be away, Isaac?"

"Well, Mr. Langley said that the wagon train was traveling to North Dakota so I guess about six months by the time we get back." Isaac was excited about his new job with Arthur Langley. Martha had tried to talk him into staying in school but this was what Isaac had dreamed of doing. He would ride shotgun with the wagon train and help with the routine chores. Isaac's marksmanship was the best Arthur had seen and the teenager was keen. They were leaving at the end of the month. Martha had been shocked to learn that Phillip Carruthers was accompanying Isaac on his first trip. Isaac was nervous and excited at the same time. He would be away from his family and Annabelle for half a year, but the excitement of the journey was overwhelming.

"You know I'll miss you terribly." Annabelle was sad to think of how long he would be gone. She would wait forever for Isaac and dreamt of marrying him one day.

"And I you, but this job is important for my future. You know how I love the west. I'm like Mr. Langley in that way. City life is just not for me and I'll be making good money for our future. Grandpap is very excited about seeing a buffalo. It is amazing that he has hunted lions in Africa but never shot a buffalo. It will be fun to hunt with him." The two held hands, watched the sunset and fished. "Mr. Langley told me that in Wyoming, farther west than Fort Laramie there is a red desert. The wagons travel through this desert for days and days and then they come to this huge rock. People stop and carve their names into that rock—Independence Rock they call it." Annabelle loved to listen to Isaac talk of the wagon trains west. His face always lit up when he spoke of the west and she knew that was where his dreams led him. She would wait. As teenagers, they were confident that they would be together forever.

Martha and Agatha had returned from a shopping trip when

Martha learned of Phillip's latest adventure. "But, Phillip, do you really think you are up to traveling by wagon train? It is very grueling."

"Don't you worry about me, my dear. I am looking forward to shooting my first buffalo. Isaac has been telling me how to go about it and I am quite excited." Phillip looked like a young boy, his eyes twinkling with excitement.

"Are you sure you aren't going just to keep an eye on my son? I am very nervous about this job with Arthur Langley. Isaac is really only a boy." Martha's concern was evident in her tone and her expression.

"Well, that is part of it, but we mustn't let Isaac know that. I have convinced him that I am going strictly as a buffalo hunter. Don't worry, I will keep an eye on him and besides, I can hardly wait." Agatha put her arm around her husband; pride showing on her face. Phillip winked at her, then added, "You should see me in my buckskins." Agatha swooned. He laughed his magical musical laugh. Although Martha worried about Phillip taking such a trip at his age, she was thankful for such a good friend and mentor for Isaac and the other boys.

Abraham, who had stayed in school, had taken a part-time job with the local veterinarian and spent his time caring for horses and large farm animals. Phillip Carruthers had introduced Abraham to the vet on one of his visits to the Carrutherses' stables. His love of animals and his healing abilities made him the perfect apprentice. The veterinarian was happy to have him. Abraham did not discuss his other special abilities with anyone but used them whenever he could. The experience with Loretta had been a life changing one for Abraham and he now happily realized that the dreams were a gift from God not a curse, and if he could control his gifts he would be able to use them to help others.

Ezekiel was devouring as much knowledge as he could and was never without a book in his hand. Martha knew that college was in Ezekiel's future. He spent time with Jeremy and was a big help with the ledgers and inventory. Phillip was advising him on possible college choices.

One day Abraham would want to go to medical school. Her business was doing well and she and Jeremy were saving money for their son's educations. Anna was a precocious little girl, much loved and spoiled by her brothers. Grandmam Agatha found Anna to be gem. The two could often be found together in gales of laughter over some secret or another.

Life with Jeremy was wonderful. He gave her support and encouragement, he was a gentle and caring lover and her dreams of a loving marriage and family had finally come true. The nightmare of her time with Jebediah was slowly fading and she seldom thought about those days.

Jeremy was on the dock checking a shipment and Martha went to meet him for lunch. As she approached, she noticed that he was talking to one of the ship's crew. Instantly recognizing the man, Martha stood in shock as she looked into the face of Richard, the seaman from the *Salvation. No, it can't be, not Richard, after all this time.* Recovering, she stomped towards the two men, fists clenched.

"You, I never thought I would see you again, you vile bastard." Martha shrieked at the man and Jeremy turned in utter surprise. Martha was usually the epitome of decorum.

"What the … , Martha, what is the matter?" Jeremy looked at the enraged face of his wife and hardly recognized her. The seaman was more surprised than Jeremy.

"You owe me an explanation. You set me up you, you …" Martha could not think of a vulgar enough word, as she pointed her finger in the seaman's face. Recognition dawned on Richard's face as he backed away. Her face was crimson with rage; his was white with shock.

"Let me explain, the bloke threatened me. One of the crew told him about the necklace and when he demanded to know what I was doing with it, I couldn't deceive him. He beat me good and threatened to throw me overboard; he was a mean bastard." Richard stammered as Martha continued to close the gap between them. "All of the crew hated him. I'm sorry but I had no choice, I felt badly but there was nothing I could do." Richard was speaking quickly, backing away as Martha descended on him with her fists clenched. A stunned Jeremy just stood and watched the events unfold, not knowing what was happening. Martha was obviously furious and what did this scruffy seaman have to do with her?

"Well, that beast beat me almost to death after you told him the entire plan of escape. I could kill you with my bare hands." Martha's face was shaking with fury and she was out of control. Jeremy decided that he better intervene before someone got hurt. He reached out and took Martha's arm.

"Let's calm down a little. What is this about? How do you know my wife, sir?" He could feel Martha's body trembling under his grasp.

Richard, still moving away from the irate Martha, related the entire story of the planned escape to Jeremy. "You can go, sir. Martha, let's go home and talk about this. Nothing else to be done here." Jeremy spun Martha around as Richard ran for the ship.

"I'll not calm down, you don't know what that man did with his big mouth." Martha, memories of the beating fresh in her mind, was still tense and not ready to calm down. "That night on the ship was the worst of my life. Jebediah was waiting for me instead of Richard." Martha related her version of the whole story and how Jebediah had intervened that fateful night. "It was a nightmare, a horrible nightmare. He hit me and hit me and I thought he would never stop. He called me every name under the sun and beat my spirit as well as my body." Jeremy pulled her close. "He tore my clothes off and raped me repeatedly, my mouth was gagged with cloth and I thought I would die. I was terrified of him. Every time he looked at me after that, I thought I would die."

She was still shaking, all of those suppressed memories fresh in her mind, when Jeremy led her into the house. He was only beginning to understand the horror she had endured at the hands of his brother. Thank God the man was dead because right now, Jeremy felt like killing him. Later that night, Martha relived her tortures once again in her nightmares. She awoke to her own scream, bolting upright in bed. Her whole body was shaking. Jeremy folded her, trembling and sobbing, into his arms.

Chapter Twenty-Five
Six Years Later

Six-year-old Anna Whittaker stood pouting at the bottom of the stairs. By the door, several cases and trunks were piled and the family was scattered through the house. Martha appeared from the kitchen with a basket of sandwiches and goodies. Jeremy and Abraham appeared at the top of the stairs and Ezekiel came from the study at the end of the hall.

"Now, Annie, no pouting. Abraham will be back for holidays and so will I. Now come here and give your brother a big hug." Ezekiel reached for the pouting child's chestnut brown pigtails and gave them a tug.

"No, I don't want you to go. I want you both to stay here with me." Anna, tears on her cheeks, stomped her foot and tried her best to get her way, but this time she knew she would not win.

"You know that we have to go to college and all that stomping will not do you any good. Now behave yourself or I won't let you come to the train station with us." Ezekiel had a natural gift with children; Anna, David and Abby Wells would do whatever he wanted.

"I'm coming to the train, Papa said I could. I'm mad at you and you too, Abraham. You are leaving me and I'm mad." She stomped her tiny foot one more time as Abraham and Jeremy reached the bottom of the stairs. Abraham scooped the little girl up in his arms and tickled her until she giggled with glee. Abraham and Ezekiel now looked almost like twins. At over six feet with blond hair, strong jaw lines and handsome features, they were very similar. Abraham was going to medical college to study for his doctorate. Everyone was surprised that he had chosen to treat people instead of animals but the family was very proud of him. Ezekiel was off to business college and then would return and help Jeremy with the business, eventually becoming a professor. Isaac was somewhere out in the west with a wagon train and was now Arthur Langley's junior partner. He spent more time away than he did at home and took wagon trains as far as the gold fields in California. Martha knew that this was the life Isaac was best suited for. She was sad when Annabelle months before, grew tired of waiting. She surprised everyone when she married the son of the blacksmith and moved away. Martha thought that Isaac and Annabelle would somehow always be together. She missed Annabelle at the dress shop as well, but her staff had now grown to over a dozen seamstresses and Ellen was an excellent manager.

The family traveled to the train station where they were met by Loretta, Austin, Abby and David. David resembled his father in every way and Abby was a smaller version of Loretta. Minnie's arthritis was acting up so she decided to stay home in her comfortable house that Austin and Loretta had bought just for her. The boys had visited the Carruthers the night before bidding them farewell. The train station was bustling with passengers arriving and departing. The youngsters ran and played and the women cried. Abby, who was madly in love with Ezekiel, gave him a small stuffed bear to take with him. "Why, I shall put it beside my bed and think of you each night," he teased her. He leaned over and pecked her cheek and she blushed bright red. The two handsome young men said their goodbyes and climbed aboard the train. Jeremy and Austin, single strands of gray beginning to show at their temples, were reminded of their own journey west years before as they watched the two young men. They looked at each other knowingly and smiled.

"We'll be back for your birthday, Mama. Goodbye. Be good, Annie." Abraham and Ezekiel's train chugged out of the station as black coal dust settled over the remaining crowd. Friends and family stood and waved until the train was out of sight.

"How long before your birthday, Mama?" Anna wanted to know just how long it would be before she got to wear her lovely new dress.

Anna loved clothes and spent as much time at the dress shop as she could. She and Abby scrutinized the *Harper's Bazaar* magazines when they arrived and usually saw them before Martha.

"Please do not rush my thirtieth birthday, young lady. Now let's go and eat at the hotel, I'm famished." Loretta looked sideways at Martha and gave her a curious look.

Days later Loretta confronted Martha with her suspicions.

"I think I might be pregnant but to be honest, I'm not sure if I'm happy or upset. I'm going to be thirty years old and I don't know if I want another child. The boys are grown and Anna is going to school now. It is nice to have some time to myself." Martha looked at her friend as if she wanted her to reassure her that she was not pregnant.

"If you are, you will have to accept it. Jeremy would love another child of his own and you are a wonderful mother. I wish we could have had more children, but after David was born, I couldn't get pregnant no matter how we tried." Loretta looked away with a sad, wishful look on her face. Seeing Loretta's reaction, Martha felt guilty for expressing her less than enthusiastic views. Loretta recovered and picked up a stack of dresses that lay on the table. "Now let's get these dresses hung up and ready for the fashion show tomorrow. These bolero jackets are most popular. I'm glad we expanded the show room because this place will be full or overflowing." Loretta carried the dresses to the rack, commenting on the new colors of magenta, electric blue and vivid yellow. Martha followed her commenting on the new aniline dyes, which had replaced many of the vegetable dyes and produced a deeper richer color.

Martha told Jeremy a few weeks later of her pregnancy and he was ecstatic. Martha, however, was not as enthused. She felt guilty for not really wanting another child, but tried to accept the situation and make the best of it. Agatha was the only person she shared her concerns over this pregnancy with. Agatha reminded her she had a birthday party to plan with Loretta and that would take her mind off it.

The party was a huge success. The country club was decorated in sparkling gold and silver decorations and beautiful red roses. The evening was warm, with a light breeze and star-studded firmament. The fragrance of roses mingled with the smell of roast beef, fresh pastries and fine cigars. Over a hundred people attended and a great deal of food and drink was consumed. Martha was dressed in a yellow bustled gown of beautifully crisp, light taffeta, which was perfectly suited for the elegant style. A gold heart necklace adorned her long neck, a birthday gift from Jeremy. Loretta wore a pink princess gown, which consisted of panels joined and fitted from shoulder to hem creating a slimmer silhouette. The two young women made a stunning pair. Anna and Abby paraded like peacocks in their own tiny designer gowns accompanied by Isabel who wore a rich golden brown pinned with emerald green plumes.

Abraham and Ezekiel returned as promised and only Isaac was missing. Martha wished he could have been with her on this wonderful day. She loved all of her sons and they were an important part of her life. The orchestra played and couples whirled on the dance floor. Ezekiel whisked the adoring Abby around the dance floor and Abraham twirled Anna as the music played. It wasn't long before several lovely young women were vying for the attentions of the two brothers. Midway through the evening, Jeremy silenced the guests and with a majestic wave of his arm invited Martha to the stage where a huge cake was waiting.

"Thank you all for coming. I have lived in St. Louis for over ten years now and I love this city and it's people. Many of you are customers as well as friends and I wish to thank you for your continued support. It is wonderful to have such wonderful friends. I must thank my family for making my life a dream come true. I have been blessed with a wonderful husband, three grown boys and a lovely little girl. I'm very grateful for all that I have." Martha paused to wipe a single tear from her cheek. She smiled lovingly at Jeremy. " Now let's eat this delicious cake." Martha lifted the knife and made the first cut in the three-tiered cake accompanied by loud applause.

"Save a big piece for me." Martha looked in the direction of the voice and there stood Isaac, bearded, tall and lean. Agatha and Phillip stood by his side, grinning from ear to ear. She put the knife down and ran to his arms. Now her party was complete.

"What a wonderful surprise. Isaac, thank you." Arm around his waist, she led him to the others. Martha stood looking at her family, Jeremy, Isaac, Abraham, Ezekiel, Anna and her friends, Loretta, Austin, David and Abby. Minnie Wells was seated to the left with Ellen and May and smiled at her. The Carruthers stood arm in arm behind Minnie. How lucky she was to have such wonderful people in her life. Her boys were no longer boys but men. She was very thankful, sending up a silent prayer.

"One more surprise, Martha." Jeremy walked to the door of the hall and when he opened it, there stood John McGuire. An older, grayer but still handsome John, dressed in country tweed entered the hall and walked to embrace his daughter.

"Happy Birthday, my dearest." John hugged his daughter and smiled at her.

"Father, oh how wonderful. Jeremy, how did you arrange it?" She kissed her father's cheek and then hugged her husband. "This is the best birthday ever."

The evening continued with great jubilation. Phillip was anxious to hear everything about the gold fields in California. He had been fascinated with the west and although he only made the one trip with Isaac, he was always keen to hear what Isaac had experienced. Isaac, exuberant and elated with his travels was happy to oblige. Agatha listened with great interest as John McGuire talked of England.

The party ended in the early hours of the morning and the tired family retired with smiles on their faces and bellies warmed with champagne. Jeremy carried the sleeping Anna up to bed. Martha was about to climb the staircase and join her husband when a sharp pain doubled her over. She was perspiring and several more pains stabbed her abdomen. She clutched her stomach, thinking that she felt something warm between her legs, she squeezed her thighs together. *Oh no, not the baby, please not the baby.* Another pain, her head swirling, she collapsed to the floor and Isaac, the last to retire, found her there.

"No, Mother, no," he screamed, reliving his own mother's death at the bottom of the stairs years before. He ran to Martha and lifted her head in his arms. Jeremy appeared above and quickly rushed to Martha's side. After a few terrifying minutes, Martha opened her eyes.

"I'm alright, I just had a sharp pain. I'm sure it is just the excitement." Martha was trying to reassure herself as well. "Isaac, are you all right, you are white as a ghost? Jeremy, just help me to bed and I'll be fine, but I think Isaac needs a stiff shot of brandy." Martha, with Jeremy's assistance, climbed the stairs and entered her bedroom. She sent Jeremy to Isaac realizing what a shock it must have been for him to see her at the bottom of the stairs. She knew it would bring back all of the unpleasant memories of his own mother's death. As she prepared for bed, she saw the blood and knew that she had lost her child. She cleaned herself up, slipped into her satin nightgown and climbed in bed to wait for her husband. She would have to tell him and although in her heart she had not been excited about the pregnancy, she knew that Jeremy would be very disappointed. She reached up twirling a lock of hair in her fingers as she waited. Her concern was in disappointing the man she loved more than in losing the child.

"Isaac has gone to bed, he's fine. Now how is my wife?" Jeremy kissed her forehead and prepared for bed. She looked at him with love and sympathy in her eyes. She took his hand.

"I'm afraid I have lost our child, Jeremy." Martha spoke softly and watched Jeremy's reaction.

"But when, what happened? Are you all right? Do you need the doctor?" Jeremy stammered as he pulled Martha close.

"I'll see the doctor in the morning and I'm afraid that is why I was in pain this evening. I'm so sorry, Jeremy, I know you so wanted another child of your own." Martha began to cry but Jeremy quickly reassured her. He let her know that she was all he needed and he would be going for the doctor first thing in the morning. Together they held each other and cried. Jeremy for their lost child and Martha for the guilt she was feeling at having been so selfish. Jeremy gave her the world and she had not wanted to give him the one thing he really wanted — another child.

The next morning the doctor confirmed that Martha had lost her baby and would require bed rest for a few days. She was very depressed and guilt-ridden. Jeremy was sad but accepting. He sat and talked to Martha, trying to reassure her that it was nothing that she did that caused the miscarriage. As usual, he was patient and supportive. Martha was very thankful for her husband but his support made her feel worse. *How could I have been so selfish?* This wonderful man would do anything for her. She put on a smiling face for Jeremy, but cried when he left the room. People came to visit expressing their condolences. Loretta took over the shop and kept Martha informed with daily visits. "Once you have recovered, you can try again. You will have many chances to have more children,

Martha." Loretta assured her. Martha could not admit that she did not want any more children, to her friend who she knew would have given anything to have one. She was more open with Agatha, who never judged her. Her older friend understood how she felt and assured her that she would feel better in time. Agatha reassured her that life was perfect as it was.

Isaac sat with her and talked of his own mother for hours. This was the first time he had ever discussed Alicia with her. It seemed that finding Martha at the bottom of the stairs had been a breakthrough for Isaac. She felt that a wall had finally been torn down between them. He was so worried about her that he refused to leave until Jeremy came home to sit with her.

"I wish Annabelle were here. She would take care of you. I miss her terribly, Martha. I understand why she left. I'm away so much and she knew that I love the west and that way of life. You have heard me speak of Independence Rock. Well, the first time I passed it, I carved our initials in that rock. I wanted to be able to show our children someday." Isaac paused, a faraway look on his face. "She would never ask me to give it up but I loved her so much and I wish she were here. It has been almost a year since she left." Isaac stared out the window, lost in his own thoughts and Martha's heart went out to this lonely man. *Will he ever find true happiness?*

The family slowly returned to their consecutive schools or jobs and John returned to England after only a three-week visit. Martha was up and around and feeling much better physically, however, she was suffering a mild depression after the miscarriage. Her feelings of guilt over not wanting the child made her wonder if she was responsible somehow. She loved Jeremy and wanted to give him anything he desired. She knew she would have loved this child and been happy once it was born and was now feeling a deep loss. She also knew that deep in her heart she would do things differently if she got pregnant again. Loretta was taking care of the dress shop and Minnie still cared for the three youngsters after school, giving Martha too much time on her hands. Even the Carruthers were not around to support her as they always did. Agatha and Phillip had traveled to Europe for three months. She found herself crying for no reason and her moods fluctuated erratically. She was worried about Isaac, who had returned to the wagon train and was somewhere in the Dakotas.

He was so lonely without Annabelle. She would inquire as to Annabelle's whereabouts from Ellen and perhaps she would go and visit her. She knew that Annabelle was married but she wanted to make sure she was happy and settled; perhaps she was wishing she had waited for Isaac after all. Martha knew how terrible it could be to be married to the wrong man. She hoped that Annabelle's situation was a good one. Isaac would just have to find someone else if that was the case. Besides she needed a distraction to fight this depression and get her back on track.

Martha was dressed and ready to go to the dress shop. She was fastening her hat to her thick upturned hair, when the doorknocker sounded. None of the servants were in the area so Martha opened the door herself. There, as if by some miracle, stood Annabelle. Martha pulled the tiny woman into her arms and looking at Annabelle realized that she had been crying.

"Annabelle, dearest, what is wrong? Come in, it is so strange that you are here. I was about to ask Ellen for your address and I was even planning a visit. Please come and sit down and tell me what is wrong." Martha ushered Annabelle into the sitting room and sent for tea. She held the young woman's tiny hand in her own and waited.

"I'm sorry to bother you, Mrs. Whittaker, Martha, but I had no one else to turn to. My husband, Allen Baker was killed in a terrible accident. He was working in the blacksmith shop and he was kicked by a horse. He hit his head on the anvil and died immediately. I'm so afraid. We had so little money and now he is gone. What will I do?" Annabelle started sobbing and Martha comforted her as best she could.

"Well you know you can come back to work for me. You were my best seamstress and I would be happy to have you back. Now stop crying and drink your tea." Martha considered the problem solved and was selfishly thinking how happy Isaac would be when he returned.

"There is something else, I have a child. A baby boy, he is with Ellen at the dress shop. I thought you would be there but when I found that you were not, I left the baby with her. I have a child to care for now and we need a place to live. My mother's house is full to capacity and there is no room for us there."

"A child, how wonderful. Not a problem, we have our own nanny,

Minnie Wells, and she loves little ones. Anna, David and Abby are all older now and not as much trouble. I'm sure she will watch the baby while you work. What a terrible shame for the child to lose its father so soon after it was born. Annabelle, I'm so sorry, please let me help you. First we'll talk to Minnie. Shall we go and ask her?" Martha had the situation in hand and was feeling happier to be helping someone else. She forgot her own depression and took Annabelle to Minnie. As expected, Minnie, much older but still healthy was more than willing to care for the baby and offered to start the next day. Martha and Annabelle returned to the dress shop where Ellen, May and the others were busy goo-goooing at the baby. Annabelle lifted the tiny boy from the carriage, hesitated for just a moment as a worried look crossed her face and then handed him to the waiting Martha. Martha looked into his little face, feeling the soft warmth of the tiny baby. It felt good to hold a baby again. She felt a stabbing pain in her chest, remembering the child she had lost. She removed his bonnet and studied his face and although the baby was chubby, immediately recognized the black hair, sharp tiny features and deep-set dark eyes of Isaac and Jebediah. *Oh, dear Lord.* Annabelle watched Martha's expression and knew that her secret was exposed. She had been pregnant when she left to marry Allen. Isaac was the love of her life but she knew a child and a wife were the last thing the carefree Isaac needed. Allen Baker had proposed to her several times and would not take no for an answer. They married and left town, the baby Thomas was born seven months later.

Chapter Twenty-Six
Isaac and Annabelle

Jeremy was in India on business and Martha was busy with the shop. Annabelle was back to work and she and Thomas now occupied a room in Jeremy and Martha's house. Isaac was expected back any day. The discussions continued between the two women with Martha trying to convince Annabelle to tell him of Thomas' paternity.

"But he doesn't want a wife and a child. He wants to travel with the wagon trains. It is best that he doesn't know." Annabelle was determined that she would not be a burden to Isaac.

"All he has to do is take one look at Thomas and he will know. Now you are fine here with Jeremy and me, and Isaac can continue with his job if he wants to. Arthur Langley has been wagon master for years and Isabel and Loretta managed quite well." Martha could see she was making a convincing argument and pushed on. "I know you will be lonely for him but it solves all of your problems. One day he will get tired of it and settle down." Martha did her best to convince the tiny woman while the chubby baby squirmed in her arms. She was very fond of this little fellow and had no intention of letting him or Annabelle leave. Thomas seemed to fill the void left by her miscarriage and even Jeremy was happy to have a baby in the house. Jeremy, too, had commented on the similarity between Isaac and Thomas. Martha and he both felt that Isaac should be told, but Jeremy

OF DREAMS AND NIGHTMARES

was more sympathetic to Annabelle's situation. The decision had to be hers and he constantly reminded Martha of that fact. It had become one of the few disagreements they had over the years and now they avoided discussing it completely. Now with her husband so far away, Martha wanted to take back every wasted minute that they had spent arguing. She reluctantly decided to put her arguments to rest after this one last attempt.

"I'll think about it. But please understand, I'm very grateful for all you have done for me but I must make my own decision. Thomas' future depends on me and I'll not be influenced." Annabelle was very grateful for all that Martha had done, but she found her overbearing at times. "I love you, Martha, and I know you love Isaac as much as I do. Just please, let me handle this my way. It might be best if Isaac continues to think of Thomas as Allen's baby." The self-reliant Annabelle, who was very much like Martha in her own way, was not going to be swayed. She would take as much time as necessary to make her decision where Isaac and Thomas were concerned.

Several days later, Annabelle who was still wrestling with her decision, ran out of time.

"Martha, I'm back. Martha?" Isaac, dusty and weary from the trail, strolled on long lean legs into the hall, calling for Martha. He stopped dead in his tracks when Annabelle appeared at the top of the stairs. "Annabelle?"

"Hello, Isaac, yes, it is I. You're not dreaming." Annabelle knew she must make a decision now.

"But what are you doing here? Where is Allen?" Isaac was happy to see Annabelle but very confused.

"I'm afraid Allen has had a terrible accident. He is dead." Annabelle descended the stairs and approached Isaac. Her heart was pounding in her chest and her palms were sweaty. Just the sight of Isaac made her heart beat quickly. How she loved this man but could she tell him?

"Dead? But what happened and why are you here?" He looked into her eyes, how he had missed her. "Not that I'm not overjoyed to see you." Isaac reached out and shyly took her hand concern and confusion showing on his face.

"Your mother was kind enough to give me my job back and let me stay here for the time being. I'm happy to see you as well." Self-consciously, she pulled her hand away gently.

"Come let's sit on the settee and you can tell me what happened. I am so sorry about Allen." Isaac dropped his dusty hat on the bench and placed his hand on her elbow urging her forward. He led her into the sitting room and could not take his eyes off of her. He was saddened to hear that Allen was dead, but at the same time, he was overjoyed to have her back in St. Louis. Isaac and Allen had been friends and Isaac, although heartbroken, wished the couple well. He knew that Allen could offer Annabelle everything that he could not. Annabelle's happiness meant more to Isaac than anything else and if another man could give her everything she wanted, then he could not stand in her way. After an hour of explanations, the two heard Martha shouting a greeting in the front hall. Seeing Isaac and Annabelle together, her heart leapt into her throat. A silencing glance from Annabelle told her that he did not know about Thomas. Annabelle excused herself and went to see to her napping son. Martha and Isaac embraced and caught up on their news. A few minutes later Annabelle entered the room, carrying Thomas.

"A baby? Annabelle, you have a baby? But it must be a newborn." Isaac approached the mother and child, stunned but curious. Annabelle, looked sideways at Martha, took a deep breath and handed the baby to Isaac. "But I'm all dusty and dirty, maybe I better not." Isaac's arms remained at his side. But Annabelle pressed the child to him. Isaac cautiously took the child at Annabelle's insistence. He felt clumsy holding the baby, as if he expected it to break apart in his grasp. He looked down at the tiny face and realized that this child was not a newborn but a few months old. He slowly took in the color of the dark locks and the set of the jaw. Dark eyes stared into dark eyes as realization dawned. A huge lump formed in his throat. But how could this be possible? Did he dare ask? With tears in his eyes, he looked up anxiously at Annabelle. "Is he? Is he mine?"

"Yes, Isaac, this is your son, Thomas. I'm so sorry that I didn't tell you before but I didn't want to be a burden to you." Annabelle, tears on her cheeks searched Isaac's face for a sign. "I love you, Isaac. I have loved you since I was a child. Please don't be angry with me." Martha, who had moved away, stood in front of the large window, hugging her arms tightly. She was crying and holding her breath waiting for his reaction.

"Hello, Thomas, my son." Isaac smiled widely and turned to Martha. "Grandma Martha, this is Thomas, my son ... my son," repeating the word son as the meaning settled in his heart. He was happier than Martha had ever seen him and he beamed with pride. "Oh, Annabelle, my darling little Annabelle. Come here, we must be married right away. You have made me the happiest man alive." Isaac reached for Annabelle with his free hand pulling her to him.

Annabelle put her arms around the tiny boy and his father and smiled at Martha. Martha let the tears of happiness flow from her eyes as she watched Isaac's dreams come true. Finally he was truly happy and all because of the impish, tiny Annabelle and a beautiful baby boy born of true and lasting love. "We can't be married right away, Isaac, because you have not asked me yet." Annabelle teased Isaac and kissed his cheek. "What about the wagon trains, when do you have to leave again?" Annabelle looked questioningly at her man and saw love and happiness on his face. "Thomas and I will not hold you back; I promise you that."

"I'm not going anywhere for a long time. I have a family to take care of and a wedding to plan. Right Martha?" Annabelle started to protest but he silenced her with a kiss. "Would it be alright if my family stayed here with you until we find a flat?" Isaac was taking charge of the situation and enjoying every minute of it.

"Absolutely, Isaac, you and your family will always be welcome in this house." Her hand rose to her hair and pushing a stray lock behind her ear, Martha acknowledged her delight at the news. How she wished Jeremy was here to see this moment. Selfishly she was happy that the friction between her and Jeremy was over now that Isaac knew. Martha missed her husband greatly over the next few days wanting to share this happy family event with him. Everything was better when she could share it with her husband.

Isaac and Annabelle were married the following month in a small church ceremony with Annabelle's parents, nine brothers and sisters, the Wells family, Jeremy and Martha all in attendance. Ezekiel came home from college and only Abraham was not in the pews. He was on a medical missionary trip to Louisiana but would be home in a few weeks. Martha made a beautiful dress for Annabelle and Isaac's face lit up at the sight of her. Anna was the flower girl in a tiny designer gown of rose pink, covered with tiny ribbon roses. Abby, in purple, was the bridesmaid and Annabelle's sister, Ellen, the maid of honor. Ezekiel stood proudly beside his brother as best man. Minnie held the tiny Thomas who howled during the service to let everyone know that he was there. Martha thought back to Wyoming and how far she had come. Isaac was once her enemy and now she loved him more than life itself as she did all of the boys. Annabelle would make a wonderful daughter-in-law and had already given Martha her first grandchild. She stroked her hair, thinking that soon there would be gray strands amongst the chestnut. *Just wait until Agatha hears that I am a grandmother.* Tears pooled in her eyes as she watched her eldest son on the happiest day of his life.

Jeremy gave Isaac his share of the trust money from England and a small cozy house on a large parcel of land was purchased on the outskirts of town. Surrounded by forest and river, it was the perfect surroundings for Isaac and his new family. Jeremy also presented Isaac and Annabelle with the portrait of Alicia Whittaker that had hug in Pheasant Run. He had returned with it from his last trip to England and he and Martha were waiting for just the right time to give it to Isaac.

Annabelle traveled into town each day to work with Martha. Minnie watched Thomas and Isaac began his new career as marksmanship instructor. Their property was just right for a shooting range and several of the city gentlemen took instruction from Isaac. Thanks to Phillip Carruthers' word-of -mouth advertising, business grew daily. Isaac kept several horses on the property, charging boarding fees. Happy with his new life, he didn't miss the wagon trains at all. On his days off, he hunted and fished and spent time with Annabelle and Thomas. Arthur Langley, realizing some of the mistakes he had made by being away so much from his own family, encouraged Isaac to settle down. Isaac would still help Arthur organize the trains and the homesteaders and now boarded the horses used on the wagon trains at a considerable profit. Life was perfect for Isaac and his family. Alicia Whittaker watched over her son and his family from her honored place above the mantel.

Abraham returned home from Louisiana. He and Martha chatted on the settee. "I'm going to continue my medical missionary work in Louisiana and Mississippi. Since the Civil War, there are many impoverished ex-slaves in the regions that need medical attention."

Martha could not help but think how handsome Abraham was and how proud she was of him. "I'm happy and content doing all I can. Martha, the dreams continue but now I can use my gifts to help the people that need it the most." She remembered all the times she had dreaded Abraham's dreams and now he was using his gift to help people. *Another of my sons has found his happiness.* "You make me very proud to be your mother, Abraham."

Isaac, Ezekiel and Abraham spent a few days together reconnecting as brothers. Noticing a new lightness to Isaac, Abraham was happy for his brother and Annabelle. He took time to check the stabling facilities and make a few suggestions as to how the horses should be fed and housed. Isaac was grateful for the advice and deeply admired his brother's selfless dedication to the sick and needy.

"Isaac, there's something we need to tell you. I've waited for the right time and I believe this is it. First you need to know that no one, including Mama knows this." Abraham sat with his brother on the fence rails of the paddock. Ezekiel stood beside them, one foot up on the rail, his arms leaning on the fence.

"What is it, Abraham? You seem rather serious." Isaac looked from Abraham to Ezekiel and he could see that they were both very serious.

"We need to tell you something important." He stopped to take a deep breath. "The day that Father died, Ezekiel and I were outside the church. We were supposed to stay in the cabin so Uncle Jeremy could surprise Father but we wanted to watch. We stood on some crates and looked in the church window. We saw Father and Uncle Jeremy standing in the church."

"We also heard what Father said. Something about some land that he had sold that really belonged to Uncle Jeremy. They were both very angry." Ezekiel interrupted. "We saw Father pull a gun on Uncle Jeremy. He said he was going to shoot him."

"Then you busted in and we ..." Abraham stopped to take another deep breath glancing at Ezekiel. Isaac stared at him in shocked silence. "We saw what happened. We heard everything you said. That Father killed our mother. He hit her and threw her down the stairs and we saw you shoot him."

"Abraham and I decided to tell you now. We don't want you to carry any secrets or any guilt. We understand why you did it, Isaac, and we hold no animosity towards you." Ezekiel reached out and rested his hand on Isaac's arm.

"He was a terrible man, our father, and you did what you had to do." Abraham stopped talking and put his arm around Isaac's shoulder. "He probably would have killed Uncle Jeremy and maybe even Martha eventually. We are glad he is dead."

"But you never said a word. You both acted like you believed the robber story all these years." Isaac could hardly believe his ears. His brothers had known all along that it was he that had shot their father.

"We both swore a vow of silence when we sat with you in the cabin afterwards. We weren't sure if you could hear us but we told you that we saw you and that we would never tell. We were scared to death that you would die too and then it would just be the two of us all alone. Ezekiel thought that maybe you would shoot us, being very afraid of you back then, but I knew you wouldn't."

"Those were scary days after Father was shot. We didn't know if Martha was just going to leave with Uncle Jeremy and Austin. We were glad when you got better because we knew you would look out for us. Even if we did think you were a big meanie and a real pain in the butt back then." Ezekiel joked, sensing the tension in Isaac's face. The humor broke the tension. The three brothers laughed together, even the air was lighter now that the secret was out.

"A big meanie, eh? Well, I was that. Sorry I treated you guys and Martha so badly." A big load had been lifted from Isaac's shoulders. He didn't have to keep his secret from his brothers anymore. They knew and they forgave him. Isaac felt free now to tell Annabelle. It was the only secret separating them. If his brothers could forgive him, Annabelle would too. Isaac would make sure that his own son would have no reason to feel anything but love for him. Now it really was over. The three brothers were reunited in the truth and would always be together.

Ezekiel returned to college for his final year. He intended to travel to England and continue his professorship studies there and Martha knew that once he arrived at Pheasant Run, he would not return to St. Louis for many years. Pheasant Run would suit Ezekiel perfectly with its large library, close proximity to the college and England's ancient history. In spite of his years in the Americas, Ezekiel was a true English gentleman.

Abby, David and Anna loved little Thomas and took turns watching him for Minnie. Although she did not have as much energy as she once did, Minnie was a perfect grandmother to all of the children and she never regretted her decision to stay with Austin in St. Louis. She was very grateful they had offered to buy her a house; she continued to live in the cozy cottage for many years.

Loretta and Martha traveled to New York to promote some of their designs and received orders from most of the upscale dress shops in New York. Although the department store, Macy's, was very popular with ladies of the middle class, upper class society definitely preferred Haute Couture. Many of the extremely wealthy purchased directly from Charles Worth in Paris, however, several other wealthy patrons were satisfied with the designs and creations of the now famous St. Louis Haute Couture salon. The designs of the tiny St. Louis dress shop were in great demand in many of the large cities. Orders were flooding in from Boston, New York, Chicago and even New Orleans. Martha's dream had taken her from seamstress to dressmaker, to designer and now to a highly revered businesswoman in the Haute Couture industry.

John McGuire passed away from pneumonia the following year. A grieving Martha, accompanied by Jeremy traveled to England to settle his affairs. The laws of England dictated that it was Jeremy and not Martha that was the new owner of Graystone, however, unlike his brother, Jeremy allowed Martha to make all of the decisions concerning the property. Jeremy always respected Martha's abilities and they were equal partners in every way. The majestic Graystone was being sold. Pheasant Run was to be maintained for the family trips to England and Ezekiel, who had returned months earlier, would occupy Pheasant Run as long as he wished. After visiting Ezekiel, Martha knew that her third son was happy and content. *Now all three of you have followed your dreams.*

She sat in her bedchamber one last time. The house felt more like an old friend revisited, than home to her now. She realized that her shop was decorated in the same colors as this room, funny how she had not thought of it before. She would miss her father but St. Louis was her home now.

Martha and Jeremy made a sizable monetary gift to Emma and old Clyde and smaller gifts to the rest of the staff. "Emma, the cottage by the river belongs to you now and you should be able to retire there for a long time to come. I love you, Emma, and I want to thank you for being here with my family for all of these years." Martha embraced the dear woman that had raised her through her teen years. She felt the tears rising in her eyes. Emma was most grateful but she would miss living in Graystone. She had been there since she was eight years old, when she had been put in service for Martha's grandfather. After receiving a sizable sum, Old Clyde, who was now over eighty, would go and live with his son in one of the miner's houses. Jeremy was surprised when Martha presented Clyde with a gold watch. He recognized it as Jebediah's but had not seen it for years. He knew she would never give it to one of the boys; they wanted no reminders of Jebediah. Clyde was very impressed. He had never owned such a valuable possession. He hugged Martha with gratitude. She never failed to surprise Jeremy. He smiled at her proudly.

"Well, Clyde, now you have a much nicer watch than I do." Jeremy pulled his gold watch from his pocket. The broken face stared up at them, causing them all to start laughing. "May your watch mean as much to you as this one does to me. Every time I check the hour, I am reminded of my father, my best friend, Austin, and the day my life was spared so that I could live to win the hand of the woman I love." Jeremy leaned towards Martha placing a kiss on her cheek. She glanced lovingly at her husband, smiling at Clyde and Emma.

Phoebe and Max would handle the disposition of the manor contents and Martha was taking only the portrait of her father as a memento. With Jeremy by her side, Martha said goodbye to her old home forever. She stopped at the mirror to check her hair before leaving. The reflection of the grand old entrance hall of Graystone surrounded her image. *Goodbye, old friend.*

She stood on the front steps of Graystone one last time, remembering a snowy night years before. After saying good night to Clyde, she stood here in this very spot. Slowly she ascended the stairs, taking in the beauty of the ice sparkling like jewels on the trees and the soft white snowflakes blanketing the manicured lawns. The ice and snow had transformed the gardens into a magical, bejeweled world that night, a world of dreamlike beauty. It was hard to believe that within twenty-four hours of that evening so long ago, her life turned into her worst nightmare. Even now the memory of it made her shudder.

Now years later, the moonlight filtered through the trees and gave the garden a soft, romantic glow. A gentle breeze brushed her skin and the smell of spring roses filled the air. Her heart was full of love and peaceful joy. She turned and put her arms around Jeremy's neck, looking deeply into his green eyes.

"I love you, my darling," she whispered. "You have pulled me out of the darkness of my nightmares and made my dreams come true."

Of dreams and nightmares, her destiny was fulfilled.

Printed in the United States
24693LVS00004B/1-51